Clash of Leaves and Shadow

ALSO BY MICHAELA RILEY KARR

The Story of the First Archimage Series
The Allyen
The War of the Three Kingdoms
Reign of Darkness
The Sorcerer's Curse

The Desire to Know

Clash of Leaves and Shadow

The Story of the First Archimage

Book 5

Michaela Riley Karr

Rye Meadow Press

Published by Rye Meadow Press, based in Emporia, KS.
ryemeadowpress@gmail.com

ISBN (paperback): 978-0-9986065-9-0
ISBN (hardback): 978-1-7355071-0-1
Library of Congress Control Number: 2021920186

Cover Design © 2021: Magpie Designs, ltd.
Photo Credit: Pixabay
Texture Credit: Sascha Duensing
Author Photo Credit: Jordan Storrer Photography
Interior Map © 2020: L. N. Weldon

Printed in the United States of America.
First Edition, 2021.

Dedication

To my children, Cassidy and Wyatt.
May you both always pursue your wildest dreams and know how much your mother loves you.

NERAHDIS

TREDENO
JOSHUUA'S TREE
LEONAR
THE KINGDOM OF
MINERALTIR
MINERALTIR CASTLE
DEMORA
TRANINI
THE
GREAT DESERT
IONDRIA
IVANN'S DELTA
N
CAPITAL
CITY
CASTLE

Archimage Palace
Ranguvariian Camp
Lunaka Castle
Lina's Old Farm
Solana
Lun
Stellan
The Kingdom of
Lunaka
Caden's Peak
Spenser's Lake
The Dome
Diagalo
Canis
The Republic of
Caark
Kingdom of
Uklia
Keilian
Auklia Castle
Kaiya
Rondeau
Calitia
The Caark Shack
Aatarilec Grotto
Nadan
Aemita
Coliare
Caenara

Family Trees

(contains spoilers)

♦ denotes marriage
◊ denotes an affair/relationship
[denotes siblings
* denotes sovereign king/queen
↓ denotes the second time a person is listed
Year 1 = Humans arrived in Nerahdis with Emperor Caden.
B.N. = "Before Nerahdis"
A.N. = "After Nerahdis"
- dates without a suffix should be considered "A.N."

Book 1: *The Allyen* = Year 344
Book 2: *The War of the Three Kingdoms* = Year 346
Book 3: *Reign of Darkness* = Year 348
Book 4: *The Sorcerer's Curse* = Year 359
Book 5: *Clash of Leaves and Shadow* = Year 360

LINEAGES OF OLD

- Emperor Caden Gornan (18 B.N. – 30 A.N.)
- ♦Empress Melodi Heid (18 B.N. – 8 A.N.)
  - Joshuua*, *the First King of Mineraltir* (4 – 58)
  - ♦Emma Rollins (4 – 64)
    - Minndosia, *the Second Archimage* (22 – 63)
    - Cilla (25 – 86)
    - Levi* (29 – 89)
      (see Mineraltin Lineage)
    - Drina (32 – 72)
    - Grace (33 – 82)
  - Ivann*, *the First King of Auklia* (5 – 62)
  - ♦Abigayle Cedal (6 – 35)
    - Felicity* (31 – 90)
      (see Auklian Lineage)
    - Dathian (33 – 88)
    - Leah (35 – 91)
    - Hyllary (37 – 82)
  - Spenser*, *the First King of Lunaka* (6 – 70)
  - ♦Laurenn Tané (7 – 63)
    - Marya (31-92)
    - Jeremie* (37 – 97)
    - Alora (42 – 101)
      (see Lunakan Lineage)
- ◊Renae Eason (15 B.N. – 30 A.N.)
  - –Ariadne, *illegitimate* (7 – 28)
  - –**Amelia**, *illegitimate* (11 – 32)
  - ◊**Rhydin Caldwell**, *the First Archimage* (10)

Mineraltin/Ranguvariian Lineage

-9 Generations Between King Levi and King Camerron-

Camerron Rollins* (279 – 325)
♦Popuri (285 – 340)

- Josip Rollins* (265 – 311)
  - – Morris Rollins* (298 – 344)
    - ♦Lyla (309 – 325)
      - – **Xavier Rollins*** (325)
        - ♦**Mira Tané** *of Lunaka* (326)
          - **Taisyn Rollins** (346)
          - **Lyla Rollins** (348)
    - ♦**Jasmine*** (304 – 348)
      - – **Ren Rollins** (330 – 348)
- Andromeda Rollins, *an Archimage* (268 – 319)
- Emily Rollins (270 – 307)
  - ♦**Clariion Arii Buiikan,** *a Ranguvariian* (19)
    - Istrii Buiikan (295 – 295)
    - Laveniia Buiikan (300 – 339)
    - ♦Viincen Owiins (297 – 333)
      - **Rachel Owens** (324)
      - ♦**Jaspen Coralii** (320)
        - – **Mathiian Coralii** (347)
      - **Luke Owens** (326 – 348)
      - **James Owens** (329)
    - Siirella Buiikan (301 – 301)
    - Siimeon Buiikan (305 – 333)
    - ◊Tiril, *an Aatarilec* (305 – 331)
      - – **Conriin Buiikan** (331)
    - Friid Buiikan (307 – 307)

Chieftess Doona (267)

- **Chieftess Jaana** (300)
  - – **Onna/Chelsea** (329)
- ↓Tiril (see above)

Auklian Lineage

-9 Generations Between Queen Felicity and King Harold-

Harold Cedal* (274 – 319)
Marissa (276 – 303)

┌ Maria Cedal* (299 – 344)
│ ♦Walter Hester (300 – 331)
│ – **Daniel Cedal*** (322 – 346)
│ ♦Lily (322)
│ – Unnamed Son (344 – 344)
└ **Dathian Cedal**, *an Archimage* (303 – 346)
♦Anne (305 – 338)
– **Sabine Cedal*** (325)
┌ **Chretien Cedal**, *adopted* (341)
└ **Willian Cedal**, *adopted* (341)

Lunakan Lineage

-10 Generations Between King Jeremie and King Adam-

Adam Tané* (295 – 348)
♦Gloria (305 – 348)

┌ **Frederick Tané*** (324)
│ ♦Cassandra Gale (323 – 346)
│ ┌ **Nathia,** *a Rounan/adopted* (343)
│ ├ **Dominick Tané** (345)
│ └ **Rayna,** *removed magically* (346)
│ (see Allyen Lineage)
├ **Mira Tané** (326)
│ (see Mineraltin Lineage)
└ **Cornflower** (333)

Allyen Lineage

Lord Anders Soreta (32 B.N. – 28 A.N.)
♦Lady Mae (24 B.N. – 15 A.N.)
–**Nora Soreta**, *the First Allyen* (7 – 59)
◊Lord Kane (37 B.N. – 38 A.N.)
♦Charles Rodgers (4 – 59)
–Myron Rodgers, *an Allyen* (36 – 92)
(see Allyen Lineage)

-9 Generations Between Allyen Myron and Allyen Saarah-

Saarah Rodgers, *an Allyen* (283 – 344)
♦Orren Harvey (280 – 325)
┌ **Robert Harvey**, *an Allyen* (305 – 348)
♦Elaine Garnett (306 – 341)
┌ **Linaria Harvey**, *an Allyen* (324)
♦**Samton Greene**, *a Rounan Kidek* (323)
┌ **Kylar Greene**, *a Rounan* (345)
└ **Rayna Greene**, *an Allyen/adopted* (346)
└ **Evanarion Harvey**, *an Allyen* (324)
♦**Cayce Dale**, *a Rounan* (325)
– **Aron Harvey**, *a Rounan* (347)
└ Jedidiah Harvey (307 – 337)
♦Marie Smith (309 – 341)
┌ ↓Evanarion Harvey, *adopted* (see above)
└ **Keera Harvey** (332 – 344)

↓Elaine Garnett Harvey (see above)
♦Liam Sanders (303 – 341)
┌ ↓Linaria Harvey, *adopted* (see above)
└ **Rosetta Harvey** (328)
♦**Mikael North** (327)
– **Erikin North** (345)

Ancestral Memory Timeline

(contains spoilers)

Year 23: Nora Soreta is thrown out of her father's house for refusing his suitor at age sixteen.

Year 28: Renae, Ariadne, and Amelia Eason flee the imperial palace. Renae is captured, Ariadne is killed, and Amelia arrives in Lunaka, meeting Nora.

Year 29: Rhydin Caldwell and Amelia begin a relationship.

Year 30: Rhydin is announced Archimage. Emperor Caden is murdered. Amelia is forced to end her relationship with Rhydin.

Year 31: Amelia lives with Nora and Charles. Rhydin becomes consumed with the decision of remaining Archimage or going home for Amelia.

Year 32: Rhydin accidentally creates an Einanhi of himself. Amelia dies; the real Rhydin is banished to the Archimage Palace. The Rhydin clone becomes emperor.

Year 33: Nora goes to train with the Ranguvariians.

Year 34: The Rhydin clone creates Duunzer in response to the Three Kings' attempted coup. Duunzer's Darkness covers all of Nerahdis except for the mountains. The Ranguvariians nearly go extinct. Nora defeats Duunzer with Arii's help, and the Rhydin clone goes into hiding.

Year 35: The Allyen lineages continues with the birth of Nora's son, Myron.

Year 59: Nora and Charles die. Myron survives.

Chapter One

Rayna

An icy breath crept down the collar of my tunic, rendering my skin into gooseflesh. Winter was like a cruel, old man whose cold heart wished to make life miserable for the rest of the world; the memories of my humid island were as tempting as jugs of sweet cream. Caark was never cold. It never dipped below seventy degrees. However, our rickety shack on the island of Caark didn't remotely compare to where I lived now.

As I sat missing the home where I'd spent the first thirteen years of my life, I hastily shut the lead-glass window. I'd poked my head out there to see how much snow we'd gotten *this* time – probably about six inches. Snow was stuff I could hardly fathom. It appeared so solid and hard from afar, yet it reduced to nothing more than powder if you tried to pick it up. My mother kept telling me that winter was almost over. That in a few more weeks the earth would warm again, and ice would stop falling from the sky.

Why in Nerahdis would someone willingly live where ice falls from the sky?

My cousin, Aron, was flung across a straw tick on the floor with his nose buried in a book, but everyone else was out for the day. When the Dome was compromised and subsequently razed, the rebellion found a new home in Lunaka Castle after a brutal battle with Emperor Rhydin's Followers and Einanhis stationed here. We'd won, but not without a gigantic cost. We lost nearly half our people either in the battle or shortly after to the new poison that Emperor Rhydin engineered for his Einanhis – his magically-created humanoids that were looking less and less human all the time.

Worst of all, I lost my father. Just a few months after us kids were brought to the Dome after being separated from our parents for eleven years. Papa had been poisoned in a fight just before we arrived, and he finally succumbed to it due to the strain of the battle.

It'd been two months now. Since it happened. My mother had been kept busy day and night being the new Kidek, acting as regent for Kylar on the Rounans' request since he's so young. She was almost never in this room that we shared with Uncle Evan, Aunt Cayce, and Aron. Nearly all the rooms in the castle held double or triple their designed capacity, especially as different pockets of rebellion from across Nerahdis journeyed to meet us here.

The Royals had talked all winter of orchestrating the final battle against Emperor Rhydin as soon as spring appears, in an effort to hopefully make the first move. Emperor Rhydin kept Lunaka Castle surrounded for a week or two after we nabbed it from him, but once winter set in, his army disappeared. However, we all understood that he'd be back once spring allowed it, when the roads were dry and the real people he did have wouldn't lose their fingers to frostbite.

Again, why did people willingly live where their fingers will literally fall off when exposed to the outside air for too long?

"Hey, Aron," I mumbled as I shoved my feet into two pairs of woolen socks and then squeezed them into my boots, "I'm going downstairs. Do you want to come?"

"Not particularly." Aron's teal eyes never left the page of his book, his most recent borrow from the castle library. The words *Nerahdis: A History* were written down the thick, cracked leather spine in gold.

I groaned inwardly, struggling to keep it to myself. Never thought I'd see the day I'd be dependent on my almost-thirteen-year-old bookish cousin to keep me from being bored. Our room was one of the smaller bedrooms in the castle, really not that much bigger than our entire house in Caark. The wallpaper was white with painted, golden flowers, and tan gossamer curtains lined the entire wall where our one window sat.

When we arrived, the furniture had been gray, covered in a healthy layer of dust. The entire rebellion spent a whole week dusting, cleaning, and rearranging as we fought to make the cold, abandoned castle into something resembling the warm, cozy cavern the Dome had once been. The white, four-poster bed was now pushed into the corner, where Aunt Cayce and my mother slept. All the other furniture in the room aside from a wash basin and its mahogany table had been spirited away to other parts of the castle to serve anyone it could. Uncle Evan, Kylar, Aron, and I were all relegated to nothing more than straw mattresses on the floor.

The door groaned when I exited the room, and the sweet, juicy smell of roasting meat wafted down the corridor from downstairs. I took a brief moment to inhale the delicious scent, knowing that was all I'd get. This might have been the first winter that no one in the rebellion starved to death, but winter wasn't quite over yet and our stock was running low. I could only imagine that a wave of salivating rebels was rushing toward that meat at this very moment. I hoped one measly chicken didn't turn into a Rounan vs. Gornish debate, or Mama and Kylar would have their hands full for the rest of the day.

I sauntered down the corridor, trying to decide what I wanted to do before my magic lesson with Uncle Evan. The halls had been cleared of any and all decoration deemed of importance to the Lunakan Royals, which was everything.

King Frederick probably doesn't trust us commoners to not stuff things in our pockets or destroy the rest, I grumbled in my mind. My footsteps echoed down the empty corridor, which was lined in absolutely nothing but an ugly, dull-green wallpaper, and I hopped down the marble steps.

I darted past the floor where Papa had died, keeping my eyes turned away as to not relive anything from that horrid day, but then my foot landed on something soft. I gasped as I lost my balance, tumbling down several stairs to the next landing, and I heard the deafening "*squawk!*" of the culprit. One of the dozens of chickens that had made the journey with us from the Dome fluttered up to the stone handrail, clucking indignantly. This one was speckled like pepper with a colorless beak tucked into crimson wattles and pale, white legs – which meant it was one of our regular layers and safe from the chopping block.

"Well, if you wouldn't perch on the stairs, we wouldn't be in this situation!" I said angrily as I pulled myself back up and rubbed the back of my head.

The hen flapped its wings and chortled like it was laughing at me, so I groaned and went about my way. Then again, maybe King Frederick was more concerned about chicken poop than rebels with deep pockets. No one seemed to be able to keep the pesky things in the stables where they belonged.

Sure enough, when I finally reached the ground floor of the castle, there was a steady stream of people headed toward the throne room, which had become the main hub of our new base. People were in there constantly, whether they were eating, mingling with others, or actually doing something important for the rebellion like decoding messages sent from the small pockets of resistance all over Nerahdis. When the shrill clattering of a dish reached my ears shortly before I heard my mother's voice ring out over the fray, I immediately changed my course toward the double doors like everyone else.

I squeezed between two lean men in Mineraltin garb, sprigs of hay caught in their woolen tunics pulled at my hair, and pushed through the crowd just far enough to be able to see and hear what was going on. My mother stood right in the thick of it, a good foot shorter than everyone who surrounded her, yet no one dared come too close to her. Papa's navy, purple, and gold-starred bandana was tied around her head, signification of her new rank.

A mouthwateringly beautiful flank of roasted goat lay on one of the tables haphazardly arranged around the cavernous throne room, but a small hunk was torn off and smattered on the floor along with a tin plate and a small, whole potato. Two small children lunged for the scraps, and I wiped my mouth absentmindedly just in case any drool had seeped forth.

"That's the last of our meat, and I was first in line!" a stout Lunakan man the shape of a pumpkin bellowed as he shook his fist.

An Auklian fellow with dark, sun-kissed skin stood defensively in front of the tempting platter of meat, not budging. "The goat was the last of my herd! It is for *my* people only!"

"That's ridiculous," the fat, Lunakan man squabbled, "we're all rebels and equals!"

"You say that when I have something you want," the Auklian replied, flashing his Rounan mark on the inside of his wrist. "The centuries have shown that you'd never do the same if the tables were turned."

Before the Auklian Rounan had even finished talking, the other man tried to stalk forward, a crooked meat fork still in his hand. After she briefly stared at something across the room, all five feet of my mother stepped in front of him without a shred of fear.

"I've heard enough," Mama declared in a much stronger voice than anyone who didn't know her would ever expect. "It's his personal goat, not the rebellion's. He can feed whomever he wishes with it."

"But! Madam Allyen," the man spouted incredulously, "these are desperate times! There is no more meat to be found, therefore we must ration-…"

"Our hunting party that left a week ago should be back any day now," Mama interrupted. "That meat will be the rebellion's, and it will be divided accordingly. I must ask you to leave the throne room."

The energy shifted in the room. The crowd became silent. The Lunakan man grimaced, glaring at my mother like he was silently probing for any weaknesses in her steely exterior. His Gornish supporters behind him watched as well, as one of their own stood up for a Rounan. Likewise, the Rounans behind my mother and the Auklian man also stared across the void, waiting to see what would happen. It was nearly a minute before a Gornish wave of people washed away toward the doors, but not without bubbling with inaudible comments and sneers.

My mother relaxed an inch as they faded away, my brother Kylar suddenly visible beside her. He was the one who was supposed to be Kidek after Papa died, but he was young and couldn't have handled it. Although, as I studied the bags under my mother's eyes and the shallow lines that were beginning to appear on her face, I wondered whether she could keep up with it either.

Before either of my family members could see me at the back of the room, I turned on my heel and exited the room along with the last of the throng of Gornish people. None of them seemed to take any notice of me, but judging from a few of their remarks, I wasn't so sure this altercation had been solved. They seemed to be discussing what they would do if this happened again in the future, and I branched away from them as soon as I could to remain blissfully unaware.

I grew up on Caark where the lines between Gornish and Rounan were all but nonexistent. Nearly everyone there was a refugee of some sort, and it didn't matter who you were or where you'd immigrated from. It still just didn't make sense to me why two labels older than Nerahdis mattered so much. Rounans had been treated so poorly for so long because of their special powers and an ancient history of slavery. They were good people, although there were good Gornish people too, obviously. My mother, King Frederick, and most of the other Royals, the new ones at least. Why should Kylar and I be treated differently simply because he had Rounan magic, and I didn't? My mother was trying to walk a delicate balance between the two as the Gornish Kidek Regent, but which side was I supposed to be on?

Instead of heading toward the towering, oak doors that led out into the courtyard, I found myself maneuvering in the direction of a certain side hallway I'd been avoiding for some time. This hallway was empty, unlike the rest of the castle that always had one person or a dozen talking, eating, or just keeping warm. A heavy iron door stared back at me from down the hall, an angry-looking torch and a helmeted, faceless guard on either side. It'd been a week since I was down here last, and last time I was too angry to talk. But I had nothing else to do.

I walked without hesitation up to knight guarding the dungeon door, and he deigned to open the lumbering door for me. King Frederick had given me permission to see my other cousin whenever I wanted, probably thinking that if Erikin had any information to spill, I'd be the one he'd tell. I crept down the damp, dark stairs as silently as possible, not wanting to alert Erikin that someone was coming. A torch lit my way every six feet or so, although I didn't have to go very far. Erikin was the only prisoner down here and therefore occupied the first cell in a long line of identical ones extending as far back as I could see.

Erikin was turned away from me when I stepped in front of the bars. He was sitting on a ledge next to the one tiny window on the back wall that was too slim for anyone to even think of trying to fit through. His dark blond hair appeared brown there was so much dirt in it, although it looked like someone had mended his clothes recently, or at least provided him something more in tune with the season. He had a cloak wrapped tight around him, but his pale hands were bare. The black ring that once allowed him to use Rhydin's magic at will had been locked up somewhere; none of the Royals had wanted to destroy it in case the magic would return to Rhydin.

If that wasn't depressing proof of our desperation to have any sort of edge over Rhydin, I didn't know what was.

"I know you're there," Erikin squeaked, his voice hoarse from lack of use. He didn't turn away from the window. "Let me guess. You have another book for me."

I didn't respond, confused, but I did suddenly notice all the random piles of books strewn around the cell along with other various items that held some amount of entertainment value. Two months in this cell. For the first time, my anger retreated a mite. I said slowly, the first real words I'd said to him in a long time, "Sorry, I don't have anything for you."

Erikin's head snapped toward me. His face was thinner than it was before, although not terribly so. Someone had obviously made sure he was eating whatever the rebellion could spare. His hazel eyes studied me briefly before dropping to his hands. "Hello, Cousin. Are you here to yell at me again?"

Anger simmered in my heart. He was the reason the Dome was destroyed. He was the reason Papa succumbed to his poison so fast. He could very well be a liability even now if any of Rhydin's Followers knew where he was. But I had nothing new to rake him over the coals for, so I sighed. "No."

Erikin seemed to sense my lack of fire, and he rotated himself on his ledge so that he was facing me. "I don't know how many more times I can give you the same apology. I'm sorrier about everything that happened than anything else in my entire life. You don't know what it was like growing up on the wrong side of things. You grew up in peace; the rest of us didn't."

"Growing up on the mainland as one of Rhydin's Followers doesn't give you the freedom to get a bunch of innocent people murdered," I growled lowly, thinking of all those who perished during the battle for Lunaka Castle after the Dome was exposed and those in Conriin's pocket of rebellion.

Erikin scoffed, "Don't you think I know that? What about *my* life? What about my parents' lives? If I hadn't obeyed Emperor Rhydin and gone out on my own to search for the rebellion, he would have cut all three of us down where we stood. When I signaled the location of Conriin's pocket, I never once thought the entire thing would be destroyed and you'd be the only prisoners taken! If you all hadn't taken me along on your escape, Emperor Rhydin would have killed me and my parents for failing."

"Huh," I muttered, crossing my arms. "I guess that was our mistake then."

"Rayna, I will admit that when I realized you all brought me to the Dome, I was ecstatic. I thought my troubles were finally over and that Emperor Rhydin would reward me and my family, but that all changed." Erikin had been slowly approaching the bars of his cell, as if I was the animal inside the cage that he feared. "You became my friend, Rayna. You became my family. I never knew you were my cousin; no one ever told me. It was obvious your mother cares about my mother, and I began to hope…"

"Hope what? That you could just blend in with us and get our guard down?" I asked hatefully.

"No!" Erikin finally clenched the bars, and I realized how close he was. "I've told you again and again…I *never* meant to signal the location of the Dome. I was trying to get *rid* of that blasted ring so that Emperor Rhydin would never find us. I hoped…that your mother would help me save my parents from him too. That we could have a different life. Everyone in Solãna hated us, Rayna. You're the only friend I've ever had in my entire life. If you'd just let me out of here, I could show you how sorry I am and how dedicated I am to making my life different. Please, I just want to be your friend again."

I was quiet for a few moments. While Erikin had indeed told me several times before that bringing Rhydin and his magically-created, Einanhi army down upon the Dome was a total accident, he'd never gone into his past before. I responded quietly, "I'm not in charge of when they let you out. King Frederick is. You have to go on trial…"

"You know they'll never forgive me unless someone important vouches for me," Erikin said, his hazel eyes pleading. "I did what I had to do to survive. Give me some punishment, I know I deserve it. But…Rayna, don't let them kill me. Please don't let them kill me for an accident."

My heart quivered. I had to look away from his shiny eyes, the brick wall around my feelings crumbling. "I…I'm fourteen years old, Erikin. No one would let me vouch for you. Nobody in my family is a Royal either, you'd need a Royal's word at this point. Even my mother's word wouldn't be enough."

"D-Does that mean you believe me?" my cousin stuttered.

"I…." My throat closed. Instead of Erikin's face in front of me, all I could see was Papa's. His long, angular face and auburn hair, the details fuzzy as if he was only a drawing like the one I'd done of him in my sketchbook. Would Papa forgive me if I forgave the one that led to his death, however inadvertently?

My warring emotions made my head pound, and I abruptly whirled on my heel with no response, unwilling to speak the words that burned of betrayal in my mouth. I was halfway to the damp, stone stairs leading back up to the life of the castle when Erikin called out from behind me, "Wait! Is it true that my father is dead too?"

I froze. With everything that happened the day the rebellion claimed Lunaka Castle, especially the death of my father, a major leader, all other news spread like molasses. My mother couldn't be found for several hours after it came out that two major Followers had been killed in the battle. Since Rhydin's numbers overwhelmingly consisted of Einanhis anymore, the few that were real people with names were all well known by the people of the rebellion, and the older rebels kept diligent track of them over the years. Coincidentally, my mother had been the one to deal the death blow to both of them.

Their names were Kino and Mikael. The former was a woman obsessed with Rhydin that many of the rebels had always wondered if there was any sort of relationship there, although that thought made me nauseous. The latter was none other than Erikin's father, the man who had kidnapped Erikin's mother, married her, and faked her death decades ago. She never left him because she loved him, but the fact remained:

Erikin's accidental actions caused my dying father to succumb to his poison earlier than he would have anyway. My mother shot a magical blast through his father's heart.

My heart hammered. Heat rushed up my neck, and my toes felt like lead. Of course, Erikin wouldn't know, having been down in the dungeon for two months. His only news came through whomever bothered to visit him or bring him food.

"Yes," I breathed shakily, before sprinting up the steps as fast as I could before I could remotely feel any sort of shock or judgment. I bolted through the iron door so fast, the guard almost thought I was an escaping prisoner or something, but I was already around the corner and out of sight before he could act.

I crashed into a quiet corner of the hallway just off the castle's main foyer, my shoulder shifting the thin, silken threads of one of the few tapestries left on the walls.

What kind of person was I? How could I be so terrible to him for two months all while harboring the information that my mother had done far worse to him? Was I really so cruel?

I had to get him out.

"Hiding from your magic lessons again, Rayna?" a girl's voice said coolly. "What a disappointment you must be."

My fingers rubbed the smooth, red-gold threads of the wheat stalks on the tapestry angrily. "Go away, Nathia," I growled. "I'm not in the mood."

Nathia chortled as she came into view, "Like you're ever in the mood anymore." The wavy, chocolate-haired girl paused in the hallway with her hip jutted out, her arms crossed over her chest. King Frederick must have somehow convinced his Rounan, seventeen-year-old ward to wear a dress that more became her station today because she was wearing a scarlet frock with a beaded bodice complete with little red slippers and a fur-lined cloak. The shock of blond hair on top of her head separate from the rest of her dark hair was just as unruly as ever.

I rolled my eyes. "You know I quit training with you Royals after I got my magic." I sized her up with my eyes briefly, knowing it would make her boil. "Nice outfit, by the way. You could have at least tried with your hair."

"You're one to talk," Nathia sneered, gesturing to the outfit I'd been wearing for maybe three days now.

Frankly, she wasn't wrong. Underneath a heavy, velvet cloak that had been a gift from King Frederick, my leather-brown tunic was too big for me, a hand-me-down from Kylar that had a couple stains here and there with some tears that had been sewn up. The hem of my knee-length, dark woolen skirt was jagged, and my worn trousers had been patched from the inside in an attempt to make them less noticeable. My boots were belted together with seams popping every which way. I'd taken my dagger to my long braid of hair after Papa died, and now my auburn locks were in uneven clumps that framed my face. Or, at least, my hair *had* been uneven until my mother hunted down a pair of scissors and forced me to let her even it out just a little past my chin.

I shrugged, "Good thing I'll never be a princess then."

"Oh, does that mean things aren't going well with Taisyn, then?" Nathia laughed mockingly.

I whirled, just about to connect my fist with her face, but I froze an inch from her big nose. The magical compass in my head was spinning; a familiar light presence that strummed like the strings on a violin manifested. I withdrew my fist, Nathia's green eyes appearing fearful for once.

"Hello, Uncle," I muttered begrudgingly.

Uncle Evan was a short, stocky fellow. Essentially a male version of my petite, brown-haired mother, which I found terrifying, but it was to be expected as twins. He had some facial hair now, so that helped. "Rayna, you're late for our lesson," my uncle's boyish voice said. Seeming to sense the tension in the air, he added, "You've come a long way in such a short time, but I still have much to teach you before spring comes."

"Don't worry. I'll be ready," I vowed through my teeth as I turned to follow Uncle Evan toward the courtyard, glaring at Nathia the whole time.

In the spring, the war with Emperor Rhydin would resume, and it was up to me to not only help the other Allyens destroy him but also to free the real Rhydin trapped in the Archimage Palace.

Apparently, I was the only one who could.

Chapter Two

Lina

The winter sky was gray and formless. It stretched horizon to horizon with no changes in its color. I supposed there must be clouds up there somewhere for it to be so gray with no sun to be seen, but anybody who didn't know that would just think the sky itself was a colorless void. There wasn't a whole lot of difference between it and the white earth below, although the earth was broken up by random spots of brown where the snow was melting or the black of naked tree branches fractured the edges of the sky.

My back was becoming numb, and my toes felt like blocks of ice. The ground was hard as a brick beneath my body, long since frozen until everything thawed in the spring. Next to me, Sam's grave was covered in snow, although I had dusted off his marker. This was the first time I'd managed to get away from Lunaka Castle in two months.

"How did you do it, Sam?" I whispered as I stared up into the big gray oblivion. "How did you lead so many people from so many different places?"

Only silence answered me, and my heart throbbed.

"I don't think I was cut out to be a leader of so many, Sam," I began to ramble, my voice high and awkward in the cold.

"Do you remember our little team of rebels we'd lead on recon missions? June and Brade and them? I miss that."

I didn't dare utter the more obvious sentiment. Saying "I miss you" out loud would render me into nothing but tears.

Sighing heavily, I leaned forward, my body slow and achy after being there for so long. My cloak clung to the snow, and its dampness made it feel heavier than it had been before. I removed one of my gloves and traced Sam's name on the grave marker, dutifully cleaning out all the snow and dirt from every little curve and nook of each letter. I had been gone too long; more than one Rounan would be looking for me by now.

I hauled myself to my feet and located my horse, who was off snacking on some decades-old hay left behind in the battered barn. I couldn't bear to say goodbye, so I slowly walked away. As I mounted the black gelding I'd borrowed from Lunaka Castle's stables, I looked over my shoulder out of habit and noticed the old house I'd grown up in. It seemed to sit on a slant with the door blasted off its hinges. There was so much pain here. I used to dream about returning to this land with Sam and turning it into a successful farm again.

That dream died the same day he did. I couldn't even fathom picking up a hoe or bucket again.

The ride back to Lunaka Castle was quick and uneventful; my mind was as blank as the white, dead world around me. It was only when the thin, dark spires appeared on the horizon that my thoughts were suddenly jarred awake. The castle's menacing silhouette draped in snow sent me spiraling back in time to the day Duunzer attacked, Rhydin's dragon-shaped creation of darkness. My heart began to pound, and I actually expected to see hundreds of people sprinting from the canyon and its pulleys as they raced to escape the encroaching Darkness and the town as it quaked.

I shook my head and tried to still my breathing, even as my old scar upon my thigh began to throb with the memory of being impaled by one of Duunzer's talons. That was a long time ago. Duunzer was destroyed, and Emperor Rhydin didn't quite have the power to create it again, especially with his magic siphoned off into so many thousands of Einanhi soldiers.

All the revelations from a few months ago came streaming back. The Rhydin I knew was an Einanhi himself, although we didn't know how or why he was created by the real Rhydin who was trapped in some sort of transparent, frozen-in-time existence within the Archimage Palace. The Rhydin I'd known all along, the one currently parading around as emperor, was nothing more than an artificial shell of magic that was becoming old and unstable. His powers had become terrifyingly unhinged, and I shuddered at the thought of how deranged and chaotically powerful he had been the last time we'd come face to face.

I couldn't wait for the day I would never have to worry about him stealing someone from me ever again. Sam, my father Robert, Rachel's brother Luke, my cousin Keera, my grandmother, the kidnapping of my sister Rosetta. It would finally come to an end in the spring, I told myself. No matter what.

After riding into the stables and caring for my horse, I found myself wandering the castle halls, making my usual rounds. Every room and hallway were perpetually jam-packed with people. Each livable room had been converted into dormitories of a dozen or more, so naturally everyone spent as much time outside those rooms during the daytime as possible, which meant lots of loiterers in the hallways. When we'd first arrived at Lunaka Castle, each hallway had been lined with crates of supplies – which had been meant for the people of Soläna but were stockpiled here instead – and the rebellion spent much of our initial days here moving those crates to the throne room where the supplies could be doled out in an organized fashion.

Of course, everything went south when the crates began to dwindle and transportation routes across the kingdom were shut down due to the onset of winter and Emperor Rhydin's forces. He thought he could starve us out. As my gaze drifted over the cold huddled figures in each nook and cranny of the castle, each looking thinner all the time, I hoped I wasn't wrong that the commonfolk of Nerahdis knew more resilience than Rhydin would ever understand.

At the end of my rounds, having already assured one frazzled woman that I would see about moving her to a different room with less snoring and helped a small boy locate a stuffed puppy made out of an old rag, I ventured toward the throne room. The Rounans preferred that I spend most of my time in there as a way to supervise the remnants of our supplies, not trusting the Gornish Royals to utilize them fairly. As soon as I opened the door, a glorious meaty scent washed over me and made me stand an inch taller. I felt compelled to move forward and discover the source, but I cringed when I noticed several others behind me do the same. Whoever was cooking or eating this meat was about to get a lot of unwanted attention, and with hundreds of hungry rebels in this castle, nothing good could possibly come from this.

I hurried toward the center of the room, Sam's Kidek bandana on my head catching on the rough wool of others taller than me as I squeezed past them, but I was too late. There were a couple quick shouts before a loud *clang* echoed around the vast throne room, and I braced myself for a fight as I pushed between an Auklian woman who smelled of rotting fish and a Mineraltin boy with smudges on his freckled face.

Everyone in the throne room, with more people on the way, was now gathered around one of the random tables we'd set up as a sort of common area. I took in everything in a flash: golden-brown chunk of goat meat lying on the table among a few potatoes, a small portion missing that was now flung on the filthy floor, and a Rounan man and a Gornish man, each flushed in the face, glaring at each other.

Perfect.

For maybe a minute, I just stood there, acting as a witness while the two revealed what had happened through their argument. The goat was the last of the dark-skinned, Rounan man's herd, who was dressed in Auklian garb, and the fat Lunakan man was demanding a portion since no one had seen meat in a couple days. I rolled my eyes. The goat was the Rounan's personal property, and it was a small, young goat at that. It'd barely feed the six children that huddled behind their father and their parents, much less anyone else.

As the altercation began to devolve toward typical Rounan versus Gornish trash talk, I opened my mouth to say something before I became distracted. Everything in the throne room had come to a standstill, but there was one, golden head that was moving. Frederick had waded through the crowd from the opposite side of the throne room, but he halted when he saw me staring at him. More lines creased his pale, wiry face than ever before, but he returned my gaze unflinchingly. He didn't even seem like the same Frederick anymore, but I suppose I had become something different as well.

We were foes more often than we were friends anymore, now that we were the leaders of the opposing parties. We hadn't spoken since he revealed he had known about Sam's deteriorating condition at Sam's graveside, and I'd been meaning to talk to him for weeks in order to apologize and finally let it go. Sam had chosen how he wanted to go out, and his temper would have never allowed him to listen to anyone else's opinion. I had come to accept that part at least. When Frederick continued to remain where he was, I realized he expected me to solve this qualm on my own.

I laid down the law. The personal goat was the Rounan's to do with as he wished; our hunting party would be back any time, and the rest of us would eat then. I sensed Kylar appear behind me, lending his support as the rightful Kidek, as the large Lunakan man stared me down. If he thought he could scare me after everything I'd faced in my life, he was sorely mistaken. After perhaps a minute of total silence and the two opposite groups daring the other to make the first move, the man and several of his Gornish friends flowed toward the exit.

Giving a sigh of relief that no one got physical, I began to relax, but a glance at Frederick told another story. His arms were folded over his chest, and he was surrounded by other Gornish people who were furiously whispering things in his ears. His icy eyes held on mine, but I couldn't detect any emotions beyond them.

I turned away from him and into the gaze of my teenage son. Kylar was looking more and more like his father all the time, despite his darker brown hair that he got from me. His poor face had erupted into small, red lumps since Sam's death, and my heart ached that he was so stressed. As his regent, I tried to keep whatever I could off his shoulders, which was what Sam had wanted so badly. But I also had to teach him how to do the job and therefore included him in everything I did as Kidek Regent.

"Never let them see your fear," I whispered up to him now that he was taller than me, "either the Rounans or the Gornish. If you pretend you're steel, you'll never be bent."

Kylar nodded quietly, not quite meeting me in the eyes, and it killed me. Sam had talked for years about how he wanted to remain Kidek as long as possible to allow Kylar to have the life he'd never had. Sam's own father had gone missing in the Quarren War when Sam himself was a teenager, and now the cycle was repeating. It simply wasn't fair.

I was broken from my thoughts by a growing volume of whispering, which slowly became regular talk before escalating to shouting.

"Is this what our future will be like? The Gornish *still* believe they can take anything they want from us!"

"Things hafta change, or we're better off leavin'!"

"No way they'd go back to hangin' us after this. We've helped them so much, surely it'll keep gettin' better!"

"Kidek Regent, you *must* fight for our rights! Nerahdis cannot go back to the way it was before!" a Mineraltin man as thin as a rake bellowed with a voice double his size.

"Alright, alright, settle down!" I shouted, moving more into the center of the small gathering. "I am doing my very best at each Council meeting to ensure that all Rounans receive equal treatment while we find ourselves under the same roof-…"

"But wha' 'bout after Rhydin is destroyed?" a teenage Lunakan girl with muddy brown braids piped up.

I inwardly groaned, and it took every ounce of my self-control not to let it become audible. "As I've said before, let's not count our hay bales before we've even swathed the field. We're not going to know what the post-Rhydin world will exactly be like until we get there, or, quite frankly, *if* we get there. We need to focus on defeating Rhydin. We don't need a civil war brewing underneath the war we're already fighting."

There was a moment of silence as many of the Rounans around me dropped their eyes to the ground, some only children while others boasted many silver hairs on their heads. Their sadness and fear were palpable around me, and I could almost feel Sam nudging me to say something more.

I sighed. "I…cannot imagine what you all have been through and what courage it took for you to join the rebellion. You've kept your lives for years, decades, by keeping your true identities unknown. I knew your fear of execution very briefly when I first became an Allyen, but that doesn't compare to what my husband grew up with his whole life, just like the rest of you."

At the mention of Sam, many of the older Rounans saluted him with a pounding of their right fists against their chests.

"I vow to you all once more than I will personally ensure that change will come. We've already come so far with the Royals we have now compared to the ones that everyone my age and older grew up fearing. I trust Frederick, Xavier, and Sabine," I said slowly, eyeing each faction of Rounans that were grouped together by their home kingdoms, "but that won't stop me from locking them in a room until we can all agree on the future laws of our land. I promise you, no Rounan shall ever be hanged based upon his identity ever again!"

All of the Rounans around me gave a vigorous shout without a care in the world for anyone else nearby. They beamed with cheer, suddenly assured just by my words that everything would turn out right. The Rounans' opinion of me had certainly done a full one-eighty in the last decade and a half. They may have hated me at first, disappointed that their pure-blooded Kidek would sully his line with the blood of their enemies, but things really changed after I brought Sam home during the war, helped save the people of our compound when King Adam and Robert razed it, and every other mission Sam and I had run together during the early years of the rebellion. It felt nice to finally be accepted, but as I eyed the older men trying to rub elbows with my shy son, I knew the second he turned eighteen in three years their opinions of me wouldn't matter anymore.

I excused myself from the hubbub, leaving Kylar to bask in the rare positive atmosphere with his people. A quick scan of the throne room revealed that Frederick had left too. The only people left besides the Rounan mob were a couple older men playing Mineraltin Blitz and a young Lunakan woman surrounded by several children of varying ages who appeared to be attempting something that resembled school.

As I walked toward the exit, I passed the spot where I'd killed Mikael in order to save Frederick's life. I hesitated there, analyzing the tiny nick in the stone where my sister's lover and his weapon had fallen. I'd never intended to kill him. I'd only fired two magical shots to knock him off balance and disarm him, but I couldn't have predicted how his body would shift between the two to make the second a kill shot. History wouldn't remember it that way.

Time seemed to slow as I looked up and suddenly imagined Duunzer crashing through the high windows with its dark talons, spraying fire everywhere. I froze, my spine like ice as my heart accelerated to the point I could barely feel the separate beats, and I took the deepest breaths I could manage without looking conspicuous until the nightmare disappeared.

"Are ye alright, Madam Allyen?" one of the men playing cards asked, his beard white as snow. "Ye're awfully pale."

"Fine," I forced out bluntly, "thank you." I tried to shake off the dark, icy feeling of too many terrible memories and walked faster toward the door.

Once in the castle foyer, I turned toward the staircase wondering if Frederick could be found upstairs, but the sound of my daughter's voice calling me stopped me in my tracks. Rayna came rushing up to me, her newly short bob of auburn hair bouncing with each step. I noticed Evan in the background, waiting for her in his heaviest cloak.

"Mama, I need to talk to you right now," Rayna pleaded, her eyes scanning back and forth for anyone else in need of my attention. "We need to get Erikin out of the dungeon. I believe him that he didn't mean to call Rhydin to the Dome."

My head quirked to the side on its own accord in shock. "Really? I thought you were determined he was guilty?"

"I…I was wrong," Rayna choked out, and I could visibly see how hard it was for the prideful young teen to admit that. "He was just trying to survive. He was trying to get rid of his magic, he never wanted to hurt us once he knew who we were to him. Please, we need to get his trial actually scheduled, and you need to vouch for him that he's telling the truth so he can be freed!"

"I see," I muttered. My heart dropped into the pit of my stomach at the thought of facing Erikin, my nephew, now that I had been the one to kill his father, even if it was accidental. Perhaps, freeing him could at least begin to make things right. "I think you are right, and I'll do whatever I can to help you. But…" – Rayna's sudden joyful expression faltered – "you'll have to find a different person to vouch for him. I'm in a…rather *odd* position at the moment. I don't quite fully represent the Rounans, and my reputation as an Allyen only gets me so far with the Gornish now that I'm serving as Kidek Regent. You need a Royal's word, especially one that is respected on both sides. King Frederick would be a good choice. He's known for being a good mediator."

My teenage daughter fully wilted now, as if that was the worst thing I could ever say to her although I certainly didn't know why. Evan was soon calling her name, and she morosely thanked me and wandered back over to where he waited. My brother met my gaze briefly across the room and gave me a rare half smile. He very much enjoyed being Rayna's magic teacher. He would never get to teach anything to his own son, Aron, who was a Rounan like his mother. While part of me ached to have that experience to myself, my busy schedule made it impossible, so I tried to let it go the best I could. Evan's happiness made it worth it.

The two disappeared through the huddled groups of people toward the castle's front gate to begin their lesson, and after a quick glance around the foyer to see if any Rounan needed my attention, I strode toward the stairs. I wasn't absolutely one hundred percent sure I knew where I was going, but I figured I could get close enough that my magical senses could steer me in. I climbed the stairs as fast as I could manage, dodging a chicken or two as I did. I shook my head at the sight of them but pocketed an egg I found anyway. If the things weren't so darn imperative to our battle against starvation, people would probably try a lot harder to keep them in the stables regardless of how cold it was.

I passed the floor where Sam spent his last hours, ignoring the icy fingers I felt reach for me even though my heart begged me to go back. *Just go peek in the bedroom where it happened. Maybe this is all a dream, and he'll be lying there alive and well.* I silenced my traitorous heart and climbed faster, past the floor with the boring green wallpaper where my family and I were staying, among many others, and all the way to the top floor where a gold and white floral design etched the walls.

While this floor was also stripped bare, it seemed even emptier than the other hallways in the castle. There were a handful of rebels that still harbored resentment against the Royals and the monarchies that were established centuries ago, so this floor had been both vacated and picked at more than any other. I'd never been up here before. As a commoner, I'd only seen the inside of the ballroom before becoming the Allyen, but even after that my experience was limited to all the random towers and ramparts outside during the battle with Duunzer. This floor was the private residence of the Lunakan Royals, and even now in its rebellion chapter of life, only the Royals stayed up here albeit not just the Lunakan ones.

I wandered down the hallway slowly, every bare cranny well-lit with a sconce on either side every six feet. The magical compass in my head was whirring. Behind the first door, I could smell the ocean of Sabine's water magic and feel the cool head of her elder twin ward, Chretien. The boys were evidently descended from some sort of noble family as evidenced by their magical powers. Willian, the younger twin whose presence always smelled of fish to me, seemed to be absent.

Farther down the hallway, I felt Mira's and Cornflower's wind powers like lace brushing against my cheek. They were in the room together along with Lyla, Mira's youngest, whose fiery presence threatened to overtake them both. The atmosphere in the room beyond the door seemed tumultuous even from here, so I tiptoed faster to leave them in peace, wondering if Xavier and Taisyn were downstairs somewhere.

Just past this doorway was an old portrait of Adam, the former king and Frederick, Mira, and Cornflower's father. I had to shove my knuckles into my mouth to keep from laughing. While the old king-turned-Follower stared seriously with his painted, violet eyes, a rebel or two had taken to embellishing the portrait. There was a curly mustache crudely drawn over Adam's neat goatee, two horns now poked out from his black curls and golden crown, and less funny were several red slashes through his pale neck. While the memory of the Crushing of the Thrones, the day Emperor Rhydin executed most of the last living Royals, still pumped fear through my veins, I couldn't help but give Frederick a silent bravo. Let the rebels work out their anger with the Royals that truly deserved every bad thing they ever got rather than the new ones trying so hard to create a different world by saving it from Rhydin.

I took a deep breath as I approached the final set of double doors in the hallway – the king's suite. Frederick's presence bounced against my mind, exuding peace and bravery along with his mighty wind powers. As my hand rose to knock, I couldn't help but remind myself that these doors had once led to King Adam's personal rooms, my first nemesis, but I steadied myself. They were Frederick's now, and it was time to put this old quarrel behind us, no matter how impossible it seemed at the moment.

Before my knuckles ever brushed the beautifully-stained wood, I heard a faint "come in." Just as I was sensing him and the other Royals, Frederick had sensed me coming. I meagerly pushed the door on the right open, taking in each bit of the suite as it became visible to me.

Piles of carefully rolled tapestries and all the other Royal knick-knacks that had disappeared from the rest of the castle along every wall, an intricate golden chandelier, several mismatched bookshelves that seemed to have been dragged in here from several other parts of the castle, deep brown corresponding furniture complete with a big four-poster bed covered in a fluffy white blanket and flowing with a snowy canopy, and a gigantic desk buried under a mountain of parchment, quills, and ink wells. Frederick sat in a velvet-covered armchair beside this desk, which looked terribly uncomfortable and more suited for a little old lady than the King of Lunaka.

"You did well with that. Down there," Frederick added awkwardly, barely meeting my eyes. He seemed thin and pale, his normally golden hair now thin, dark, and flat. I suddenly found myself wondering whether anyone was making sure he was eating. If one didn't know Frederick, one would think there was a subtle hint of sarcasm to his statement, but in the last two decades, I could count on one hand how many times I'd witnessed anything remotely resembling sarcasm coming from Frederick. I knew he meant it.

"Uh…thank you," I uttered automatically as I took a couple more steps into the room and closed the door behind me. "I'd like to talk to you, if that's alright. If you're not too busy, that is."

Frederick didn't respond, but he pushed himself to his feet, the bones in his hands suddenly more noticeable, and procured another, almost identical chair. He placed it at least six feet away from his, then he silently returned to his own seat.

I sat on the very edge of the hard chair, feeling the need to be at least a little bit closer to him. I cleared my throat and said, "Frederick, I'd like to apologize to you. I'm sorry for the way I've treated you ever since Sam died. You've been nothing but gracious to me and my family, and…" – I swallowed hard; I may have meant it, but it was still difficult to say – "…I've forgiven you. That you didn't tell me. I know, more than anyone, how stubborn Sam can be…*could* be…" I had to stop. There was abruptly something lodged in my throat. I hadn't slipped up on using the correct tense since the first week.

He was looking at me now, his eyes clearer than I'd seen in weeks, although heavy-lidded and underlined with red. He leaned forward as he replied barely above a whisper, "I should have told you as soon as you arrived at the battle that day. He told me during the trip from the Dome to Lunaka Castle, and I had plenty of opportunities to tell you as we made our way into the castle. I am sincerely sorry, Lina."

"I…" My voice broke. I shook my head, drowning in frustration. "You hadn't even known that long! And for me to hold that against you…I just… W-Why couldn't he have just told m-me?"

Frederick instantly leapt up as I dissolved into tears. He knelt at my feet and tucked his thin, wiry hands around mine, not saying a word. He didn't have to because I knew he understood my pain. His late wife, Cassandra, had died during childbirth after a long, horrific illness about which Frederick was mostly kept in the dark.

After a few minutes and I had embarrassedly scraped myself back together, he stared at our hands before meeting my gaze. "He knew your fear of losing him. I know it is hard, but I will ensure that you and your children are taken care of. I promised Sam, and I promise you now."

I was barely listening. "Don't you see?" I asked squeakily, my anger rising. "I was so afraid of losing him that I lost him altogether."

"I know, Lina" Frederick breathed, and he stayed in his position for a moment more as I swallowed my grief for the time being. Then, he returned to his chair, although he did move it a couple feet closer to a friendly distance rather than the type of distance reserved for strangers. "Now, I think we probably need to talk about the donkey in the room."

I groaned, still venting. "I'm fed up, Frederick. I'm ready for somebody to just outlaw the words 'Rounan' and 'Gornish.' Why can't we all just be Nerahdian? My son is both Gornish and Rounan, but everyone only sees him as Rounan. I don't want him to have some opportunities extended and some withheld simply because the world only sees half of his blood."

Frederick nodded in understanding, then asked cryptically, "What about Rayna?"

"I-I mean Rayna too, of course…" I stuttered, flustered. Of all people to make that comment in front of, Frederick was not the one. "She is also half-Gornish, half-Rounan...*now*. I'm sorry, that didn't come out well."

The blond-haired man hesitated, his icy gaze on the floor. It was still painful for him that Rayna, the child Cassandra died giving live to, was born his blood, but our need for a new Allyen to rejuvenate the magic was too dire. "Think nothing of it. I will always support her, no matter what happens."

My shoulders went slack, awed and heartbroken at Frederick's tremendous sacrifice. We spent the next hour or so discussing the attitudes and goings-on of our respective people, trying to nip any issues possible in the bud and preparing different plans to mitigate any possible rumblings of civil war. I decided to leave the Erikin issue to Rayna, although I did vaguely hint to Frederick that Rayna would likely be seeking him out to talk to him soon. When I left Frederick's chambers, I felt lighter than I had in ages.

Little did I know, whatever semblance of a life I had tried to put together in Sam's absence would come crashing down around me at the next Council meeting.

Chapter Three

Rayna

"Excellent job, Rayna," Uncle Evan mused as he studied my adorably fluffy puppy perfectly perched on its hind paws with a stick in its mouth. "Your Einanhis are always flawlessly executed even as we continue to grow their size. You should try a full-size dog next."

I grumbled moodily as I mentally found the magical tether tying me and my power to my creation. The ash-gray puppy reduced to a golden orb of magic as I repossessed it, and without skipping a beat, I immediately imagined a larger dog, a midnight-colored Mineraltin hunting hound like I'd seen in Caark once. The siphoning of my magic began instantly as it filtered through the air invisibly, growing another golden orb bigger and bigger with several offshoots, before I abruptly felt that sweet spot where I knew the Einanhi had attained the perfect level of magic. Not too much as to lose control, and not too little as to be too weak.

I whispered the magic word, "*anadlu*," which meant "breathe" in Gornish.

The ball of magic popped like a bubble, and in its place was a tall, sleek Mineraltin hound the color of coal. It shook its body as it adjusted to the cold and waited obediently for its first order. The first Einanhi I'd ever made was a rat that was too limp to stand, but all the other ones I'd made were excellent rule-followers.

"Fetch," I declared in a bored tone, pointing to a thin tree branch lying in the corner of the courtyard. Instantly, the hound trotted directly to the branch, snatched it up, and dutifully brought it right back and laid it at my feet.

Uncle Evan shook his head incredulously. "You know, if your mother ever sees how easy Einanhis are for you, she'll be very jealous. She never was able to get it right."

"Uncle Evan," I groaned, "if we're going to have lessons every single day to get me caught up, we might as well work on the death spell! *Alytniinaeran*. Einanhis are easy, and I'm not going to need to know how to make one in order to destroy Emperor Rhydin."

"Mm, you don't know that," my uncle replied, folding his hands behind his back. "If Emperor Rhydin is truly an Einanhi gone wild with too much power, all the Allyens will need to know the inner workings of Einanhi creation better than anyone. Or, the two of us will need to, anyway."

"But if I can't perform my end of the death spell, my knowledge of Einanhi creation isn't going to matter that much!" I whined, crossing my arms angrily.

Uncle Evan took a deep breath and paused a moment before he settled his heavy hand on my shoulder, his fingertips calloused from years of violin playing. "I have full confidence in you. My worry is having the opportunity to perform the spell, not whether we'll get it right or not. But come. We'll run through it, and you can be done for today."

I nodded appreciatively, and we took our places, leaving an imaginary spot for my mother like the third point of a triangle. Uncle Evan waited for me to begin, and as soon as my right foot swept outward in the first movement, he was paralleling me in the dance-like spell. We circled around each other, arcing our arms as we stepped with our corresponding feet.

Two small, golden balls of magic appeared, and as we dragged them through each movement, they grew larger and larger. It took a couple of minutes to finish the spell, and my cold lungs were breathless when we came together for the final move, pushing our charged magic together into an absolutely huge central orb. The built-up magic lasted a few moments before it disappeared in a flash of light like lightning, and I could only wonder what it would look like when all three of us were present. Would our combined magic shoot toward Emperor Rhydin? Would we have to aim it at him? Would something else happen? None of us really knew.

Perhaps, the real Rhydin Caldwell locked away in the Archimage Palace as an invisible specter knew.

Uncle Evan dismissed me without much ado, and I bolted back into the warmth of the castle and toward the main staircase. I felt a desperate need to talk to King Frederick as soon as possible about Erikin, and I also wondered about asking yet again to be allowed to travel to the Archimage Palace. I hadn't forgotten my promise to Rhydin Caldwell, that I would return to him as soon as I could. He had been alone for oh so long, and I just *knew* that there was more to the story of the two Rhydins that he could tell us.

I took the stairs two at a time, hopping over chickens and one or two weary rebels as I did. I had been up to the top floor of the castle a couple times before to find Taisyn, my only true friend in this place, but I'd never been past King Xavier and Queen Mira's door. Anxiously, I passed a vandalized tapestry depicting a man I didn't recognize and was just about to reach King Frederick's door when I suddenly realized I could sense my mother's light magic within.

What on Nerahdis was she doing in King Frederick's room? Was she talking to him about Erikin for me?

I crept closer, hoping I'd be able to hear whatever was going on in there, and jumped when my mother's voice suddenly became loud. She sounded frustrated as she said, "I'm fed up, Frederick. I'm ready for somebody to just outlaw the words 'Rounan' and 'Gornish.' Why can't we all just be Nerahdian? My son is both Gornish and Rounan, but everyone only sees him as Rounan. I don't want him to have some opportunities extended and some withheld simply because the world only sees half of his blood."

Well, she had a point. The labels certainly seemed outdated to me. King Frederick must have said something back that I couldn't hear because my mother's voice now stammered, "I-I mean, Rayna too, of course! She is also half-Gornish, half-Rounan…*now*. I'm sorry, that didn't come out well."

My brow furrowed. What did that mean? I was half and half "*now*."

"Think nothing of it," King Frederick said, barely audible as I pressed my ear so hard to the door that I lost feeling in it, "I will always support her, no matter what happens."

I stumbled backward from the door as the two inside switched to a new topic of conversation. What was with the weird serious tones? Surely, my mother was simply more focused on Kylar because it was more dangerous to be a Rounan, right? She obviously meant all the same things for me; it just wasn't that big of a deal since the world saw me as Gornish. I didn't have an angular mark on my wrist. I was an Allyen. I could do anything I wanted with my life…right?

That had to be it. And King Frederick only made that vow because of what he already promised Papa. I mean, he gave me a new winter cloak; I knew he cared. His apparent devotion to me was just a product of his long friendship with my parents. Nothing more.

Yep, that makes sense, I thought to myself as I anxiously rushed back down the hallway toward the stairs. I didn't *need* to talk to King Frederick right now anyway, I could wait maybe another day.

I hustled down the stairs to the floor where our room was and flew through the door, swinging it shut behind me. Aron barely bothered to look up from his book, a different one now, and I briefly wondered how anyone could literally just sit and read all day long.

"Want to talk about it?" Aron asked monotonously, his nose already buried again.

"Nope," I replied firmly, as I approached my younger cousin still sprawled across his straw tick on the floor, desperate to get my mind off the conversation I'd just heard. "What are you reading now?"

Aron chuckled, "That history book Aunt Lina keeps thinking she can hide from me. I don't know why she even bothers anymore. It's like the rarest book ever, it has Rhydin Caldwell's real history in it."

"*What?*" I gasped and threw myself down next to him, my eyes soaking up the pages.

"Yeah, I mean, it's just a few chapters, but it tells how Emperor Caden was searching for a young noble with the ability to receive magic to become the First Archimage," Aron said, suddenly flipping through pages too fast for me to read to my chagrin. "Rhydin Caldwell was only eighteen, but I guess he was the perfect candidate. They pumped him full of all three of the main types of magic, but then it ends and skips to when he's replaced by the second Archimage. I guess even this book has been censored." Aron sighed pitifully.

"But that's not what happened," I murmured, more to myself than anyone else. "He wasn't just replaced by the next Archimage. He somehow accidentally created an Einanhi of himself that stole every drop of that power he was given, and he disappeared. Became that specter trapped in the Archimage Palace for centuries."

"Hmph. There definitely has to be more to the story than that," Aron grumbled as his page flipping began to slow. "Nobody just 'accidentally' creates an Einanhi for no reason."

"Maybe there was a reason, and we just don't know it! A really good reason that went wrong!" I snipped defensively. I was exhausted of the Gornish rumor going around that Rhydin

Caldwell was even more evil than Emperor Rhydin the Einanhi, and he did it all on purpose.

Aron rolled his eyes like a child just as he finally came to a stop on a page with a full portrait two men. My breath left me as I first recognized Rhydin Caldwell on the right, nearly a spitting image to the apparition I had met in the Archimage Palace months ago. He looked a year or two younger, but his brow was drawn and he stood so straight it was like there was a rod in his back. The caption underneath listed him as "the new Archimage-in-training," so it made sense he looked a little younger and less weary than he did now as a specter.

He hadn't seen everything yet that he'd seen now.

Next to him was Emperor Caden, whose image I knew well from history lessons in school. He was dressed more regally than any Royal I'd ever seen, and his long, lined face was framed in a tidy, graying beard. He looked like he'd seen a lot in his life too, and I abruptly recalled that he was murdered. I wracked my brain, trying to remember when it happened. Emperor Caden was in the process of breaking Nerahdis into the Three Kingdoms so that his sons wouldn't go to war, but of course my education had included nothing about the secret Archimage position.

Who killed Emperor Caden? And how long after Rhydin Caldwell became the First Archimage did it happen? Was his death possibly linked with the creation of Rhydin's Einanhi clone who was reigning as emperor now? Most people just assumed anymore that the evil clone killed him, but was that really true?

The room started to spin. Aron, his book, and the bedroom around us melted away into nothing but colors. My heartbeat accelerated as the colors rearranged themselves and changed hues to mostly browns, some black and red, and one spot of brilliant, ocean blue. All at once, I found myself in a small room walled with logs with a crude table in the middle. A quaint, black kettle sat on a roaring fire, and I abruptly realized I was taller again and dressed in the dark green garb of a hunter. I stared at my new leathery, scarred hands before sound returned to my ears.

"Nora, I've been told the most *horrendous* news!" a young woman in a pretty purple day dress had just burst through the front door. Her long tresses were the bright blue color I'd just seen as the ancestral memory took hold.

Amelia Eason. The woman I saw in another memory once before when Nora met Rhydin Caldwell, Amelia's new beau, for the first time, and the woman whose name was written upon the grave where Nora had been mourning. Who was Amelia Eason, and why was she so important?

"What do you mean?" a full, throaty voice escaped from my lips. Nora's voice. "What's wrong?"

"Rhydin, he…he…he's going to be taken away!" Amelia cried, her eyes shimmering with tears. She was clinging to me – Nora – now, sobbing hysterically.

"Why?" Nora's voice sprung from my mouth again. My hands braced Amelia's shoulders, and I suddenly felt very protective of this girl. "Is he in danger?"

"I-I-I don't think so…but he's…he has to go away," Amelia wept, barely able to remain understandable, "with the *emperor!*"

Nora's entire demeanor changed in a flash; I could feel it inside me somehow. Her tone turned dark and defensive. "What does Emperor Caden want with Rhydin? Does he know you're involved with him?"

"It's that Archimage thing," Amelia declared in a solid voice, her anger rising. "Remember when the emperor printed all those notices a few months ago looking for someone of noble blood to fill that new Archimage role? Apparently, Master Caldwell signed Rhydin up for it, and he's been chosen!"

Nora took control of my hands and guided Amelia to sit on a stool under the table as she perched on the other. She took a deep breath before responding. "The town crier made it seem like being this Archimage thing is an amazing opportunity. Is it really a bad thing that Rhydin might become this Archimage?"

"Y-You don't understand," Amelia blubbered, beginning to dissolve into tears again as her ocean blue hair fell in front of her face, "he has no choice but to go…and he'll be expected to meet with Emperor Caden and his sons…f-for the rest of his life."

"And you can't go with him," Nora finished quietly. "They'd never let you live if they saw you. Not after what they did to your mother and sister."

Amelia collapsed in a heap upon the table, her blue tresses fanning everywhere. Nora gently set her hand on Amelia's head. The girl whimpered, "I-I love him, Nora…w-we were going to get m-married."

"I know," Nora whispered.

The room burst into colors again, whirling around and re-shaping themselves back into the bright bedroom at Lunaka Castle. I was being shaken when things finally settled, and I found myself rolled onto the floor with Aron above me.

"Finally!" Aron grumbled, although his eyes were wide with fear. "What's the big idea, huh? I thought you were in a *coma!*"

I touched my head, feeling dizzy and breathless. "I…I saw another of Nora's memories."

My younger cousin froze. My family, of course, had been informed of the ancestral memories I was seeing, but Clariion Arii had convinced us that they needed to remain strictly secret. I didn't understand why, but apparently, he thought they wouldn't go over well with the rest of the rebellion. Aron's teal eyes grew large with wonder. "Really? What did you see? You haven't had one of those in a long time."

I looked down and rubbed my eyes. It was true. I hadn't had any ancestral memories since the day Papa died and I witnessed Nora's memory of grieving at Amelia's grave, vowing to avenge her. Promising that even if she failed, her descendants would see it through – the birth of the Allyen line.

I clutched my knees to my chest as I said, "I saw Nora's memory of when Amelia told her that Rhydin was chosen as the First Archimage. The two of them were in like a log cabin or something. It seemed like maybe it was Nora's house. Amelia was...like *devastated.* They were already betrothed."

"Why?" Aron's brow furrowed. He briefly glanced back at my mother's old book, flipping a couple pages. "There's no mention of Amelia Eason at all in this book. Why would she be devastated that he would be chosen for such a big deal?"

"That's what doesn't quite make sense. For some reason, Amelia couldn't go with him. Nora even suggested that if Emperor Caden or any of his sons saw her, she'd be killed. Apparently, they'd done the same to her mother and her sister...but why?" I shook my head in confusion. I stared at the gray, cobbled ceiling for a few minutes before my eyes landed on Aron's book again at the sound of his rapidly flipping pages. "If there's no mention of her in that book, she really must not have gone. She broke off their betrothal. Wouldn't she be mentioned, even indirectly, if the First Archimage had a wife?"

"It's hard telling. Women weren't mentioned much back then. Nora's not even in this book," Aron scoffed, his annoyance obvious. "We may never know what actually happened."

"That's not true." I grumbled. "These memories help a lot, but they come so randomly. It'd be better just to go ask the firsthand witness himself."

Aron blanched a little. "Who, Rhydin Caldwell? He's stuck in the Archimage Palace, and the entire rebellion rejected the idea of going there to talk to him months ago. How would you get there?"

"I'll walk if I have to!" I insisted before jumping up to grab my sketchbook out of the small bag containing my whole world – including the little metal bird Taisyn had sculpted for me using his fire magic – and returning to the straw tick to sit next to my cousin. "Alright, Aron. You've read practically every book in Lunaka Castle since we got here. Tell me everything you've ever read about Rhydin Caldwell, Emperor Caden, Amelia Eason, and Nora Soreta."

To my dismay, of the hundreds of books Aron had ever read both here and back home in Caark, the information available on these people was very limited, although it varied a lot by person. There was absolutely nothing about Amelia, which semi-confirmed my suspicions that she never went with Rhydin when he became Archimage. If she had, she surely would have been mentioned *somewhere* once she was a part of the highest, most exclusive social circle there was. Women weren't even listed by name on any of the first few censuses of Nerahdis, only as tally marks under their fathers or husbands. I groaned. Why was history so frustrating?

It seemed that my mother was so protective of her history book simply because it was the only book to reference Rhydin Caldwell, however briefly and incompletely. He was a noble's son who grew up in Diagalo, a town that no longer existed near Lake Spenser in Lunaka. According to a census Aron found in another book, there had been a Benjamin Caldwell living in Diagalo for many years with only one child ever tallied, so we decided that was likely his father and Rhydin had been an only child.

While there was no mention of Nora in the same book as Rhydin, Aron had read about her in a couple other places, although she seemed to be swept under the rug. Most people hadn't heard of the Allyen before my mother destroyed Duunzer – the person was only a myth – so I supposed that made sense. All Aron could remember was that she grew up in Soläna and lived most of her adult life alone before meeting her husband, Charles Rodgers, much later. I wondered how alone she'd actually been if Amelia had been in her life for however long.

Emperor Caden was another story. As the first ruler of Nerahdis and someone who was generally adored by all, there were *tons* of sources listing the usual information about him.

He was the youngest of the emperor of Gornan's nine sons and came to Nerahdis with hundreds of others seeking a better life as Gornan, another continent thousands of miles away, experienced drought, famine, and disease.

He and his wife, Melodi, had three sons – Joshuua, Ivann, and Spenser – who each inherited Mineraltir, Auklia, and Lunaka respectively, leaving Caark and the Great Desert ungoverned. Then, he was mysteriously murdered. That much was common sense to any person in Nerahdis. But who murdered him? What was his relationship like with Rhydin Caldwell? The only thing I learned about him that I hadn't been taught a hundred times before was that his wife died when Spenser, the youngest son, was only two years old, and she'd been sick since his birth. That didn't help me a whole lot.

Books weren't going to help at all. Only one person could fill in the gaps now.

Aron and I spent the rest of that day digging through books and cross-referencing whatever sources we could find. Actually, to be more precise, Aron spent the day scouring books while I sat next to him as moral support, absent-mindedly doodling the memory I'd just witnessed into my sketchbook. He thoroughly enjoyed the project I had created for him, but I only found myself more and more exasperated and was almost too frustrated to sleep. Rest couldn't claim me until I promised myself that I would broach the topic of returning to the Archimage Palace at the next Council meeting just days away, along with petitioning them to announce a trial date for Erikin. There was no way I'd take "no" as an answer either!

The next few days were utterly uneventful, which just made them feel even longer. I spent the hours doing lessons with Uncle Evan, steering as clear of Nathia as humanly possible, sending notes down to Erikin in the dungeon to let him know I was working on it, and wandering around the castle with Taisyn in search of King Frederick. To my dismay, the only times we seemed to find him were when he was in the thick of a Gornish/Rounan conflict and not available to talk. I wished Taisyn could just be Erikin's Royal voucher – he was the heir to the Mineraltin throne as King Xavier and Queen Mira's firstborn, even if he hated the idea – but if my own Allyen mother wasn't good enough, the rebellion would never take the word of a teenager. Blind or not, Taisyn was the best listener in the whole castle. He knew when to press for more information and when to leave me be. He'd certainly come a long way from the sore jerk he'd been when we'd first met in the Dome.

"Are you ready for the Council meeting? Have you figured out what you're going to say?" Taisyn asked, his fingers glowing as we hustled down the stairs. Whenever he used his pyromage powers, Taisyn was able to see outlines and silhouettes around him, which allowed him to use the stairs on his own.

I groaned as I hopped over a salt-and-pepper-colored chicken, "Ugh, I think so? I'm not sure it's really a matter of *what* I say, but whether I'll get to talk at all!"

"True, these meetings just get uglier and uglier." Taisyn shrugged as we reached the bottom of the stairs. He ran a pale, freckled hand through his coppery hair and quickly brushed his face, his nervous tick.

"You look fine, I swear," I tried to reassure him as we joined the throng of people migrating toward the throne room.

Taisyn scoffed. "My father will find some hair out of place, I'm sure. Even if he has started allowing me to use my fire during lessons."

I sighed heavily. "One problem at a time, Taisyn. One problem at a time."

We hurried into the throne room, which was filled to bursting. All the extra tables had been pushed to the walls to make as much room as possible, but people were still practically standing on each other, aside from the detectable gap that separated the Gornish from the small, Rounan minority. All of our leaders were already standing up on the dais, well in front of the thrones as if to minimize their presence. The Council meetings used to be held around a large table and were mostly public discussions between the leaders themselves with an audience that typically stayed quiet aside from a question or two. Anymore, the table was abandoned, and the Council spent more time policing debates in the audience than actually talking to each other.

Everyone was already fighting about the same old thing as Taisyn and I squeezed toward the front of the dais. We bounced between the Rounan side complaining that they wanted control over their own set of rations and the Gornish side arguing that the Rounans were smaller in number and yet receiving preferential treatment. To my chagrin, we ended up standing with all the other Royal children – Dominick and Nathia of Lunaka, Chretien and Willian of Auklia, and Lyla of Mineraltir – as well as Chelsea, our Aatarilec friend currently in her human form. I did my best to avoid eye contact with Nathia even as Willian sidled over to me. He whispered in my ear with a smirk on his face, "Missing you at lessons, Rayna. Where have you been hiding?"

"Right under your nose, Willian," I grumbled, hoping to shut both him and his annoying remarks down.

"Oh, don't be like that," he grumbled before his grin returned. "If you don't want to spend your lessons around *Nathia*, I completely understand" – at this, Nathia rolled her eyes theatrically – "but we should find some time to hang out anyway. Just you and me, you know?"

While my face screwed up into an incredulous expression, I was sadly unable to give him a piece of my mind before the shouting consumed the entire room.

"We deserve to keep track of our own food!"

"You're no better than the rest of us! None of us keep our own food!"

"But your Gornish Royals do! Our Kidek Regent should be given the same power as the Three Kings!"

"That's *outrageous!*"

I cringed at the thought of my mother being ranked the same as the Three Kings. That was as good as making me a princess like Nathia and Lyla, and the thought made my stomach churn.

"*This* is why we need an Archimage!" a loud-mouthed Mineraltin woman shouted, the usual proponent of the topic. Her black hair was streaked with white, and her dark face was heavily lined. "Then *one* person can make all the decisions the rest of us are held to, and it'll be fair!"

A gigantic thunder of denials and negative responses rumbled through the Rounan side of the room, along with a couple comments on how it'd only be fair if the Archimage was a Rounan, or at least mixed. Others reasoned that it should be put to a vote whether to install an Archimage or not. Taisyn was rolling his eyes as I turned to look for poor Princess Cornflower. She was a beautiful young woman with golden curls, not quite thirty, and she was the only traditional Archimage candidate we had as a Royal not in line for a throne. She was King Frederick's youngest sister with Queen Mira of Mineraltir in the middle. King Xavier and Queen Sabine didn't have any siblings.

Princess Cornflower was wringing her skirt behind her back to at least make it a little less obvious that she chafed at the idea of being propelled above all of her siblings and cohorts. I didn't blame her. Being Archimage was what tore Rhydin Caldwell apart, seemingly in more ways than one.

As the rebellion continued to point fingers and the Royals on the dais attempted to retain control, I knew there was no point in opening my mouth. None of the Royals would ever hear me over this chaos. My best bet was to track down King Frederick when he was alone about both Erikin and returning to the Archimage Palace to hear Rhydin Caldwell's story.

"I have a solution to propose," a clear, mellow voice echoed around the room, amplified by magic.

The entire rebellion silenced almost immediately, the Gornish fear of magic palpable. I was shocked to see Clariion Arii, the pointy-eared leader of the mythical Ranguvariians, striding into the room toward the dais, the crowd parting for him instantly. Aunt Rachel, his human-looking granddaughter and my mother's best friend, followed in his wake, dressed in an elaborate orange robe identical to Clariion Arii's.

King Frederick, so weary it seemed he might drop over dead any second, seemed grateful for a break in the cacophony. He cleared his throat and asked, "Which problem does your prospective solution address?"

"All of them," Clariion Arii replied seriously, no trace of a smile on his leathery face. His Ranguvariian eyes were a stale green color, utterly unindicative of any emotion he could possibly be feeling.

The room itself seemed to begin murmuring. Even the Royals eyed each other uncomfortably. I glanced at Taisyn briefly, and he, too, was trained carefully on Clariion Arii. If a solution existed that would solve all our problems, how had we not found it already?

"What is this solution?" Queen Sabine of Auklia asked skeptically as she placed a strong hand on her hip.

Clariion Arii seemed to meet each of the leaders' eyes in turn, lingering a beat longer on my mother's than anyone else's. He took a deep breath before carefully enunciating, "I propose that Allyen Linaria, the current Kidek Regent, be joined with King Frederick of Lunaka in marriage."

Everything in the room, including my own heart and time itself, stopped.

Chapter Four

Lina

I was frozen, my eyes glued to Arii's face. What had he said? Did I hear him properly?

I didn't dare turn to look at any of the other Royals, especially not Frederick. Surely, my ears were mistaken. Then, I saw the look on my daughter's face; blanched, agape, and a hint of preposterousness in her eyes. Kylar, too, seemed paralyzed next to me. The distance between us seemed to open up in a chasm even though neither of us moved an inch.

My heart hammered.

Then I heard the major shift as the chatter of the rebellion resumed around us. So many…*intrigued* expressions. Nodding. On *both* sides. The Gornish seemed appeased that the Kidek wouldn't be given their own separate throne. Grins were spreading across most of the Rounans' faces as the prospect of more power and influence loomed. Pro-Archimage opinions were suddenly silent.

"Our Kidek Regent…a queen! And our next Kidek a Rounan *and* a Royal!"

The room began to tilt. Xavier happened to catch the corner of my eye, and I barely registered his stern yet consigned look, his bad arm bundled away within his emerald cloak – his old injury from when he and Sam were caught in an avalanche during the war.

No.

Before I could help myself, I found my feet scurrying off the dais and out the side door into a blissfully cool hallway. My breaths were ragged now, my lungs heaving for air like there wasn't enough in the whole castle. I paused briefly, pressing my back into the cold stone like it might clear my head. What was Arii *thinking?* Suggesting such a thing! Sam had barely been gone two months. There was no way I could ever do anything like that ever again.

A door creaked open as the Council meeting adjourned within the throne room, and I took off again. I sprinted toward the stairs, my third of the locket hot as it bounced against my chest. Unbidden tears welled in the corners of my eyes until they streaked down my cheeks, and that just made me more furious.

I threw myself into the room my family shared and slammed the door. It was empty thankfully, although I hadn't noticed Evan, Cayce, or Aron in the throne room. I began to pace, unable to still myself. *Too hot, too hot.* I couldn't take it anymore. I stalked to the one window and pushed it open, flooding the bedroom with crisp, icy air.

The bedroom door opened so quietly I barely heard it. I whirled, my magic reaching my fingertips like lightning, and Arii himself towered just inside the door frame, having already ducked in. I turned back to my window, trying to breathe. "Leave me alone."

"Lina," Arii said gently as he closed the door behind him, the beads on his ornate, orange robe rattling, "I wish to speak with you more on this matter. It is very important and personal."

I faced him and couldn't stop myself from shouting, "If it was personal, you would have come to me about this ridiculous notion *privately* instead of announcing it to the entire rebellion!"

"Yet, I knew you would need to see the positive reaction the idea would generate," Arii replied softly, still not speaking at his regular volume, "if you were to even consider the idea."

"I'm *not*," I grunted through gritted teeth. "I'm never getting married again."

"Please, let me speak unhindered, so that you may at least understand my reasoning." Arii carefully approached me, like one would someone about to jump off a cliff, just near enough to sit cross-legged on the floor. The one chair in our room was far too short for him, and I could tell he was trying to disarm me by no longer looming several feet above my head.

When I remained silent, my gaze hard on the floor, he continued, "This proposal contains several advantages for many parties. You, Frederick, Cornflower, your children, the rebellion, and therefore all of Nerahdis."

I rolled my eyes. Sure, it did.

"The strife between the Gornish and Rounans must end. They are on the precipice of civil war, which puts all of Nerahdis in danger of remaining under Emperor Rhydin's rule. The Rounans will be appeased with both their Kidek Regent and Kidek-in-training permanently linked to the Royals, while the Gornish see this as a better outcome than making the Kidek position like a fourth king. If both sides feel adequately represented and treated fairly, then this Archimage bickering will disappear as the leaders are better able to do their jobs themselves," Arii began his list of positives.

"Sure, they'll be appeased for now," I scoffed. "Doesn't mean it'll last if other things don't change too."

"But it will open the door for more change. All of the Three Kings need to mend their relations with the Rounans, but Frederick must do so much more than the others. His father, King Adam, executed ten times the number of Rounans than either of his foreign counterparts. Frederick is stretched too thin, Lina, as a solo ruler. He is not doing well," Arii insisted, but I cut him off before he could continue.

"Sabine seems to do it just fine. Frederick is a great king," I muttered loudly, before Arii gave me a look pleading for fewer interruptions.

"I did not mean his leadership skills," Arii clarified a little sternly, really fixing me in his green gaze. "Perhaps, you have not noticed, but his health is deteriorating. I have looked into the future, Lina, and if his status remains as it is, his health will decline to the point where it cannot recover. Lunaka will be left without an adult king, and someone I have always thought was a dear friend of yours will not live long enough to sit on the throne upon which he was born to sit."

My breath left me as the gears of my mind reluctantly kicked into motion. Frederick had looked older than his age for nearly as long as I'd known him, and it was true. When I sat down to apologize to him the other day, I *had* noticed the worsening of his appearance. His thinness, his lack of color, the dullness of his hair and eyes, the bones sticking out of his hands, his palpable exhaustion. I turned my head as if Arii had struck me. "You're…you're exaggerating. Sure, stress isn't good for you, and we've all had our fair share. But Frederick isn't *dying*."

"No, he is not currently dying," Arii responded matter-of-factly as he tapped his knee. "But if his trajectory remains as it is now, if he continues walking the path that he is walking, yes. He will die in the near future, and not as an old man."

I had to lead against the wall behind me. The cold was suddenly too much, and I grasped for the handle to pull the window closed. Could it be true? My visions of the future definitely always came true. Always. I stuttered, "H-How does marrying me fix that? Stop that from happening?"

"Multiple ways," Arii answered simply, as if it was the easiest thing in the world. "It alleviates part of his burden. He has a queen to help him make decisions and a mother figure for his children. Likewise, your children would gain a fa-…"

"Don't say it." I squeezed my eyes shut.

"A…male figure, who can contribute a significant amount of safety through his position," Arii adjusted his words. "Plus, you cannot leave out Rayna in all this. Giving Frederick the ability to provide for her and act…as that male figure toward her…can only bring him, and you as well, I think, healing."

I pressed my hand against my mouth to stop me from speaking. From just shutting the whole entire thing down while I still could, even though the other half of me was still screaming to do so. Why did this have to be happening?

"Please know, Lina, that I would not be asking you to do this, much less proposing the idea in front of the entire rebellion, if I didn't think it was one hundred percent necessary," Arii said quietly as he rose from his place on the floor and slowly moved toward the door, his orange robe flowing lightly. "For all of our sakes," he added, barely audible, just before he ducked through the door frame and pulled the door closed behind him.

Now that I was truly alone, I curled into a ball on the window seat with my back to the door, and my breath fogged up the cool glass. The now translucent glass just made the white, snowy world beyond it that much more feature-less and muddled. I covered my eyes with my hands, trying to find solace in the darkness. Sam's long, angular face came to me unbidden – tanned from days working out in the sun like in the better days when we were still able to farm, not thin and pale like the final days underground – and that all too familiar pang in my heart threatened to choke me. I desperately tried to read his expression like he was truly there in front of me. Was he mad? Did he understand? Could he forgive me if I went through with this?

Sam's face was replaced by different memories of Frederick. Serving alongside him on the Council during the past decade and then some, saving his life at the Crushing of the Thrones, all my letters asking for help translating the lofty language of the history book detailing Rhydin Caldwell, the aftermath of Rayna's birth and the war, and our time stuck together in the basement underneath Luke Owens's old livery in Soläna where he was my first magic teacher. All the way back to when we'd unknowingly met as children, and I inadvertently stopped him from running away. Made him want to be king for the first time.

Perhaps, marriage wasn't just something for two people in love. Maybe, it could also just be for two life-long friends trying to take care of each other and the people they served.

Didn't most Royal marriages fall under that category anyway?

I took the deepest breath I could manage, letting the air reach the farthest recesses of my lungs before I slowly let it out. Then, I uncurled myself from my fetal position and stood, straightening my black tunic and the knee length skirt I wore over my earth-colored trousers and tightened my scarlet sash, which concealed my blade.

Frederick was one of my dearest friends, and Rhydin had stolen far too much from me already. If it was within my power to save even one of my friend's lives, I knew I had to take it. Even if it meant doing something for which I wasn't remotely ready.

Frederick watched Clariion Arii leave his chambers in silence. He hadn't moved since the Ranguvariian entered, who had just come from speaking to Lina. Frederick wished he could say that he felt numb about the entire thing, but the honest truth was that he had felt numb for a very long time before this and that didn't look to be changing anytime soon.

Still frozen in place and not ready to entertain any of the ideas Arii had proposed, Frederick let his gaze wander. His desk was piled with roll after roll of parchment and a dozen quills, half of which had been snapped. He caught bits of pieces of the different writings he had received and was working on sending off. Requests for aid and reinforcements to the various pockets of rebellion around Nerahdis, news from the leaders of a couple pockets that Rhydin had wiped them out, various personal notes to himself about Dominick and Nathia as he kept failing to keep up with his son and ward.

His fingers absent-mindedly reached for the top drawer of his desk and withdrew an oval, stained-wood frame. Within it was a painting of a midnight-haired woman with a heart-shaped face and shining blue eyes. Tucked into her hair was a red rayna flower pin, which she had worn daily. Frederick's heart throbbed within the empty shell of his body, yet he couldn't remember what Cassandra had looked like in real life anymore. She'd been gone for fourteen years, and she hadn't bothered to inform him that she wouldn't survive her secret pregnancy. Frederick had always liked to think that if he had been there instead of being off in Auklia helping Daniel lead his kingdom that he could have stopped what happened. But maybe it was time for him to stop blaming himself, even as the guilt crept into his soul once more.

There was the lightest of knocks at the door, and suddenly Lina herself appeared. She had her color back now after going white as a sheet after Arii's proposal, but Frederick was too lost in his own mind to absorb much else.

"Um, I saw Arii leave," she said tremulously, her hand still on the door knob. "Can we discuss this?"

Frederick couldn't answer. Didn't know what to say and afraid to say anything before he knew what Lina's thoughts were. Of course, Arii hadn't told Frederick quite everything he had told Lina, but Frederick didn't know that. While Frederick knew his health probably wasn't the greatest and that more things were slipping through his fingers than he preferred to admit, he was told nothing about Arii's vision for his future.

Lina cautiously closed the door and perched on the same chair she'd sat in just the other day, back when it seemed like their friendship was going to finally go back to normal. She folded her hands diplomatically in front of her, and Frederick already hated where this was going. She said matter-of-factly, "I am prepared to do this if you are on board."

Numb or not, Frederick's jaw just about fell to the floor. His brow furrowed as he tried to process the response he'd never expected. "You…You are?"

Lina nodded, not quite meeting his eyes. "It seems to be what is best for everyone," she replied, a little too vaguely as far as Frederick was concerned.

"I…I don't want to force you into something you don't want," the king said carefully, still trying to read the Allyen's guarded expression. "You can simply live in the castle and enjoy your status as a Royal, nothing more."

Lina didn't respond, staring at her knees. The numbness around Frederick's heart was beginning to fade ever so slightly. He hadn't wanted to admit until this moment that while he had panicked at Arii's original proposal, the Ranguvariian's reasoning later had awakened a part of Frederick that had been slumbering for quite some time. The notion of a partner – a companion his age with so many common experiences – was more tempting than he dared to admit after so many years of only his much younger sister and children for company.

It was then that Frederick realized that he wanted this proposal to come to fruition.

"Sorry," Lina suddenly spoke again, jarring Frederick from his thoughts. "It's going to take me some time to get used to that…being a Royal…myself. You don't really understand what it's like growing up as a commoner to fear anything a Royal could possibly ever do to you."

"I understand," Frederick responded too quickly. "Just…let me know if there's ever anything you need…to help you through this. I'll grant you any freedoms you desire."

Lina gave Frederick a funny look after his last few words, and Frederick briefly wondered what he'd said. Then, she nodded again, this time meeting his gaze. She stood abruptly, as if she had reached the limit of however much of this notion she could handle for the day. She muttered a quick "thank you" and then disappeared out the door without much ado.

A beat after she was gone, Frederick pushed himself out of his uncomfortable chair, his joints creaking as he did. He moved to the door and poked his head out into the hallway, watching Lina's dark form in stark contrast with the white wallpaper retreat toward the staircase. As he watched her go, rubbing his unshaven face, he couldn't help but begin to hope.

Maybe, just maybe, Frederick wouldn't have to spend the rest of his life alone after all.

Chapter Five

Rayna

"Plus, you cannot leave out Rayna in all this. Giving Frederick the ability to provide for her and act…as that male figure toward her…can only bring him, and you too I think, healing," Clariion Arii's voice lilted through the door as I found myself eavesdropping on my mother's private conversations for the second time that week. As soon as the Council meeting was over, I had rushed upstairs to talk her out of entertaining any sort of notion of remarrying – *ever* – but that thought had been derailed quickly by the first words I'd heard.

There was no denying it now. There was something linking me to King Frederick that no one was telling me. First, his vow to take care of me, and now this suggestion that providing for me would somehow bring him "healing." Healing for what? Why just me, and not Kylar too? Why were Kylar and I constantly being considered differently when we were siblings and only a year apart in age? Was it the fact I was a girl? If so, King Frederick had something coming for him.

Nerahdis would freeze over before I let *anyone* take my papa's place.

Someone approached the door on the other side, and I panicked. I raced back toward the staircase before I could be seen eavesdropping, found Taisyn where I'd abandoned him in the castle foyer, and whisked us both out into the chilly courtyard where I shouted in frustration. "This is *ridiculous!* I can't believe this is happening!"

"It did sort of come from nowhere," Taisyn replied as he wrapped a green scarf around his neck from his cloak pocket, "but you have to admit, it might really help things."

I glared at him, making sure to draw out the silence since he couldn't see that I was glaring at him. "I'm going to try and forget that you said that. Lucky you."

Taisyn chuckled, "Relax. We don't even know if it'll happen yet. Even if they did go for it, there's no way they'd do it so soon. Royal weddings are something else, it took nearly a year for my parents' to happen."

"Yeah, and that's if they could even pull it off with how little resources we have right now since Emperor Rhydin is trying to keep us cut off from the world." I suddenly felt at ease. There was no way to make a Royal wedding happen right now, and by the time it was feasible, my mother and King Frederick would have no reason to get married anymore.

Taisyn and I remained out in the courtyard talking until Uncle Evan appeared for our usual, daily lesson. Taisyn hung around to partake in the lesson with me, curious for a new point of view after so many years of training with the other Royal children.

It wasn't until the next day when everyone was convened in the throne room again for the usual lunch ration of hardtack and boiled potatoes that the announcement came that my mother, Allyen Linaria, would be marrying King Frederick of Lunaka.

In a *week*.

I bit my tongue instead of my rock-solid bread. Taisyn gulped in front of me, preparing for my reaction. I kept my head down even as my ears grew hot, and nearly everyone around us became suddenly cheery. Nathia caught my eye at the other end of the table, and if looks could kill, I'd be dead on the spot. Her green eyes were like liquid lava, and her tin fork was bending in her grasp.

Of course, my mother and King Frederick themselves were absent.

I rapidly finished the rest of my potatoes and shoved my hardtack into my pocket for later. Once upon a time, I would have balked at such a meal, but it sure beat letting my stomach try to digest itself.

The castle around me was a blur as I stalked out of the throne room and up the stairs. Anyone I happened to pass gave me a wide berth like they could see the steam pouring out of my ears. I charged into my family's room only to find it empty, which just made me see red.

There was only one other place she could be.

I raced back to the stairs and up to the top floor, dodging more than one chicken, and I banged my entire fist on King Frederick's set of double doors. Before there was even time for a response, I immediately sensed my mother beyond the door, and I let myself in. As I seethed in the doorway, the sight of my mother and King Frederick huddled together over his desk about sent me through the roof. There were pieces of parchment sprawled across the desk appearing to concern the governance of Lunaka and the state of the rebellion. Their improper alliance was already beginning, and both of them stared back at me with the audacity of appearing confused.

"How. Dare. You!" I yelled hotly, my hands clenching into fists. "This is not going to solve *anything!* How could you even *consider* doing this to Papa?"

My mother straightened and took a step towards me. There may have actually been pain in her expression, but I was far too gone to see it. "Now, Rayna…"

"*No!*" I screamed. "Papa has barely been gone for a season, and you do *this?* Did you ever love him at all?"

My mother's face turned to stone. King Frederick rose from his chair and tried to gesture for me to come further in with his bony hand. "Rayna, let's all sit down and talk about this. You're taking this the wrong way-…"

"I am taking this the perfectly correct way, thank you," I snarled, my voice morphing into something even I did not recognize. "I will *not* play any part in this, and *you*" – I pointed menacingly at King Frederick – "will *never* replace my father! No matter how long he's gone!"

The king flinched as if I'd wounded him with a blade rather than words. My mother's eyes darted back and forth between the king and me, but when she took a step toward me, I backed up and slammed the door without another word.

I ripped my hands through my short, choppy hair, tracking my way back down the hallway in a zig-zag pattern. *I'll never speak to them again*, I thought to myself. There was no way I could go to King Frederick about Erikin now; I'd have to ask one of Taisyn's parents or *something*. I groaned loudly. *What in Nerahdis were they thinking??*

"I see you beat me to it," a familiar voice said mockingly, which just made my blood boil even more. "Trying to put an end to this ridiculous political stunt too, I take it?"

"Oh, for once, Nathia, just *leave me alone!*" I growled, throwing my hands up in exasperation.

Nathia rolled her green eyes. "Oh, believe me, I'm just as furious as you are. We're being shoved into the same boat for a plan that'll never work, and I intend to put an end to that immediately."

"Well, then. I can honestly say that I wish you the absolute best of luck," I muttered, as I side-stepped her in the hallway and tried to go about my way.

"Quit acting like you're better than the rest of us!" Nathia called after me, her sly smirk suddenly gone.

I whirled on my heel; my anger barely contained. "What in Nerahdis are you *talking* about?"

"Your private lessons, your Kidek father and now brother, your Allyen mother. If you become a princess too, it'll just swell your big head even more," Nathia growled, her arms crossed tightly over her beaded bodice.

Now, I really tilted my head at her. "You're totally nuts," I declared. "My family's roles don't decide who I am! I can be whoever I want," I insisted, trying to leave again.

"That's the most Gornish thing I've ever heard. We Rounans can't just 'be whatever we want.' You're just like the rest of the arrogant, selfish overlords," Nathia said haughtily as she finally moved toward King Frederick's door. She added over her shoulder, "Your father would be so disappointed. I bet he was devastated when you weren't born a Rounan."

I couldn't see her anymore. I lost my hold on my anger altogether, and my hands were pumping with hot magic in a flash. Jumping into a rapid stance, I fired everything I had at Nathia. My third of the Allyen locket was warm against my chest before suddenly its heat vanished. The hallway swirled around me, its white, dull colors melting down and changing hues instantly.

The whites of the hallway reformed into a plain gray sky above me while dry, brown prairie grass sprung up beneath my feet. My ragged boots stitched themselves together and grew taller before my eyes, and my reaching fingers suddenly brushed against the rough, bark of a tree that wasn't there a second before. It took only a beat before I recognized this feeling and realized that I was Nora once more, getting ready to view something that happened over three centuries ago.

A woman screamed. A high-pitched scream that curdled my blood. My head moved on its own accord, long brown hair flowing over my shoulder. There was a slight, grassy hill ahead of me, and Nora immediately left the safety of the tree and began to jog up the hill. I even felt winded when we reached the top even though Nora's breathing in my lungs was unchanged.

I lost my breath altogether when I witnessed what was just beyond the knoll.

Three people were spread across a small clearing, two on one side and one on the other. In between, a bright rainbow of magic swirled through the air, lit by tiny charges of what looked like purple lightning every so often. It twisted and moved like something I'd only been taught about in my Caarkian school, a strange weather phenomenon that only occurred in Lunaka and the Great Desert: a twister.

The strange funnel of magic – which began as several colors and morphed into familiar-looking, amethyst-colored power at its destination – was being siphoned toward the person who stood by himself. Emperor Rhydin was clad all in black, although his hair was much shorter than it was during my time, and he stood motionless as he absorbed his new dark energy. My chin snapped to the other side as I finally realized there were *two* Rhydins in front of me, and the other was flung on the ground as his rainbow of magic bequeathed to him by each of the Three Kings was sucked out of him and twisted into darkness. He was wearing an old-fashioned white tunic and plain breeches, his hair in the same cut as his clone.

Rhydin Caldwell. He looked identical to the specter trapped in the Archimage Palace.

Huddled next to the real Rhydin Caldwell was none other than the ocean-haired Amelia, and I felt Nora's ire rise as she took in the massive blood stain decorating the belly of her bodice. Crimson seeped from Amelia's lips too, and heat flooded my neck. That wound could be nothing but fatal.

"What is the meaning of this??" Nora screamed, her strong, full voice twisting into something much darker than normal. Her thoughts broke unbidden in my mind, circling her confusion and ultimately denial that she was seeing two Rhydins.

The Rhydin dressed in black didn't respond, totally focused on his siphoning of magic from the real Rhydin Caldwell, the swirling power diving directly into his pale fingertips. Amelia tried to stand, but couldn't, her hands still clutching the front of Rhydin Caldwell's bloodied, white tunic. He was lying in front of her, as if he had tried to protect her.

Just as Nora moved to draw her sword, my hands following her every impulse, something happened that my mind struggled to make sense of. As more and more magic was leeched away from Rhydin Caldwell to the black-clad Rhydin who would become the emperor I knew, Rhydin Caldwell's feet began to shatter like glass. The pieces were sucked right along with the amethyst twister as the bright colors of Rhydin Caldwell's original magic faded away. His knees soon followed suit and then his hips. He whispered rapidly to the bleeding-out Amelia, his words lost over the roar of magic in the air.

Then, he was gone, and the magical siphon in the air cut off as the last bits of power soared into Emperor Rhydin's hands. Only I knew he wasn't actually gone. Just so low on power than he'd been rendered invisible. I glanced as far toward the mountains just beyond us as I could, unable to move my neck with Nora trained intently on where Rhydin Caldwell had once been. The Archimage Palace stared back at me in the distance, its windows like empty eyes.

It had just begun. Rhydin Caldwell's three-hundred-year-long sentence to invisibility, loneliness, and being frozen in time, unable to reverse whatever it was that just happened.

Nora finally found her footing and raced for Amelia, who now lay by herself as her life's blood left her. The light in her sapphire eyes was gone by the time we reached her, and a mountain of fury overtook Nora. Anger clouded her vision, and she gave a heart-wrenching roar of both rage and grief. Those emotions echoed in my own heart, exactly what I'd been feeling just before being sucked into this ancestral memory.

"*What have you done?*" Nora roared at the remaining Rhydin as she drew her menacing blade and took up a stance above Amelia. "How could you do this! She *loved* you!"

The evil Rhydin leveled his amethyst gaze at her, his blank, Einanhi-like expression cracking into a smirk. "Only what must be done in order to make Nerahdis strong again."

"You are *mad!*" Nora yelled. "Emperor Caden is gone. The Archimage doesn't have that kind of power!"

"I shall become the new emperor then," Rhydin stated simply as he drew his own sword, "but having anyone in my way is not an option. Not even you, Nora Soreta."

Rhydin leapt toward us, charging a wickedly powerful burst of purple power into his hand. As Nora stepped forward, armed with nothing more than her blade – after all, I'd already seen her tell Amelia's grave that she was headed to the Ranguvariians to create her Allyen magic, and that obviously hadn't happened yet – I felt pulled back from the impending duel by my collar. As their blades clashed, the world melted away and morphed back into the dimly-lit, white hallway in Lunaka Castle.

I was sprawled on the floor, my chest heaving as I gasped for air. *I can't believe it*, I thought to myself. Nora was *there*. She witnessed the two Rhydins *and* the thievery and transformation of the real one's magic by his own Einanhi, yet she didn't realize which was real and which was fake. She didn't have magic or understand it yet. If only she had discovered the truth, then perhaps none of this would have ever happened.

But she never saw the creation of the Einanhi clone. There were already two in that memory, and something huge had already gone down between Amelia's mortal wound and the real Rhydin's defeat. How in Nerahdis did she even survive dueling the evil Rhydin without magic?

Only one person was left to tell the tale. No more waiting for permission.

"*Rayna!*" Taisyn was suddenly hovering over me, his freckled face drawn with concern.

I glanced around anxiously as Taisyn helped me lean forward. Nathia had vanished, likely afraid I was going to kill her, I thought smugly to myself. Judging by the amount of arguing coming from the end of the hallway, she was already addressing my mother and the king, her guardian. I remained silent, my mind still lost in history.

"What did you see?" Taisyn asked hesitantly, not needing to see my face to know what had occurred.

"Two Rhydins," I blubbered semi-incoherently as I replayed the memory over and over in my mind. "The evil one stealing the original's magic, and it becoming dark magic. Amelia's death. Rhydin Caldwell's disappearance. Nora fought the Einanhi without magic, but she obviously survived somehow."

"Whoa," Taisyn breathed as he hauled me to my feet. "That's a huge chunk of the story. So, who killed Amelia then? And why was the evil Rhydin created? Did Rhydin Caldwell say anything in the memory to suggest the reason?"

"I don't know," I replied as I brushed the dirt and dust off my clothes. "She was already wounded, and the magic-stealing was already happening by the time Nora showed up. It's time to go, Taisyn."

"What?" Taisyn's copper brow furrowed.

"We're going to the Archimage Palace. We need to know what really happened before it's too late if we're going to be able to save Rhydin Caldwell. Before spring comes and with it, Emperor Rhydin," I started talking really fast as I dragged Taisyn down the hallway toward the stairs.

"But the Council still hasn't approved it, and I doubt our parents would let us go," the prince responded worriedly. I couldn't help but roll my eyes.

"Well, then it's a good thing this castle is about to get *really* wrapped up in planning a Royal wedding, isn't it?" I said in a sing-song voice. "And guess who else will likely arrive just in time for this wedding to help us get there?"

Taisyn halted for a second, pulling his hand from my rebellious grasp. "Who?"

I grinned maniacally, remembering my Ranguvariian friend with whom we'd grown up in Caark, Aunt Rachel's son. "Mathiian."

Chapter Six

Lina

"Sam!" I cried as I sprinted through the dark castle hallway. "*Sam!!*"

Thundering crashes came two at a time from the outdoors, and I caught a glimpse of the gleam of the shiny, magical shield the Lunakan Royals were projecting above the castle, trying to keep Duunzer out. Crimson red eyes peered in through the smoky black Darkness beyond the shield.

I had the arrow, I had my locket, but Sam was nowhere to be found.

I couldn't do this without Sam.

The shield above the castle was suddenly smashed into a million pieces, shards raining down like glass as I burst through the next door out into the courtyard. Duunzer let out a screeching roar as it pushed over one of the castle ramparts like it was a tower of blocks. I drew my sword with quivering fingers, feeling like a tiny ant on the ground about to be stomped.

Sam, Sam, Sam, Sam. My heart beat out a desperate, unsteady rhythm. I looked every which way around the courtyard, frozen in place.

Duunzer lifted its massive, scaly paw toward me just as I saw a much younger Frederick lying dead in the corner, a sword wound to his chest. Then, I realized that my own blade was now blood-stained….

I screamed. My tunic was plastered to my chest with cold sweat, and goosebumps erupted on my arms as I realized I was huddled along the icy, marble steps of the main castle staircase. I focused on breathing for a moment, confused as to why I was out here and not warm in my bed, but my old leg wound from Duunzer throbbed as if its talon had impaled me all over again. The images of the Einanhi dragon and Frederick dead seemingly by my hand wouldn't leave my mind.

But what did they mean? I'd had dreams of the future before, but never dreams of a skewed memory. Sam had never gone missing during the battle with Duunzer, and I'd never entered the castle proper. And Frederick certainly never died.

Grasping my freezing arms, I tip-toed two floors back up the stairs, side-stepping slumbering chickens the entire way. Each step was like an electric shock, the marble was so cold on my bare feet. I quickly shuffled through our bedroom door, which I had apparently left ajar, and jumped back under the covers of the small bed I shared with Cayce, my sister-in-law. Trying not to shiver too hard and wake her up, I scanned all the straw ticks strewn about on the floor. Evan was just a mound, facing the wall by the door, while Kylar and Aron were both sprawled on the tick they shared. One tick was empty, and I sighed heavily as I tried to bury deeper into my pillow.

Rayna had been avoiding me the entire week, ever since the announcement that Frederick and I had agreed to marry. She spent all her time on the top floor with Taisyn, only coming down for her lessons with Evan. Usually, I'd see her at least once per day, just from afar. Yesterday morning, I'd seen her downstairs welcoming Mathiian, Rachel and Jaspen's son, who had traveled to Lunaka Castle with several other prominent Ranguvariians for the occasion. I hadn't seen her since then.

The minutes trickled by, and sleep evaded me. I rolled toward the window and watched as the nighttime spilled away like sand in an hourglass. The window grew lighter inch by inch, and I knew it wouldn't be long before the castle began to wake. After all, there would no doubt be last minute preparations going on in the throne room below.

It was today. This morning. My wedding day.

Second wedding.

I remained burrowed under the covers as everyone else in the room stretched, rose, dressed, and left for the day, one by one. I momentarily wondered if I could just hide all day before the door to our room opened long after everyone else had left. The person's warm, motherly presence that smelled like tea let me know exactly who it was who had walked into my room, and it was only seconds before she gently pulled the covers away from my face.

"Oh, Lina," Rachel sighed, already dressed in her nicest Ranguvariian-style robe, "come on now."

Rachel pulled me to my feet, and my body followed her like a stiff doll. She propped me in front of a floor-length mirror that had magically appeared in my room at some point in the last week and silently began working a brush through my snarled, mud-colored hair.

I kept my eyes on the floor as she worked. My heart ached as I remembered her doing this for me last time. For my *first* wedding, I tried to correct myself. We'd been in the small house Sam and I had just built in the Rounan Compound, the one room to ourselves. She had left my hair down then, graced with a simple crown of white wildflowers, and my face plain. She had sewn my dress for me that day too. A loose, sky-blue one with darker blue patterns along the cuffs and hem.

Today, I couldn't have looked more different. Rachel had managed to transform my bedhead into a hairdo worthy of a Royal, an intricate bun threaded with pearls. She had smeared my face with powder, which I thought made me look older than I was, and she had added color to my cheeks and lips somehow while also darkening my eyes with kohl.

Someone must have raided Queen Gloria's old closet because a few different dresses lay before me as options, but Rachel had already thrown the one she knew I'd choose over my head. It was white, of course, the color reserved for the Lunakan monarchs, and my skin crawled at the feeling of wearing someone else's skin. The one Rachel chose was the least gaudy. While the other two were dripping in gold or jewels, this one was more subtle. Pearls and clear gems were sewn into the tight, corset-like bodice, which Rachel tied mercifully loose. My third of the locket lay exposed upon my breastbone, strung along the chain Sam had given me. The translucent sleeves draped long over my arms, and a silver sash dangled toward the floor, my feet entirely hidden. Rachel was rapidly whipstitching the hem upward about six inches as I took in the reflection of someone who wasn't me.

"What am I doing, Rachel?" I whispered as I numbly touched one of the diamonds embedded along my stomach.

My oldest friend finished her stitching and stood once more, her head well above mine. She met my gaze and held it firmly. "You're the following the best path you can. For everyone."

The image of Frederick dead at my hand flashed in my mind yet again. Was it my insistence on searching for Sam that led to his death? I breathed, "Even me?"

Rachel hesitated for a moment, and then answered assuredly, "Even you, I believe."

After I took one look at the silver, strappy things Rachel claimed were shoes and chose to go barefoot underneath the voluminous gown, we headed toward the door. It was time. Just before we left, Rachel suddenly went back and snatched something from my bedside table. She smoothed out the worn Kidek bandana, folded it nearly over itself several times, and then tied it around my head like a navy, purple, and gold crown, not covering my entire head like usual. The public reminder of what this marriage meant. The unification of the Kidek Regent and the Lunakan king.

I'd worn one of these on my first wedding day too, around my shoulders, as the wife of the Kidek himself.

I found it hard to move, but Rachel did not. She softly but firmly wrapped an arm around my shoulders and guided me toward the stairs. The hallways and foyer below were totally abandoned, which was extremely abnormal. Heat seemed to exude from the throne room door as we approached it, and I gulped as I realized the whole entire rebellion and then some were just beyond. My hands and feet went cold as if they weren't already before.

Rachel released my shoulders, but she turned and held both of my hands in hers between us. She moved her head until she could meet my downcast eyes. "You're doing the right thing. It will all be okay," she said in soothing tones. "At least it's a good friend and not a complete stranger!"

"A friend," I repeated absent-mindedly. Would our friendship survive such a change in status? Yet, Frederick himself wouldn't if I refused.

Rachel must have taken that answer as reassurance that I could handle myself because she gave a quick rap on the throne room door with her knuckles and proceeded to disappear within. She was immediately replaced by Kylar, who bowed out into the foyer with me. My teenage son was wearing a borrowed suitcoat, which looked similar to something Frederick used to wear at that age. He, too, was now wearing another Kidek bandana that a Rounan must have made for him to wear today, and the sight of him with his long face just like Sam's framed by an identical head covering about pushed me overboard.

"Are you ready, Mother?" Kylar asked, ducking his head closer to mine. He truly meant it too, I could tell.

I nodded numbly, touching his face like he was still my baby. "Are you okay with this?"

Kylar looked down and shrugged half-heartedly. "I mean, I understand why it's a good idea. And I'd much rather you marry a friend of yours than me marry *Nathia* to bring the Royals and the Rounans together…or Lyla of Mineraltir for that matter. Or *anyone* really. I'm only fifteen."

A smile broke my stern mask, and Kylar chuckled, holding out his arm to me. As the huge, heavy doors to the throne room finally opened, unleashing a wave of blistering heat, Kylar tossed in a quick remark on how he was sure Rayna would get over it eventually, and we started our walk.

There was an uneven gap down the middle of the room between the Gornish rebels on one side and the Rounans on the other, although there were plenty of Ranguvariians and a handful of Aatarilecs present as well. Looking at hundreds of faces was far too overwhelming, so my gaze traveled to the ceiling where every single candle, sconce, and chandelier was lit for the first time we'd been here. The image of the stone room with fire everywhere jarred my memory of the last time I'd made such a walk…although the first had been by myself, which was Lunakan custom. We'd been surrounded by newly green prairie grass and wildflowers that day that I walked toward Sam. Nothing living adorned this room – it was winter, after all – although it was decorated as well as possible with random furnishings from around the castle. I found it odd that Kylar was walking with me. Yet another reminder that this wedding was for show. Kylar was the real Kidek; we couldn't have people forgetting the real reason behind this marriage, could we?

It finally occurred to me to look toward the dais, our final destination. The golden thrones were front and center once more, and the sight of those alone made my heart plummet into the pit of my stomach. Clariion Arii was dressed in his full regalia, a long orange robe decorated with every Ranguvariian pattern with half a dozen different colored sashes tied around his waist with crystalline ornaments. He stood next to Frederick, who was as pale as his crisp, white tunic that was hemmed with gold. Upon his fading blond hair was the silver crown of wheat heads that I myself had placed on his head the day we founded the Dome and made him, Xavier, and Sabine the new official monarchs – not the traditional Lunakan crown likely somewhere in this castle. My heart quivered at the sight of it, remembering how nervous I'd been to touch that crown and be the one to place it on his head.

Along the dais were the rest of the Royals, like some sort of reminder as to which elite club the Kidek line and I would be joining. Xavier and Sabine were both wearing their silver crowns from the Dome, his like woven branches with leaves and hers like a single wave, and I noticed that Mira was actually wearing one that matched Xavier's that I'd never seen her wear before. Aside from that, the rest of the Royals were all wearing their usual attire, probably not to flash their wealth too much, which could be dangerous. Sabine's twin wards, Chretien and Willian, flanked her on either side, while Lyla stood with Xavier and Mira. Cornflower, Dominick, and Nathia stood just behind Frederick as his immediate family, but my attention suddenly went back to the Mineraltin grouping.

Taisyn wasn't here, who was like my daughter's shadow.

I instantly began to search the crowd as discreetly as humanly possible, but Rayna didn't seem to be present. She certainly wasn't up on the dais.

Was she truly that angry with me that she wouldn't even attend?

Arii began to speak, "We are gathered here today to witness not only the union of these two people but the alliance of the two peoples across Nerahdis that they represent…"

I tuned it out. I couldn't listen. Kylar took his leave to stand upon the other end of the dais with Evan, Cayce, and Aron, and it was up to me to climb the two steps and join Frederick. It seemed like an eternity went by in my mind as I struggled to put one foot in front of the other to leave the level where the rebels stood and enter the level of the dais where all the Royals were – which was *far* more than two steps in all actuality.

Frederick reached out to me with his hand, and the action of taking it with mine seemed long and drawn out. His hand was clammy, but strong. Arii continued making some sort of grandiose speech about unions and peace and the future being a brighter place.

Frederick was paler than I'd ever seen him before, but while I was beginning to feel nauseous from the constant motion of my mind, he surprisingly seemed very sure. His icy-blue eyes were no longer glazed over, as they had been for some weeks if not months, and his hands were steady, strong from years of swordsmanship but without blemish, a reflection of his privileged life even in exile.

Cruelly, my mind kept blipping back and forth with my first wedding, replacing him with Sam. Suddenly, it was Sam in front of me against a backdrop of prairie grass. Sam, in his best shirt and breeches, which had both seen better days. Sam, with his warm, brown eyes gleaming and a smile so large no one would ever know it was usually lop-sided. His face decades younger, his callused, tan hands gripping mine, abused from decades of farming.

Arii was now apparently giving some sort of history of Frederick and I's supposed romantic relationship. Our time together as children, which was heavily expanded, and our rekindling when we were in hiding together the year before Duunzer attacked. My saving his life when King Adam tried to throw him off the castle balcony, and our continued connection over the years even after we both married other people. The hairs on the back of my neck seemed to stand on end as simple facts that were actually true got spun into an intricate spider's web of half-truths detailing a decades-long passion, which was only serving as a way to convince the people it was totally okay that I was remarrying just a few short months after my husband's death.

First husband, my mind brutally corrected. I cringed.

"Now, for the vows," Arii declared, finally turning to face Frederick and I for the first time during this entire ordeal. "Will you, King Frederick Tané of Lunaka, hold up your sword to defend this woman and her people, Kidek Regent Linaria Harvey Greene, until you breathe your last?"

I blinked at Arii a couple times, jolted back to the present. I'd never heard these vows before. They certainly weren't the ones that commoners made. Sam and I had vowed to love each other in plenty and drought, in plague and blessing, until our coal went out. I supposed those were all things that only normal people experienced. Royals only experienced plenty and blessing, and coal, Lunaka's main export and the product that employed at least ninety percent of the capital city, had absolutely nothing to do with their lives. These must be the vows Royals take at their weddings, which almost always united kingdoms and *usually* prevented wars.

Frederick was quick to answer, his voice firm and sure. "My sword is ready."

Arii then turned to me, his eyes soft and green. "Will you, Kidek Regent and Allyen Linaria Harvey Greene, hold up your sword to defend this man and his people, King Frederick Tané of Lunaka, until you breathe your last?"

My breath caught in my throat. This was it. This was the moment from which there was no return. I opened my mouth at least twice before sound actually came out, and ultimately the drastically different words of the vow were probably the only reason I was able to get it out, as if I wasn't betraying Sam with every word.

Even though his coal, the light of his life, had indeed gone out.

"M-My sword is ready," I said breathily, but the words still managed to be carried out into the rest of the room. The Rounan side of the room was beaming ear to ear. These vows were exactly the kind of verbiage they wanted so much to hear, and I suddenly began to wonder whether Arii had written these himself rather than being the typical Royal's vows.

"To symbolize the new unity between Gornish and Rounan, Royal and commoner, husband and wife, King Frederick has elected to bestow a ring upon Linaria," Arii began to say before he launched into another long speech detailing the meaning of alliances, rings, and the general histories of Nerahdis.

As Frederick released my hands and began rummaging through his pocket, my heart sank into the pit of my stomach. Heat flooded my face and chest as I looked down to see Sam's ring, its plain, silver band still glinting on my finger with its too-tiny-to-see stones. It had belonged to his mother, he told me the day he'd given it to me. I'd never taken it off. Suddenly, all I could see in front of me was my shaking hand. I had to take it off. It was like ripping off a piece of my skin.

Don't be ridiculous, Lina, I struggled to chide myself, *it's just a piece of jewelry.*

Before I could even begin to reach toward the ring, Frederick took my other hand softly with a knowing expression on his face and seamlessly slid his ring onto my third finger. I stared at it numbly for a moment, still processing Frederick's swift, subtle decision to allow me to keep Sam's ring. Twin, golden stalks of wheat reached around my finger to encircle a dainty, opalescent pearl. It wasn't nearly as gaudy as I might have feared, and I couldn't stop a small smile coming to my face in gratefulness for Frederick's knowing me so well.

The feeling vanished rapidly as I realized Arii wasn't talking anymore and everyone was staring at us in silence. Frederick finally appeared uncomfortable for the first time throughout this ordeal, and I remembered what was supposed to happen next. I lost all feeling in my hands, which Frederick held, and I felt like a marble statue.

Neither of us moved. In all reality, only milliseconds were slipping by, but it was an eternity in my mind. Arii eyed the two of us and made a subtle hand movement, hidden by the ceremonial lantern he held in his hands. *Get it over with*, he seemed to be saying.

Frederick finally moved at long last, although he was now dripping in anxiety. He deftly leaned forward, slowing when his narrow, pale nose was only an inch from mine. I did not move to meet him, still frozen, and my eyes unwittingly closed as if that could transport me miles away from here. I steeled myself, only to suddenly feel Frederick's kiss on the corner of my mouth – mostly on my cheek, instead of my lips – on the opposite side from the audience so they would have no idea it wasn't the real thing.

I still didn't move, but he didn't linger there long. When I opened my eyes again, Frederick was gazing down at me forlornly, even as the rebellion broke into applause and cheering. I could tell he was thinking of Cassandra just as I was thinking of Sam, but there was something else in his eyes. He inspected his boots for a second before meeting my gaze again, and I still saw it there. A glimmer. Of quite what, I didn't know, but even as he plastered a fake, political smile to his face, his hand was confident as it found my waist to turn us toward the audience. My own hands no longer trembled. Arii grinned approvingly at the spectacle we were creating, and then he gestured to the golden thrones behind us.

It was then that I truly became nauseous.

Frederick moved slowly, carefully using one hand to guide me toward the throne on the right. If my knees hadn't already been so weak, I couldn't have sat upon it. Cornflower suddenly appeared from the sidelines to flush out the trail of my skirt to fan elegantly at my feet, and before I knew it, Frederick stood in front of me, slightly off-centered so that the audience could see, with none other than a crown in his hands that was the mirror image of the one on his own brow.

This was so backwards. *I* was the one who placed the crown of wheat onto the rightful Lunakan king's head just a little over a decade ago. *I* was the one that Frederick claimed inspired him to actually want to be king as children. Now, *he* was putting a matching crown on *my* head, on top of the bandana crown I already wore. Now, *I* was his queen, a position his real wife and love of his life never even got to hold. The silver was cold against my forehead, yet it burned like fire.

As Frederick continued to stand next to the throne and took my hand tightly instead of going to sit in his own, Arii announced triumphantly, "Long live King Frederick and Queen Linaria of Lunaka!"

As the room erupted into victorious chaos, the sea of smiling faces waving tumultuously, Kylar and the rest of my family came to stand on the other side of my throne while Cornflower, Dominick, and Nathia joined Frederick on his side. Trying desperately not to vomit, I was wondering for about the hundredth time where Rayna was and why she wasn't here, when I noticed Rachel approach the dais from the side door. Her freckled face was pinched with worry, her hands grasped Rayna's worn, leather sketchbook, and suddenly I knew.

Rayna wasn't just hiding from me. She wasn't in Lunaka Castle *at all*.

Chapter Seven

Rayna

The Archimage Palace came into view abruptly, its sprawling complex tucked into the northern mountain border of Lunaka, mostly camouflaged. Mathiian had dropped out of his transportation spell just moments before, and we were now sweeping toward the darkened palace with every flap of his glowing, shard-like wings. It was twilight, the eve before my mother would make the biggest mistake of her life, and the sun was falling rapidly beyond the mountains to the west where Mineraltir lay.

"You've gotten a lot better at transporting!" I called over the whistle of the wind as I remembered the last time Mathiian tried to transport anyone when us kids left Caark. "I didn't get wrung through the wringer or sopping wet!"

Mathiian chuckled, his long, dark hair swept back in the breeze, "well, it certainly helps when there isn't an entire city between point A and point B! Don't say anything more, or I'll slam your boyfriend into a mountain on the next trip."

"He's *not* my boyfriend!" I growled as Mathiian swiftly rode a strong current of air over the next peak and rounded toward the oceanside of the palace.

"I'd be willing to wager he's interested in changing that, especially with that Auklian show-off keeping tabs on you," the teenage Ranguvariian cackled as he pulled up to a large balcony about mid-level.

"Oh, *whatever.* That's preposterous," I grumbled as we hovered over the balcony.

As soon as my feet touched the ground, Mathiian waved a finger at me and said, "Alright, I'm headed back to get Taisyn. Just *please* actually wait for once. It'll take like five minutes, max. I'm doing you a gigantic favor, y'know."

I rolled my eyes. "Yeah, yeah, yeah, fine. Thank you, I appreciate it. I'm definitely glad you chose to help the cause rather than witness the completely pointless solution Clariion Arii pulled out of thin air."

Mathiian sighed, his eyes turning a tinge blue. "I never said the wedding was a bad idea. My mother thinks it could really turn things around, for the rebellion, King Frederick, *and* your mother. All I said was this sounded like more fun than dressing up and standing in one place for however many hours a Royal wedding goes for."

I grumbled incoherently as Aunt Rachel's son vanished in a flash, his wings wrapped around him. The sound of the waves crashing to shore several stories underneath me drowned out any other noises, which gave me a brief flashback to when I was hurled over a different balcony toward them and my magic awakened. When I turned to face the Archimage Palace, there wasn't a single light in any of the hundreds of windows. My eyes fluttered shut as I reached out with my senses, searching for the real Rhydin Caldwell. I had no time to lose.

There was no telling how long we had before someone realized Taisyn and I were missing. Of course, my mother was pretty accustomed by now to my staying with Taisyn's family overnight, and we'd told Queen Mira, Taisyn's mother, the opposite story. Therefore, we should have been good through the night, but there was always the chance our mothers would talk. However, I was banking on them both being way too wrapped up in putting on this sham of a wedding to notice we were gone until at least tomorrow morning when they might realize we weren't around getting ready. In all reality, they could be barreling towards us any second.

No little pings of the ancient, friendly presence bounced back at me, and I felt a twinge of fear. Why couldn't I sense him? He was surely still here, being cursed after all. Was his power too weak? Were we going to have to walk around the *entire* palace to try and get close enough to sense him? We certainly didn't have time for that.

There was a blitz of light, and Mathiian swooped down once again with Taisyn dangling from his arms. Taisyn's blank blue eyes were wide with fear, his chest heaving rapidly, and I suddenly cringed as I realized how terrifying flying must be for a blind person. Mathiian set the teenager's booted feet gently on the balcony floor, and I touched Taisyn's elbow lightly. "I'm so sorry. I wasn't thinking about how frightening that could be."

At my touch, Taisyn grasped my hand as he tried to regain control of his breathing, like my hand would anchor him to the ground. "No, no," he panted breathlessly, "it's fine. T-Totally fine. No big deal."

"Alright, then. Let's get started," I said decisively before turning around to give Taisyn some space. I cracked my knuckles and focused on pushing my magic outward, ready to test the boundaries of my abilities.

Instantly, I felt the familiar pull on my power as not one, not two, but *three* golden orbs of pure energy sparkled in front of me – the most I could apparently conjure. The drain on me seemed gigantic. I was losing power left and right, and I scaled the size of my future Einanhis way down. Three small dogs were way too much to handle, but that perfect strum of balance came all too soon. I changed the shape yet again in my head and whispered the magic word to bring them to life, "*Anadlu.*"

The magical spheres popped like starry bubbles, and there were three identical songbirds staring back at me, a Caarkian breed that made my heart ache a little. Mathiian quirked his brow and asked, "What are you doing?"

"I can't sense Rhydin Caldwell from here, and we don't have time to search the entire palace ourselves. These little guys are going to help us out," I explained, proud of myself but exhausted nonetheless. The amount of power Emperor Rhydin possessed in order to animate hundreds of humanoid Einanhis was completely beyond me.

Mathiian seemed impressed. "Good idea."

Taisyn just smiled.

"Let's go, boys," I declared. "The night isn't getting any younger."

The three of us entered the palace doors, and my three little birds instantly flew off into different directions. I took off into a run, trying to make up as much lost time as possible, and soon we were all spread out around the dilapidated palace. I didn't bother checking any doors or going into any rooms, convinced it was a waste of time unless I finally sensed Rhydin Caldwell's presence. At some point, I passed the main hall where the Archimage's mist swirled high among the rafters, its violet color a little more pronounced than the last time we were here. *He's definitely here*, I thought to myself, *but where are you?*

An hour ticked by. Then two. I'd long given up running, my lungs burning for air. The Archimage Palace was *a lot* different from Lunaka Castle. It had wings off into every direction practically, and the seven floors didn't help matters much. Why in Nerahdis did one person need such a big palace if they were a total secret from the rest of the world besides the Royal families, anyway?

I paused briefly in the main hall once again, staring up at the moving, magical mist. My mother told me once that the Archimage could use it to view anyone anywhere in all of Nerahdis, and I wondered if the real Rhydin had enough power now to wield it again. Who did he look in on? Did it make him more or less alone to witness the rest of Nerahdis moving on through time without him?

Lightning jolted through me as I found myself wandering more toward the east. A quiet presence whispered into existence in the back of my mind, old but peaceful. My heart instantly sped up as I instantly reabsorbed the three little songbirds that were in the dungeon, the kitchens, and the attic respectively. Bellowing for Mathiian and Taisyn, I took off toward the library, kicking myself for not checking there sooner.

I hesitated a moment before turning the ornate, golden doorknob. What would I see once I opened the doors to the library? I was still messing with a power I didn't understand. Taking a deep breath, I grasped the doorknob firmly and thrust the doors inward, their creaks loud enough to wake the dead.

The library appeared largely unchanged from the last time I'd been here with Clariion Arii and my mother. The pile of monstrous books even still sat beside the velveteen armchair in which Clariion Arii had perused them looking for information on why the Archimage's mist had reappeared. The walls were lined with bookshelves upon bookshelves, each almost blue with cold and strung with cobwebs. My breath gathered in puffs of vapor in here as the grand, central fireplace lay dead. Rhydin Caldwell's presence was practically screaming in my head now, and I tiptoed further in until I noticed a small, flickering light in the far corner of the room, hidden by various dusty, plush furniture.

I wandered through the fancy chairs, settees, and desks laden with books like a maze, trying to build my courage. The sound of a quill scratching parchment reached my ears as I approached, and it wasn't long before a glowing, midnight head of hair appeared over the back of the next chair.

He looked exactly the same as the last time I'd seen him, as well as in the last ancestral memory I had witnessed. Old-fashioned white tunic with a lacy collar, plain breeches and boots, his hands and face very pale, the entirety of him lightly aglow as the specter he was, although the flickering light came from a stubby candle melted to his desk. He was turned away from me, busy writing something. I meant to say something to announce my presence, but the words were caught in my throat. The last ancestral memory where he shattered like glass in front of a dying Amelia as his Einanhi clone stole all his power and turned it to darkness kept replaying in my head. Such a quick moment that went on to define much of Nerahdis's history – only nobody knew it. I just couldn't help but stare.

Rhydin Caldwell's quill suddenly stilled, and his head snapped toward me, his amethyst eyes wide in shock. His gaze relaxed a mite at the sight of me, but a sadness overcame him. "You…you came back," he said softly, barely audible.

At first, I could only nod. I struggled to clear my throat, suddenly feeling emotional at the thought of being alone in this palace for so many years…centuries. "Yes," I replied through the frog in my throat, "I'm sorry it took so long."

Rhydin settled his quill and capped his ink well, giving me his undivided attention. "Not that I am not pleased to see you…but why are you here? In the night and alone?"

"I'm not alone," I said coolly, trying to shrug it off. "My friends are around here somewhere. I'm here to help you, that's what matters."

The specter shook his head despondently. "I am not sure anyone can help me anymore."

"That's not true!" My passionate tone surprised even me. "My mother and my uncle and I are preparing to perform the death spell on Emperor Rhydin, but I need your help. How do I make sure that your magic returns to you? How do I save you?"

Rhydin looked away from me for a moment, firelight dancing in his glassy eyes. I realized with a jolt that he really wasn't that much older than me. Perhaps, nineteen or twenty, tops. He spoke slowly, "I always wondered if anyone would figure it out. The spell to destroy my other half. I always knew the Ranguvariians were designing something based on rumors that came into the Archimage, but never much. Not until Clariion Arii left me a note anyway."

"A note?" I gasped. "He left you a note? When? What did it say?"

"Only that this spell…'Al-yuht-nee-nai-rahn'…" – Rhydin shrugged as he horribly butchered the five-syllable Ranguvariian word for "death by three lights" – "was finally powerful enough when performed by three Allyens? And that the Ranguvariians do not quite know what will happen or how my power will return to me rather than vanish…. He left me the note before you all returned to your Dome the last time we met because he needed my help."

"Your help for what?" I asked again before the sound of footsteps reached my ears. Rhydin's gaze shifted toward the door, a stoic expression going over his face like a mask. I looked around to see Taisyn and Mathiian hurrying toward me. I crossed my arms indignantly. "It's about time you two showed up! Look, I found him!"

Mathiian's dark brow furrowed as his eyes darted left and right, his irises sinking through the color spectrum into a buttercup yellow. Taisyn, too, seemed confused, although his eyes remained stationary. The Ranguvariian boy said softly, "Rayna…there's no one here. I don't sense anything."

"Me neither," Taisyn added slowly.

My heart began to sink. It was the same as last time. Neither my mother or Clariion Arii could see the real Rhydin either. I turned back to the ancient specter. "Why am I still the only one who can see you? Your mist makes it seem like you have more power this time."

"A little bit more, yes, but not enough to be able to maintain my visibility to you long enough to answer the most important questions," Rhydin explained. "I told you before, you and I are the only two people in all of Nerahdis with the exact same type of magic. Magic given to us by others' choices, not by blood. Your mother will have to explain the rest, as I do not have the power."

The memory of that conversation came flooding back. It was directly after I'd awakened following the coming of my magic, and I hadn't understood an ounce of what he'd told me. Now that I had months of magic training under my belt, his words tried to settle into my mind more. Why were he and I the same? I *had* been born with my Allyen magic, passed down to me by my mother. He had to be confused, and there was another reason the boys couldn't see or hear him.

"Y'know, I think I'm going to wait outside," Mathiian declared abruptly, his gaze shifting all over the place now. "This is too freaky." He looked to Taisyn briefly, but it became clear that he would stay with me, so Mathiian headed to the door by himself.

"Okay…so," I began to ramble, scratching my head nervously, "We need to know the rest of your story. Who's Amelia? Why couldn't she go with you when you became Archimage? Why were the Three Kings trying to kill her? Why did the evil Rhydin kill her? How was the evil Rhydin created? Why-…?"

Rhydin's eyes about bugged out of his glowing, translucent head. "How in great Gornan do you know all that already?"

Heat flooded my cheeks. I suddenly felt embarrassed beyond belief and looked back at Taisyn. His fingers were glowing, and he magically saw my need for support. He spoke awkwardly, probably feeling like he was speaking to no one. "She's been witnessing memories of Nora's. We're not really sure why. She's seen several of them now, and she's drawn them out in her sketchbook."

My sketchbook. I smacked myself in the forehead. *Why* hadn't I brought it? I'd added the most recent memory and left it safely in Taisyn's family's shared room.

Rhydin covered his mouth with one pale hand. He stared at the floor for a few moments, his glow seeming to flicker, before he asked, "What have you seen?"

"Um," I stuttered, trying to remember them all, "I saw the first time Nora ever met you, and I saw her grieving at Amelia's grave. Most recently, I saw Amelia devastated that you were chosen as Archimage, and the moment the evil Rhydin stole all your power and you disappeared."

Rhydin was silent, his eyes darting back and forth like he was reliving it all in his mind. I couldn't imagine how much those memories tormented him. It was several moments before he even moved, and when he moved his hand to brace himself against the desk, it was tremoring horribly. His glowing form was now flashing brighter and dimmer repeatedly, as if he was a candle threatening to go out.

"I want to tell you all of it, I truly do," Rhydin struggled to say, each word dimming his appearance, "but I am afraid I only have so much power left for today. I need to tell you how to help Clariion Arii…what the spell will do and how to return my power to me."

Disappointment rippled from my head to my toes, and I sighed. "Alright…what does Arii need help with?" I groaned.

"According to the Clariion, the spell will not just conjure a fatal charge of light magic…the opposite of the dark power into which my clone twisted the magic he stole from me. It will summon his greatest weakness…*my* greatest weakness…which will effectively tear him apart." Rhydin was beginning to mumble, his voice losing its tenor. He was groping his pockets now as if he was losing his vision or sense of feeling. Finally, he withdrew a slender, shining object with a gem twinkling on one end and offered it to me. "Once the death spell has been performed successfully and my clone is rendered into sand, you must use this vial I have constructed to recapture the freed magic before it vanishes…. Then, you must bring it directly here to me so it will restore me to true flesh and bone."

"Okay," I breathed, nodding as I tried to make sure I understood. I cradled a glass vial with silver wire wrapped around it and its jeweled stopper in my hands. "Hasn't some of your magic come back already? Why not just wait for it all to come back on its own?"

"Yes, by happenstance, but my clone won't lose any more on his own, or it'd endanger his life. The vial must be used to ensure enough of it comes back to me to restore me, and *you*, Rayna, have to be the one to use it," Rhydin reiterated, even as he seemed to be sinking back into his chair. His voice was becoming quieter. "No one else. The magic will be drawn to you, like to like…."

My eyes narrowed, and I began to open my mouth to ask him to tell me why in Nerahdis it was only *my* magic that was just like his rather than my mother's or uncle's. But one look at his vacant expression and fading eyes told me he was all but out of the power required to be visible even just to me. I chose my next words carefully. "What is this weakness? What should we expect to happen when we perform the death spell?"

Rhydin was beginning to completely disappear, beginning with his feet, just like he had in my vision although without any glass. "Amelia," he whispered, his eyes falling shut as his lower half became invisible. "At least, her image anyway… Not the actual one. She…could not marry me…could not go with me…because her parents were-…"

Just as Rhydin vanished altogether, the room began to twist and morph. The dark blacks and browns of the musty library transformed into bright greens and livelier browns as a forest sprung up through the marble floor all around me. Taisyn fell away from me, and I found myself growing taller into the form of Nora once again. As my mind fought to orient myself in this abrupt, new landscape, I found myself familiar enough with the process to be wondering what I would be seeing this time.

I was in the midst of dozens of thick, towering trees when the world settled, and salty air stung my nose. My muscles suddenly felt sore, and my limbs were heavy. Nora panted for a moment before she threw her arms out ahead of her, which resulted in two tiny charges of golden light that spiraled to the ground before fizzling out like dying fireflies. As she did so, I saw pink marks all over her hands like healing wounds that I'd never noticed before. Had she always had scars on her hands?

I hadn't seen them in any of the recent memories I'd had. Her voice growled from the pit of my chest, "*Arii!* This isn't working! I'll never be able to cast this spell of yours if I can't even light a candle!"

"I know," a calm voice replied from somewhere behind me, but it certainly wasn't Arii's voice. Or, at least the Arii I knew.

Nora angrily spun us around to face him, and my jaw would have dropped if I'd been in my own body. Standing there was a young Ranguvariian boy who vaguely resembled Mathiian, although younger. Perhaps, twelve? I was iffy on Ranguvariian ages since they were all so tall. Arii was so young, but his high cheekbones and perfectly straight nose could be none other than Arii, obviously well before he halted his aging as Clariion. He was even wearing an orange robe as a member of the Clariion line, although no thin band of silver was yet along his brow.

"How am I supposed to avenge Amelia and kill Rhydin if you can't help me get my magic seed to grow? I've been here for months!" Nora raged on. "Your people saw me swear I'd avenge her and brought me here to help you, but at this rate, I'm not going to be able to help anyone!"

"It *will* work, you just have to keep trying. You have magic deep within you from an ancestor, you only need practice. We would not have asked for your help otherwise. A great mage is not simply born a great mage," Arii insisted, and I couldn't help but size him up. Nora was quite a bit taller. "I know you will be able to save us from Rhydin's poisonous magic. Here, I have just had this made by our silverer. It will act as an amplifier for your new power and help you gain your footing as you learn and grow."

I gasped as Arii held out none other than the Allyen locket on a throng of leather, whole in one piece, its face shinier than I'd ever seen. The grooves of the swirling design were crisp and clean, and the pieces of embedded amber shone like sunlight. Nora touched it delicately with her fingertips, having no clue whatsoever that so many Allyens after her would handle it too. She whispered, "It's beautiful."

"Hopefully, with this amplifier, you will be powerful enough to perform the spell I have designed to tear Rhydin's darkness apart by summoning his weakness," Arii explained like no other twelve-year-old in the world, and I began to wonder just how many months Nora had been with the Ranguvariians. "From this day forth, we Ranguvariians shall call you *Alyen*, 'bringer of light,' for this reason."

"Allyen, huh?" Nora murmured, as she took the locket with her scarred hands and tied it around her neck. She took her rudimentary stance again, and when she focused this time, a much larger ball of light magic appeared in the palms of her hands. "I guess whatever it takes to make Rhydin pay for what he's done and get him out of power."

Nora began to run through the movements of the death spell that were now very familiar to me, and I found myself anticipating every move she made with her limbs, which were also my own in a way. To my surprise, nothing much else happened in the memory, but it didn't come to an end either. She spent hours practicing her new powers there in the forest, which must have been just outside the Ranguvariian Camp judging by how many of them periodically stopped by to watch silently from afar.

At some point, a tall, dark-haired human man showed up to keep her company, but that was about it. Nora called him "Charles" a little while later, which meant he was her husband whom I hadn't actually met yet beyond seeing his grave next to hers at my family's ancestral farm.

As time continued to tick by, I began to worry. Could I get stuck in one of these memories? How did they work exactly? Did I usually do something to get out of them? To my relief, the memory did finally come to an end what seemed like an eternity later, and Nora's body transformed back into my own as the colors of the landscape morphed back into the library at the Archimage Palace. When I opened my eyes, I was flat on the floor, and sunlight was now shining through the windows high above the bookcases. It was *morning?* Was real time the same speed as time spent in those memories?

Taisyn hovered over me, his copper brow knit with concern, but it didn't seem to just be for my welfare. Mathiian, wouldn't meet my gaze.

"How long was I out?" I asked groggily as I struggled to lean forward, rubbing my eyes.

"Oh, long enough," Taisyn whispered with an ounce of fear. He gave the barest of nods toward the other end of the room.

I forced myself to turn slowly and see, but I already knew what sight awaited me. Still standing as if they'd just arrived were none other than my mother, King Xavier, and Aunt Rachel looking frazzled and worried, but it wasn't until I noticed King Frederick in my mother's shadow that my blood began to boil.

Chapter Eight

Lina

Rayna's eyes finally opened, and while some small part of me felt relief that she was okay, my anger threatened to boil over. I stalked toward her, barely giving her enough time to take in the fact that she'd been caught. "Rayna, what is *wrong* with you? Do you have any idea how dangerous it is for you to go off by yourself without telling anyone? And especially *here* of all places?"

My daughter's expression grew hard. She snapped, "Wrong with me, *really?* You sure don't have a right to start *that* what with your new husband already at your beck and call" – she threw her hand in Frederick's general direction – "and besides, I wasn't by myself. I had Taisyn and Mathiian with me. We were *fine!*"

Frederick's wiry face grew pained, even though I had warned him again that Rayna had not been remotely on board with this idea whatsoever. I crouched down so that only she could hear me and said darkly, "You will give Frederick the respect that he deserves, if not as a family member, then as your king."

"He will only *ever* be my king. *That's* it," Rayna growled back, too low for anyone else to hear. She stood indignantly; her hands clenched into fists. She declared, "What matters now is what I've learned from Rhydin Caldwell! Arii asked him for help on making sure the death spell is successful, and now he's relayed that information to me." Rayna fumbled in her pocket a few moments before realizing that Taisyn held out what looked like a vial to her, a slender glass tube wrapped in silver wire with a glittering stopper.

Xavier suddenly piped up from behind me, "Did you find out why he created Rhydin the Einanhi? Or how it happened?"

Rayna lost her look of confidence. "W-Well…*no*, but-…!"

"Or if he's somehow remotely controlling his Einanhi from here?" Rachel asked, her red brow skeptical as she pinned her son in her gaze.

"Look, he still only has a fraction of his power, he could only tell me so much before he disappeared, but I have no reason to believe that he's evil!" Rayna became defensive, and I could see the desperation in her eyes as she argued with people more than double her age.

Xavier and Rachel had obviously both heard enough, and they moved away to reprimand their respective sons in their own way, which left Rayna and I staring at each other in an impasse.

Rayna accused stubbornly, "Of course, you don't believe me, do you?"

I sighed, trying to vent my anger. "I don't know what to believe," I replied quietly. "All I believe right now is that I'm thankful you weren't hurt and that we need to go. We can talk later."

Rayna glared angrily at her boots. I could practically see the steam rising off her head.

"I believe you," Frederick said out of nowhere, which made me jump a little. I'd forgotten he was with me.

I pinched the bridge of my nose. *Thanks for making me look bad, Husband.*

Rayna only rolled her eyes before staring forlornly at a writing desk nearby.

Rachel summoned Jaspen and Bartholomiiu from their posts keeping watching outside, and I volunteered to stay behind on the first round of transportations home. The four Ranguvariians, including Mathiian, took Rayna, Taisyn, and the two kings back to Lunaka Castle while I tried to take advantage of the perhaps five minutes I had for myself before one of them returned for me. I paced around the library, remembering the last time I'd been here when Rhydin Caldwell had written out the rest of a cipher for me, although I'd only seen a floating quill. It had read, "the throne of sand must meet its end to break the curse that shrouds the First. But do hear me this, should the curse remain, for all Nerahdis just death can be gained."

We knew the meaning now. That Emperor Rhydin, now known to only be an Einanhi that would dissolve into sand, had to be destroyed in order to break the curse on the real Rhydin Caldwell, the First Archimage. If we didn't, Emperor Rhydin would systematically wipe us all out. But there were still so many questions that didn't have answers, and as I found myself sitting at the very writing desk with which Rayna had been so absorbed, I realized I was jealous. Why was Rayna the only Allyen who could see Rhydin Caldwell? After all my little brushes with him as simply a helpful presence in my head, why couldn't I see him too? Perhaps, if I could see him, it would all feel more real.

Rachel flew back into the library before I was really ready, her short red hair windblown. She quietly moved toward me and set her hand on the back of my chair. "I'm sure my grandfather will really want to talk to Rayna now, although he won't be back for another week. I want to believe her…I really do."

"I do too," I whispered back as I stood, "but after everything that Einanhi has put all of Nerahdis through in the last three hundred years, we have to be absolutely sure."

Without much ado, Rachel summoned her beautiful wings and took me back to Lunaka Castle. I'd almost managed to forget that the wedding was only this morning before I saw the remnants of the hullaballoo in the throne room. I barely got a glimpse of the room and the two shining, golden thrones in the background before doing an about-face and heading toward the hallways where my usual rounds waited.

The people along my route seemed brighter than usual, the events of the morning still fresh in everyone's heads. More than one older Rounan clasped my hands as they gushed about how wonderful it was to finally have representation among the Royals, oohing over Frederick's ring on my finger, and while I tried to nod and smile, my mouth seemed to always be glued shut. Several of them came up to me like a child tattling to a teacher, informing me of any recent Gornish slander, destruction, or dare I say it "mischievous looks." A few of them wanted me to start working right away to establish a Rounan-specific stockpile for rations and supplies, and it always made the skin on the back of my neck crawl. *More* separation didn't seem like the answer to their troubles, and their expressions didn't seem quite as cheery whenever that topic came up and I didn't give a firm "yes, absolutely, right away."

Of course, none of them ever bothered to ask if I *wanted* to be queen. Marriage was far more permanent than my temporary position as Kidek Regent, although it would still tie Kylar to the Royals forever.

I didn't make it through my entire walk. All the hundreds of faces lining the hallways, whether they were positively aglow or bent on abusing this new power, were far too much today. Wandering toward the staircase and the upper levels, my mind submerged into a fog, utterly thoughtless. I didn't feel the cool marble against my fingertips; I didn't see the chickens scatter as I approached or the whispers of the Gornish and Rounans alike as I passed by – aside from one word, repeated over and over.

Royal.

It couldn't be true. It just wasn't possible. I'd feared Royals and their powers and their executions all my life. I couldn't be one. I didn't *want* to be one. Impossible.

As I stepped off the stairs onto the top floor of Lunaka Castle, I finally looked up and came nose to nose with a face from my nightmares. King Adam was suddenly staring back at me, his pale face much younger and round with privilege, his eyes like violet fire. He was dressed in the same fancy velvet suit he'd worn the night he tried to murder Frederick when we were only nineteen. I gasped and fell backward as he cackled and stroked his midnight goatee right there in the tapestry. His voice echoed strangely off the walls as he laughed, "Now, you are no better than I once was! You will forever be tarnished by the title of *Royal.*"

"No!" I cried. My hands went to my temples, but only felt the crown of wheat heads still on my brow and my fingertips suddenly felt seared. "You're dead! You died at the Crushing of the Thrones! I will *never* be like you; I will never put people to death!"

"You already have. Death has claimed many because of you," King Adam sneered as he aged before my eyes into his appearance the last time I'd seen him. Streaks of silver in his curly hair, his golden crown faded to silver as one of Rhydin's underlings, deeper wrinkles along his face, and dressed plainly as one about to face the noose in Rhydin's amphitheater of death.

Images flashed in my mind as fast as lightning, all of faces. Grandma Saarah, Keera, my parents, Cassandra, Queen Gloria, Luke, Robert, Kino, Mikael, Sam.

"*No!*" I screamed, squeezing my eyes shut, "No, no, no, *no!*"

In a flash, there were hands gripping my forearms, and I thrashed, thinking they belonged to the former king. "Lina, *Lina!*" a voice that was not Adam's shouted in close proximity to my ear.

My eyes snapped open, and I sucked in a breath of air. Frederick was crouched low next to me, his face replacing King Adam's but not entirely. His bony nose and wiry build mirrored his father's, and for a split second, I felt fear at the sight of him. By some miracle, I was able to clench my teeth to keep from uttering anything I'd regret. After a moment or two of just the two of us huddled in the hallway, Frederick's eyes locked on mine as I desperately searched for my anchor to reality, my ragged breaths becoming even again. My gaze fell to the ground in embarrassment.

"You don't have to tell me," Frederick whispered as he gently released my arms. They throbbed where his hands had been, and heat flooded my face and neck as I realized just how hard I'd fought against him thinking he was Adam. He added a mite awkwardly, "Just know that you're safe. And that I'm here to help you."

I dipped my head once or twice, just willing the entire thing to be over. Frederick helped me to my feet, and then he suddenly became bashful, his throat bobbing as he gulped. "Rachel moved your things into my…o-our chambers…to the queen's suite. Don't worry, it's uh…it's separate. I'll let you go see to your things."

I was all too grateful when he disappeared up the hall and down the stairs in a flash, not waiting for a reaction. As I rubbed my pounding head and groaned inwardly for what seemed like the hundredth time that day, I made my way down the hallway, very carefully keeping my distance from the vandalized tapestry of the former king who was apparently very much alive in my psyche, and paused in front of Frederick's set of double doors.

Fighting the urge to knock, I pushed them inward to find that Frederick had tidied up significantly since the last time I'd been in here. The heavy, velvet curtains had been drawn open and tied back to allow the winter sun to illuminate the room in a far nicer light than the usual chandelier. Everything had been given a good dusting, and every book, knick-knack, and piece of décor seemed to have a richer color while there were no dust bunnies floating through the sun beams. The tile floor was now spotless, and every book that had once been lain aside forgotten in random nooks and corners was now returned to a place on a neat shelf. The surface of Frederick's desk was visible again, although there was still a terrifying stack of paperwork on one end, corners of parchment sticking out here and there. His bed was made with a fresh set of blankets that seemed newer and less worn, but that was as far as my train of thought got before I promptly turned toward the next set of double doors that had appeared along the wall where I was pretty sure a book shelf had been before.

They were already opened into a room adjoining Frederick's that I'd never seen before, and I briefly began to wonder whether it was Frederick that had done the cleaning or Rachel. This room smelled musty, although a window had been left open to try and dispel that odor. There were large purple flowers painted on all four walls, which were interconnected by healthy green vines dotted with dainty leaves. Aside from a bookshelf with glass doors, a smaller, more feminine writing desk, and a canopy bed with gauzy drapes, it appeared that much of the other furniture had been moved out of the room judging by the discolorations on the floor. This room had obviously not been inhabited in a significant amount of time, perhaps even before Queen Gloria died.

My things were spread along the bed, although I had very little in material possessions anymore. I briefly closed my eyes and imagined the quaint tent Sam and I had called home for over a decade in the Dome, filled to the brim with furniture Sam had built by hand along with a vast assortment of items we'd collected along our missions. All of it was ash now, of course, aside from what lay before me, what Sam had been able to pack and carry on his horse when the rebellion evacuated the Dome after discovering Erikin had signaled its location to Emperor Rhydin.

Rayna had the Allyen journal now, learning from it just as I did before her, so in front of me lay only one change of clothes that I recognized – the rest were probably the plainest gowns of the queen's wardrobe that I had no intention of touching – as well as the history book that contained Rhydin Caldwell and a tiny pot with a sad-looking Lunakan moon plant that Sam and I had experimented with growing together in the artificial glow of the Dome. All of my other possessions – my blade magically hidden within my sash, my locket, Sam's Kidek bandana – were all on my body all the time. Emperor Rhydin had destroyed every home I'd built, and this was all that was left.

Ignoring the pile of queen-like clothes Rachel had selected for me, I plucked up my book and my plant to find them homes. I set the book flat against one of the glass-covered shelves so that it wasn't visible, and then I found a quill to shove into the dry soil hugging my poor little plant that Sam had saved for me. I ripped a few pieces of cloth from the tail end of my sash and used them to tie the green stalk to the quill, and then I retrieved the pitcher of water from a wash basin in Frederick's room to give it a drink. I placed it on the window sill, blanketed in the golden sunset, and it already seemed perkier. Nodding in approval that I'd been able to at least set one thing right in the world, I closed the doors joining my new room to Frederick's and tossed myself onto the fluffy bed, kicking the gowns and my new crown to the floor as I did. My eyelids felt weighed down by bricks after such a long, arduous day that had begun with a wedding I'd once sworn would never happen.

The castle shook, and my eyes snapped open. An eerie light was shining through my window now instead of the sunset, which bathed my Lunakan moon plant in blue-gray. I leapt from the bed, my head spinning with so much dark power in the air, and bundled my sash into my hand to magically summon my sword from within it. I clutched the red-clad handle to my waist, leaning the blade against my collar bone as I dared to peek outside. Above the castle like a giant dome was the shining, magical barrier, all that kept us safe within from the Darkness outside.

Duunzer was *back*.

I sprinted through the adjoining doors, through the blackness of Frederick's room, and out into the hallway. My sword glinted in the low-light every time I happened to pass a window, and I flew down the stairs, my heavy cloak streaming out behind me since I'd never taken it off. The castle hallways were utterly abandoned, and I hesitated at the bottom of the stairway.

Where are all the people? This place should be cram-packed with all the survivors from Soläna. Are they trapped outside? I have to save them!

My hand was on the big, metal ring of the heavy door leading out to the courtyard when I heard a moan behind me. I turned slowly, and there, standing in the hallway leading toward the dungeon and painted in the strange blue-gray light pouring through all the windows, was Luke. The arm holding my sword went limp, and its point tapped the stone floor. Rachel's brother was dressed exactly like I'd seen him last, but his orange, Ranguvariian-style tunic was ragged and there was a sheet – *oh* that sheet – around his shoulders that was covered with dirt and old, dried blood.

"No," I breathed, shaking my head. "You died. Rhydin *killed* you in his imperial palace when we were captured together…*used* you to break all the Ranguvariian magic's secrets."

Luke shook his shaggy brown head slowly, his freckled face unnaturally pale. "No, Lina. I would have never died if you hadn't run off that night. You robbed me of my future, my siblings of my presence. Why did you run away from camp? Why did you let me die in that dungeon?"

"I-…! I'm sorry! I didn't mean to!" I cried as my sword clanged to the ground. "I never meant for anyone to die!"

Suddenly, Luke began to shift. He shrunk two or three feet, and his long brown hair shortened and lightened. In his place, it was now Erikin standing in the hallway leading toward the dungeon, dressed in Luke's torn clothes and bloody sheet. He stared at me, his eyes wide and empty. He mumbled, "Help me, Aunt Lina. You already killed my father. What would your sister Rosetta think?"

My young nephew vanished as I collapsed to the floor, shoving my face into my knees. Was this what I had been reduced to? Nothing more than a ball of past trauma and guilt?

My magic abruptly alerted me that someone was coming, but I stayed huddled where I was hoping that maybe it was just a random rebel searching for the water closet. Instead, torchlight grew ever closer before it stopped right next to me, and the presence of Frederick settled on the floor next to me.

He sat there in silence for a little while. I could feel his warmth radiating upon my bare arm, so he was close, but I never lifted my head from my knees. After a few minutes went by, he whispered, "I have nightmares too. It's not just you."

I lifted my head just enough to see him out of the corner of my eye. Frederick looked weary, dark circles under his eyes, and his new thinness was dramatized by the dancing flame of the torch in his hand. A warm cloak was thrown on over his night shirt, which meant I'd probably woken him up on my way through his room to the hallway.

"I see Cassandra most of the time," Frederick mumbled, his blue eyes staring off into space. "She's always asking me, 'why didn't you come home?' or something similar. I see my father, too, yelling at me that I'll end up just like him. Sometimes I even see my mother, but she only stares, which is somehow worse than any of the others. She didn't deserve to die the way she did at the Crushing of the Thrones."

"No," I replied hoarsely. "No, she did not."

I was just about to open up and tell Frederick about the things I was seeing – how being in Lunaka Castle again was dredging up memories of Duunzer attacking but also of King

Adam and Luke – as well as try to ask about freeing Erikin when shouts began to echo down the corridor. Both Frederick and I jumped to our feet, that familiar adrenaline beginning to race. It was only a second or two before the words bouncing toward us clarified into the solitary word of "*fire*."

We both sprinted toward the direction of the noise without a word, although my ignorant mind could only wonder how an all-stone building could catch on fire. All the fires I'd ever experienced were back in my pre-Allyen days or when the Rounan Compound was razed, both of which involved the typical wooden building. It was then that I realized that fires didn't just start accidentally within a stone castle.

They were set.

Black smoke was rolling along the ceiling as we approached, and around the next corner, people appeared, some of whom with buckets but not nearly enough of them. The hallway was scorching hot from the temperature of the fire inside one of the rooms, and angry orange light flickered and flashed through the open doorway.

I sheathed my blade and barked to Frederick, "Go get Sabine and the twins! The nearest water source is too far, we'll never get it out like this!"

My new husband nodded and hightailed it back the way we'd come, and I threw myself into working alongside the other rebels. There were Gornish and Rounan here alike, dressed in all the different nationalities of Nerahdis, but I didn't realize the gravity of the situation until I got a good look inside the flame-engulfed room.

This wasn't just a random side room squeezed full of beds and cots and straw ticks like practically every other room in the castle. This was one of two rooms where we kept all our supplies. Whatever non-perishable food we had like sacks of beans and flour. We'd even transported part of the castle armory into this room in order to split things up as a safety precaution.

My stomach flipped over. With a blaze like this, there would be nothing left.

Who could have done such a thing? And would the rebellion survive its aftermath?

Chapter Nine

Rayna

Someone was jiggling me, my dream of being back on the beach in Caark suddenly rocking like the powerful ocean waves. "Rayna! Rayna, wake up!"

I grumbled, stretched, and groaned some more. "Kylar, it's not even light out. Go away." I tried to roll over on my thin straw tick and go back to sleep.

"No, *Rayna*," my brother whined as he shook my shoulders again, "this is serious! I need you to come with me right now, the *entire* rebellion just called a Council meeting. There was a fire; we might be done for!"

"A fire?" I asked skeptically, trying to clear the sleep from my voice as I levelled my gaze at him. He'd always been a worrywart, but this was a little much from him. "You had to have been dreaming. A stone castle doesn't just catch on fire."

Kylar finally lost his patience and yanked me forward onto my feet, and then he promptly shoved my boots into my arms. "And neither does it conveniently take place in one of our biggest supply rooms. Let's go, we need to help Mother."

Gravity seemed to pull extra hard on my heart as the news sunk in. In seconds, I had my boots on, and I grabbed my winter cloak rather than take the time changing out of my nightshirt. It was only on the way out of the room that I realized both Uncle Evan and Aunt Cayce were missing. Aron remained safely cocooned in his blanket, blissfully unaware that any such disaster had occurred. Must be nice to not be anyone important.

The smells of smoke and ash assaulted my nose the instant we entered the hallway. As we flew down the stairs, all the chickens were missing, and inky smoke collected along the rafters high above our heads. We could hear the arguing from the upper floors.

"What time is it?" I hissed more to myself than anything, astounded that literally the entire rebellion was up and arguing at this hour.

"Does it really matter?" Kylar griped back. "The food situation was already bad *before* this happened, and now half of what we had is ash! Somebody might die today, and it may not even be the person who did it. This arsonist just destroyed whatever time we had to find a solution that Mother's wedding bought us."

I gulped.

We crept into the throne room through the side door, our motions sound-less simply because the cacophony in the room about instantly made one deaf. My mouth fell open at the sight of everyone so bedraggled. Most of them also had smears of black soot across their faces streaked with lines of sweat. Absolutely every one of them were pointing fingers.

"*She* did it!" one Mineraltin woman thrust a bony finger at an Auklian woman across from her. "She told me just yesterday that our food supply wasn't safe!"

A dark-skinned man who didn't quite look like he belonged to any of the Three Kingdoms roared, "The Rounans *had* to have done it! They were angry they didn't get their own personal stores and took it out on all of us!"

"We did no such thing!" a Lunakan woman bellowed back, her fists planted on her wide hips. "The Gornish are just mad that our regent was made queen!"

"Silence!" King Frederick roared over the chaos, now standing upon one of the tables in the middle of the room. King Xavier, Queen Sabine, and my mother all rapidly followed suit, issuing proclamations of their own to their respective peoples. My mother was the dirtiest of them all, as if she had been on the front line of battling this fire, but Queen Sabine appeared the most exhausted. I could only guess it was her water magic that had extinguished the blaze.

There was once a time where the people would have listened. A time when their respect for the new, younger Royals who were so different from their predecessors was so high that they would have instantly shut their mouths and waited for instructions and clarity.

That time had been burned away with however many provisions had been in that room.

Voices shouted, fingers pointed, shoulders were roughed up, hundreds of names were named. Just for kicks, I threw an accusatory finger in Nathia's direction, simply because all meaning associated with that gesture had been lost now. She glared at me, but to my surprise, it wasn't as hateful as it'd been in the past. She quickly lost my gaze and resumed a very uncomfortable-looking stance right next to Princess Cornflower, who was white as a sheet.

"*Hey!*" my mother shouted so loudly at the top of her lungs that her throat instantly went hoarse. When the volume faded just a little, she declared, "Does anyone have any *actual* evidence to point us toward a suspect?"

The room quieted a little more, and hundreds of arms shot up into the air.

My mother groaned and rolled her eyes unapologetically. "Did anyone actually *see* who started the fire?"

Every single hand went down, one by one, some more hesitant than others. The Royals standing on the table looked at each other in turn, a silent conversation buzzing through the air between them. Queen Sabine was the one who spoke first, her cropped, emerald hair disheveled. "We have no choice but to move on for the time being…" – a gigantic groan rippled through the crowd, along with a few shouts of anger – "*just* until evidence comes forth. We have no way of questioning every single one of you, nor would we discover the truth until a witness comes forward. We promise you all that we *will* get to the bottom of this."

"That's all fine and dandy," a Lunakan man announced, "but what do we do *now?* Where will we get food?"

"Spring is right around the corner," King Frederick answered, his voice rising as the murmurs of the crowd grew. "We'll send out another hunting party."

"The last hunting party only came back with one deer! We're going to *starve!*" an Auklian woman cried hysterically. "Spring will be here in only a few weeks, and the roads will allow Emperor Rhydin to pick us off one by one!"

Suddenly the room was pulsating with dozens of different ideas. Leaving Lunaka Castle, staying at Lunaka Castle. Foraging for food here, traveling to Auklia where fish were easy to procure. Splitting the final stockpile between everyone to fend for themselves at Lunaka Castle, or stick together. The Rounans should leave the Gornish to their destruction, after all there's no way they're going back to letting the Gornish put them to death. The conversations rapidly transformed into the same topics the rebellion had debated since day one concerning the world after Emperor Rhydin, and I crossed my arms in anger. These people were so consumed with the future that they couldn't focus on the now.

One man's voice rang out above the rest, sight unseen, "This isn't working! This system of governance is a disaster!"

To my dismay, the entire room was nodding. I watched as every one of the Royals' faces fell, some of them going a mite pale. I couldn't say I was their number one fan, especially right now, but it wasn't their fault the people weren't agreeing or didn't want to go along with their choices. They were giving the people more say in decision-making than any commoner had had in *centuries*, and they got no thanks.

"Archimage" began to circle the room for the hundredth time, and I shook my head. These people just wanted one person to make all the decisions for everyone so there was no more disagreement and drama. The old way of thinking.

Yet, it was the old way of absolute power that landed us here.

A chorus made up of the single word "vote" reverberated throughout the throne room. Princess Cornflower was stoic now, her usual fear hidden behind a stony mask. She folded her dainty hands in front of her and lifted her head high, but she never said a word. Kylar and I glanced at each other briefly, and my brother was cupping his chin with his hand, cleverly disguising whatever feelings his face might display unintentionally. Typically, only the members of the Council voted on things, which were the Royals, the Allyens, and the others like the Kidek, James as ambassador for the Ranguvariians and Chelsea, the Aatarilec ambassador. However, if only those people voted, the outcome would be an obvious no. That wasn't the kind of vote the people were chanting for.

King Frederick looked as weary as an old man as he turned to speak with the other Council members, his wiry hand going to his little sister's shoulder. My mother looked like she was going to be nauseous as they broke their huddle, and Queen Sabine plumb left the table, letting herself down to the floor and walking away. She knew the pain of an Archimage first hand, since the last one was her father.

I wasn't sure why they even bothered. As soon as King Xavier uttered the words, "all in favor of an Archimage," about ninety percent of the hands in the room lifted to the ceiling.

Princess Cornflower put on a brave face and took a couple steps forward on the table, projecting a firm, regal tone I didn't know she had. "Thank you for your confidence, Nerahdis. I will do my best to serve you as Archimage."

The entire room was quiet now, waiting for the youngest adult Royal to say more. There was a slight quiver to her pale hands as she took a deep breath and announced, "We shall stay here in Lunaka Castle and request more help from our allies to send out extra hunting parties both to the forest and town. The Aatarilecs can hide the presences of the Ranguvariians from Rhydin to allow them to move more freely. I do not think we should go to Auklia. It would take over a week to move everyone there, and we would be left exposed and unprotected without this fortress. Instead of waiting for Emperor Rhydin to come for us, as soon as spring rears her head, we shall go to him. We shall not allow him to starve us out."

A tremendous cheer went around the room. No discussion, no arguing, no talking back. It was absolutely surreal.

I could only shake my head as I backed away from Kylar's side slowly and inched toward the door. There was no way I was going to watch anymore of this. The rebellion was about to test that old saying about being ignorant of history, and I had no desire to watch it play out.

Princess Cornflower continued addressing questions from the audience as I pushed toward the door. My hand barely touched the metal of the handle when someone in the crowd asked rather loudly, "Since we're takin' the fight to Rhydin, will the Allyens be ready? 'Specially the kid one?"

Heat flashed through my chest. I could suddenly feel several sets of eyes on the back of my head, and I realized how bad this probably looked that I was caught leaving before the meeting was over. My anger only grew though. How dare they pretend they had *any* idea what went on in my lessons with Uncle Evan!

My hands clenched into fists, but before I could whirl around and defend myself, I heard my mother proclaim, "We are *all* ready. You have nothing to fear-…!"

I stopped listening and ushered myself out the door. Immediately, I threw a punch into the stone wall next to the door as if that would help me vent. After pausing in that position for a moment, waiting for the throbbing in my hand to stop, I dug around in my pocket for Rhydin Caldwell's vial. It gleamed as I pulled it out, its shiny glass tube adorned with silver wire, especially the fancy stopper I could only wonder where Rhydin had found it. I could detect a very faint magical signature emanating from it, but my mind didn't know how to identify it. It was unlike any other magic I had sensed before; certainly nothing like Emperor Rhydin's dark magic that I'd sensed within his Einanhis.

"I'm not just ready to perform the death spell," I whispered myself as I caught my stretched reflection in the vial meant to recapture Rhydin Caldwell's magic. "I'm ready to put all this to right. Save Rhydin Caldwell and learn his story so that *none* of this *ever* happens again."

Suddenly pleased with myself, I tucked the vial back into my pocket and aimlessly started wandering in the direction of the dungeon. It'd been a long time since I'd visited Erikin, and I was curious to hear his opinion of this fire and ridiculous vote. I was just about to leave the room when a loud knock resounded on the heavy door leading to the outdoors.

I froze mid-step. That was odd. It was still pretty early in the morning, although there was finally a faint glow coming from the eastern windows. Wasn't everyone at the Council meeting? I tip-toed over to toward the gigantic front door as lightly and quickly as I could as if the ground was going to give out underneath me. No sounds came from beyond the door, but I reached out with my magic and there was definitely a person on the other side.

Just one person, but they didn't give off any sort of presence in particular. Just blankness.

Another knock came, and I jumped unintentionally. Surely the guards already inspected the person, right? They had no real presence, which meant they had to be magic-less. There were rebels out on the ramparts and by the gates every hour of the day and night. Maybe it was a rebel who got locked out?

For right or wrong, I yanked on the heavy handle, and the door let out a long, arduous groan. A crack of daylight flooded the castle foyer as the door on the opposite end of the room opened as well. A slow trickle of rebels began to flow out of the throne room, so I felt a little less fearful as I pulled the front door wide enough to see who was on the other side.

A middle-aged woman swamped in a black cloak stared back at me with hazel eyes. Sprigs of dark blonde hair stuck out of her hood alongside her pale, thin face, and her cloak swallowed up any other identifying features. There was something familiar about her face though, something I couldn't quite put my finger on. When she continued to stand there unflinchingly, her eyes pinned to me and obviously not a rebel, I stuttered, "C-Can I help you?"

"Rosetta?"

My mother's voice sounded from right behind me, and I moved away from the door with a jolt as if I'd been caught doing something I wasn't supposed to. There was a look of utter shock on my mother's oval face, her mouth partially agape. My gaze happened to wander over her shoulder to see King Frederick, who appeared far from pleased.

Well, good!

"I…I don't understand. How are you here?" My mother stumbled over her words as her hands suddenly fidgeted with her sash.

The woman outside finally gave some sort of restrained smile. Her voice was a little hoarse as she replied, "I always told you I'd come back as soon as I could…and, well, Mikael died when Lunaka Castle was attacked….er, reclaimed. I'm here to join you."

"That…That's great!" gushed my mother, a grin splitting her face like very few I'd seen before. "I just can't believe you're here!"

I cleared my throat rather loudly. It was like my mother had forgotten anybody else was here. "Mother, who is this?"

To my intense frustration, it was King Frederick that responded to me, a look of grave concern plastered upon his face. "This is Rosetta, your mother's younger sister." Then he added, "half-sister, actually. She's been living among Rhydin's Followers since before you were born."

His words made my heart quicken and the blood drain from my face.

"Wait," I mumbled, abruptly finding it difficult to speak, "you're Erikin's mother?"

"Yes," Rosetta bobbed her dirty-blonde head, and her expression turned fearful. "Where is he? I've been trying to find him for weeks, ever since I heard his father was killed."

"Killed," my mother repeated in barely a whisper. Her smile vanished, and she became motionless. Her tone almost made it seem like a question, but I knew it wasn't. Not *everyone* in the rebellion knew that my mother had killed both Kino and Mikael the day we took Lunaka Castle, but it wasn't entirely a secret either.

Rosetta's face was flooded with emotion, her hazel eyes found the floor. "Yes…they were all killed, the ones who were here guarding the castle and all the town's resources for the emperor. I just still can't believe he's gone, after all these years. Anyway" – she straightened and fixed her gaze on mine with a flash, which rapidly made me feel like she could see through my skin or something – "where is my son? I need to see him, as soon as possible."

I scratched my cheek awkwardly and hem-hawed around for a second before admitting where exactly Erikin was and had been for months.

"He's in the *dungeon?* Lina, you put your own nephew in the dungeon?" Rosetta gasped, incredulous. My mother attempted to make some sort of explanation, but she was cut off. "I need to see him right now!"

The newcomer tried to storm away, but King Frederick was instantly in her path. He declared rather firmly, "I am afraid I cannot let you pass. You've just come from being among our enemies, we cannot just allow you to roam the castle until we ascertain your motives."

My mother's eyes flew open, astounded. She hurried over to King Frederick and muttered embarrassedly, "Frederick, this is my *sister!* Let her go see her son!"

King Frederick looked down at her apologetically and said, "I am sorry, but I can't. I have to keep all these people safe." Then, much louder, he called for some guards to take Rosetta upstairs and keep her in an unoccupied bedroom.

My mother glared hatefully at him as several rebels rushed forward to forcefully escort my newfound aunt upstairs. She followed in their wake, which left King Frederick and I standing together awkwardly as the rest of the rebels in the foyer milled about doing their daily routines. Before he remotely had a chance to talk to me, I took my leave and hurried out the closest door into the castle courtyard.

Perhaps, this sham of a marriage would fall apart on its own without any further objection from me.

Chapter Ten

Lina

Sixteen years. Sixteen years had it been since my little sister was taken from me, abducted by Mikael, who had joined Rhydin's ranks of Followers and made me believe that she was dead. She had been sixteen herself at the time, so young and naïve. Aside from when she'd briefly helped us escape Rhydin's prison tower in the Great Desert where Sam had been held and tortured, I hadn't seen her in all that time.

I ran after Rosetta as she was pulled away by some rebels pulling guard duty, not willing to let her out of my sight. There was no way I would allow Frederick to do this to her. Had he gone completely paranoid?

The guards settled Rosetta in what looked to me like a small closet with a shelving unit stripped bare of any supplies it may have once held on one side and a meager cot on the other. It was like this room had been held in wait for just this sort of scenario. My cheeks flushed with heat in embarrassment. This was just adding insult to injury.

Once the guards left us alone in the closet turned jail cell, locking the door behind them before instructing me to knock when I wanted to leave, my words tumbled out of my mouth.

"Rosetta, I am *so* sorry about this. I will be speaking to Frederick immediately, this is ridiculous!"

"Don't worry about it," Rosetta replied hesitantly, flapping her hand around as she took a seat on the plain cot. "I just want to see my son, that's all."

"Yes, yes, of course." I nodded my head like my neck was a spring. I sat down next to her, aching to feel that sisterly bond again. "Oh, Rosetta…there's so much I've wanted to talk to you about over the years. I'm sorry I kept so much from you back then.… Maybe if I hadn't, I could have kept Mikael from stealing you from me."

"That was a lifetime ago, Lina," my sister said as she stared at the floor. "I don't regret any of the choices I've made."

I stared at her for a few moments, studying her face which was thinner than I'd ever seen before. I supposed that was a fair statement, that people usually came to a place of acceptance for the things that happened in their lives, but it also didn't open things up much. I just had this fierce desire to talk to her about *everything*, especially before I needed to tell her that it was me who took Mikael's life. I giggled awkwardly, "Do you remember when we were kids? And we would play with Papa in the corn field for hours racing and hiding in the rows?"

Rosetta was quite for a moment, and then asked as if she hadn't heard me, "When can I see Erikin?"

My brow furrowed as disappointment lodged itself in my throat. Was our relationship truly so irreparable? I hauled myself to my feet, feeling the strain as if my bones were twice their age. "I'll talk to Frederick. He can't keep you locked up here forever if I have anything to say about it."

Rosetta gave some sort of half-snort, her hazel eyes suddenly lightening a bit. "I don't know if this whole rebellion thing has made you forgetful or not, Lina, but a king can do whatever the heck he wants without a care in the world for what two peasant girls think. That's Royals for you, in case you've forgotten. Exactly what Rhydin was trying to rid Nerahdis of."

I paused for a moment, my eyes narrowing upon her. "How is Rhydin's absolute dictatorship any better than what the Royals did in the past? The new ones have proven their difference time and again."

"Not trying to start an argument." Rosetta held up her hands, but her sly smile remained. "Just curious what this hold is that you seem to have over our 'new king.'"

"I…" I stuttered, finding it hard to actually say the words. I hadn't had to say them to anyone yet; everyone in the rebellion already knew, and the tell-tale crown was somewhere on my bedroom floor. "I'm the queen, Rosetta. Queen of Lunaka."

Rosetta's eyes widened into saucers, and her mouth went agape. She paused that way for several seconds like her brain just wouldn't process the information I was telling her before her gaze went directly to each of the rings on my hands, Sam's silver and Frederick's gold. I bolstered myself for her inevitable first question, but that didn't make me any more ready for it when it came. Her forehead crinkled as she asked skeptically, "What happened to Sam?"

I told her the whole story. How he'd been poisoned by an Einanhi's blade, how there was no cure even after months of Ranguvariian research and experimentation, and how he withheld the entire thing from me until the very end. To my surprise, it may have been the first time I was able to tell what happened without being reduced to tears, if only for my hope that any sort of shared experiences could help us reinstate our bond.

"So, Sam died right after the battle…and you just married the prince, like, yesterday," Rosetta replied monotonously, like she was mulling it around in her head.

"I know it sounds bad," I tried to say, readying to launch into the spiel that Arii had given to me, but I never got the chance.

"No, no," Rosetta chuckled, her mouth twisting into a strange smile, "I would have done the exact same thing. You executed quite the power grab, I'm sure your family's thrilled."

I shook my head so hard it hurt. "No, that's not what it was! I didn't even *want* to! But it was the right thing to do for everyone.... You're my family too, y'know, in case you forgot."

"Oh, I'm definitely thrilled," Rosetta responded smugly, tucking her hands behind her head confidently. "You're the queen of this castle, which means you have the power to pardon me, don't you? Regardless of what your new kingly husband has to say."

"Y-...You have an *excellent* point," I declared as the epiphany went off in my head. I was a *queen*; I had just as much power as Frederick did. Feeling victorious, I waltzed up to the door and rapped my knuckles upon it. When the shaggy-haired, unshaven guard unlocked the door, I said firmly, "Your services are no longer required. As queen of Lunaka, I pardon this woman."

The guard eyed the other one out of sight hesitantly, but he ultimately gave a gruff acknowledgement before the twosome disappeared down the hall, key ring in tow.

"Royal life is going to be nice." My little sister winked at me. "Now, about my son..."

I sighed, my feeling of victory fleeting. "Erikin won't be so simple. He's actually committed a crime, whether purposeful or not. You were just a victim. I'll speak to Frederick, I promise. We'll have to get the entire Council's approval to free him, and I'm trying to get Frederick to vouch for him. In the meantime, we can move you up to my room?"

"Eh," Rosetta glanced around the tiny closet briefly as she drew her black cloak around her gaunt body, "here's fine. I don't need to interrupt the honeymoon phase."

My nose wrinkled inadvertently. "Well, surely you can stay with Evan and Cayce, I mean, he's your brother too after all-…"

"No, seriously Lina, I want to stay here. I like my space," Rosetta replied a little crudely, not meeting my gaze. "All I care about is seeing Erikin. That's it."

"I…I understand," I said glumly, wishing I actually did. I promised her I would work on arranging a visit, then I slowly withdrew myself from the room, hoping in vain that she would ask me to stay and talk longer.

My feet moved automatically even as my mind entered a fog. Was this just the way we'd be from now on? Our relationship permanently altered? She hadn't even seemed sorry for me that Sam died, although I hadn't really had a chance to talk to her about Mikael either. If this was the way our relationship was like before I could confess to accidentally killing Mikael, there'd surely be nothing left afterward.

Why did this have to happen? Why did Mikael have to steal her from me sixteen years ago? It was starting to feel more and more like Rosetta truly died that day. Why did I have to lose *everyone?*

Before I knew it, I was planted squarely in front of Frederick's double doors – which now were considered mine as well. Fuming, I slapped the palms of my hands against their cool wood and slammed them open, each of them banging off the opposite, stone walls. Frederick was seated inside at his desk, and he jumped at the sudden intrusion, knocking over an ink well that spilled blackness onto the floor. He remained frozen in place as I roared, "Are you *trying* to make her hate me? What is *wrong* with you?"

Frederick quickly righted the ink well and rubbed his blackened fingers on a cloth rag on his desk top. He sighed heavily, cavities appearing along his collar bone, and replied, "Lina, it's just standard protocol. We can't just let someone in whose been living among our enemies for years. Once we make sure all is right, I'll let Rosetta out, I promise."

"That's ridiculous! This is my *sister* who was abducted, not some loyal Follower! This isn't Kino or Mikael or any of the others we've dealt with. Besides, she's no longer your problem," I declared as I crossed my arms indignantly.

The king's icy gaze narrowed. "What have you done?"

"What you should have," I accused. "I pardoned her."

"You *what?*" Frederick leapt to his feet, a rare anger flaring forth. "Have you lost your mind? We don't know if she's safe, if she's actually here for the reasons you think she is! Not to mention how bad it looks for you to undermine me! As queen, you're supposed to support my decisions, not overturn them!"

"Undermine you," I scoffed, rolling my eyes. "I am *not* your mother, Frederick! I will not just blindly go along with your every whim like she did for King Adam! I have my own voice, I always have since becoming an Allyen!"

"As an Allyen, you could do whatever you wanted because you did not have a people to directly represent, please, and lead. Being a Royal is *very* different; you can't just do whatever you want if you want to be a good leader!" Frederick came closer, the veins in his pale neck popping like his father's used to.

"I already did," I growled lowly, not budging. "She's pardoned. She's free to go about the castle. You may be king, but I'm the queen, not just some pretty face you keep around for company."

"Then start acting like you serve someone other than yourself or your family," Frederick replied darkly as he stared down his nose at me.

My cheeks burned. I felt like I'd been slapped. I opened my mouth to contradict him, but he beat me to it.

"And I understand that you're different," he said quietly, his eyes abruptly softening. "You're not my mother or any other submissive female Royal in the history of all time. I *like* that you're different. But *talk to me* before you make big decisions like this. I deserve to at least be consulted. You would've talked to Sam first on a Rounan issue, wouldn't you?"

With that, Frederick took his leave, grabbing his cloak off the back of his chair as he did. I stood as still as a statue as he passed, feeling nothing as he stalked toward the door and shut it behind him. Time moved strangely around me. I could see the change in the sun's light outside and the burning down of the solitary candle on Frederick's desk, but everything seemed so still that surely time wasn't moving at all.

Was he right? Did I only care about my own family? That couldn't be entirely true, not when I normally spent every waking moment making rounds around the castle to be available to the Rounans. Was it because I didn't do the same for the Gornish? I would only be Kidek Regent for a few more years until Kylar came of age…I'd be spending the rest of my life as queen of one of the Three Kingdoms, directly in charge of thousands of Gornish citizens.

But it was my sister. I had absolutely no reason to doubt her. She had promised to return one day the last time I'd seen her in the Great Desert, although at the time she had hoped to bring Mikael with her. I hadn't sensed anything amiss in her, just the usual vague presence that every magic-less human gave off when near enough.

I started nodding to myself. My decision was totally justified. Frederick would have done the exact same thing for Mira or Cornflower. And that comment about Sam? Seriously? He and I were a well-oiled team, not two people just thrown together. *But* – I held up a finger like I was conducting an argument with another person – I would start to act more like the queen. The people of Lunaka, my own people that I grew up with, deserved to have a good queen, and one that worked well with the king. Queen Gloria would be a hard act to follow, her lack of action against King Adam aside, but I would do everything in my power to make their lives better. It was what I would want from my queen if the situation was different.

Suddenly feeling empowered and weightless, I changed out of my ruined, sooty clothes, slapped my wheat head crown on top of the bandana on my head, and trotted out of the cool suite and down the hall in search of any Lunakan I could help.

It was nearly lunch time, however, so the halls were pretty bare. I couldn't decipher the scent wafting up the stairway from the throne room, but it seemed slightly potato-like. Our reserves were nothing but potatoes anymore, until Cornflower's new hunting party came back anyway. However, I'd spent more than one winter living off potatoes as a child just as any other commoner had at one point or another, so I changed direction all the same. Anything that kept my stomach from trying to gnaw at itself all hours of the day was good with me.

As I hustled down the stairs and dreamed of transforming one of our rebellious chickens into something fried, the magical compass in my head alerted me to the presence of my daughter on the floor which housed the room she still sometimes shared with Evan and Cayce now that I'd moved out. I halted on the landing automatically, my foot still mid-air. Why was she up here during lunch? Was she not eating? I didn't sense anyone with her.

I swept down the hall as silent as the wind and placed an ear against the door. To my surprise, it wasn't my daughter's alto voice that reverberated through but Arii's tenor. "How fascinating," the Ranguvariian leader mused, and I could imagine the sweet smile on his wrinkled face. "I was certainly a precocious child. I still remember giving the locket to Nora. I wasn't even Clariion yet."

"Really?" I heard Rayna ask, her voice full of wonder. "You seemed so in charge in that memory."

Arii chuckled, "My father was Clariion at the time and too busy with our war against the Aatarilecs to spare any time. He knew cultivating Nora's power was important, and he entrusted that task to me as his heir. I became Clariion a year later when Rhydin created Duunzer the first time in response to the coup d'état mounted by Caden's sons. My father and half our people were on campaign when the Darkness came, and they were all instantly killed. That is why my people fear Rhydin so. Our camp is so close to the mountains, where no magic works, that the rest of us were able to evacuate in time and survive."

There was a beat of silence beyond the door, and my heart clenched. Arii had never told me any of this before, and I wondered if Rachel knew, although I remembered her sheer terror when Rhydin created Duunzer during our lifetime as he worked to establish his empire.

Rayna finally replied, echoing my own thoughts, "So what happened? You all were safe but had no magic. How did you take down Rhydin and Duunzer the first time without any help?"

I squished my ear to the door. Their tones were getting softer, and I was desperate to hear the answer.

"It took a week for Nora and I to travel through the mountains. I flew her as much as I could, but even that magic was limited. On the way, we studied together and brainstormed ways we could destroy such a large, magical being without the help of our own power. By the time we got there, we had designed the arrow meant to carry the Allyen locket, the one shred of magic we had at our disposal, through Duunzer's shadowy heart," Arii explained, and I briefly wondered whether Rayna even knew what he was talking about.

Arii went on, "What we didn't anticipate was that when we arrived at the old imperial palace where Caden's Plain is now, neither Rhydin nor Duunzer knew we were there. It was then that we originally discovered that Rhydin couldn't sense Ranguvariians, or anyone with a Ranguvariian. Between the arrow, the element of surprise, and our own swordsmanship, we were victorious. Duunzer dissolved into nothingness, and Rhydin disappeared. We had hoped for good. However, …you know how that turned out."

"Wow," Rayna breathed, and I had to stop myself from doing the same. "I wish more people knew that story."

"Perhaps, someday they will," Arii responded quietly, seeming to be lost in thought. "Now, you told me that the real Rhydin has answered my message asking how to ensure the death spell successfully returns his power to him and what weakness it will muster. What did he say?"

"He gave me this." There was a pause, and I could only assume that Rayna had withdrawn that strange vial she'd gotten at the Archimage Palace and given it to Arii. "He made it to recapture his magic once the death spell destroys the evil Rhydin, but *I* have to be the one to use it. No one else, or it won't work. The magic will only be drawn to me for some reason."

I cringed. Did she know what that meant? Had she found out the truth? Arii, too, was quiet for a few moments before asking in a grave tone, "And his weakness? What will that be? What should we be prepared to see?"

Rayna answered sadly, "Amelia. The woman I keep seeing with Nora and Rhydin in those memories. Just her image though, it's not like she's being brought back from the dead or something like that." – I shuddered involuntarily – "I think maybe because they loved each other? But they couldn't marry because Rhydin was made Archimage, and she was the daughter of someone who didn't like that or something? And if Caden's sons saw her, they'd kill her? I don't know, that part isn't clear at all."

"I never had the pleasure of meeting Miss Eason, and Nora rarely spoke of her, so devastated as she was. Her husband, Charles, told me once that she was never the same after Amelia's death, but I never knew her before," Arii murmured.

"Arii..." Rayna was suddenly pleading, "you have to explain to me why *I'm* the only one who can do it. Why am I the only one who can see him or collect his magic? Why does he keep telling me that he and I are the only two people in the world who were given magic the same way? He keeps saying

I was given my Allyen magic just like him, but I wasn't. My mother and Uncle Evan are way more capable Allyens to be entrusted with this stuff. It just doesn't make sense." After silence filled the room for a couple of seconds, Rayna added, "What aren't you all telling me? There *is* a reason, isn't there?"

My blood froze in my veins. I could scarcely feel myself breathing, much less summon the power to move.

"Well, Rayna, I think you know that you are a special Allyen. It just took a little more effort to give you your power when you were born, that is all," Arii tried to explain vaguely, and I inwardly thanked him for not spilling the beans.

"But *why?*" Rayna insisted from beyond the door, her voice growing higher like she was approaching the act of pleading. "I keep hearing people talk about me like I'm different. My magic is different, and I'm somehow different from my brother, and that there's some sort of link between me and King Frederick. Will you please just tell me, Arii? I know there's something there. I'm not stupid."

I took in a ragged breath as my heart stuttered in my chest. I was a fool to think we could hide it from her forever, but I never once imagined having to tell her before she was a full-grown adult. Especially not without Sam at my side to help lessen the blow.

Nonetheless, it was time. Time to tell my daughter that she wasn't born my daughter.

Chapter Eleven

Rayna

Clariion Arii was staring at me with plaintive eyes now steeped the color of the ocean when the door to my family's bedroom suddenly opened. My mother cautiously stepped inside, dressed now a plain brown gown that I supposed must be a part of her new wardrobe as queen. Her mud-brown hair was pulled back into a high bun, unlike her usual half-down hairstyle, which made her new crown on top of Papa's bandana obvious and raised my ire. I looked away from her, not liking the changes. It was like she'd ceased being the mother I knew upon marrying King Frederick.

"It's time we told you," I heard my mother say in a shaky voice.

There was the sound of a chair creaking. "I will let you two discuss this in private," Clariion Arii murmured softly, barely audible.

When the door closed once again, ushering in a wave of ringing silence, my skin began to crawl. It'd been an eternity since the last time my mother and I had been alone together. I couldn't help but glare at her as she carefully smoothed her skirt over her knees. "How long were you listening?"

"For a little while," she breathed, then she seemed to try and change the subject. "Your ancestral memories sound fascinating. I wish I could experience one with you, and I'm proud of you for how you've studied them so diligently to help us."

I rolled my eyes mercilessly. "Sure, whatever. Are you going to tell me why Rhydin Caldwell seems to think we're the same or not?"

My mother took a deep breath and blew it out slowly like she was blowing out a candle. "Arii is right. When you were born, you…you weren't born an Allyen. Arii had to help me transfer some of my magic to you to grow as your own. That's why you're the same as the real Rhydin, because you weren't born with your magic inherently there. If we hadn't given it to you, you would have never been an Allyen. In fact, the Allyen magic would have ceased to exist altogether."

"Okay, so…what's the big deal about that? Why would the Allyen magic cease to exist?" I asked, shrugging as I crossed my arms over my chest.

"Because…because the Allyen magic even since Nora has depended upon being renewed each generation with the birth of a new Allyen…and Evan and I messed up the system. We were the first Allyens to marry Rounans, which is a dominant trait, so all our children we could ever have would be Rounans too," my mother replied hesitantly.

"Ah, so if you hadn't changed me into an Allyen, I would have been a Rounan then? I guess that makes sense," I mused. Some of the pieces seemed to be falling together.

"N-No," my mother choked out, her Allyen eyes squeezing shut, "actually, you would have been an aeromage."

My brow furrowed. "What? Why? There's no wind magic in our family."

"Rayna…in order to transfer the magic, we needed a newborn. A newborn born with…with *Gornish* magic. Kylar was born a Rounan, and all either Evan or I's children could only ever be Rounans," my mother warbled.

Understanding started to dawn on me. I hated the tremor in my voice when I asked accusingly, "What are you saying?"

Tears streamed down my mother's thin face as she whispered, "You weren't born to Sam and I…but we've been your parents and loved you as our own from that very first day."

I was instantly in motion, pacing from one side of the room to the other, not daring to look in my mo-…in *her* direction. My hands grew hot, and if I'd been a pyromage like Taisyn, something probably would have been on fire. Memories flashed in my mind, my earliest memories of my so-called parents, and images of my papa…*Sam*…about put me overboard. I whirled on her and growled, "So whose kid am I then, huh? D-D-Did you *steal* me or something? And why do I look like you and P-Papa if not, hmm?"

"Arii changed your appearance at the same time for the sake of your safety. Your blood is *our* blood," the woman in front of me who apparently was *not* my mother croaked. "We didn't steal you, we just didn't want anyone to-…"

"To what? To think the Allyen magic so weak as to die out?" I roared angrily as I continued my frantic pacing. "*Who am I, Mother?*"

It was then that the bedroom door opened, and I about launched the nearest side table at Arii's head when he came through, only it wasn't Arii. Standing there with eyes wide in desperation was none other than King Frederick, and it only took me a beat to realize his attention was on me and not his new wife.

Aeromage. His insistence on providing for me.

"*No!*" I bellowed, as I raked my hands through my short auburn hair.

"Please, Rayna." King Frederick tried to approach me as my former mother just cried in the corner. "I've always loved you and wanted to be in your life, believe me I have. If you could just let me into your life in some way-…"

"*You're* my father?" I shouted incredulously, tears now leaking from my eyes, and then I pointed at the pitiful woman in the corner. "Is this why you *married* him after Papa's *barely* been dead? Because he's my 'real' father even though he obviously gave me up?!"

"Rayna, I know this is hard to understand…it's *still* hard for me to understand even fourteen years later," the balding king said quietly. "I told you once that my wife, Cassandra…she died in childbirth when having my daughter. That was *you*, Rayna. I didn't even know you existed back then. I was away in Auklia during the war. All those decisions were made for me."

I cringed briefly, remembering that conversation back in the Dome, but I was too angry for logic. "What, so your wife died, you were out of town, and my so-called parents just took me? That's real great."

"It was *necessary*, Rayna," my fake mother suddenly re-entered the conversation, her voice so hoarse it was unrecognizable. "If we hadn't made you into the new Allyen, our magic would have died, and Nerahdis would have been lost to Emperor Rhydin forever. Can't you see? You weren't 'given up' at all! We just had no choice!"

"No choice but to take in an abandoned Royal baby just to solve your problems. Yeah, I get it." I scooped up my bag that contained my sketchbook, the little metal bird sculpture Taisyn made me back in the Dome, and a few other meager possessions in one fluid motion, heading for the door and ramming my shoulder into Frederick on the way. I declared loudly, "As far as I'm concerned, I'm an *orphan!*"

Both of them called after me, but I ignored them. I ran haphazardly down the hall, my disoriented steps mirroring the jumble of thoughts in my mind. *My parents aren't my parents. They raised me because they had to save the Allyen magic. My real mother willingly gave me away without even telling my real father that I existed. Did Papa ever truly love me, the daughter that wasn't his?*

Who am I? Does anyone actually want me for me?

I was at the stairs by the time I realized the castle walls were melting around me. The definition of the stones seeped away into nothing but dark colors that shifted into lighter grays and browns before redefining into a totally different landscape. I was standing in a doorway, the cold outdoors behind me as I peered into a well-built, well-furnished home. There were silver spoons and porcelain dishes in cabinets, as well as intricate rugs and furs keeping the smooth, shiny floors warm. The fireplace and chimney were crafted of hewn, rectangular stone instead of the random, natural rock to be found outside. Whoever lived here was obviously very wealthy.

Only seconds had I been within this ancestral memory, hesitantly hovering in the doorway, before a tall, middle-aged man crashed into the picture from another room. He was dressed in a fancy suit with a frilly collar and thick, woolen coat, and his brown hair was perfectly tied back into a ponytail like the people of Gornan did in history book illustrations. He bellowed at me – at Nora, "What have you done, you ungrateful child?"

My body shook on its own accord, and Nora's voice sprang from my mouth, much younger-sounding than any of the other memories I'd so far witnessed. "Father, *please*. I cannot marry Lord Kane, I refuse!"

"Daughter, Lord Kane is the wealthiest man in this new country!" the man shouted back, his face turning beet red, "Do you not understand how this can help our family remain in power? We left behind all our power and influence when we left Gornan, you *must* perform your duty as my only child and establish our security! Lord Kane is very taken with you, and I have assured him of your fertility. He is not even requesting a dowry!"

"Father, he is nearly *sixty* years old, and I am only sixteen," Nora pleaded, and I was rocked as she moved to kneel in the navy satin dress she wore. "I will *not* marry him for anything in the world."

"Anything, eh?" Nora's father repeated as he stared down his long nose at Nora and I. "Your mother would be ashamed of you if she had lived to see this."

In a flash, the middle-aged lord had stomped forward, hauled Nora – and therefore me – to her feet, and forcibly shoved her out the door so hard that she fell backwards into the dirt. My head collided with the hard ground, and the sound of screaming horses as they dodged us in the middle of the road was deafening. When Nora was able to pull herself up and her father came back into view, he yelled, "You may only re-enter this house after I hear word of your betrothal to Lord Kane! Good-bye, Nora."

Nora stood, and my hands moved with hers as she brushed the dirt off her dress. No scars in this memory, I thought to myself briefly. She sniffled a little and moved out of the road, and I studied our surroundings in confusion. Lord Soreta's house was the largest one on the block with quite a bit of space between it and the other houses and shops nearby. The road was plain dirt, and none of the buildings looked more than fifteen or twenty years old. Besides being in Lunaka with the mountains in the distance, the prairie grass, and the general lack of trees, I couldn't place our location until I spotted a huge structure on the horizon. A stone building was sprouting a couple miles from where we stood, its base encased in wooden scaffolding that betrayed the scope of the project as workers laid stone by stone.

Lunaka Castle was being built before my very eyes. We were in Soläna before it had become a mining center, and the town descended into the man-made canyon along with all its workers.

Suddenly, I was pulled back from Nora's point of view, and I could see her standing in the road below me like I was hovering over her head. She looked so young and small, but she brushed her hands together and walked away from her father's house with whatever dignity she had left. Then, time seemed to move faster. People and horses rushed up and down the dirt road, and lamps in houses flashed on and off as the sun and twin moons raced each other up above.

Nora, on the other hand, seemed to move at a more normal pace even as the world sped around her and Lunaka Castle grew ever taller. She spent her days on the road begging for money or working small jobs for whatever shopkeeper was willing, and she never once went remotely close to the area of town where her father lived. Her satin dress disappeared quickly as she sold it, and she began to wear very plain, rough clothes. Once she had saved up enough, she purchased a used bow and quiver of arrows, which she used to hunt and sell meat and fur to the people of Soläna. I wondered if she'd been taught archery as the daughter of a lord based on her immediate skill, or she could have been a fast learner, I didn't know.

Years seemed to be going by as both Nora and the town aged and grew beneath me. She was starting to look like the Nora I'd encountered in other ancestral memories, the rough and tumble huntress as opposed to the young noblewoman I'd never known she'd been. She saved every copper piece she gained and slept under the stars every night, but I couldn't help but notice how alone she was. She had no one to spend her days with. No friends, no family, and she threatened to shoot any man that dared approach her.

I was beginning to wonder how long this strange montage would go on until one day, five years into the memory based on how many times I'd seen winter turn into spring – although I probably hadn't been in the memory more than twenty minutes – Nora was hunting in the forest a few miles southwest of Soläna. When the sun began to move normally again and I found myself once again within Nora's body, I knew I was about to see something important.

We crept forward, an arrow nocked and ready for anything. Nora had her grass green hood low over her head as she fiercely stalked forward, ready to fire at the first living thing that burst into the meadow. As if on cue, the brush to our left began to rustle, and Nora drew back her arrow, the muscles in her chest feeling strong within my own.

But it was no deer, rabbit, or squirrel that fled into the meadow, or anything that had fur for that matter. A young woman tripped and fell as she pushed through the bushes, a once beautiful gown on her person torn to shreds, and her limbs were crisscrossed with red. Her hair was as blue as the ocean back home in Caark, even matted and threaded as it was with sticks and leaves.

Amelia, I thought to myself in shock as Nora narrowly changed her aim just as she loosed her arrow. It struck a tree with a *thud*, and Amelia's head instantly shot up. Upon sight of Nora, she scrambled to her feet, which were bare, muddy, and blistered, and she tried to run toward us. "Help!" she screamed hoarsely. "Please help me, please!"

Seconds later, half a dozen male guards burst into the meadow clad in old-fashioned armor that gleamed in the daylight. Every one of them held spears, and etched onto their breastplates was a crest I only knew from history books. A large, shining sun behind a sword pointed to the ground.

It was the old seal of ancient Gornan. Emperor Caden's personal emblem.

Nora took one look at the situation, and I already knew what was going through her mind after witnessing the past five years of her life in such quick succession. Injured young girl being pursued by faceless men in armor?

The six of them were dead in only moments, a single arrow buried in each.

Amelia was pretty much hyperventilating on the ground now, and as Nora approached her, she gazed up at us in fear. "P-Please…th-thank you, but d-don't hurt me."

"You have nothing to fear from me," Nora replied, her voice now the gruff tone I remembered. "Nobody was there to protect me once. I vowed to never leave someone defenseless like I was. What's your name?"

"A-Amelia," the blue-haired teen answered awkwardly. "Amelia…E-Eason."

Nora's and my hands moved together as she motioned to the bodies, but Amelia couldn't bear to look. "Why is the Emperor's Guard after you? Steal the crown jewels or something? I wouldn't blame you if you had."

"N-No." Amelia shook her head as she finally stood and caught her breath. She began to inspect the various scratches along her pale arms. "They want to kill me…for something I didn't do."

"Fair enough." Nora shrugged, the reason evidently not bothering her. "Do you have any family I can take you to for tending? It's nearly dark, and you really ought to treat those."

Amelia clutched her arms to her chest and hid her face behind her hands in a child-like way. Her voice warbled as she answered, "W-We all ran together. We didn't even do anything wrong! T-The guards captured my mother, and they *killed* Ariadne…m-my sister. I have no one. Not anymore."

Nora shifted slightly on her feet and took a deep breath. Then, she slung her bow over her back and reached toward Amelia with an outstretched hand. "You can come with me. I don't have much, but you don't have to be alone."

The young girl nodded, and the two began to walk back toward town together, leaving the bodies where they lay. I was pulled up out of Nora once again as time began to speed up, and I only saw one last thing before the old world began to melt away. After a few weeks, Amelia shared a large purse of money with Nora, and pooled with Nora's savings, they bought land in what would become the Southern Canyonlands. My ancestral family farm was purchased by none other than Nora and Amelia together, and nobody had ever known.

Lunaka Castle re-materialized around me, all the colors going back into their normal shapes. I had to stand there on the staircase for a little while, thinking about the huge chunk of time I had just witnessed. Nora had felt the same way I did once, that nobody wanted her because her father abandoned her, and it was those very feelings that led her to Amelia. The two of us were a lot more similar than I'd ever realized, and Nora was beginning to feel like a real person to me. Like a friend.

I walked down the stairs in a haze, sort of like I was sleep-walking, my mind still buried deep in the memories. More answers, yet more questions too. Why was Emperor Caden's personal guard after Amelia, her mother, and her sister? She said they were innocent, but such a high-level squadron wouldn't have been sent after just anybody, especially to eliminate them. This obviously connected to why Amelia felt like she couldn't go with Rhydin when he became Archimage, that the Three Kings would kill her if they saw her.

But why?

"Hey, Rayna! You okay?" a familiar voice broke me from my thoughts.

I looked over to see Kylar, leaning nonchalantly against the wall with his elbow propped out. Next to him was Dominick, King Frederick's blond-haired heir who was the spitting image of him. My heart rate accelerated as I was brought back to the more pressing issues of the present. They appeared to have been deep in conversation, but now they both stared at me. With every second that ticked by, they looked at me, standing there still clutching my bag with all my things, more and more like I was something exotic.

One was my brother at the moment of my birth, and the other had been raised as my brother. My blood matched the latter, but I was born matching the former. Which one was actually my brother now? Or did it even matter with this new convoluted marriage?

I scurried away from them with no response in search of respite, changing directions once when I suddenly saw Willian heading my way. I had no desire to deal with the weird attention he always seemed to give me, whether it was showing his magic off like back in the Dome or insisting on spending alone time with me.

On the other side of the foyer, surrounded by dozens of people just milling around, I caught a couple glimpses of Taisyn and his family. Judging by the loud protestations from his father, King Xavier, and the defiant look on Taisyn's face, I was pretty sure they were fighting about the usual topic. Taisyn had no interest in being king; he thought his little sister Lyla would do a better job. But Mineraltir was a much more traditional kingdom than Auklia was and didn't allow for a girl to inherit, even if she was born first. The second Archimage, Minndosia of Mineraltir, was a prime example of that.

King Xavier better start re-writing some laws, I thought to myself, because Taisyn was stalwart in the matter. It was time they caught up with the times anyway. Auklia had had several queens inherit in the last few decades, like Queen Maria and Queen Sabine, and they'd all been widely successful.

As I watched Queen Mira set a gentle hand on Taisyn's shoulder, I shuddered. Perhaps, I needed to be more thankful that my blood was totally changed magically. Otherwise, Taisyn would be my first cousin.... My cheeks momentarily flushed with heat before I trotted right along so they wouldn't see me. I was skirting along the edge of the room toward the dungeons when a hand suddenly shot out of nowhere and grasped my arm through my cloak, causing me to almost drop my things.

When I whirled around, my anxiety racing, my brow furrowed at the sight of my mother's sister. Wasn't she supposed to be locked up somewhere? I stuttered, "Uh...h-hi?"

"We weren't properly introduced earlier. I'm your aunt, Rosetta," the thin, black-clad woman said, her hand still strangely tight on my arm. "I can tell you're my sister's daughter. You look a lot like she did at that age, although your coloring is all Sam."

I shrank involuntarily. "Thanks," I huffed, my eyes sliding to the side as I discreetly tried to shake her hand off. It was still odd to me that she didn't seem to give off much of a presence, but I chalked it up to not knowing her very well. I began to pull away from her and said, "I was just going to see Erikin."

"Oh, you won't have to wait much longer then! He's being released today," Rosetta replied cheerily, although her body language seemed to exude something else entirely.

"He…he what?" I gasped, my arms going limp as the crowd around us grew thicker. My bag fell on the cold floor with a *clunk.* "I don't understand. Has there been a Council meeting?"

"Just the Three Kings and Queen got together and decided it a couple hours ago," my aunt explained. "I'm so excited to see him!"

For a moment, my heart felt light. Erikin would be free! Even after I'd hopelessly failed to get that ball rolling myself. I almost forgot that my arm was still in a shackle hold as my eyes glued themselves to the dungeon door just a few feet away from us, the usual guards absent.

Only seconds later, the door opened. My sandy-haired cousin stepped into the light, dressed in a clean blue tunic and mended trousers. Relief flooded me at the sight of him, and he smiled at me, his freckled face much thinner than before. However, that smile was instantly replaced by confusion as his hazel eyes moved to the woman next to me, and he slowly crept toward us.

I gushed, "I'm so glad you're out!"

But Erikin took one look at Rosetta's beaming face and her hand clasped around my arm before declaring, "You're not my mother! Who are you, what are you doing h-…?"

Before he could finish, Rosetta lashed out with unhuman speed, attaching her other hand to Erikin's wrist. I panicked, yanking hard against her grip, strong as metal, but it was too late. Amethyst smoke appeared at our feet, and the world vanished in the blink of an eye, replaced by an empty, white void.

This isn't a memory, I thought to myself. *This is transportation magic.*

When the void disappeared, Lunaka Castle's gray, featureless foyer had been replaced by a dark, damp dungeon. Three walls were dirty bricks while the fourth consisted of metal bars. I'd landed on my knees, my head woozy from transportation, but I jumped to my feet and back into a corner as I saw Rosetta for what she really was.

Standing in her place was a strange human-like creature that was black as midnight with sharp, thin limbs and empty white eyes. I reached out with my senses, trying desperately to learn anything I could about this terrifying being, but *nothing* bounced back at me. Not even what little she'd had before with the presence of a human at least.

"I know where we are," Erikin said so quietly that I barely heard him. He seemed to be becoming smaller by the second, shrinking into another corner.

"What?" I halfway shrieked. "What's going on? Where's your mother?"

Erikin shook his head and whimpered, "I don't know, Rayna. But that's not her, and we're in big trouble now. This is Emperor Rhydin's dungeon."

My heart felt like it plummeted fifty feet.

"You are correct," a smooth voice came from the darkness beyond the bars to our cell, which sent shivers throughout my body.

A man dressed in a gold-trimmed, black tunic stepped forward into the light of the torch fastened to the wall above our heads. His hands were ridiculously pale as they touched our bars, and long black hair curled over his shoulder in a ponytail. Purple eyes glared at us, even as his lips curled into a smirk, and raw black power emanated from him like lightning about to bolt. I would've known who he was even if I hadn't met the man whose likeness he had. After all, his portrait was plastered on nearly every newspaper and poster from here to Caark.

Emperor Rhydin.

Chapter Twelve

Lina

Rayna flew out of the room with her things and slammed the door, leaving Frederick and I alone in her rocky wake. Anger bubbled up inside of me, and my hands began to shake. "I don't know why we thought this ridiculous marriage would help," I growled as I launched myself out of my chair. "This is a disaster!"

"We couldn't have kept it from her forever," Frederick replied defensively as he unconsciously touched the arm that Rayna had rammed on her way out. "It was only a matter of time."

"But why did it have to be *now?* When the only father she's ever known has been taken from her so fast after coming back into her life and when our fight is at its most critical point? She's fourteen years old, Frederick!" I seethed.

Frederick leaned against the bedpost; all the wind vanished from his sails. "What's done is done. We can't undo that Rayna knows now, and we can't undo our marriage."

"So what?" I replied angrily, "We just grin and bear it? Move on? Forget that any of this has happened or the permanent stains left on our lives?"

"Of course not, but we have to keep moving forward. We have enough mire weighing the two of us down as it is, we certainly cannot allow it to tie us down altogether." Frederick shrugged like that was the easiest thing in the world.

I scowled. "Is that what helps you sleep at night? Just forget it all and keep moving, so it doesn't catch up with you? Your wife, your mother, their memories forgotten? Good to know I'll never be mourned by *either* of my husbands."

Suddenly, there seemed to be a snap within Frederick. His face flushed red, and a vein pulsed in his temple. He took a step or two toward me and shouted, "*I had to keep going*, Lina. I am *king* of an entire kingdom with thousands depending on me, balanced upon *my* shoulders alone. I had to give up my daughter for this fight. I had to lose my wife, my mother, my home. What good would it do if I crumbled? Lunaka would only be lost too. I *know* that you are struggling, but you have got to pull yourself together. If you don't, not only will the people who follow you not have a leader, but you'll lose yourself, too. I, for one, don't want to see that."

My cheeks burned, and tears stung my eyes. Heat flooded my chest as my heart spewed blackened thoughts. "Don't pretend you care about me, Frederick. Not after everything I've done to you," I murmured, abruptly unable to summon any sort of volume. "You married me for your kingdom, and nothing else."

Frederick groaned and rubbed his head. "Lina, life isn't clean. It's dirty. Good things happen to bad people, and bad things happen to good people. Things of all kinds happen all the time that are outside of our control. If you need me to forgive you for taking Rayna and raising her as your own, then you have my forgiveness. I don't *blame* you for what happened. I am so sorry that Sam died, but he wouldn't want you to be stuck in that mud for the rest of your life either, just as Cassandra wouldn't have wanted me to be."

I was quiet for several moments, letting his words sink deep into my skin. My mouth opened and closed several times before I was able to formulate any sort of words. "I…I have agonized over what happened with Rayna for her entire life. Every time I see you I…am reminded of what we did while you were in Auklia."

"It's not your fault," Frederick whispered as he crept closer to me inch by inch. "I've never once blamed you or Sam. I know it's what had to be done. I only wish to move forward and have any kind of relationship I can with her now." He continued to stare at me even as the floor held my gaze. After a few seconds, he added, "Moving on does not mean forgetting. I think of the people I have lost every day, knowing that by moving forward I am doing exactly what they would want me to do. It would hurt them if I wallowed and became stuck."

I nodded numbly, knowing that I was standing at a precipice. Could I move on? Could I let go of guilt I'd housed for fourteen years? And move on from…from Sam? My eyes finally found Frederick's.

No. There was no moving on from Sam. Ever. I couldn't do that to him.

But I could still turn things around. I could still make things right with Frederick, by helping him keep up as king and cultivating a relationship between him and Rayna.

At the same time, Sam never wanted me to spend the rest of my days alone. He had ensured that with his final request that Frederick care for us. He certainly couldn't have imagined it like this though, right? We could just remain friends, as always, and keep each other company.

Frederick glanced downward before carefully meeting my eyes again. His voice was a low rumble as he said, "I did not just marry you for my kingdom. Lunaka benefits from it, the Rounans benefit from it, and so do Dominick, Rayna, and Kylar, of course. But I would be doing you a disservice if I didn't tell you that the idea of our marriage gave me hope for the future again…and that I have made the decision to love you. Both for your sake and for mine, whether you return it or not."

My mouth wouldn't move. It had been glued shut.

"Just...so you know, that's all," Frederick said again, his voice seeming a little constricted. He backed away from me quickly and headed for the door. "I need to be downstairs. I met with Xavier and Sabine privately just an hour ago, and I was able to convince them that your nephew meant no harm. He'll be free shortly. I hope in turn you might forgive me for my treatment of your sister."

He was instantly gone. Didn't even wait for a reply.

Love? "Made the decision" to love?

What in Nerahdis does that mean?

I wandered from the room, my thoughts in a jumble. Frederick had "decided" to love me, whatever that meant. He'd gone to Xavier and Sabine on his own to free Erikin to make up with me even though *I* was technically the one who'd gone behind his back to pardon Rosetta in the first place. I certainly didn't deserve any favors right now.

What was with this man?

The foyer seemed more chaotic when I reached the ground floor. Sure, there was the usual bickering and private conversations filled with backhand comments pointed toward either the Gornish or the Rounans respectively. Perhaps, the two peoples would never see eye to eye, regardless of the Royal marriage or Cornflower's promotion.

But as I moved through the room, people seemed to part for me like I was a carrier of the Epidemic. People of all types hushed as I neared and moved toward the closest wall, their eyes wide with anxiety. Once there was enough distance, they would start their chorus of whispering again, so the room never truly became quiet, but as Frederick's golden head appeared among a huddled mass of other Royals, Ranguvariians, and a couple Aatarilecs, I knew more than ever that something had changed. Something had happened. The only question was what.

Frederick seemed to steel himself as his blue eyes flashed to mine. Worry emanated from him as he rapidly quit the meeting and made his way over to me. He spoke firmly but quickly as he said, "We have a situation. Rayna and Erikin have been kidnapped."

The world seemed to freeze around me, even down to the beat of my heart. I shook my head in disbelief. "That…that's not possible," I chuckled slightly as the impossibility of it all. "Surely, he was freed, and they ran off to go talk in private or something."

Frederick touched my arm gingerly and pulled me closer to the wall. In a tone barely above a whisper, he said, "There are several witnesses, Lina…she took them right in the middle of the room. There is no doubt in any of our minds where they've been taken."

"Sh-She…" I mumbled, my mind refusing to compute. "She who?"

The king's eyes fluttered shut like he hated to have to utter the words. In the most innocent, non-accusing tone he could likely muster, he breathed, "You already know."

My hand covered my eyes. *It can't be. She would never do this to me.* We were mending our relationship. She had promised to come home. My words were garbled. "No…she's my sister. She'd never betray me."

"She may not have had a choice," Frederick replied firmly as his eyes bored into my mine. "We won't know the truth until we catch up to them."

I crossed my arms and looked away, readying myself for the angry explosion that was certainly imminent. "I suppose you're going to tell me 'I told you so'?"

Frederick's brow furrowed for a minute. I mean, he did have every right to tell me that this could have all been avoided if I hadn't gone behind his back and pardoned my sister before she could be checked out. "No," he responded lightly, starting to turn back to where the others awaited, "That wouldn't be productive at this point. Right now, all that matters is getting Rayna back."

As he returned to the Ranguvariians and other Royals, anxiously and rapidly spouting out ideas and plans for recovery, I couldn't help but feel like I'd been knocked off my feet. Very few would ever say anything negative about Sam, but the man was known for his temper. He would've let me had it, and rightly so. Rosetta may have betrayed me, but it wouldn't have happened if she'd been locked in her room like Frederick ordered. As I stared at Frederick, totally engrossed in his own meeting, I began to realize that I didn't truly know him as much as I thought I did.

I let that thought pass me by and looked inward. I focused on the ball of magic heavy in my chest and reached out with my senses. Of course, Rayna's presence never pinged back at me, but I had to try. She was nowhere in Lunaka Castle, nor in Soläna just a mile away. I couldn't try sensing for Erikin since he didn't have magic, but there was no point in questioning it. Several rebels were huddled around the inner Royal mass yelling their version of what happened. While each story varied slightly, they circled the same core truth.

My sister had grabbed her son and my daughter and disappeared in a puff of purple smoke. Emperor Rhydin's dark magic. Even more whispers speculated that she had been the one to start the fire to turn us against each other just hours before she arrived, which made me feel even more sick.

Two more Ranguvariians flew in overhead, and I found myself doing my familiar tics before a battle. Tightening the sash around my waist that magically held my sword, tugging and centering my piece of the Allyen locket on my breastbone, tapping the toe of each of my boots against the stone floor.

Sister or not, I was going to get my daughter back.

The crowd finally began to disperse, a decision evidently made, and Frederick moved back toward me. In the blink of an eye, Rachel and Jaspen landed right in front of us, each of them armed to the teeth with every weapon known to both man and Ranguvariian, long-tasseled décor hanging from each handle. Frederick was now buckling a heavy leather cuirass over his chest, and Rachel scowled at him. "Is there *anything* I can say that would convince either of you to stay here while we go get Rayna? We could even grab some Aatarilecs and go in undetected."

"No," we replied in unison. I eyed Frederick warily as he tightened his baldric, his sword winking at me from over his shoulder.

"The Council agreed the fewer people the better in case things go wrong," Frederick explained as he armed himself. "You Ranguvariians will only last so long at the imperial palace because of all of Rhydin's magic there, we don't have enough Aatarilecs here to rectify that. Besides, we can't ask any others to risk themselves-…"

I cut him off, firmly meeting Rachel's eyes. "She's our daughter. So, we will go."

Rachel held my gaze a beat too long before a look of realization crossed her face. She hissed, "You told her? *Now* of all times? What are you thinking? What if the rebellion finds out we've *lied* to them for so many years?"

"They'll never find out," I declared. "When we say 'our daughter,' people will only assume we mean through this marriage Arii's designed. Now, can we please stop bickering about labels and go save Rayna? I don't want to start imagining what Rhydin's plan behind all this is."

"I'm sure he just wants her third of the locket to stop you Allyens from performing *Alytniinaeran*," Rachel responded matter-of-factly.

"Or, he can kill her!" I started to yell.

Frederick stepped forward and placed a hand on my shoulder. Then, calmly, he turned to the two Ranguvariians. "If you could please transport us to the imperial palace now, we would appreciate it."

Rachel and Jaspen shared a look of frustration, obviously not wanting anything to do with getting either the king of

Lunaka or an Allyen killed, but they acquiesced, nonetheless. Rachel put a hand on Frederick while Jaspen took my arm.

I caught a quick glimpse of an anxious, upset Taisyn across the room, a steaming Willian not too far from him. As even more proof of what had occurred, Taisyn was clutching the bag, a small metal bird, and other personal items with which I'd just seen Rayna exit the room upstairs. Her sketchbook was among them, the one item she would never *ever* just drop on the floor. I lifted my hand halfway to give Taisyn a wave of reassurance before I remembered he wouldn't be able to see it, which just filled me with more dread at the reminder of what Rhydin was willing to do to children. It was Rhydin's decree that Taisyn be blinded as a baby – to taint him with his dark power and keep us from turning him into the next Allyen.

The flood of the Ranguvariians' transportation magic gushed through my limbs as the world went white around us, their shard-like wings cocooning us. When the world reappeared, we were deep in the forest, trees every which way towering over our heads. This corner of Lunaka was so southwestern that Mineraltir's climate was a little more at play, although the lack of any leaves whatsoever clearly pointed to these being Lunakan trees. Snow crunched underneath my boots, and I found myself yearning for spring for the hundredth time. Warmth, green, rain, sun, leaves, plants. My hands ached to till the earth and sow seed within it, but that dream still felt lifeless without Sam.

Nestled among the mountains was the sprawling imperial palace, Emperor Rhydin's seat of power. It didn't look anything like any of the castles of the Three Kingdoms, which all had high, fortified walls. It was like the design of the palace mocked us with its luxury and apparent lack of defenses, even though one had to be absolutely mad to try breaking in there.

All four of us began to hustle toward the great, towering center of darkness. The last time I'd been here was the day Rachel's brother Luke and I were captured, before the Dome had ever been established. Emperor Rhydin had gruesomely murdered Luke, conducting his study in order to break all the Ranguvariians' magical secrets. I would have died if my father, Robert, hadn't changed his ways and helped me to escape.

I knew what this evil Rhydin was capable of better than anyone else, and while every bone in my body screamed at me to go the other way, there was no turning back.

I would not let Rayna suffer Luke's fate even if it was the last thing I ever did.

Chapter Thirteen

Rayna

"I see you have met my newest experiment," Emperor Rhydin crooned as he gestured to the strange, featureless being that had replaced Rosetta during our transportation here. "I have not only cracked how Ranguvariians are presence-less but have created my own version, a new and improved Einanhi that can transport multiple people while being undetectable by mages."

My skin crawled at the sight of this new, unnatural Einanhi until it suddenly dissolved into sand out of nowhere, the piles pooling where its odd, pointed feet had once been.

"Come, Erikin," the dark sorcerer commanded, his smile reappearing, "you have done well, and I look forward to hearing everything you have to tell me about this absurd rebellion."

The heavy, iron-barred door to our cell popped open on its own, swinging to the side with a screech. Erikin's breaths shortened, and beads of sweat appeared on his brow out of nowhere. "I…I won't go. I have nothing to tell, I was in a dungeon the entire time."

"I am sure there is something I can glean from you," Rhydin said harshly, his face going slack. "You would not want to disappoint your poor mother, would you?"

My cousin swallowed hard and barely glanced my way before woodenly placing one foot in front of the other until he was out of the cell, albeit as far from Emperor Rhydin as he could manage. Fear began to overtake me as I realized I was about to be left in this cell all alone, but that couldn't compare to the sheer panic that erupted when Rhydin took a step into the cell.

I grasped for words, anything that might slow him down. "I know the truth, y'know!" I shouted, failing to hide my desperation. "I know that you're *fake!* That you're just an Einanhi created by the real Rhydin Caldwell!"

The sound of his maker's name slowed his step a little. I kept going, even as I unconsciously continued to back away. "I know about Amelia too! Why'd you kill her, huh? She never did anything to you!"

"She was an obstacle," Emperor Rhydin growled lowly, his violet eyes narrowing as he paused a moment. "She stood between me and the power to save Nerahdis from the corrupt Royals. Nothing more."

"What, so Rhydin Caldwell loved and adored her, but none of that transferred to you?" I accused. Emperor Rhydin began to approach me once again, and I moved backward again in response. "Rhydin Caldwell didn't want to take over Nerahdis, so why do you?!"

Something within the evil clone seemed to come unhinged. "*Caldwell* didn't know what he wanted! He wished to be in two places at once so that he could have everything he desired. Instead, I took *everything* from him and made the choice for him. *I* am the real Rhydin now," Emperor Rhydin sneered. "All that remains is to use the power of the Allyen locket to seal my reign and destroy the last remnant of that past once and for all."

The wall was cold and unforgiving when I finally backed into it, and there was nowhere left to run. I summoned my quickest attack spell, a charge of glowing, golden energy materializing in my hands, but a lone, half-trained Allyen was no match for the deep depths of power wielded by a magical being with three hundred years' worth of practice.

Emperor Rhydin's amethyst-colored magic crackled as it appeared, unstable in his hands even though its power absolutely dwarfed mine. He knocked my hands down and thrust me up into the wall in one fluid motion, my feet dangling. I choked for breath as his magic seemed to burn my skin, attaching to me like leeches. Rhydin dropped me almost instantly, and as I crumpled to the floor, purple flecks of magic embedded in my arms like splinters. Unchecked fury seemed to grow in him.

"It is true, then. You are just like Caldwell," the emperor scoffed, "and Nora Soreta for that matter. A human who can absorb magic. A forger."

My consciousness teetered on edge, but my tongue remained sharp. "I'll steal it. I'll steal *all* of your magic and destroy you."

The last thing I heard before the world began to melt around me was Rhydin cackling, "Those who forge their own magic, or are forged upon by others, are the ones to be pitied. Caldwell rots in the Archimage Palace, and not even the great Nora Soreta could escape her fate. Neither will you."

Even as I lay flat on the floor fighting to stay awake, the colors of the dungeon cell morphed all around me until they reconfigured into another stone room. This one was breezy with a huge window letting in the first rays of the sunrise, which illuminated the various scientific equipment littered around the room. Much of it, I couldn't even begin to try and identify, but I did recognize a few astronomical tools like a sextant and a sundial. The rest of the shining metal and glass was a mystery.

A loud shout and groan led me to try and roll over, pain ricocheting around my body. At the big wooden desk along the far wall of the room was a slumped figure, which was turned away from me. It wasn't until he began to speak that I realized who it was. He moaned, "What do I do? I cannot go on like this."

It was Rhydin's voice. But which one?

He stood abruptly and began to pace. His dark hair was short, not long and grown out like the evil Rhydin's was in my time. The dark circles under his eyes and the twitchiness of his pale hands suggested that he'd been agonizing over something all night long, if not for much longer. He wore robes unlike any I'd ever seen with multiple layers, colors, and adornments that clashed pretty hard. It was like all three cultures of the kingdoms had vomited their fashions upon him at once. I began to wonder if this meant he was still Archimage, if the creation of his Einanhi clone hadn't happened yet.

Rhydin had made several laps around the room muttering to himself before his thoughts erupted into words. "I could run away! This job is too much for one person. Surely, she would take me back? ...But then what would come of Nerahdis? Caden passed two years ago, and his sons still bicker like children. If they are left to their own devices, they will tear Nerahdis apart, and the destruction of Gornan will happen all over again..."

He continued to think out loud, his words becoming louder. "The Royals will never get along! Nerahdis can only be saved if one person is kept at the helm...but who? If I suggest one of the Three Kings over either of the other two, the others will murder him. They have already proven capable of murdering their own siblings..." – he paused, as if some truth was sinking in – "I must do it. I am the only one with the power...but if I do, I can never see Amelia again...yet I shall die without her!"

Rhydin threw himself against the wall next to the window, shouting unintelligibly as tears leaked down his face. I'd never seen one person in so much turmoil before. He continued to rant and rant for what seemed like an hour, weighing the decision of disappearing to wed Amelia against taking total control of Nerahdis in order to save it from the Royals' ruthless fighting. I hated to admit it, but his argument wasn't unsound. Joshuua, Ivann, and Spenser obviously couldn't get along and could easily be the ruination of Nerahdis if they'd already attempted assassinating each other. Their murder attempts must have failed since the three brothers obviously lived.

Suddenly, there was a *boom* like thunder, and a rainbow of incandescent smoke burst forth from Rhydin's core to fill the entire room. Everything was obscured, although I could hear Rhydin coughing. I used what little strength I had left to push myself forward and peer around, and I noticed that the tiny shards of Emperor Rhydin's magic were still embedded in the skin of my forearm, although they were smaller than they'd been before. Were these the source of this strange memory? It certainly was completely unlike any of the ancestral memories I'd experienced from within Nora's body.

The thick, heavy smoke began to suck inwards toward the center of the room like an explosion in reverse. The glittering dust congealed into a human shape only six feet away from where Rhydin was revealed to still be standing near the window. His pale face was confused and terrified even as he leaned on his knees and fought to catch his breath. He stared at the pillar of dark purple dust as it slowly refined itself into his mirror image, and my jaw dropped.

Rhydin the original gasped, "What is this sorcery?"

The magical clone paused, still coming to life. He replied, "I am…you."

"What, an Einanhi of myself? I did not create you nor utter the incantation. This is a mistake, now be gone!" the original

Rhydin commanded as he turned back to his desk, beginning to shuffle papers and put things to right. I cringed.

The Einanhi stared at his hands for a moment, the gears visibly moving in the mind that would someday become the emperor of my time. He said monotonously, "That is not an option. I have enough power that you are no longer my master, but I shall not stop until I accomplish the task that provoked your powerful magic to give me life."

Rhydin Caldwell turned back toward his clone, his brow furrowed. After a beat, fear abruptly filled his violet eyes. "Wh-What task?"

"I shall usurp Nerahdis from its treacherous Royals and become its emperor, and I shall eliminate the one person who stands in my way," the evil clone declared before he disappeared into a puff of smoke.

The real Rhydin stared at where he'd once been for a few seconds, still embroiled in confusion. Then, an idea seemed to strike him like a bolt of lightning as his eyes doubled in size and he said panickily, "Amelia." Then, he too vanished as he transported away, desperate to stop what I already knew was coming.

Amelia was going to die, and the evil Rhydin was going to steal the rest of his creator's magic.

Now that I was alone, the scene shifted slowly back to the dungeon in the belly of Emperor Rhydin's imperial palace. I still lay outstretched along the back wall of my cell, but both Rhydin and Erikin were gone. My head throbbed as I carefully leaned forward, my arms clear of Rhydin's magic. I reached for my breastbone, but my fingers only met empty space. I threw my fist into the damp bricks, although I didn't know why I expected anything different.

Emperor Rhydin had my third of the locket. There would be no way to perform the death spell, and the rebellion would fail.

I roared in frustration, not caring how loudly it echoed around and how far it reached. I plucked myself off the filthy floor and anxiously plodded back and forth. There was no window, and the dungeon sounded like it was empty aside from me. Emperor Rhydin didn't seem to be the prisoner type.

My mind revolved back to what I'd just witnessed, the first memory I'd experienced outside of Nora's personal point of view. Had I stolen pieces of Rhydin's power? When those flecks burned into my skin? Was I really a "forger" like he said?

I shook my head. The "how" didn't matter right now. What truly mattered was that I'd finally seen the critical moment that everyone had been debating for weeks, terrified that Rhydin Caldwell was even more evil than his artificial counterpart. The creation of the Einanhi clone certainly hadn't seemed purposeful to me…but at the same time, Einanhis didn't just create themselves, did they? That was a process I understood perfectly during my own magic practice. That one would need more clarification.

As my thoughts jumbled together, replaying the memory over and over to glean any other information I could from it, I noticed that a sliver of parchment had been nailed just to the side of the bars to my cell, and I immediately stalked forward and ripped it down.

Allyen Rayna – Execution: Late Winter 23rd

Nope. Not the prisoner type. That was tomorrow, and it was stamped with the imperial insignia I'd seen all my life: a golden flame surrounding a red circle.

I shredded the parchment and then yanked on the metal bars with all my might, sending deafening crashes reverberating throughout the dungeon. Of course, they didn't budge, and I found myself sinking back to the floor. What was the point, anyhow? Rhydin had my share of the locket. Even if I managed to escape this cell, I'd never get it back or get out of this fortress alive with it. Everything I'd learned from these memories would die with me, yet without me there was no hope of ever destroying the evil emperor and saving Rhydin Caldwell.

"You are *awfully* loud for one person, you know that?" a voice hissed in the darkness beyond the tiny perimeter the one torch could light.

I jumped, feeling blind without the amplification my locket gave my power. When my cousin slowly came into the light, dressed in a brand-new imperial uniform and shrouded in a midnight cloak, I crossed my arms. "Well, that didn't take long. Did you spill all our secrets?"

Erikin rolled his eyes. "Seriously? You really think after everything we've been through, I'd go right back to this again? You're ridiculous."

"Just asking," I grumbled, still sitting under my dark, metaphorical cloud. "What do you want? Here to rub it in that our positions are reversed?"

"Uh, I'm here to save your skin, dummy," my cousin replied goadingly as he started to inspect the iron hinges of the cell door. "You could be, like, *thankful*, or something. I meant it when I said you're my family."

"Forget it. There's no point." My voice fell to a whisper as my eyes fixated on a certain black brick missing a corner in the wall across from me. "Even if we got out, we wouldn't have my piece of the locket anymore. We're doomed."

Erikin groaned loudly as he braced a metal spear he'd nicked from somewhere against the top hinge of my door. "Well, aren't you dramatic? If I've learned anything from you lot, it's that we'll cross that bridge when we get there, and getting your scrawny neck off the chopping block is priority number one. The locket can wait for another day, but priority number two can't."

My brow furrowed as I finally turned to face him again. "What's number two?"

Erikin suddenly shoved the spear inward and upward, hefting the door a few inches off the ground on top of the small gap that had already existed there. He screeched at me through gritted teeth, "Crawl under there, I can't hold it!"

Instinct took over, and I scrambled to where the new gap between the door and floor had appeared. I lay flat on my back and pulled myself through, rotating my head to fit as my clothes dragged against the dirty floor. I barely scraped my hips through, the spokes of the bars threatening to impale me at any second. Lucky for me, my legs were all that was left when Erikin's strength gave out and the door clanged back into place. My skinny shins and ankles narrowly shifted between bars, but there was no way my boots were going to fit through the gaps left behind. Without thinking twice, I reached through and chucked them off back into the middle of the cell.

There. Let him burn my ragged boots in the morning if he wanted!

Erikin gasped for breath, exhausted from holding the door. He sputtered, "We're getting my mother out too. I know where she is."

"The real one, I presume?" I muttered facetiously.

"Just c'mon, will you?" Erikin moaned, and then tossed me his cloak. "And put this on. You'll stick out like a sore thumb between your clothes and your bare feet."

I was wrapping his cloak around my filthy, disheveled clothes when a racket broke out up above. Erikin and I eyed each other, and he retrieved his spear from where it'd clanged to the floor. As we crept toward the torch-lit staircase, I whispered, "I don't suppose Emperor Rhydin gave you another magic ring, did he?"

Erikin scoffed almost soundlessly. "If he did, do you think I would have just nearly chopped your feet off?"

I cringed, and we inched faster and faster up the stairs toward the door. The banging noises grew louder and louder, mixed in with shouting and screaming. My hand shakily found the latch to the door, and I tried to assuage myself with the idea that maybe whatever this ruckus was would give us a good distraction to escape.

Sheer panic spread through me like wildfire when the door was wrenched open from the other side, and white sunlight spilled into the dark stairway, temporarily blinding us. I blinked rapidly, willing my eyes to adjust faster, as the person beyond the door yanked me through it and against the wall. However, when my vision did clear, I was quite sure the sun was still playing tricks on my eyes.

Instead of one of Rhydin's Followers threatening to run me through on the spot, King Frederick was hollering through the chaos that he'd found me even as he shot blast after blast of wind magic in each direction, bowling Followers over left and right.

I finally started to believe my eyes when I saw my mother a short distance away with her sword embedded in an Einanhi's sandy chest, as well as Aunt Rachel and Jaspen lending support from above.

They've come for me, I thought with wonder ever so briefly before another battalion of Followers and Einanhis swept into the hall, and my heart lost hope.

Chapter Fourteen

Lina

I cleaved an Einanhi in two and caught the briefest of glimpses of Rayna standing beyond Frederick before dozens more ushered around the corner. Rachel and Jaspen dove downward, taking out the front line as I dashed toward my daughter. I swung my sword with both hands against any foe that popped up between her and me, and I roared with every thrust. Frederick flattened any Einanhis that came near, and both Rayna and Erikin stared at the scene in front of them with their mouths agape.

My heart quivered at the sight of Rayna wrapped in a Follower's cloak with bare, filthy feet sticking out from underneath, her cheeks red and smeared with dirt. With one hand, I touched her head to prove to myself that she was okay, my fingers hesitating along her auburn hair, the same shade as Sam's. As Frederick continued firing wave after wave of wind magic, I bellowed over the chaos, "Are you alright?"

Rayna nodded silently, her golden-speckled eyes growing large as they veered to the floor. It seemed like an eternity since the tumultuous events of the morning, and I desperately hoped that she didn't still feel like an orphan.

Rayna wheedled, "He took my necklace. I don't know where it is, and without it-…"

"We'll figure it out," I said before she could finish. "I'm just glad you're alright." Then, I announced over my shoulder to Frederick, "Let's get out of here!"

"W-Wait!" Erikin warbled, "Please…can we go get my mother and take her away from here?"

Heat arose in my chest, and my heart hammered unsteadily. I growled as I tried to pull them toward the exit, "Why would I go get her after what she's done? She betrayed us all! She obviously wants to be here. Where do your loyalties lie, Nephew?" I eyed his new, crisp uniform in disgust.

Erikin flushed a deep red, and Rayna jumped to his defense, "He was taken same as me! He's the one who busted me out of the dungeon, so don't you dare leave him behind! Besides, the Rosetta that took us wasn't the real one. It was some new experiment of Emperor Rhydin's."

I stopped in my tracks, feeling afraid to even hope that my sister possibly didn't betray me.

"Lina!" Frederick called now from several feet away, doing his best to take on any attackers with Rachel and Jaspen's assistance. "I can't do this forever! We need to go!"

"Please," Erikin begged, his hazel eyes desperate, "I know exactly where she is, just please let her come with us so we can be free."

My eyes darted back and forth between the desperate teenagers in front of me and Frederick narrowly keeping our enemies at bay several times. Could I make another decision to trust my sister so rashly without proof? What if they were wrong, and it was another trap?

But then, what if it wasn't?

"Fine!" I groaned loudly, albeit wondering if this would be the final nail in my coffin. "Lead the way, Erikin."

The boy didn't need to be told twice. He instantly sprinted toward the far end of the hall with Rayna fast on his heels. I dove into the fray surrounding Frederick just long enough to create an opening in the fight, and then I pushed him along in front of me in the direction the kids had gone.

Frederick sputtered in confusion as Rachel and Jaspen suddenly veered from their flight paths to follow, "What are you doing? The exit is the other way!"

"We've got one more to save," I answered vaguely. While that thankfully seemed to be enough for him, the Ranguvariians weren't as convinced.

"Lina!" Rachel hollered from above, exasperated. "It's bad enough Jaspen and I are already going to have to make two trips to transport you all home, we don't need another passenger!"

I didn't have time to answer her; more Einanhis came barreling into the long hall just as Erikin and Rayna disappeared behind a dull, wooden door. My sword clashed with three different thin, needle-like blades before I charged a blast of light magic to flatten the two Einanhis that stood between me and my daughter.

To my dismay, I flung open the door to discover a set of wooden stairs within the wide, rounded base of what could only be a tower above our heads. Moisture must have seeped into this area of the palace because the wood was sagging and warped, and the smell of rot was strong. I only gave a second to these observations before a big *boom* resounded behind me, and Frederick flew through the door and latched it behind him. Soot spotted his wiry face, and his hair was darkened with sweat.

"What was *that?*" I gasped as he ushered me toward the stairs. After a few glances at the locked door behind us that was now attempting to stand up to far more force than it'd ever been designed to hold back, I started taking two stairs at a time.

Frederick replied breathily with bewilderment, "The Ranguvariians apparently have some new toys to buy us some time. Hurry up, or we may not have a ticket out of here when we get back down!"

We climbed the steps as fast as we could, huffing and puffing as we willed the door below to remain on its hinges. Every so often there would be a landing with a wooden door braced with iron, and I found myself wondering what in Nerahdis this tower was used for. I had to brush that thought away, however, in order to focus on sensing for Rayna so we didn't accidentally pass her. Her presence suddenly chimed in my head just as we reached a landing where the door was ajar for once, probably around halfway up the tall spire.

I stopped and gasped for air, abruptly hesitant. Frederick was immediately behind me, but there was no one to be seen inside the door. A nearly featureless living area stared back at us. The back wall of the room was the curved stone of the tower while the other two walls were the same rotten wood as the stairs. Along the stone wall was a large window, the glass rippled within diamond-shaped panes. As Frederick and I inched closer, a rough-hewn chair and bed came into view, the only two pieces of furniture in the room. I relaxed at the sight of Rayna and Erikin huddled around a third person in a plain linen shift sitting on the bed, and I approached them carefully even as the banging from the tower door below continued to echo upward.

The woman sitting on the edge of the lumpy straw tick looked very different from her Einanhi imposter, which seemed to have been a glorified version based more on how I'd seen her last. Her sandy blonde hair was faded from the vibrance of her youth, slowly melting into a medium gray that was far beyond her years. It was coiled into a thick bun at the back of her head while wisps of gold and silver framed her heart-shaped face that had a certain permanent tiredness to it. Her hazel eyes, however, were bright as ever, and they filled with tears upon sight of me, even as I felt immense confusion radiating off of Frederick behind me.

"Lina," my sister whimpered before she threw herself across the room and into my arms. I'd forgotten she was taller than me.

I couldn't speak, only held her tight like I used to when we were little and the big storms came. All of my fears washed away, and I could have stayed there for an eternity if it weren't for Frederick.

"Lina, we need to go. There's plenty of time for this later," my new husband said, his hand cautious and gentle as it grazed my shoulder. "We still need to get out of here alive."

I nodded against my sister's thin cheek and tore myself away from her. "You're coming with me this time," I said softly, my voice at its breaking point.

Rosetta cracked a smile and a sob at the same time. "I'd like nothing better."

My sister grabbed a worn leather volume off her pitiful-looking bed, probably a journal of some sort knowing her, and then the five of us were hurdling down the stairs as fast as we could. A few of the other doors had opened now, revealing similar plain living spaces complete with a few thin, nondescript faces. Was this where Rhydin's Followers lived? Or their relatives? I couldn't stop myself from feeling appalled. It seemed more like a prison than a home.

The tower was eerily silent by the time we reached the bottom. The door was still on its hinges, although a few bolts hadn't made it through the fight. A prickly feeling arose along the back of my neck. No presences pinged back at me from beyond the door, but my senses as a whole felt cloudy in a way I'd never experienced before. Rayna glanced at me, her eyes filled with fear for what may have been the first time since our reunion, and Frederick tightened his grip on his sword while drawing another small dagger from his boot.

Something wasn't right. But this was the only way out. And our enemy knew it.

Frederick and I pushed toward the front, keeping the kids and Rosetta to the back. I wiped my sweaty palms on my trousers and took a deep breath, readying myself the best I could. As I reached for the latch, Frederick eyed me and whispered, "Lina, if I fall today…"

"Nobody's dying today," I responded harsher than I'd intended before I thrust the door open as hard as I could, raising my sword in readiness.

On the other side was a small army. Columns and rows of blank, black humanoids, their thin arms bearing their needle-like blades. Likely poisoned, I added mentally as the memory of Sam's blackened ribs flashed in my mind. Rachel and Jaspen were nowhere to be seen, while standing ahead of the first row of Einanhis was none other than Emperor Rhydin himself. His pale face was a mirror image to the first time I'd seen him over fifteen years ago; his midnight hair was just as black without even the faintest streaks of silver. The amethyst fire in his eyes shone no less bright.

Once, I feared his lack of aging and the power it must take to maintain his youth. Now, I knew the truth. He was an Einanhi. Frozen in time. His physical being was incapable of change, as hard and unmoving as stone. That much was true. But his mind and his magic were another story entirely, and it was time to see how much more he'd destabilized since the last time I'd seen him.

As every single one of the hundred or so Einanhis raised their blades, I bellowed, "Stop! I want to make a deal."

Frederick looked at me like I was nuts.

A crooked grin appeared on Emperor Rhydin's face. "You are vastly outnumbered. What could you possibly offer me?"

"This," I replied simply, as I looped my third of the Allyen locket over my head. "You've already taken my daughter's. I know you still need them to destroy the real Rhydin and steal the rest of his power."

Rhydin laughed darkly. "You foolish girl. I will pluck that little token from your dead body. It is not a bargaining chip."

Without hesitation, I held my locket outward with one hand and charged a crackling ball of golden energy into the other hand, directly underneath it. "How about now?" I asked mockingly.

The Einanhi emperor's eyes narrowed. He crossed his black-clad arms over his chest, his bony fingers twitching awkwardly. "What is it that you propose?"

"Fight me, one on one," I declared, even as Frederick hissed my name and Rayna hovered closer. "You kill me, you get my part of the locket, but everyone else gets to leave safely."

"You did not say what the outcome would be if you killed me." Rhydin's smile returned. His teeth were the same color as his skin.

I faltered for a moment. I knew I couldn't kill him. The death spell was off the table between Evan's absence and Rayna's loss of her locket, and I wasn't powerful enough on my own. But I needed to keep this going for as long as I could. It was the only plan that offered a chance as survival.

"No point in stating the obvious benefits of your death," I goaded him, as I made a show of placing my locket back over my head, hoping it'd be enough to tempt him. Would the old, calculated Rhydin fall for it? Probably not. But this Rhydin was unstable, his power erratic and unpredictable as his creator slowly grew in strength hundreds of miles away.

Frederick grabbed my arm. "I'm not going along with this!"

I shoved him off and pushed him in the general direction of the door. I barely breathed through gritted teeth, "Find Rachel!"

"So be it," Rhydin announced before abruptly conjuring twin bolts of unhinged purple energy in his hands, which crackled and shifted like wildfire.

He fired mercilessly, and I narrowly lifted my blade to divide one blast while ducking to avoid the other. Out of the corner of my eye, I saw Frederick haul Rayna toward the door with Erikin and Rosetta closely following, expressions of fear on both their faces. Then, suddenly it was just me and Rhydin in the room, all other background fixtures and the Einanhi army fading away.

Anger bubbled in my veins as Rhydin stole one of his creation's swords and leapt at me with cruel precision. I ran my weapon along his, diverting its path as I drew my own magic into my palm, golden and hot. I chucked it at him with a grunt, but Rhydin shoved my blade downward and spun in a circle faster than my mind could process, catching my spell in his long, thick cape. A surprise purple blast came flying out the other side of his cape, searing my arm as it mostly went haywire into the stone wall behind me. I clutched my burnt sleeve momentarily before desperately raising my sword to block the swing of Rhydin's sword.

We were locked together, pushing against each other, and Rhydin's breath was strangely cold as he huffed, "You were but a child when we crossed paths first, Linaria. Now look at you. Decades have passed for you while I have remained eternal. I shall outlast all of you!"

"You're not real," I grunted, as I shoved backward against his poisoned weapon. "You are not eternal, only a monster given too much leash. Even if I die today, we'll never stop until Nerahdis is free!"

Rhydin's eyes narrowed in fierce hatred, and he threw several more rounds of attack spells in my direction as we broke apart. There were no more words as we attacked and blocked, attacked and blocked. Time lost all meaning for me as I worked to keep up with everything he threw at me. His magic was imbalanced and unpredictable every time its purple hue buzzed to life, but his sheer amount of power was still almost impossible to keep up with. Adrenaline fueled my muscles and my magic more and more as my body tired, but even that couldn't last forever.

I stalled for a moment, heaving air into my lungs and swiping wet, sweaty hair out of my face with fingers I could barely feel.

"Need a respite, madam?" the Einanhi emperor crooned, looking delighted with himself. "If you give me your locket willingly, I suppose I could let you leave with your companions."

As I breathed, unable to quite respond yet, my mind actually entertained the idea for the briefest of moments. Give him mine, he already had Rayna's but not Evan's, and go home to fight another day. But then Sam flashed before my eyes, his long face thin and contorted with the pain of his poison. Everyone else I'd ever lost were standing just beyond him, staring me down with vacant expressions as they stood shoulder to shoulder. Robert, Keera, Grandma Saarah, Luke, my mother and step-father. Beyond them were others I'd known that had died due to Rhydin's hand: Queen Gloria, Archimage Dathian, Rachel's father, and still others I didn't even know.

Did any of them experience mercy?

They did not.

"No!" I roared, and on a whim, I fired light magic at the hanging cord of a gigantic tapestry depicting a map of Nerahdis unbroken by kingdom boundaries. The heavy fabric fell forward, rippling through the air like a huge ribbon, and while a human army would disperse and run, the Einanhi army remained squarely where it was. As Rhydin whirled to watch half his reinforcements draped with the tapestry, I leapt forward, sprinting with my sword held high.

Behind me, I heard the sound of glass breaking and crashing to the floor, but there was no stopping me now. I swung downward at Rhydin's neck, already envisioning the gash that would appear upon any human after such a blow, but what happened next was beyond what my mind was ever capable of imagining.

I'd only seen Rhydin wounded a handful of times before. Once when Sam struck his cheek with a dagger during his murder of Archimage Dathian, and once during the last mission Sam and I led when his blade rebounded into his shoulder. Both times, he'd broken like stone, no blood to be seen within the dark cavity. An Einanhi so powerful and established, his sand had solidified, Arii had theorized once. Yet, that wasn't the part that caught me off guard. Instead, it was the fact that Rhydin stepped into my swing, allowing my weapon to carve into the stone of his shoulder where it met the base of his neck.

Cracks radiated out from the wound, appearing at Rhydin's collar, and I froze in shock. I met Rhydin's eyes, and they glowed with the fire of a madman. Milliseconds passed before a fierce burning sensation buried itself into my gut, and I looked down as if in a dream to see Rhydin's pale hand cramming a bolt of sizzling violet energy into my abdomen.

The emperor grinned wildly as I stumbled backward, my sword sliding out of the new, uneven groove in the rock of Rhydin's shoulder. I pressed my hand to my charred stomach like I would a normal blood wound, but that just made the pain exponentially worse. The edges of my vision went black, and I struggled to draw air into my lungs.

I had the power for just one more blast. With my opposite hand, I conjured the largest orb of light magic I could muster and fired in Rhydin's direction. He blocked it of course, but its size at least kept it from splitting in two and pushed him several yards away from me. Then, my mind went blank. I felt myself falling, but there was nothing I could do to stop it. The sensation of two rock-like hands threading themselves through my arms was the last thing I'd remember before succumbing to the blackness.

Pain greeted me before my eyes could even open. Absolute silence surrounded me, and I felt afraid to open my eyes even as my nose registered the familiar scent of Lunaka Castle – damp with a mix of live chicken and baking bread.

I had to be dead. But was death supposed to be painful?

My eyes fluttered open to slits, distrustful of everything. The familiar furnishings of my room gazed back at me, although there was a gray tone to everything with the curtains drawn. Someone had noticed my pitiful Lunakan Moon plant on the windowsill though, because it had been tucked into the corner where it could still receive some sunlight even as the rest of the room was kept dimmed.

I tried to lean forward, and pain erupted across my stomach. I lifted the nightgown someone had dressed me in, its cool silk like a balm across my flushed skin, and I found bandaging tightly wound around my abdomen. It was mostly clean aside from some yellow places, and it was then that I realized a glass Ranguvariian feather was dangling above my head.

Upon seeing it and wondering about its healing properties while absent a user, my hand flew to my collarbone. To my great surprise, my piece of the locket was still there, and I stared at its one silver, amber-studded face for several moments in disbelief.

How could this be? I reached out with my magic, and Rayna's presence bounced back to me from just downstairs.

A snore broke the silence, and I jumped, causing more pain to blossom in my middle. I groaned a little unintentionally, which caused the slumbering person in the wing-backed chair off the side of my bed to shift a little. Frederick looked exhausted; darkness circled his eyes and his hair laid funny due to how the sweat had dried. Like he hadn't dared leave the chair in days.

My shoulders relaxed as I looked at him, innocent in sleep. *He really does love me, doesn't he?* I thought to myself, still mulling over what that really meant. Guilt wrapped around my heart like a coiled snake ready to squeeze the life out of its prey. He cared so much and had done so much for me and my family, but could I ever give him the type of companionship he clearly desired?

Memories of Sam came in unbidden flurries. Our childhood together growing up on poor, neighboring farms in the Canyonlands south of Soläna, and our early marriage in the Rounan Compound. We were the same, he and I. Love for him had come easily. We were passionate about the same things and were so similar. Sure, he had a temper, and I could be stubborn as a mule, but being with him and loving him had been as easy as breathing.

Frederick was my opposite. He'd grown up wanting for nothing. He'd never feared death like the poor did, whether from starvation or from the Royals. Money was no issue, and work was something you did with your head, not your hands, if done at all. He'd said in the past that he never understood Sam and I's desire to work the land simply because we wanted to. He was my friend, so of course I cared about him. I wanted him to have a happy ending.

But could I love him? I stared at the two rings on my hands. Would I be torn between their givers for the rest of my life?

Frederick stirred in the chair, stretching his neck like he'd gotten a crick in it as he rubbed his thin face. When he saw me awake and upright, he sprouted from his chair a little too fast, losing his balance a bit. Relief flooded his expression even as he looked a little woozy. "You're awake!"

I couldn't manage to give him any sort of smile. "How did we get out?" I whispered. "What happened?"

"I found Rachel outside, recovering from being around so much of Rhydin's dark power," Frederick replied softly. He thought for a moment of approaching my bedside, but then seemed to think better of it. "She had sent Jaspen for Aatarilec help to offset the effect of Rhydin's magic, and they arrived just in time to get us out of there. They busted through a window to get to you. If you hadn't pushed Rhydin so far away from you, it would have been too late."

The sound of glass shattering echoed in my ears from when I'd heard it toward the end of my duel with Emperor Rhydin. I allowed myself to relax a little as the answer washed over me. "The others. Are they okay?"

"They're all fine. *We're* all fine," Frederick amended, his throat bobbing, "thanks to you."

"Good," I breathed awkwardly, my energy quickly sapped. Warring emotions played out upon Frederick's face as he seemed to debate what he should do next. I finally gave him a small grin as I gently settled myself back down onto my pillows. "Go get some food, Frederick. You look awful. I'll still be here when you get back."

He snorted, but I caught a glimpse of his smile before he turned toward the door. "You should see yourself."

Once he was gone, tension left my body that I hadn't known was there. A dream-less sleep claimed me rapidly as I rolled to face Sam's little plant up on the windowsill catching the last few rays of sunlight.

Chapter Fifteen

Rayna

"You *saw* it?" Taisyn gasped, his forkful of potato mush pausing mid-air. "You *saw* the moment that Rhydin made his Einanhi?"

"I did," I said hesitantly, "but it's not like what everyone thinks. It didn't make a lot of sense. It looked like an accident, it happened out of nowhere. He never started dividing his magic or said *anadlu* or anything."

"Just…poof? Is that even possible?" Taisyn asked incredulously through a full mouth now. "Wait a minute. You've only ever seen Nora's memories because she's your ancestor. How did you see one of *Rhydin's?* Nora wasn't there, was she?"

I shook my head, my eyes glued to my plate. "I'm…not sure," I lied, even as I felt the lingering prickle of what Rhydin's solidified magic had felt like embedded in my arms.

Erikin had been preoccupied shoveling his own mystery, potato-based meal into his mouth, but now piped up, "Have you told anybody that you saw the moment it happened?"

"Not yet," I groaned as I twirled my fork absentmindedly, my stomach in knots. "Clariion Arii wants to talk to me in a bit though, so it'll probably come up."

My gaze began to wander. We were in the throne room in the belly of Lunaka Castle eating what really couldn't be called "supper" with pretty much the rest of the rebellion. While the last hunting party had in fact returned with some meat in the form of rabbits, squirrels, and one majestic stag, that meat had gone ferociously fast. Supposedly, there was some meat in the bowls of mush we were eating, but if there was, it was an ant-sized serving.

My mother's sister, the real one, sat on Erikin's opposite side, giving the three of us space but still a part of our table. King Frederick had procured some different clothes for her, an embroidered blue tunic over a plain set of trousers that looked like they may have once belonged to Queen Sabine. The queen was a muscular woman, so the garments hung loosely on Rosetta's thin frame. She kept glancing around like an owl at all the people around us, huddled around their own tables scraping their bowls clean in no time flat for at least a chance at seconds. Others stared at her, convinced she started the fire that burned up all our food even though King Frederick told everyone the other Rosetta was a fake. I wondered if she recognized any of the people here. She'd grown up in Soläna, and so had Erikin. Surely, there were a few others from Soläna here.

"I'm sure it'll be fine. Clariion Arii isn't that scary," Taisyn mused as he made several loud scrapes against his wooden bowl with his spoon, trying to lick up every morsel. "I'm just glad you're back and you're safe."

"Yeah?" I muttered softly, bringing my attention back to our table. Erikin suddenly struck up a conversation with his mother, pointing out the other Royal children across the way.

"Well, yeah," Taisyn shrugged. "You and your mother are probably the only two people to come back out of Emperor Rhydin's dungeon alive. We know plenty of others who haven't or didn't even make it that far in the first place."

Disappointment bubbled up in my heart, although its existence made me feel confused. "Sure," I answered simply, as I finally took a bite of my dinner in an effort to end the conversation.

Taisyn couldn't see my face, but his copper brow knitted together even as he continued to stare unseeingly off into the distance. "You know I care…don't you?"

"Mm-hmm." I nodded my head rapidly, which was stupid because he couldn't see it. "You're my friend, I'd be concerned about you too for sure."

"Rayna," the prince's voice lowered as Erikin continued to chitchat loudly with Rosetta. I wished we could meet eyes, although his hands were glowing now so his head was at least pointed in the right direction. "You're not just a friend to me."

I suddenly squeezed my eyes shut. *This isn't happening. Why was I upset it wasn't happening, and now I'm upset that it is?*

My mouth opened to respond, but a big rock-hard hand settled on my shoulder before I could. I already knew what he was going to say as Clariion Arii's pleasant voice lilted downward. "Rayna, would now be a good time for our talk?"

"'Course," I answered shortly, pushing my bowl toward the center of the table for anybody who wanted it. My stomach was churning far too much to appreciate whatever nutrition it could possibly offer.

Taisyn's head turned away, his mouth becoming a thin line. Erikin mouthed the words "good luck" to me as we turned to leave. I followed Arii out of the throne room, narrowly missing a famished-looking King Frederick as he entered, and down the hallway toward a less-frequented area of the castle.

Nearly every room and inch of hallway was full of rebels milling about their daily routines, but Arii turned into one of our remaining supply rooms for some privacy. This one had crates lining every wall, although the towering stacks had been reduced to haphazard collections here and there. I almost felt sick when I peered into an open one to see hundreds of moldy spuds staring back at me.

"How is your mother doing?" Arii asked politely as he settled his seven-foot frame upon a stack of three crates, his orange robe draping elegantly.

The word still jarred me a little, but after all the events of the previous day, I was a little more willing to consider her my mother again. "Fine, I think," I answered numbly as I touched the side of a rough crate. "Your healers think she should wake up soon. They said she was lucky to be wounded with magic and not the poisoned blades."

"Yes," Arii answered simply.

There was no need to remind me that there was still no cure for the lethal poison all of Rhydin's Einanhis used.

"When you returned," Arii continued on almost seamlessly, "we talked only long enough to understand what happened at the imperial palace. Now that things have settled down a bit, I would like to hear more about the memory you saw in the dungeon, as well as what Rhydin himself told you."

I shrugged, feeling jittery. "I was trying to trick him into telling me anything at all. I called him fake and mocked him about Amelia. He told me that she was in the way and that the real Rhydin Caldwell just wanted to be in two places at once. Then, I actually saw the memory of the Einanhi creation."

Arii asked a question or two about Rhydin's desire to be in two places, how he wanted to go home and marry Amelia but also save Nerahdis from the brand new, quarrelsome Three Kings. Then he started asking more magic-specific questions that I wasn't sure I could answer. "When the creation of the Einanhi occurred, did you see the original Rhydin begin to siphon his power to the new being? Did you hear the incantation?"

"No. It happened out of nowhere. Even Rhydin was confused as to how it happened," I replied as if in a daze, seeing it happen again in my mind's eye. The horror on Rhydin's face as he realized his clone was no longer under his control. "The Einanhi said that Rhydin wasn't his master anymore, and he wouldn't stop until he accomplished the task that made Rhydin's magic give him life. The Einanhi took the side of taking Nerahdis from the Three Kings and killing Amelia, the only thing that'd been holding Rhydin back."

Arii stroked his hairless chin. "Could that be possible?" he mused. "Could Rhydin have been filled with so much unnatural power when he was made Archimage that he lost control of it?" The ancient Ranguvariian continued hypothesizing to himself in deep magical theory far beyond the boundaries that my mind – or any human's, for that matter – could understand.

"I still think there's more to it we don't know," I grumbled as I leaned against a crate. "There's parts to this that still just aren't clicking. Especially Amelia."

"I agree," Arii responded, popping back out of his own mind, "but why Amelia?"

"Well, it's her situation that caused her to break off her and Rhydin's relationship when he was made Archimage, which then led him to be so torn," I explained. "We're learning more and more of Rhydin Caldwell's story, but Amelia's still a shot in the dark. Who was she? Why did the Three Kings want to kill a random teenage girl and her family?"

Arii dwelled in silence for a few moments thoughtfully, mulling over my words. "Yes...Amelia's story is the actual riddle to solve in this mystery, I see your meaning. As I said before, Nora never spoke of her to me. What have you learned of her story?"

I slowly imparted everything I'd learned over the last few months. I tried to place all the ancestral memories in some sort of order for him, starting with one of my more recent visions of when Nora and Amelia first met. She was on the run from Emperor Caden's personal guard, who were intent upon killing her after already capturing her mother and murdering her sister, called Ariadne. Amelia claimed she didn't know why they were after them but also said that she was innocent of whatever they thought she'd done, which didn't quite go together.

She obviously came from some sort of money because she gave Nora a bunch of money, which allowed her, essentially a job-less homeless woman, to purchase all the land that was now my mother's family farm. Rhydin Caldwell had suggested that she was the daughter of somebody important, but he hadn't been able to identify whom before he used up all his energy. With the Emperor's Guard after her, it was no wonder she couldn't go with Rhydin once he was Archimage, even if we didn't know her crime. I started spinning a story that maybe her father was on bad terms with Emperor Caden and his sons – perhaps stole something from them, even the huge bag of money she had on her when Arii finally interrupted me.

"Rhydin Caldwell also had you relay to me that it would be Amelia *Alytniinaeran* conjured. That she would be the evil Rhydin's undoing, just as she was his," Arii mumbled pensively to himself.

I bobbed my head, beginning to feel the weight of it all. "Y'know, for a woman who's not mentioned even once in any historical account *ever*, she sure drove Nerahdis down the path it's on today. She's the reason Rhydin split in two, the reason Rhydin Caldwell lost his remaining power and visibility, *and* the entire reason that you all found Nora and helped her create her magic to get vengeance and save you all."

Arii nodded, but it was obviously he was hundreds of miles away in his own brain.

It took a beat for me to realize that Arii had frozen, the broad lines of his face and robe becoming slightly blurred. The stone walls around me lost their definition, the individual bricks fading into nothing but colors, but the world didn't melt away entirely and reshape like to what I had become accustomed.

My head was suddenly full of noise like the continuous rumble of a great thunderstorm. Voices were speaking among the roars and grumbles of the thunder, and there were so many of them I couldn't help but throw my hands over my ears, which did nothing to stop the noise. A small tug in the corner of my mind honed me in on a particular voice, a high soprano that I recognized immediately as Amelia's.

"Nora, please, you have to help me…" her voice resounded, even as another person responded in a low alto, which had to be Nora's although it sounded muffled. "I need your help. I want to save my mother. Joshuua, Ivann, and Spenser will kill her if we don't get her out of the palace…whether the emperor condones it or not."

The only part of Nora's response that I could make out were the words "too dangerous."

"Fine! But I cannot sit here and do nothing. I am not as defenseless as you think!" Amelia's voice retorted. Nora ultimately uttered a groan, which seemed to be agreement, before a few seconds of silence ensued.

During that time, wisps of color materialized before my eyes like smoky shadows. A collection of earthen-toned smoke gathered on one side of the room while a column of ocean colors approached from the other side. Nora's voice shattered my ears, suddenly crystal clear and loud with a hint of desperation. "Amelia, I was keeping watch, I didn't see what happened in that room. What did you see?"

The earth-colored wisp seemed to shake the ocean-hued one.

Amelia's tone was quite the opposite, barely above a whisper. "You'll hear soon enough."

"*The emperor is dead!* Struck down in the night by an unknown murderer!" a male voice bellowed in the manner of a town crier as the two wisps before me disintegrated.

"Rayna?" Arii asked, his smooth tenor bringing me back to the present. He no longer appeared blurred; time was moving normally again. "Have you seen something?"

"I…I don't know. I-It was different this time." I touched my head gingerly. A cold feeling was spreading along my shoulders and down my spine as panic gripped my heart. "We definitely need to be looking at Amelia. Not just Rhydin. She might not have been as innocent as she seems."

Arii's leathery brow furrowed, but after evaluating my face, he decided not to press me about it. Instead, he cleared his throat and changed the subject. "Before we adjourn, I would like to hear about these new Einanhis of Emperor Rhydin's. The ones that cannot be sensed by mages."

I shrugged, starting to feel exasperated. "That's all I know, Arii. He's invented some new Einanhi that doesn't give off a magical signature. Wouldn't surprise me if he's overhauling his whole army with them."

The ancient Ranguvariian sighed sadly. "I have feared this day for many decades, especially after he took my grandson and…." Arii tapered off, and I didn't push him either. I didn't know much about Aunt Rachel's other brother, Luke, but I knew it was a sore subject for practically everyone I knew. Arii added as he rose from his place on a crate, "He must have finally figured out how to employ our secrets against us. We will need the Aatarilecs' help more than ever."

The Clariion was headed toward the door, but one last burning question tugged on my heart. "Arii, what's a forger?"

He stopped in his tracks, and his eyes were a tinge closer to yellow when he faced me again. "A forger? Why do you ask?"

"Emperor Rhydin called me one. And when he tried to touch me, pieces of his magic broke away and stuck in my arms. That's how I saw his memory. He said the real Rhydin Caldwell and Nora were both forgers too," I explained slowly, watching his expression carefully.

Arii's mind seemed to be racing. "It's…it's an archaic term, one no longer used. I'd forgotten all about it, none of my books even mention it…but he's correct." He levelled his gaze at me, suddenly a fierce white color. "In nice terms, a forger is simply someone who is able to create or take on their own magic. In other cases, they are someone who steals the magic of others to become something else."

I met his eyes hesitantly. "Like someone who forges a Royal seal?"

Arii breezed back into the room and took my hand. "Rayna, you may be a forger, but you are not fake or bad. You are good, just like Nora was."

Then, he was gone all at once. I touched my hand where he'd held it so softly. Emperor Rhydin's words were ringing in my ears. "*Those who forge their own magic, or are forged upon by others, are the ones to be pitied. Caldwell rots in the Archimage Palace, and not even the great Nora Soreta could escape her fate. Neither will you.*"

Nora had died on the younger side. I knew that from her grave marker. And her husband, Charles, died in the same year, which was suspicious. Two middle-aged people didn't just up and die the same year of natural causes. What had her fate been? I realized with a jolt that I really didn't know. Part of me didn't want to know. Surely Arii knew…if I ever got up the gall to ask.

I wandered out of the storeroom slowly. This area of the castle was devoid of life, and the sight surprised me before I remembered there was a Council meeting this evening. I had absolutely no desire to be any part of that, so I headed the opposite direction, yearning for sleep. Even on the back route, I could hear the echoes of yelling and shouting bouncing down the corridors. I didn't envy whoever was in charge of the meeting tonight.

King Frederick suddenly came to mind accompanied by a split-second worry that he was the target of all the anger tonight. I shook my head, trying to get that thought to clear. He came for me in the imperial palace, sure…but he probably only did that to try and win my mother over. He didn't care about me. He didn't try to get me back when I was baby. He had never been any sort of father to me, and he never would be.

Yeah.

I made my way straight to my bed in Uncle Evan and Aunt Cayce's room, also abandoned, and was claimed by fitful dreams filled with images of Rhydin Caldwell shattering to bits, Nora on the run from strange shadows chasing her, and Amelia wielding the storied sword that struck down Emperor Caden in the night.

"The ground is beginning to thaw! We must rally our forces across Nerahdis, or we won't be ready when the emperor comes!"

"We are *not* ready! We should get to the mountains while we still have a chance to run! We cannot compare to Rhydin's new, magical army!"

Cornflower collapsed into one of the Lunakan thrones on the dais as the room erupted once again into chaos and argumentation. The Three Kings and Queen of course began their usual dialogue of trying to soothe their respective peoples, but without Lina present, the Rounans were extra tumultuous at this meeting. Cornflower eyed Lina's young son, who was sheepishly wringing the hem of his tunic as he stood among the other leaders, and wished he was about ten years older. They had only just put the fire issue to rest – what with no one but Rhydin to punish – when the next argument sprang up in its place.

The princess rubbed her temples before covering her eyes, even though she could hear her old lady's maid usual reprimand. *"A princess does not show her emotions in public,"* she used to say whenever Cornflower began to cry after being scolded one too many times. The young woman certainly did not miss those poise and etiquette lessons, which had come to an abrupt end when she left Lunaka Castle with her brother, Frederick, shortly before the war. Sometimes, she still found herself missing the normalcy of them.

If the world had been normal, she would have never left Lunaka Castle and would have continued her lessons until her parents arranged a suitable match for her, likely the son of some noble either in Lunaka or abroad. While that future had never been that enticing to Cornflower, it at least allowed her a glimpse at what would come. The future she faced now was murky; would she have to remain Archimage even after Rhydin's reign came to an end? She didn't really want to. But then, what use did the rebellion – or the world, for that matter – have for a princess with no throne?

Yet, an even murkier future was the one staring down at her if the rebellion continued to run and hide.

"No more hiding," Cornflower said, the words bursting forth from her mind. The room stilled a moment, not having quite heard her over the ruckus. In that new space, she declared more confidently, "Are we a rebellion or a bug? We are useless if we do not do for what we have gathered. We *must* rebel. We must force the emperor's hand to meet us at Caden's Plain where we can have the advantage of choosing the terrain."

Half of the room cheered victoriously, their eyes gleaming with passion, which was almost enough for Cornflower to ignore the rest of the room.

Almost.

A cacophony of rebuttals resounded. "We don't know what we're up against!" "These Einanhis are too new; what if he has something else we don't know about?" "It's suicide if we go now." "If we're going to get out, we have to leave *now!*"

Cornflower slammed her hands on the table as she launched herself out of her seat. The other Royals turned to stare at her, unused to this kind of display. Mira and Frederick, her siblings, seemed to eye her with pity, and that made her skin chafe. Her fragile mask hiding her emotions was beginning to shatter. Her voice wheedled. "What was the point in making me Archimage if you all are still going to bicker and keep us at a stalemate? I don't even *want* to be Archimage!"

The room fell quiet for the first time. Cornflower didn't dare search the crowd for individual faces as hot tears threatened to spill forth. "What's next, huh? Make one of us emperor so that decisions can be made? You all are no better than those who made Rhydin Caldwell Archimage and then allowed his clone to be emperor."

The princess didn't wait for a response. She hurried away from the dais, the crowd parting for her like she carried the Epidemic. The castle foyer was significantly cooler than the heated throne room, but it wasn't enough. It still smelled like the same musky, dank rebel stench that Cornflower had been breathing for years. Her lungs constricted and shook, desperate for a breath of fresh air. She stumbled toward the heavy, wooden door leading to the courtyard, but it had already been barricaded for the night after the arson incident with the Rosetta look-alike. Struggling to breathe, she raced down a short hallway to a side door and pushed it open.

Glorious evening air embraced Cornflower like an old friend. Cool wisps scented with the first smells of spring soothed her airways. Never had the smells of fresh mud and new leaves been so wonderful. The sun was just setting to the west, heating the sky above Mineraltir a blood red color, and Lunaka's twin moons were already fast on the ascent, both full.

Cornflower wandered over toward a large stone situated beneath a very old, thick tree, one of her favorite spots as a child since it was outside the main courtyard where guards' eyes could never be lost. She perched upon the rock, spreading the skirts of her gown and pretending she was still no more than the average Royal lady, not a rebel leader.

She didn't see the amethyst glow of the mage behind her until it was too late.

Chapter Sixteen

Lina

The sound of the bedroom door opening woke me several hours after Frederick had left, the room plunged in blackness now that the sun had set. Unable to see, my hand blindly reached for the side of the bed, and my fingers curled around the sleek handle of the dagger I'd hidden between the mattress and its frame. My mind played tricks on me as the silhouette of a dragon rose upon the purple-flowered wall. I was just about to raise my blade when the golden light of a candle was struck into existence, and Rachel's fiery head of red hair appeared in the doorway.

"Ah, I see we are slowly returning to ourselves!" Rachel laughed throatily as she waltzed into the room. "Put that thing down, I don't need to tend to any more patients today."

I reluctantly did as I was told, feeling a little embarrassed. I hadn't even told Rachel about the nightmarish visions.

Rachel lit a few more lights around the room before she claimed the chair at my bedside and tapped the Ranguvariian feather dangling over my head. As she hummed her magical tune and the feathers began to glow, she chattered between musical phrases, "What, no 'thanks, Rachel, for saving my life *again*'? Are you feeling any pain?"

Her healing magic was spreading a warm feeling through me, kind of like a warm bowl of soup on a freezing day. The wound on my abdomen stung as the magic moved through me, but that pain was becoming weaker with every passing moment. Instead, tension seemed to sprout in my heart, and Frederick's relieved expression from earlier filled up my mind's eye.

"You're trying to divert my magic, Lina," Rachel said suddenly, her tone lower. "I can't heal broken hearts. No magic can."

"I…" I sputtered, ashamed. "I didn't mean to…I didn't even know that could be done."

Rachel sat back in her chair, and the feathers above my head stopped glowing. The lovely warm feeling circulating my veins vanished. "That's the funny thing about healing magic. It goes to where the body needs it most. Most of the time, that's a physical wound, but sometimes the worst wounds are the ones people on the outside can't see. Wounds of the mind, heart, or spirit."

I stared at my hands for a moment, twisted up in the beautiful quilt on my bed, two rings glinting upon them. Everything from my last conversation with Frederick came roaring back. I finally whispered, "This is a total disaster, Rachel."

"Why?" my friend asked nonchalantly, as if it was the easiest question to answer in the world.

"B-…Because!" I stammered, unprepared. "I was pushed into this before Sam had been in the ground for even a season, and now Frederick thinks he loves me!"

Rachel remained quiet for a few moments, mulling something over in her mind. I appreciated that she didn't just immediately spout a rebuttal or jump on the same speech I'd been given when this marriage was proposed. Her blue eyes were gentle when they met mine. "Do you think it impossible that he has learned to love you? Do you not think his feelings are real?"

"W-..." I sputtered, "Th-That's not what I meant! How should I know if they're real or not? We've been acting the act; he may just be feeling that way because we're playing marriage!"

Rachel leaned back on the chair, gracefully propping her pointed chin atop a pale, freckled hand as if she were a noble lady. "Well, how do you feel, hm? Are you just 'playing marriage'?"

I groaned. Slow bubbles of compassion rose up within me like a stew just beginning to think about boiling. "I don't know what I feel. I can't even think about it. I do *care* about Frederick, but Sam hasn't-..."

"You're not betraying Sam," my friend interrupted softly, and I could tell she truly meant the words and wasn't just saying them to make me feel better. "Contrary to what you may think, you don't have to let go of the old in order to embrace the new. Sam will always be a part of you for the rest of your life, just as Cassandra will always be a part of Frederick and Luke will always be a part of me. Your pursuing a new form of happiness and companionship with Frederick will never *replace* what you had with Sam or dishonor him. You're human, Lina-..."

I jumped in, feeling angry even though in my heart I knew I was being obstinate. "What if I never fall in love with him, hmm? We're so different!"

"Sometimes, love isn't something you fall into. Sometimes, love is something you decide to do." Rachel gave me a sad smile, like she knew from experience. "Every love story is different. They're not all the romantic, sweep-you-off-your-feet type."

I jutted my jaw out in annoyance. Rachel was grinning a little larger now, but to her credit, she mashed her lips beneath her teeth and made a move to return to her healing duties. She'd seen right through my false words, but she at least had the decency to not push me about the apparent truth that I was, in fact, beginning to possibly – maybe – consider the idea that I *might* have feelings for Frederick. Maybe.

All of a sudden, Rachel's face went slack, her hands freezing where they hung above my wound. The *matrii* print on her cheek glowed softly for the briefest of moments, the link between every Ranguvariian and their mate.

"What is it?" I asked as the atmosphere of the room changed. "What's Jaspen saying?"

My friend immediately stood and yanked back my covers, throwing clean clothes over my head like I was a toddler. "Downstairs. Now."

Only seconds later, Rachel was moving as fast as she could toward the throne room downstairs with me slung over her back since anything faster than a snail's pace was too much for my wound. It didn't take long to realize just how wrong things were, even if I didn't yet know why.

The castle was still. Normally, it hummed with life, and sounds drummed up and down the corridors like a rapid heartbeat. People walking, people talking, people cooking, playing, cleaning, training. The stone walls reverberated and amplified every sound, which always made the castle seem like it had taken on a life of its very own. Now, it all had fallen silent to the point where I actually wondered if the entire rebellion hadn't just vanished into a puff of smoke.

We didn't pass a single soul on our way to the throne room, and when Rachel flung open the side door, it revealed a sea of people within pressed shoulder to shoulder. As Rachel waded through them, gently tapping arms or touching the heads of children in order to create a path, my heart didn't know whether to sink or rise.

Perched upon a Ranguvariian's back, I had a much better vantage point than most, but I couldn't see it. The divide. The gap that always existed between the Gornish and the Rounans, the people who wanted to fight and the people who wanted to run. There was *always* a physical separation halving our rebellion at every Council meeting and meal time, although the lines fluctuated from time to time.

Instead, every square inch of space was filled as everyone huddled close to one of the tables in the center of the room. The dais was empty. The room itself seethed tension, like the entire castle was holding its breath.

My eyes snagged on the Royals gathered around a table within the fold of the rebels. This, too, was odd, seeing as usually the rebels kept their distance from the Royals up on the dais, creating yet another divide within our rebellion. Sabine was off to the side with her twin wards, blended in with the rebels around her. Xavier was physically holding Mira up, her arms wrapped around his broad shoulders, and his icy eyes met mine even though there was no real emotion emanating from them.

At the sight of Mira, my mind started going down the list. Taisyn and Lyla were right behind their parents, the elder with an arm draped supportively around the younger who had tears in her eyes. Kylar was off in the crowd standing with Evan, Cayce, and Aron, but there was no sign of Rayna anywhere. This made me nervous, but with them all off to the side and not looking traumatized, Rayna's absence couldn't be the issue. I barely spied Rosetta and Erikin at the very back of the room, Chelsea nearby.

Nathia stood halfway between her adoptive cousins and the table, but I almost didn't recognize her without her usual angry or smug expression. She seemed stunned, her chocolate-colored hair loose around her face. I followed her gaze to the other side of the table where Dominick abruptly turned to face me, something I couldn't see behind him. His blue eyes were reddened, and his face – becoming more like his father's every day – was flushed.

Time seemed to slow. Rachel was no longer moving forward, and my patience snapped. Fighting the desire to just shout at them all to tell me what was going on, I pushed downward out of Rachel's grip and slid to the floor. Pain rippled through my middle, causing me to almost double-over, but I inched toward Dominick and whatever was behind him. As I maneuvered around him, I realized there was a large, long item on the table draped with a bed sheet, and crouched directly behind him was Frederick, kneeling at the table with his head in his hands. My heart stammered at the sight of him in such turmoil before the realization that we weren't all here hit me at long last.

Where was Cornflower?

Just as I placed a hand on Frederick's shoulder, beginning to say her name, I caught sight of one golden curl upon the table that hadn't quite been covered by the bedsheet. My heart plummeted right through my stomach and down between my feet.

"Wha-…?" I tried to ask, my voice becoming shrill as my pain seemed to triple.

Xavier's eyes had never left me since I entered the room, and he tossed something in my direction. He growled, "Emperor Rhydin happened. That's what. She was found just outside."

I tore the piece of parchment off the table, and heat bubbled in my veins at the sight of the handwriting. It matched the riddle Rhydin Caldwell had written for me. The words were written under a doodle of a periwinkle-blue cornflower with a snapped stem.

Long live the First Archimage

The parchment crumpled in my hand before my mind could hardly process the words. The message was clear enough. Rhydin thrived on our rebellion's discord, and therefore he had removed the person we'd put up as our unified leader. But more than that? We weren't safe even just outside our walls. I gripped Frederick's shoulder tighter as it began to quake, and it killed me that he continued to hide his face from me in his hands. I seethed, "We're going to make him pay for this."

Suddenly, the room was overflowing with shouts of agreement. Awestruck, I and the other Royals looked around at the rebels flanking us. Every last one of them had revenge written upon their faces. A Lunakan man stepped forward, fingering the hilt of his sword as if it begged him for blood. "We must avenge our Archimage! She only wanted peace among us!"

"Yeah!" a Mineraltin woman yelled as she raised her copper fist in the air. "Cornflower was the very *last* of us that deserved such a fate! She cared about *all* of us!"

"Like she said, no more hiding," a teenage Auklian boy near me declared gruffly, his Rounan mark on his wrist in full view. "If we're not safe here, there's nowhere in Nerahdis that's safe. It's time we take our fighting to the emperor and meet him on Caden's Plain!"

Someone in the audience I couldn't see proclaimed, "To Caden's Plain!"

"To Caden's Plain!" the words echoed. One after the other, all the rebels took them up. The words rippled into each other until they were in unison; the entire room continued to chant them as they lifted their fists into the air or beat them against their chests like a fierce battle cry.

I couldn't stop the smile coming to my face as my eyes jumped from rebel to rebel. Their resolve was contagious, and I found myself tapping my fist against my breastbone alongside the beat of their declaration. Finally, I could no longer resist, and I added my cry to theirs.

"To Caden's Plain! To Caden's Plain! To Caden's Plain!"

Xavier and Sabine sprang into action. They began a discourse concerning all the details of this next move. When would we march? How would we ensure we gained the best defensive position at Caden's Plain? What would our strategy be? Plans were suddenly being made left and right, and the speed of it all and everyone's total willingness left my mind spinning.

I glanced once more at the covered body on the table, the euphoria of the room exiting my system. Cornflower had only been twenty-seven years old. Still a young woman in her prime; the youngest of her Royal generation. She had so much life ahead of her, so much opportunity as we re-wrote Royal duties and expectations to bury the closed-mindedness of kings like Adam and Morris. This fueled my anger still as my gaze shifted to the Royal heirs, as well as the young faces in the rest of the rebellion. They would know a different world than the one I knew, I promised myself.

Rhydin wouldn't walk off Caden's Plain. Even if I didn't either.

The rebellion kicked itself into gear, scattering to the winds to ready weapons and supplies as spring threatened to show her warm face in less than a week. The roads could be thawed and cleared enough to travel any day really. Even as I watched the activity with sad pride, I jumped when Frederick abruptly stood from his place at Cornflower's side, knocking my hand off his shoulder. He didn't even look at me as he made for the nearest exit, and I instantly moved to follow him, slow as I was, unable to let him go alone.

Frederick turned down the nearest hallway, away from the tide of rebels flowing toward the supply rooms and closets that held all our extra artillery. I limped after him, unable to fully extend my left leg or the pull upon the muscles of my lower stomach was unbearable. I hobbled along as fast as I could, becoming afraid that I would lose him to the labyrinth of the castle. After maybe a minute, Frederick happened to catch sight of me out of the corner of his eye, and he called to me hoarsely, "Leave me be, Lina. I need to be alone."

The gruffness of his voice tore at my heart. "No…you don't, Frederick," I gasped in response, even as he continued to move away from me. "I'm just going to…keep following you…until you stop."

Frederick's steps began to taper off until they halted altogether. His shoulders slouched, and his long arms dangled helplessly. It was a minute or two before I caught up to him with my awkward gait, sucking air between my teeth to keep myself going through the burning in my ribs. We were well away from all the activity now, the shouts and cheers like only whispers after echoing so far.

I didn't wait to catch my breath. As soon as I could reach him, I tugged on his sleeve to make him turn toward me. He kept his eyes shut, like he was ashamed for anyone to see him grieve. His pale face was flushed with emotion, or perhaps the rubbing of tears away before anyone could possibly see them. I'd never seen him like this; when Gloria died, he was filled with anger. Now, his heartache for his youngest sister was laid bare, and it made my own heart hurt to see him so devastated. He was finally crumbling after staying strong for so long, and I hated it.

No words would ever suffice. I knew that from experience by now. Without thinking, I reached up with both hands and touched his face, sweeping a few wisps of faded gold hair back into place as best I could. Frederick was a couple inches shorter than Sam's height of six feet, but he was still well above my meager five-foot frame.

Part of my mind felt surprised at the tender actions my hands were doing on their own, but the rest of me didn't, which was surprising in itself. It felt...*right*. To soothe him. It *hurt* to see him in pain. And when Frederick's eyes finally opened, staring at me emptily with no more strength to give, I wrapped my arms around his neck and hugged him as tightly as I could. Like I could squeeze all his broken pieces back together into some semblance of the brave young prince I remembered from long before any tragedy had ever befallen us.

It was several moments before Frederick responded. He started by gently placing his thin hands upon my shoulders. After a few moments more, it turned into him wrapping his wiry arms more securely around my back. Then, as he melted into his grief, he let out a suffocated sob as he pressed me closer. My ribs began to protest, but I ignored them. His ear was right next to my lips, and I whispered, "I'm so sorry. She didn't deserve to die."

Frederick sputtered a little after waiting a moment. His voice was so croaky that I wouldn't have recognized it if he wasn't right next to me. "You're the first person to say that without saying her death is a good thing for us."

My brow furrowed as I tried to choose my next words carefully. "It shouldn't have taken the death of the most innocent of us to bring everyone together. Her death is wrong, no matter how anyone spins it."

His golden head bobbed once or twice before my new husband pushed it against mine to stop me from seeing his expression crumble.

"I know you had a special relationship with her," I whispered softly. "You two have always been together after Mira married Xavier, through the war and before the rebellion and in the Dome. She helped you so much with Dominick, too."

"I *failed* her," Frederick choked. "I didn't protect her."

I shook my head against his, and the weight of my own words was heavy on my heart. "Sometimes all we can do is the best we can."

Silence embraced us then. Even the ruckus from the other part of the castle seemed to fade away. I didn't let go until he did, trying to give him whatever time he needed. When Frederick pulled away, there was a different look on his face. His eyes were heavy and pensive, and his mouth was slightly agape. I tried to smile at him, one of the small ones that people typically did when they were trying to make someone feel better, my hands still on his forearms. Then, without a word, Frederick slowly reached up, cupped my neck, and placed a kiss just in front of my ear – before walking back the way he had come.

Stunned, I touched where his lips had just been. My emotions began to war with each other. Surprisingly enough, I didn't feel any anger. Only shock…yet that wasn't completely true. I knew what I was feeling, even if I didn't want to put a name to it just yet. It only felt safe to say that I hadn't been ready for him to walk away just yet.

I did an about-face and hobbled back down the hallway, past the wave of energized rebels sharpening and polishing their various weapons, and up the stairs. Tucking away my confusing feelings for Frederick, I felt consumed with the desire to find my daughter, who hadn't been in the throne room where Cornflower's body lay. She needed to know what had transpired, and I needed to know she was safe.

It wasn't hard to find her at all. I saw her immediately upon pushing open the door to Evan and Cayce's room, curled up on her straw tick down on the floor. Her face seemed so young as she slept, her auburn hair wild upon her pillow, and a memory of her as a tiny baby asleep in my arms flashed in my memory. Satisfied and not wanting to wake her, I turned to make my leave, suddenly hyperaware of all the noise echoing up from the ground floor. The door was nearly shut when I heard her croak, "What's going on downstairs?"

I sighed, contemplating telling her it was nothing and to return to sleep, but I knew I'd be angry if someone told me that tonight. "The rebellion is preparing for battle. Emperor Rhydin murdered Cornflower tonight."

Rayna shot up out of her bed, her Allyen eyes wide. "*What?* H-How?"

"I…I don't know the full story, but apparently she went outside the castle walls for some reason. It shouldn't have been possible," I muttered as I drew close to her, aching to soothe her fear. I withdrew the crumpled piece of parchment I abruptly remembered; I must have absentmindedly shoved it into my pocket when I went after Frederick. I put a hand on Rayna's shoulder as I gave it to her.

She studied it a couple moments, then glared at it. I opened my mouth to ask what she was thinking when all at once, I began to feel funny. Looking up from Rayna's face, I noticed that the room was turning strange as well. It was blurring before my eyes, and I panicked that something was wrong with my vision. My fingers tightened on Rayna's shoulder, but she didn't seem surprised as she looked up and around.

"What's happening?" I asked her fearfully.

Rayna's head snapped toward me, her eyes full of shock. "You can see it, too??"

The black colors of the room transformed into dull, natural tones. Prairie grass sprung up beneath our feet, and a vault of gray, cloudy sky opened up above our heads. Then, before my very eyes, a young woman with long, ocean-blue hair materialized out of nowhere.

My breath left me altogether. This was one of the memories that Rayna had been seeing.

"That's…," I whispered, unable to tear my eyes away from her. She was kneeling in the grass, her sensible, Lunakan dress a pool of brown at her feet. She seemed to be combing the grasses for small flowers or herbs, stuffing small stems into her apron pockets every so often.

"Amelia," Rayna finished for me, her gaze darting back and forth between the young woman from centuries ago and me. "I can't believe you're seeing this too…but why do I feel like I've been here before?" Then, she looked down at her hands, which were see-through. "That's strange. Usually, I'm always in Nora's body. The only time I've ever been myself is when-…"

A black-clad figure suddenly appeared within a puff of violet smoke, and my heart began to race, forgetting this was a memory of something that had already happened and therefore posed no threat to us.

Rayna's face fell slack as she took in the evil Rhydin – albeit with a much shorter haircut than I'd ever seen him with – stalking toward Amelia, whose back was to him. Rayna whirled around, looking off into the distance where a small forest sat on the other side of a grassy hill.

"No," she whispered, "I've seen this before. Nora's over there…in the trees. She didn't see this part, so…how are we seeing this?"

"Seeing what?" I hissed to her under my breath, as if the figures of memory could hear me.

Rayna couldn't tear her eyes away. "The evil Rhydin is brand new, Amelia is about to die, and Rhydin Caldwell is going to lose the rest of his power. This is the day that determined Nerahdis's entire future."

Chapter Seventeen

Rayna

"R-Rhydin? What are you doing here?"

My words died on the wind as Amelia noticed the false Rhydin's arrival. She stuffed her hands behind her apron, her chin angled toward her toes in bashfulness. "I-It's been a long time. You look…different, but well. I hope the last two years have been kind to you."

Rhydin's eyes narrowed, and he didn't respond right away. I studied everything in front of me fiercely. The way the Einanhi moved and his simple black clothing. Amelia's expression and poise, obviously trying to make a surprise reunion with her former swain the least awkward as possible. Once or twice, I spared the fastest of glances toward the trees behind us, but I already knew that Nora wouldn't appear until after the fatal wound had been delivered.

Amelia's blue brow furrowed, and her movement to run her fingers through her hair betrayed her discomfort at seeing him. She seemed to begin talking just to fill the uneasy silence, her tone steeped in anxiety. "I…I am sorry. Again. For what happened between us. I truly abhor how it ended…I never wanted it to end." She stopped, looked down briefly, and then cleared her throat. "I have missed you. I hope these years have helped you come to understand why I couldn't go with you."

An idea suddenly struck me. What if the reason she couldn't be around the Three Kings was because she was the one who killed Emperor Caden? My mind jogged with this theory a bit until I remembered that Rhydin had been made Archimage before Caden's death. Whether Amelia was Caden's mysterious murderer or not, that hadn't been the reason she couldn't stay with Rhydin because it hadn't happened yet at that point.

"Foolish woman," the Rhydin clone that would someday create Duunzer and become emperor in my time spoke at last. "I shall never understand why he loves you or would let you stand in the way of his power. I will not make the same mistake."

Amelia's face twisted in confusion, and when Rhydin began to stalk toward her, she instantly stepped backward in fear. I stepped forward myself, the fierce desire to help her rippling through me, before I remembered that this had already happened. These events were written in the stone of time and couldn't be stopped or changed.

A third person abruptly materialized in the middle of things amongst another puff of power, and I heard my mother gasp as Rhydin Caldwell landed in the prairie. After all, she'd never seen him before. I didn't dare turn to her to explain anything, too enraptured by what the next few seconds would show.

The real Rhydin rapidly took in the situation in front of him. He looked from his mistakenly-created clone to the woman he loved, and his gaze hung up on her. Two years it'd been since they'd seen each other last. He glanced at his Einanhi once more, the gears in his scientific mind churning as he made a decision in a fraction of a second. I'd always wondered how an Einanhi – even one given far too much of his creator's power upon creation – could best his master and steal the rest of his power from him.

It was because he was underestimated.

Rhydin chose the wrong person to run toward.

Of course, we'd never know what would have happened if Rhydin Caldwell had made the decision to turn toward his Einanhi and deliver whatever magical might he still retained. Or why he thought his Einanhi would wait or wouldn't fight, or whatever it was he believed in that moment. All that was forever lost to history.

Instead, he turned toward Amelia, desperate to put his body between hers and her murderer-to-be. His back still facing his enemy, the Rhydin clone stretched out both of his hands like lightning. One hand flung a throwing knife deep into Amelia's belly, and the other whipped up the violet twister of magic that latched onto Rhydin's back like a leash and thrust him to the ground.

Amelia screamed. The high-pitched, grating sound that would bring Nora running. She lurched forward, falling to her knees just a couple feet from where Rhydin Caldwell had fallen. Blood leaked from her wound and began to dribble from her mouth. She dragged herself to where her lover lay, and it was *her* blood that fell onto his crisp, white shirt. He hadn't been wounded, as I'd wondered.

Barely a minute went by before I heard Nora's voice. "What is the meaning of this??" she bellowed. My mother's attention was on her now, the brown-haired huntress standing several feet away, heartbroken confusion all over her fierce features.

I halfway expected the memory to end here. I was caught up with what I'd seen before from Nora's point of view. Rhydin Caldwell shattered like glass into a mere specter, Amelia bled out, the evil Rhydin gained his full dark prowess, and Nora drew her sword. My mother watched it all unfold with her mouth agape, and I briefly found myself wondering if this was what she envisioned my ancestral memories to be like.

"I shall become the new emperor then," the clone said monotonously, as if it was the simplest notion in the world, "but having anyone in my way is not an option. Not even you, Nora Soreta."

Rhydin summoned an absolutely gigantic charge of amethyst lightning, and Nora stepped forward to meet him. Their blades came together with a *clang*, just as I'd seen before, but then the memory continued as Rhydin threw his spell at Nora. She narrowly jumped out of the way, her muscular frame moving like a willow tree. They continued to duel for several more minutes wordlessly, the only noise erupting from their swords each time they met. However, as Rhydin's movements became angrier and harsher, I realized he was losing his patience. Nora wasn't backing down though, no fear present on her face regardless of how soundly outmatched she was. Finally, Rhydin reached the end of his artificial tolerance.

"Enough!" he bellowed. "You will never be anything more than a magic-less peasant, and your time has run out."

Nora opened her mouth to reply, but she never got the chance. Rhydin dropped his sword and used both hands to charge the largest orb of magic I'd ever seen, nearly as large as a wagon wheel. Then, he threw it like it was as light as a feather, and its size alone made it impossible to escape. Unable to dodge it, Nora held up her blade, the flat of it facing Rhydin, and braced herself. My mother and I could only stare in frozen horror as Nora faced the magical blast head on.

Her sword blocked the bulk of it, saved her face and her chest at least. She was thrown backwards several feet, but her arms and hands bore the brunt of the blast. Tiny wisps of smoke rose into the air from her tattered, smoldering sleeves, her cloak was in ruins, and her hands were red and charred. *The source of her scars*, I gasped inwardly. Nora groaned and twitched on the ground; I could barely believe she was even alive.

Rhydin sheathed his sword, a confident look returning to his expression. "If you survive, the next time you see me, I shall be your new emperor."

"That will *never* happen!" Nora roared violently as she struggled to push herself off the ground. "You will regret this day, I swear it! I will end you even if it's the last thing I do!!"

The evil Rhydin chuckled, the preposterousness of a magic-less woman being remotely capable of killing the most powerful sorcerer in the land evidently too much, and then his smile vanished instantly. "Amelia was my target, not you. If I ever see you again, you will join her in death."

A male voice started calling from afar, "Nora? Nora! Nora, where are you?"

I saw Nora shake her heavy head and mouth the word "Charles," her husband's name, but Rhydin didn't care to notice. He gracefully walked across the clearing to where Amelia's body still lay, seeming to double-check that she was in fact dead. Once satisfied, his gaze traveled to the horizon where the Archimage Palace was just a small dot, and I wished I could know what he was thinking. Happy the real Rhydin was locked away? Concerned that he needed to kill him too? Either way, the Einanhi clone seemed to decide that his business was concluded, and he vanished in a puff of purple smoke.

The memory ended there, and the grassy hills morphed back into the small dark room in Lunaka Castle. My mother's hand was still on my shoulder as we both stood silent and processed what we'd seen. I could see it all in my mind's eye so vividly, and my fingers itched to add this memory to the others in my sketchbook. I was mentally knee deep in the question of how we'd seen what we saw when my mother abruptly spoke, jarring me from my thoughts.

"I never imagined that your visions were so…real," she whispered, like she was afraid of being overheard. "I'm sorry I've never given them much heed before now."

I shrugged, and her hand finally dropped to her side. "It's fine. You've…been busy."

Mama's expression filled with sadness. "I'm sorry for that too."

I let that one roll off, too, moving on to my questions that seemed far more critical at the moment. "How do you think Nora ended up with the Ranguvariians between this memory and her at Amelia's grave saying they're going to help her get her vengeance? How did they find her?"

"Arii told me this story once a long time ago," my mother murmured as she limped over to sit on the bed. "A Ranguvariian scouting party happened to be nearby when that memory happened, and they were drawn to it, what with all the noise they were making and the magic in the air. By the time they reached the source of the noise, Nora and Rhydin were already dueling. They heard Nora swear her revenge, and after a month or two of tailing Rhydin and observing what kind of emperor he planned on being, they knew he was planning something drastic to make Nerahdis submit to them. They knew, by then, that his magic was like poison to them. Fearful for their lives, the Ranguvariians went to her and discovered she had the ability to grow her own power. So, they chose her, and took her with them to train her as the first Allyen."

"Wow," I breathed. I wished I could see *that* memory; Nora's reaction to seeing the seven-foot-tall Ranguvariians for the very first time on her doorstep. That one had to be memorable.

We fell into silence, still lost in what we'd just seen, and I seated myself next to her. It was strange to wonder what our lives would have been like if the Ranguvariians hadn't found Nora, or if she hadn't been born with the capacity to grow her own magic. A forger, as Emperor Rhydin called it. Someone just like me – although apparently, I was forged upon and given the powers of an Allyen when neither of the previous Allyens' children inherited the power. He had told me about that right after seeing bits of his power leave him and stick to my arms, and I found myself promptly consumed with inspecting the skin where they'd been.

I said slowly, my eyes still glued to my forearms, "I've seen one of Rhydin's memories before when I was in his dungeon…but that was when I accidentally stole some of his power. It was like crystals along my arms, but they absorbed into my skin during the first memory I saw. I thought they were gone, but…do you think I still have some tiny piece of his power within me? And that's how we saw what we did, things that happened before Nora came?"

My mother shook her head helplessly. "That level of magical theory is beyond me. You should ask Arii. If it's happened before, then I suppose it makes sense. But how did you 'steal' his magic?"

I sighed and gave her a quick rundown of mine and Arii's last conversation about forgers. She seemed shocked and confused for what this meant about me, but she was more interested in our shift in focus to Amelia and my theories about her. She was quiet for a few minutes, her eyes trained on a corner of the dark room as she thought, before saying, "We need to figure out the rest of Amelia's backstory."

"That's what *I* said," I huffed, crossing my arms like the indignant teenager I was, "but there's only one way to do that anymore."

Mama met my gaze. "Ask someone who actually knew her. Who loved her."

I eyed her hesitantly, afraid to get my hopes up. "What are you saying?"

She stood abruptly, which resulted in a wince as it pulled her wound. Then, she declared determinedly, "We'll go to the Archimage Palace together this time. Before the battle. We need to know what we're walking into if the death spell is going to conjure Amelia."

I couldn't help but smile giddily before an entire castle's worth of anxiety perched upon my shoulders. "Wh-When do you think the battle is going to be?" I stuttered.

"Well, spring is all but here, and we don't want to risk missing our opportunity and having Rhydin pin us in here. It'll take three days for every rebel in Nerahdis to march to Caden's Plain to claim the high ground of Lunaka's mountains before intercepting the might of Rhydin's army as they travel from the Great Desert." My mother eyed me cautiously as she realized why I'd asked. "We leave tomorrow."

There suddenly didn't seem to be enough air in the room. So much hinged on my ability to perform the death spell. The rebellion's survival, Emperor Rhydin's destruction, Rhydin Caldwell's salvation.... I stammered, "B-But, Emperor Rhydin has my piece of the locket...how am I supposed to do my part?"

To her credit, my mother didn't let any fear come over her face, whether she felt some or not. "The Ranguvariians have been watching him from afar. He wears it; he's never put it down. I think he knows we would swipe it if he did. So, he'll have it on him when we face him on the battlefield. We'll figure it out from there."

That didn't make me feel any better. My breaths were still ragged. "But what if we can't get to it? Or what if we *do* get to it, but then I mess up the spell? What if-...?"

"Hey. You've got it down. It'll be okay," my mother whispered soothingly. "Now, get some sleep. We'll leave for the palace tomorrow too."

She may as well as said don't be afraid of water to someone who couldn't swim.

When she closed the door, the room was blanketed in darkness once more. I stood from the bed and dragged my straw tick closer to the window where I wouldn't be a tripping hazard for anyone coming to bed later. I lay there for a while, my mind racing. At some point, I must have fallen asleep out of sheer exhaustion for some amount of time, because the next thing I knew, I could hear the slumbering breaths of Uncle Evan, Aunt Cayce, Aron, and Kylar.

I tossed and turned for probably hours. I mentally went through each stance of the death spell, but my mind continued to ebb and flow into the realm of sleep. On one mental run-through of the death spell, I was halfway through when Emperor Rhydin suddenly snatched my third of the locket from my collar. On another, I was just getting ready to join in the center for the big finish with my mother and Uncle Evan when my foot went down a gopher hole, and my third of the spell dropped to the ground and shattered like a heavy glass orb. Then, an image of the battlefield flashed in my mind, littered with bodies. Various faces of different rebels I saw day to day stared back at me unseeingly, their lifeless eyes everywhere I looked.

But it was the dead eyes of Kylar, Taisyn, and my mother that made me shoot up out of bed.

"No more sleep, no more sleep," I repeated to myself as I squeezed my eyes shut and ran my hands over my face, trying to wipe away the images forever.

To my surprise, after a moment or two of composing myself, I saw the first gray light of daylight when I opened my eyes. The room was just beginning to lighten, and a couple songbirds were greeting the sun together in their tree just outside our window. *Spring really is coming to life*, I thought to myself.

I cautiously turned toward the rest of the room, fully expecting to see an annoyed relative or two that I'd awakened. Instead, there was nothing more than empty beds, each nicely put back to rights which meant that their former occupants wouldn't be returning. Except Kylar's of course, which made it seem like he'd lost a wrestling match with his pillow.

Panic kicked my heart into an unsteady rhythm. I threw my cloak over the wrinkled clothes I'd slept in and tugged on my boots as I staggered into the hallway. Rather than making for the stairs, I rushed the opposite direction where a few doors down I burst out upon a balcony blanketed with the morning sun just barely over the mountains. Moisture clung to the air in a way I hadn't felt since autumn, and I froze in place at the sight of what lay beneath me. This balcony overlooked the far side of the courtyard, mostly out of the way.

There were so many people littered about the courtyard that the ground wasn't visible. They were a rainbow of colors, all interspersed like someone had dumped a tray of paints. Earthen-toned Lunakans, emerald-clad Mineraltins, and colorful Auklians. The ones with Gornish blood indistinguishable from the Rounans. Sword hilts gleamed on the back of nearly every one of them, and some also had a quiver and bow or perhaps a battle ax alongside them. Even children as young as maybe ten were being handed daggers.

The oldest and youngest of us were down there hefting tall banners over their heads that they must have spent the night stitching together. They weren't the separate emblems of the Three Kingdoms I'd seen a thousand times either; these were new. They were gold with red borders, and upon them were all the kingdoms' usual symbols combined. A great tree off-centered with the ocean at its feet and twin moons high above it. However, it wasn't until I saw another detail standing on the shore that my mouth fell open. The big white body, slender blue bill, and golden crest of a sun crane, which was Caark's usual ensign. Had people from Caark come to help us during our fateful hour? Was *all* of Nerahdis truly united at long last?

A command circled the courtyard, and the people began to stir. They slung their supplies across their backs or over their shoulders and began to exit the front gates. Several were horsebound, but there weren't enough for everyone. As the rebels slowly trickled out toward the southwestern road, I noticed dark shapes on the horizon approaching from the north and east. For a second, I feared they were armies of Rhydin's, but when I squinted, I recognized the same ragtag jumble of colors and supplies as the people below me.

They're the pockets, I thought with a start. The small groups of rebels spread out all around the Nerahdian continent. They were coming to join us at last, just as we'd always planned. Over time, the pockets meshed seamlessly into the flow of rebels from the castle, joining the march toward Caden's Plain. There were even a few here and there that made their way from Soläna, the city deep in Lunaka's canyon. It was like an ocean of people, and the sheer size of it was almost too much to take in. Yet, it would continue to grow even larger as pockets from Auklia and Mineraltir – and the Ranguvariians and watery Aatarilecs too – met up with us closer to the battlefield.

"Hey! Rayna!" a voice called from down below.

I jumped, quite frankly forgetting I could be seen. The balcony was only a few floors above the ground after all. I stepped forward, flexing my hands from gripping the stone of the railing so hard, and my eyes immediately pinned to the copper head of hair below.

"Taisyn," I said softly, forgetting he couldn't hear me if I didn't yell. Seeing him done up in leather and armor with the first weapon I'd *ever* seen remotely near him made everything I was seeing that much more real. I wasn't prepared for him to leave without me.

He was smiling. "I expect a full report of everything you learn from him when you get to Caden's Plain!"

The edges of my mouth twitched upward, but my heart was still gripped in a vise of fear. To banish the emotion from my voice, I summoned my best bossy voice and hollered at him, "You stay out of trouble until I get there, y'hear Taisyn Rollins?"

The teenage prince's shoulders were moving. He was laughing, but I couldn't hear it. "Oh, you know me! I'll be fine."

My heart continued to sink. He looked so small from up where I stood, and my mind started to spin. *What if the battle begins before Mama and I get there? What if he gets separated from the other rebels? What if there's so much magic in the air that he can't use his powers to see? What if he di-…?*

No. I shook my head. We'd get there in time, and I'd find him, no matter what. I said firmly, "I'll be there as soon as I can."

All too soon, Queen Mira was gesturing for her son to come along. The courtyard was nearly empty now, and Taisyn gave me a quick wave before mounting the horse his sister rode, settling behind her in the saddle. He must have said something about me because Lyla suddenly looked up in my direction. An unknown remark passed between the two of them before she waved as well, and they were on their way.

I watched them until they exited the castle gates and were absorbed into the stream of rebels, lost to my sight. Feeling like I was dreaming – certain that this couldn't actually be happening – I wandered back to the room and dressed myself properly this time. I pulled on a clean tunic and pair of trousers, my old, threadbare set I'd worn from Caark, and cinched my belt tight. Best to wear old clothes to battle, I figured detachedly. Battle was likely messy business, just like painting. Before leaving the room, I dug around in the one drawer assigned to me and unearthed the sleek, shining vial that Rhydin Caldwell had given me from a mess of holey socks desperately in need of darning. I tucked the artifact into my pocket, not giving myself the time to wonder whether I was ready to wield it and recapture the Einanhi Rhydin's stolen power, before my eyes happened upon Taisyn's little metal bird that he'd returned to me after I returned to the castle from Emperor Rhydin's dungeon. After a couple seconds of decision, I settled it into my other pocket, and I felt an ounce more secure than I had moments prior.

The halls were eerily quiet as I went in search of my mother. She wasn't hard to find, but I had to stop in my tracks when I saw the first patch of bird droppings on the marble staircase. I stared at it in confusion before looking around like an owl for the chickens. For weeks, I'd dodged chickens while climbing up and down these stairs, and now not a single one was to be found. I slowly got going again, lost in the wondering if the rebellion had decided to take them along on the journey, just as we had when we left the Dome.

When I reached the bottom, I instantly saw my mother standing at the large wooden door leading out to the courtyard, which stood ajar. She was gazing out toward where the rebellion had vanished, and I couldn't help but wonder what she was thinking. She was dressed in clothing I hadn't seen since before her and King Frederick's marriage, just simple brown clothing with a black skirt over her trousers, her usual red sash tied tight. It was like a breath of fresh air to see her in her old clothes instead of the gowns Aunt Rachel had her wearing since becoming queen.

She turned to me, a little misty-eyed. "Are you ready to leave? Mathiian is waiting outside."

I nodded, suddenly unable to speak as I took one last look at the castle foyer before following my mother out into the dawn. Mathiian was stone-faced today, his usual joking attitude absent. He transported my mother first, and as I waited for my turn, I suddenly heard some scratching and clucking. Six or seven hens were clustered around the nearest tree with several more beyond that.

They'd been freed and left behind.

I struggled to breathe. I choked down air, and it came sputtering back up. I didn't even see the flash of light as Mathiian reappeared, but soon there was a rock-hard hand on my shoulder. "Rayna?" he asked, "What's wrong? What happened?"

Embarrassed, I tried to blow air out with my lips to regain control. "N-Nothing…ju-just the chickens."

Mathiian's dark brow furrowed, his eyes seeping into a golden color. He stared at the feathered creatures a second or two in confusion. He appeared to be trying to formulate some sort of response, possibly to inquire about my sanity.

I sighed. "It…it just means…they're not needed anymore. They've been freed. The rebellion doesn't plan on returning."

"Well, yeah," Mathiian replied lightly, not getting it. "Once we destroy Emperor Rhydin, Nerahdis will be free too. All these people who have lived underground for years in order to preserve their lives will be able to go home and get their lives back."

"Or, they don't see themselves coming back from Caden's Plain," I moaned quietly, clutching my elbows.

The Ranguvariian boy paused, considered his words for a minute before taking my arm and readying to transport. "Both are possibilities, it's true. But every single soul in the rebellion knows what they signed up for. It's not like you're forcing them to fight for you. Whether we win or lose, many of us will be lost, and you cannot blame yourself." Mathiian leveled his gaze at me, his slitted pupils growing larger. "This much I believe: you are fully capable of pulling off *Alytniinaeran*. If we die, we died doing the right thing."

Instantly, the world flashed white, and I felt thankful that Mathiian cut off the conversation so I didn't have to respond. I didn't want to think about people dying. I didn't want to imagine any of the rebels that I'd been surrounded by for months could not come back from Caden's Plain, even if everything went off great. My fingers absent-mindedly touched the cool hilt of my dagger, the one Uncle Evan had given me just before the rebellion took Lunaka Castle months ago. I hadn't used it since I defended my dying father while he lay on the ground struggling to breathe. Was I ready to use it again?

Mathiian was evidently still improving on his transportation skills because he managed to land us right at the massive front doors of the Archimage Palace, their wood carved and painted to blend in with the mountain terrain. I gripped my dagger harder and took a deep breath before pushing the doors open. My mother waited just inside, gazing up at the swirling mist along the rafters of the great hall. It had grown since we were last here, its lavender color more defined, which meant Rhydin Caldwell was still growing in strength even as his counterpart grew increasingly unstable.

This time, I thought to myself, *I'm leaving with all the answers*.

Chapter Eighteen

Lina

A chill made my bones shudder as I entered the Archimage Palace. The air seemed stale, and healthy layers of dust covered every surface. The place just oozed death everywhere I looked, a far cry from the opulent residence it'd been when Archimage Dathian was still alive. However, the magical mist churning above my head was a different story. It was proof that life still remained in this cold, stone tomb.

"Come on, I bet he's in the library again," Rayna said as she entered the hall. "He seems to like it in there."

"I'll just wait here," Mathiian announced to nobody in particular as he perched upon a fallen column. "Enjoy your creepy ghost talk."

Rayna rolled her eyes before beginning to walk across the vast room in the direction of the library.

"Okay," I breathed awkwardly, and I moved to follow her. The realness of her memories may have been mindboggling to me, but I could only imagine what Rhydin Caldwell must be like to her. He had only ever been an invisible, voice-less presence to me over the years, albeit a very helpful one. As we walked to the other end of the massive room and turned down the hallway leading to the library, I tried to think of ways I could be helpful to Rayna since I wouldn't be able to help ask any questions or clarify any answers.

When the big library doors swung open, I stopped in my tracks. The presence that once warned me that Emperor Rhydin was coming back when Rayna was only a baby popped up in my mind, stronger than I'd ever felt before. It felt ancient yet young, smelled of parchment, and was incredibly lonely on top of everything.

"Yep, he's here," Rayna declared.

"I can tell," I murmured, my eyes glued to the floor as I focused on his presence.

"You can sense him?" Rayna gasped

I cringed a little. In all my jealousy in the past that she could see and hear him, I'd forgotten that I hadn't told her that. "Um…yes. I've been able to for some time, since the first time I was ever here. But only if there aren't a lot of people around," I explained slowly. "He's always tried to help me, even if I had no idea what or who he was. He's the one who guided me to that history book I know you and Aron like to take and read."

Rayna flushed red, but she tried to sidestep the fact I'd known she was taking my book. "No one else I've ever brought here could sense him. I wonder if it's because you're an Allyen too? Just not like me though. You're not a forger. Just descended from one, I guess."

"Perhaps," I muttered. Magical theory would never my best subject.

At that, my teenage daughter hurried farther into the library toward the back wall with the magnificent stone fireplace. I sighed and moved to follow her at the pace of a snail, failing to completely squash my frustration that she could see him and I couldn't. I was just giving myself a mental speech about remembering what was truly important – healing my tenuous relationship with Rayna since her discovering that I wasn't the mother who gave birth to her and gleaning the information we needed from Rhydin Caldwell – when I heard my daughter exclaim a heartfelt greeting.

And the tenor of a young man's voice responded.

For a second, I was certain I'd imagined it. Rayna jabbered on with news of the rebellion as I hesitantly made my way around the chairs and piles of books toward her. I slowly rounded a dusty marble column, and my knees went weak. There, sitting at a sleek writing desk and dressed in a fashion not seen in centuries, was a young, dark-haired man with a quill in his translucent hand, and when he glanced up at me, my world about stopped spinning altogether.

Adrenaline instantly pumped through my veins as I stared down the face of my enemy. The sorcerer who had hunted me as a child, who engineered the disease that orphaned me, who created Duunzer, who tore the Three Kingdoms apart. He looked *just* like him, aside from a couple very minor differences such as the cut of his hair and the set of his jaw.

Rhydin Caldwell appeared a little fearful – an expression I'd never witnessed before on any face of Rhydin's – and his violet eyes darted between Rayna and I a few times as if he was just as shocked that I could see him.

I cleared my throat uncomfortably as I stationed myself on the very edge of a winged armchair so dusty there was no telling its original color. "Rhydin Caldwell, I presume?"

Before he could manage a response, Rayna gasped, "You can see him??"

"Trust me, I'm just as surprised as you two are," I huffed, unable to take my eyes from my old "helpful presence."

Rhydin's voice had a slight tremor to it as he said, "My power has been strengthening in recent days…and you were always able to sense me if there were not too many other magical presences around to hide me, as a descendant of Nora's. Perhaps, I must have enough substance again that you are able to see me as well, even if others still cannot. A thief was here just yesterday to prove that point."

"Perhaps," I repeated dully. I was swimming in disbelief, and I couldn't fight the instinct that he couldn't be trusted. Not with that face.

Rhydin looked as uneasy as a swain on his true love's front porch waiting to meet her father for the first time. His boyish looks that his evil counterpart didn't quite share certainly lent a lot to that comparison, which brought me back to our purpose here. He stuttered, "R-Rayna tells me the rebellion is on the march…that battle is soon at hand. I wish to help however I can."

"Good, because we need information-…" I attempted to jump right into the vigilante scout role I had filled for a decade in the rebellion, but Rayna instantly cut me off.

"Skies above, Mother, you're talking to him like he's not even a person!" my daughter declared, as Rhydin's face went through about sixteen shades of red. "Just…let me do the talking, okay? It's thanks to me we even know as much as we do, and he's *my* friend."

My mouth clamped shut. What had I said? I motioned for her to take over and occupied myself with giving Rhydin the third degree visually if I couldn't audibly.

Rayna grinned proudly before pretending that I was no longer present. She turned to Rhydin with a gleam in her eyes that I hadn't seen since before Sam died. "I'm glad you have more power because we have a lot of questions for you…"

Rhydin chuckled awkwardly, "That does not surprise me."

"…about Amelia," Rayna finished her sentence.

"That *does* surprise me." The young man ogled at us, color flushing his face again. "Why Amelia?"

"Well, she *is* the whole reason all of this happened," Rayna declared matter-of-factly, suddenly appearing very scholarly. "One could argue that if she'd just married you, none of this would have ever happened. No evil Rhydin, no banishment for you, no Allyens, no Duunzer…."

Rhydin grimaced. Even three hundred years later, the pain still seemed fresh upon his face. "I see your point."

Rayna started counting off on her fingers. "We know she came from money since she purchased Nora's farm, we know the Three Kings were trying to kill her for whatever reason but she believed she was innocent, her mother was captured, her sister was murdered, and I'm not so sure that she's not the one who killed Emperor Caden!"

I stared at Rayna bewildered. I hadn't heard any of that information, and that last revelation was difficult to stomach. However, with what I now understood of her visions, I believed her. After a beat of silence, I saw Rhydin genuinely laugh for the first time, which seemed very odd.

"Amelia?" he asked breathlessly as he tried to rein himself in, "Kill Caden? That is absurd. She could never harm even a fly."

"But she was there!" Rayna replied defensively as she stood and pointed at him. "She was there the night he was murdered with Nora! But Nora wasn't in the room where it happened, so I didn't see in there."

The smile slowly left Rhydin's face, his amethyst eyes filling with sorrow. "You are correct. She was there and witnessed it. She asked Nora to help her because I was here training, but she told me about it just before she broke things off between us."

I found myself leaning forward in my seat. Rayna looked like she was about to explode in anticipation. Both of us were frozen, barely breathing. The question of who killed Emperor Caden had been a mystery for centuries; it was the event that effectively established the Three Kingdoms and set our history in motion.

"Amelia didn't kill Caden," Rhydin said slowly, his eyes on the floor. "Her mother did."

"Her…her *mother?*" I burst, unable to stay silent any longer. "Why in Nerahdis would she do that? How did she even get into the palace?"

Rhydin swallowed, lifting his eyes to each of ours as he chose his words carefully. "Renae was one of Empress

Melodi's ladies-in-waiting for years until she died, even back in Gornan. She and Caden had a...*close* relationship during Melodi's illness and after she died. Amelia had gone to the palace to rescue her from the dungeon, but Renae had already escaped. She killed Caden for many reasons, but namely because he failed his daughters-...."

"Wait, wait, wait. His *daughters?*" Rayna interrupted. "What are you saying? Caden didn't have any daughters."

"Not...officially," Rhydin replied sheepishly, as if it was a taboo subject.

Rayna and I looked at each other as the information hit home. This changed *everything*.

Amelia was Emperor Caden's daughter. His illegitimate daughter with Renae.

Rayna had to sit down. I covered my mouth with my hands and leaned backward in my chair. It explained everything. Where Amelia had gotten the money to give Nora, why she couldn't be around Emperor Caden or his sons, and therefore why she'd broken off her betrothal to Rhydin. Why she was on the run in the first place, and why she believed herself to be innocent. It *all* fit.

"The real kicker is that Caden was already dying. That was why he was working so hard to find an Archimage to help his sons through the coming transition. He told me so himself, but absolutely no one else knew," Rhydin continued, appearing to be hundreds of miles away, "Renae was really just trying to reason with Caden, but he was so fragile at that point. Amelia swore to me that she truly believed her mother did not mean to kill him, but we will never truly know. Like I said, Renae's biggest motive for killing him was that he'd left their daughters absolutely nothing in the division of Nerahdis. Renae didn't expect kingdoms for them, just parcels of land as dowries to help them find suitable husbands despite their illegitimacy. She tried to get Caden to bequeath the Great Desert to Ariadne and Caark to Amelia, but he refused. Caden did not want Nerahdis to know of his infidelity or to suggest that his wife died due to his betrayal. Melodi died a couple of years *after* the affair began. With his death imminent, he wanted Nerahdis to be united and to trust his sons as their leaders. He feared that the girls would create instability in the brand new Three Kingdoms."

"What, so he tried to *kill* them? His own daughters?" Rayna gasped, desperate to know the answer.

"No, no, not at all." Rhydin was quick to answer, finally back in the moment. "It was the Three Kings who wanted them dead, who hunted them. Caden was perfectly happy to let them disappear into the world, but his sons didn't want any chance of them returning to take any portion of their inheritance. Amelia knew that from the start. She told me who she really was a few months after meeting her, much to Nora's dismay. She constantly lived in fear that one of her half-brothers would show up and kill her any second of the day, just as they did to Ariadne. It only became worse after Renae murdered Caden because then they also desired vengeance on top of wanting to eliminate her claim to any part of Nerahdis."

"That's why Nora was so fiercely protective of her," Rayna mused sadly, "aside from seeing herself in Amelia. A girl alone in the world."

The smallest of grins appeared on Rhydin's face. "Yes, it is. Nora was a force to be reckoned with. She didn't care that Amelia had magic; she killed more than one stray member of the Emperor's Guard whenever they came too close."

Rayna was nodding, the information still seeping in. I glanced between the two of them, wondering if I'd heard something he hadn't said. I stuttered, "I-I…I'm sorry, maybe I misheard you. Did you say *Amelia* had magic?"

"Well, of course," Rhydin answered simply. "She was a daughter of Caden. She possessed her own incredibly powerful type of Gornish magic never before seen. Just as Caden's sons had three very different, very powerful magics – fire, water, and air – Amelia and her sister did too."

"Really?" I exclaimed. I couldn't hardly believe it. "What kind of magic was it?"

Rhydin leveled his gaze at me, smiling at the memory of it. "Foliage."

"Foliage," I echoed in confused disbelief, "as in…leaves?"

Rayna made a face. "She must have gotten the short end of the genetic stick."

"Oh no, she was immensely powerful," Rhydin contradicted, his eyes wide like he was remembering something specific in particular. "Terrifying, in fact, although all magic was terrifying to me at the time. The biggest mistake those who hunted her made was to underestimate her. She was particularly adept with vines."

"What about Ariadne then? How did the guards kill her if she had magic too? And Renae was captured?" Rayna asked quizzically.

"The three of them ran from the palace when Joshuua, Ivann, and Spenser learned of Renae's intentions to give parts of Nerahdis to Ariadne and Amelia. They tried to kill them in the night, and they managed to escape. They had just reached the Lunakan border when a hundred of the Emperor's Guard caught up with them. Renae told the girls to run, but she was magic-less and Ariadne refused to leave her behind," Rhydin explained. "Ariadne had the power to shift the earth, throw boulders, and open up chasms. They told Amelia to run, and when she tried to stay, Ariadne used her magic to suck Amelia's feet into the earth and whisk that piece of earth miles away. They were so outnumbered; they had no hope regardless of Ariadne's power. Renae was already in custody when Ariadne spirited Amelia away, and Amelia felt her sister's magic die around her. She knew what had happened, so she kept running deeper into Lunaka…."

"Where she found Nora," Rayna finished for him, "and you."

Rhydin nodded sadly.

The three of us sat in silence for a few moments, Amelia's story complete. I shook my head in disbelief at how it'd all gone down. My old primary school teachers had always loved to come up with different theories of who killed Emperor Caden. One of his sons wanted all of Nerahdis, not just a third. A rogue Rounan who wanted to be in charge. A disgruntled servant. Actually, that one wasn't too far off. If only I could tell them that the perfect, golden Caden was trying to preserve his reputation, and his mistress killed him for it.

"Any other questions?" Rhydin asked suddenly, seeming keen to move on from the subject.

When I looked up, there was a hint of a gleam coming to his eyes. *Even after all this time,* I thought to myself, *he's still in love with her*.

"What happened to Renae then?" I asked.

"Renae told Amelia to run after she saw what her mother had done. Amelia was barely out the door and reunited with Nora when Joshuua came from the other direction. Renae did not leave that room alive," Rhydin answered darkly. "Joshuua handled it all himself, so nobody in the palace could ever link Caden and Renae. Thus, the mystery was born."

I nodded as I took it in. The desire to remain unblemished continued on.

"I've got one," Rayna announced, interrupting the moment. "I saw the moment your Einanhi was created. It happened out of nowhere, and you never said the incantation. How did it happen?

Rhydin suddenly looked down as if a wave of nausea overcame him. He shook his head, the muscle in his jaw tensing a couple times. His voice tremored, barely in check. "He…he filled me so full of all their different magics – Caden did. It was far too much. I had to *constantly* keep it in check, every day and night. It was like treading water in a sea of magic with weights attached to my ankles, and I succeeded in keeping my head up for two whole years."

"Why didn't you tell someone?" I found myself asking. Thankfully, my tone seemed more of motherly concern than accusatory.

"Caden wanted me to have the same powers as his sons and to be more powerful than them. That was the whole point of creating the Archimage position, what he envisioned for the role for which he chose me." Rhydin shook his head, becoming angrier by the minute. "He did not give me the powers his daughters inherited from him. He did not want me to be another Caden, only a mighty shadow keeping his sons in check. He should not have given me any at all. If only he could have grown my own capability for magic as the Ranguvariians did for Nora, this would have never happened."

Rayna and I glanced at each other, unsure of what to say.

"That day, I was in turmoil. I was miserable as Archimage. I so desperately wanted to go home to Lunaka and Amelia, but I *knew* I could not abandon my job. Caden was not wrong to create the Archimage position. His sons were so greedy and hated each other so much, they would have torn Nerahdis apart without supervision," Rhydin sneered in disgust. "I…I became so mentally consumed with the decision of whether to stay or go that just for a few seconds, I forgot to keep swimming. My head slipped under, and the magic broke out to solve the problem of wanting to be in two places at once. The Einanhi created itself. Then, he made me his shadow."

A memory came rushing back at me. It was when I'd been with the Ranguvariians last autumn for the meeting with the Aatarilec chieftess, and Sam had been there trying to secretly heal his poison. Arii had given me an in-depth lesson on the types of magic, and when he'd explained Rhydin, he filled a cup with a bead – which represented Rhydin's capability of creating or taking on magic – with several different kinds of other liquid. This turned the glass black and murky, and it caused it to overflow.

"This is what happened to Rhydin Caldwell. We know from the history book you found that he was made Archimage at eighteen years of age. Rather than cultivating his aptitude for magic as I did with Nora, Emperor Caden pumped him full of all three Gornish magics together. He was overwhelmed with powers unnatural to him, and as the cup loses its bearing on its water, so did Rhydin."

Of course, Arii designed this lesson before we knew that the Rhydin acting as emperor was actually an Einanhi – and before we knew there were actually *five* Gornish magics, for that matter – but he wasn't too far off in reality. Rhydin lost his bearing on his magic, and the Einanhi was born of that brief loss of control.

Rhydin sat quietly in his chair, shame written all over his face. I didn't know what to say; it was hard to not feel angry with him, even if I knew better. Why didn't he tell someone it was too much? Why did he let his feelings distract him? Why did he even agree to be Archimage in the first place?

"For the record, my father signed me up for the opportunity to be interviewed by Caden's Archimage search team," Rhydin suddenly piped up as if he had read my mind. "He could never pass up the opportunity for attention or prestige. 'Father of the Archimage' was evidently too good to pass up. I was clueless until they showed up at my doorstep and spoke to me. Caden had given them a tiny portion of his power to help sense whether the Archimage candidates had the magical proclivity they sought. I was the only one they ever found who could do it, so I lost my choice in the matter."

Rayna fell into a chair, immediately slumping backward with her arms crossed over her chest. "So stupid," she huffed.

I groaned quietly as I leaned forward and raked my hands through my hair. Then, I just held my hands against my face for a few seconds, letting it all sink in. The fact that we knew all the answers at long last. The history that our forefathers had so tirelessly tried to wipe away was finally laid bare.

"At least we know now," I mumbled as I folded my hands in front of me. "We can't change the past. This knowledge will help us go toward the future the best we can manage." I turned to Rhydin, meeting his eyes for longer than a millisecond for the first time. "Thank you for your honesty. I'm sure it wasn't easy."

"It is nice to have a reason to use my voice," Rhydin replied sardonically, a fake smile plastered to his face.

"I'll do you one better," Rayna said gruffly before staring him down, "I'll free you. I promise."

Rhydin nodded sadly. Disbelief plagued his expression, and I hoped Rayna couldn't see it. "I wish you all the success in the world," he responded quietly.

I took a deep breath, still in the throes of absorbing Amelia and Rhydin's story. A tale of heartache and deception. Then I stood, stretching, feeling sorer than what seemed possible although still much improved after Rachel's last healing session. My wound felt better than it had in days. "Looks like we'll make it back to the rebellion with plenty of time to spare before the battle."

Rayna only bobbed her head once or twice, her eyes immediately falling to her lap.

It was then that I caught sight of the windows along the very upper rim of the library walls. The deep colors of sunset were pouring in from above the towering bookshelves, and I could hardly believe my eyes. "It's already evening," I gasped. Had we really been that enraptured by the tale of the emperor's daughter?

Neither Rhydin nor Rayna acknowledged me, but I began digging through my bag for the food I'd packed anyway. My stomach was suddenly as ravenous as a bear coming out of winter hibernation. I was just about to sink my teeth into some of the salted pork, my hand outstretched to Rayna with the other half of what I'd brought, when Rayna suddenly asked, "How did Nora die?"

I paused with my food just inches from mouth, confused. Where did that come from?

Rhydin seemed surprised too, his translucence fading a bit. He glanced at me for barely a second before swallowing hard and meeting Rayna's gaze.

"She was hanged."

Chapter Nineteen

Rayna

"Hanged?" I echoed in shock. My mother's hands fell back to her lap along with her food. "Why in Nerahdis was she *hanged?* She saved them all from the evil Rhydin and Duunzer!"

Irritation and annoyance were written all over Rhydin Caldwell's glowing translucent face. "No one knew that. There were no witnesses to her fight against my Einanhi and his Einanhi dragon. Twenty-five years had passed since that time, and by then, the new narrative was established. My existence was struck from every corner of life. Books were rewritten, and portraits were burned. My clone murdered my parents and razed my hometown of Diagalo during his first reign as emperor. The people who lived during that time became terrified of magic and imparted that fear unto their children and grandchildren. Most importantly, the First Three Kings determined that commoners possessing magic should be illegal and put to death."

The blood left my mother's face. She looked like she was going to be sick.

"What's wrong, Mama?" I asked her. I knew her upbringing was different than what mine had been on Caark among all the Rounan refugees, but still.

She started wringing her hands, her food totally forgotten in her lap. "That…that law has caused so much pain. I've seen people be executed in Soläna's central square just on the *suspicion* of having magic, almost always Rounans. I spent my first several months as an Allyen terrified that I would be taken and hanged too. I lived underneath the Owenses' livery for weeks with Frederick. I never understood why they couldn't just check them for the Rounan marks, but suddenly it makes sense. People like Nora and Rhydin – and us Allyens too – don't have any physical signs. They weren't just persecuting Rounans-…"

"They were trying to ensure that someone like us would never exist again," Rhydin finished for me, his mouth in a flat line. "Just, over the generations, the 'why' was forgotten."

"So, Nora was killed for having magic?" I repeated back. *For forging her own magic*, my mind added. "What about her husband, Charles? I saw their graves, and he died the same year."

Rhydin scowled. "They were hanged side by side. Guilty by association. Nothing more. Neither of them deserved to die the way they did, but Nora was too stubborn to leave her land and go into hiding. I was relieved to learn their son was away when they were arrested. He survived."

"Would that be Allyen Myron?" my mother asked. "Arii told me his name once."

"Yes," Rhydin answered. "Nora's land remained abandoned for decades, but a rumor came into the Archimage later that someone had come to claim it. Myron returned to Soläna under a different name with his adult children. No one knew he was an Allyen too; I assume he must have hidden the locket to greatly lessen his magical presence. The title became a myth over the centuries."

The library suddenly melted around me into a different scene altogether. I was back in Nora's body. The roar of a crowd surrounded me, but I couldn't see much beyond the noose that dangled ahead of me. Up beyond their blurry bodies, I could make out the dark walls of the canyon in Soläna. Nora rotated her head to the left where a man stood next to her on a wooden stage, a noose facing him as well. He was an average height – not tall but not short either, although I wondered whether Nora might be taller than him – and had dark hair streaked with silver.

Nora was shaking with anger. I could feel it in how she fought against the bonds tying her scarred hands behind her back. No locket graced her breastbone; it must be with Myron. More memories were flashing through her mind as Charles smiled sadly at her. They'd met in the forest one day shortly after Amelia came into Nora's life. She was hunting; he was fishing. Nora spent the first year of their association ignoring him and making sure he knew how much she found him annoying. But he was always around. He fought alongside her whenever the Emperor's Guard came close to finding Amelia. He mended her arm when she broke it falling out of a tree once and brought her fish. He helped her through Amelia's death and went with her to the Ranguvariians. It took a year for her to call him friend and years more before he was anything more. It wasn't hard to see that she wore the pants.

As Charles stepped up to his noose and nodded to her that it was okay – whispering that he'd do it all over again – I could feel the depth of Nora's love for him, her desire to sweep in and save him. I briefly wondered why she didn't until she glanced behind her and I got a view of what waited behind them.

Hundreds of armed soldiers, if not thousands. What appeared to be three generations of Lunakan Royals all with their hands outstretched toward her. Even with the help of the locket's amplification, their escape would be iffy. Without it, there was no point in even trying. Nora's eyes skimmed the rim of the canyon up above. No Ranguvariians. Either too little in number from their population being decimated by Duunzer, or no idea the aging Allyen was in danger in her own home.

Something prodded Nora in the back, and as she hesitantly approached her own noose, I was transported to yet a different memory. A small, dark room in what appeared to be a log cabin greeted me, and Nora was sprawled out on a bed, cradling something in her arms. It didn't take long to figure out that it was a baby, some twenty years before Nora would face the noose.

"That's the only one you get," Nora grunted in her husky tone as Charles approached her cautiously, and she slid the baby into his arms. He was much younger, maybe mid-thirties, with jet black hair.

"Oh, come now. You make it seem like he's the last cookie or something," the man laughed. "He at least looks like he could be my son."

Nora grumped and rolled her eyes, but she seemed happy on the inside. Based on the memories I'd seen, their relationship seemed to be founded on giving the other as hard a time as possible. But something dark suddenly settled within her as she gazed at her child. She was serious for once as she said, "He's another Allyen, Charles. I can feel it."

Charles's dark brow furrowed. "How is that possible? Your power is created, not genetic."

"When Arii helped me grow my magic, it was based upon my desire for vengeance," Nora mused quietly, her eyes trained off into space which made everything blurry to my viewpoint. "If my magic has been passed on, I think it means Rhydin is still alive. That I have not yet accomplished my revenge for Amelia."

"How is that possible?" Charles asked slowly, still processing her words. "You destroyed Duunzer, and he disappeared too. You killed them both."

Nora noiselessly rolled over in bed away from Charles and baby Myron, tucking the blankets around her into a cocoon as she did. She whispered, staring at the now white scars on her hands, "Maybe I failed."

All at once, I was back in the library at the Archimage Palace. The vast room had become eerily dark now that the sun had set aside from one small oil lamp that my mother must have lit. She gazed at me expectantly while Rhydin Caldwell seemed anxious as he looked me up and down.

"What did you see?" Mama asked. Her food was still untouched in her lap.

I rubbed my head, still fuzzy from the memories, and tried to string words together. "I saw…two things. I saw the day they died. They were…hanged in Soläna, surrounded by a gigantic crowd and hundreds of soldiers. Myron had the locket, and no Ranguvariians were there to help." I shuddered, still reeling from her feeling of inevitable death. "Then I saw Myron's birth. Nora was surprised he was an Allyen. She thought it meant she had failed to kill Rhydin."

Rhydin Caldwell blinked once or twice. "Well, she was not wrong. Her magic has lived as long as my havoc-wreaking Einanhi has."

My mother briefly gave him a look before staring at her lap and whispering, "How sad."

Emperor Rhydin's voice droned through my head yet again. "*…not even the great Nora Soreta could escape her fate. Neither will you.*"

I shuddered again.

Silence consumed us. After a few moments' worth showed us that we were all out of questions, my mother stood, handed me half of the food she had packed, and expressed the desire to get some fresh air before finding a place to sleep for the night.

My eyes followed her out of the room until she was out of sight, and then stared at the food I'd been given. Salted pork, an apple, and a small roll of bread. I felt too distracted to eat, but my stomach wasn't taking no as an answer. I bit off a chunk of apple, appreciating its crisp sweetness first before taking on the chewy meat and the stale, bland roll.

It was a few moments before I realized Rhydin was awkwardly eyeing me every so often from where he sat at his desk. I struggled to swallow, feeling self-conscious. "What is it? Do I have food on my face?"

A mite more color came to Rhydin's pale, translucent face, although it really couldn't be called a blush. "No," he chuckled nervously, "I just never dreamed I would ever miss food so much."

"Oh…" I breathed. My heart dropped into the pit of my stomach as my eyes dropped to what was left of my meal in my lap. "I'm so sorry. I didn't realize-…"

"Do not apologize. Please eat," Rhydin replied. He nodded at me and smiled once more before I was willing to pick it up again. I began eating as quickly as I could manage without making it appear that I was doing so as Rhydin looked back to his papers. "My mother used to make these amazing apple turnovers when I was a boy. I used to make her so upset when I would smear Mineraltin nut butter on them. She thought I ruined their flavor that way, but I always that they were delicious."

I tossed my apple core, swallowed the rest of my bread in one scratchy bite, and nibbled on my pork from behind my hands. "Sounds pretty tasty to me. I'm sure you miss her."

Rhydin nodded sadly. "She was a good mother, but she was just as afraid of my father as I was. Our best days were when he was away checking on his workers in Diagalo. Our manor was just outside the town right next to the lake you all now call Spenser's Lake."

"It must seem strange to you," I mused, thinking out loud, "that we've idolized the First Three Kings so much that we named landmarks after them. Caden, too."

"Not that strange." The specter shook his head. "I am the only outsider that truly knew the Royals personally. The

Archimages who came after me were all second-born Royals, already privy to their secrets. Sometimes, I wonder if that is another reason they erased me."

My head bobbed up and down on its own accord, my mind lost in history.

"While I thoroughly enjoy having someone with whom to talk, I recommend you get some rest, Rayna," Rhydin said as he stood from his desk, a small smile on his face. "You will certainly need it for the coming battle.

I sighed, my anxiety flaring. "I'm sure you're right," I groaned. I stood, ready to go in search of my mother and an intact bed somewhere in the palace.

Rhydin walked with me toward the main hall, his translucent form pulsing in brightness with every step. He had a couple books tucked under his arm, which were fully tangible. Likely proof of his growing power. Corners of maps and charts with various dots and designs on them stuck out of the books haphazardly, and I wondered what they detailed. We reached the midnight-colored grand staircase, which slowly transformed along the spectrum of grays until it reached a snow white at the very top. A couple floors up, Rhydin gestured and said, "Your mother is on this floor, one of the last doors on the right. It was her room when she stayed here once. You were barely a year old if I recall."

I studied him briefly – what must it be like to have seen so many come and go? So many generations born and die? I thanked him and began walking down the hall, but I stopped when I realized Rhydin began to climb the staircase again instead of going back down. I called after him, "What do you do at night? Do you sleep?"

Rhydin chuckled. "I rest sometimes, especially when I run out of energy to be visible like this, but I usually do what I always wanted to do while growing up."

"What's that?" I asked, my curiosity overtaking me.

He smiled. "I have been alive for three hundred and forty-nine years, and I have charted the stars every night for just shy of that time. I never wanted to be Archimage. I wanted to be an astronomer."

I eyed the books stuffed with hand-drawn charts again as I remembered all of the astronomy tools I'd seen in the palace tower the day his clone came to life. "I'd say you *are* an astronomer."

Rhydin's face slackened with surprise, and I could have sworn his amethyst eyes became a little misty. Then, he put on a brave face, whispered a quiet "thank you," and went on his way.

I fumbled through the dark hallway until I saw Mathiian standing outside one of the bedroom doors. He nodded at me, resulting in the *clink* of unseen armor under his buttercup-yellow tunic. I almost shuffled past him with nothing more than a smile, but then I thought better of it. I threw my arms around his lanky form, and he stiffened in confusion. The memory of Nora scanning the canyon rim for any Ranguvariian who could save her played in my mind. Was Nora's untimely death the reason the *Alyen nou Clarii* was created? The Allyen bodyguards that I'd never been without during my whole life? And my mother's and uncle's lives?

"Tell every *Alyen nou Clarii* you know thank you for me," I said softly into his pointed ear before disappearing through the black doorway and sliding into the four-poster bed next to my slumbering mother.

Before I knew it, the hours flew by, and the gauzy curtains draped over the eastern windows were faintly aglow with the pink hues of sunrise. I briefly considered rolling over and trying to sleep a couple more hours, but there was no hope of that after I realized I was alone in the bed.

My mother's short, muscular frame was stark against the lightening windows, and she turned to face me when the bed squeaked as I leaned forward. As my eyes adjusted, I realized that she was wearing armor now, which I'd never seen her wear before. A tunic of chainmail reached halfway down her thighs with sleeves as long as her elbows. Thick leather vambraces were belted to her forearms, but her hands were left bare for magic. She wore a fitted, heavy leather breastplate over the chainmail, but her regular, old trousers poked out from underneath. A coil of dull brown braids topped her head, which were wrapped around Papa's navy, purple, and gold bandana, the tails touching her back. The hair style revealed silver wings of hair around her ears, which usually weren't visible, just beneath the silver crown of wheat that matched King Frederick's.

My heart quivered at the sight. "You look as if the battle is today."

"If the Rhydin I have fought for my entire life has taught me anything, it's to be prepared for anything," she answered, before she reached out to me. "Come. Mathiian has brought armor for you too. I think it would be best if we rejoined the rebellion as soon as possible."

I nodded and let her take me by the hand. I stood awkwardly in the middle of the room as my mother dragged a similar set of chainmail over my head. My mind wandered aimlessly as she buckled a nearly identical set of leather armor on top of my chainmail, and then she methodically attempted to do something about my short, unruly waves of hair that I'd chopped so fiercely after Papa's death. She settled on braiding back several chunks of it at a time before twisting it all up in the back, and I watched her hands bob back and forth, her two wedding rings from her two husbands blinking at me. When I saw my reflection in the mirror, I looked more like my old long-haired self than I had in a long time, even if my outfit was totally foreign aside from the familiar edges poking out from underneath the chainmail.

"I forgive you," I said, out of nowhere, "for remarrying. And for not telling me the truth about my birth."

She seemed surprised. "Oh? I am grateful, but what brought that on?"

I thought for a moment, considering the weight of my words. "Everything you and Papa have ever done has been to keep Kylar and I safe, which meant leaving us in Caark for twelve years. It's not like you had an opportunity to tell me the truth during all that time away, and I'm not mad at you for it. You let us grow up and have a normal childhood. To at least experience normal life a little. Then, Papa asked Frederick to make sure we were taken care of, and you married him to bring peace to the rebellion even though you didn't want to."

I stopped briefly and met her eyes. "Do you know the real reason Rhydin and Amelia's story is so sad and why all of Nerahdis has had to deal with the fallout? Those two were pretty much set up for failure by people who were only thinking about themselves, and the whole world has had to deal with the consequences ever since. Caden wanted to keep his reputation. Rhydin's father wanted the honor of being the Archimage's father. Caden's sons didn't want to share Nerahdis with their two illegitimate sisters. You've only ever acted for others."

My mother's eyes were wide, and she blushed before looking down. "I'm not a saint, Rayna. I've made decisions I'm not proud of in my life, before and after you were born. It's easy for people to argue that I stole you from Frederick and that I only married him for security-…"

"People who don't know you or the whole story," I insisted as I lay my hand on top of hers. "I don't envy the choices you've had to make. I just wanted you to know that I don't hold them against you anymore. You did the best you could."

Mama's chin quivered. She wrapped her short arms around me, our chainmail making a crunching sound. I was the same height as her, I realized just as she pulled away. She cleared her throat and met my gaze. "Are you ready?"

We weren't speaking of the past anymore. It didn't matter anymore now that the crux of the future was at hand. I forced myself to nod as I slid my faithful dagger into its sheath. "Yes."

The two of us left the room after one last look and made our way downstairs. Both Mathiian and the translucent

Rhydin Caldwell stood in the hall awaiting us. Mathiian was adorned in a little more battle gear than he typically wore on the daily over his yellow tunic while Rhydin stood awkwardly to the side. My mother paused a moment in front of the specter as their eyes met, and an entire unspoken conversation seemed to occur between them. I kept waiting for her to give some sort of parting remark, such as an "I'm sorry for what happened to you" or "don't worry, we'll be back," but nothing more than "thank you for all your help" ever passed her lips. Rhydin's eyes fell to the floor, emotions warring for control of his face.

No sooner than Mathiian disappeared with my mother did I approach Rhydin. Instinctually, I put my hands on his and almost jumped. He was more solid than I'd expected at this point, but his hands were like coldest ice. They were soft though, the hands of someone who had never labored in his life, of someone whose passion lay with quill and parchment. I mumbled, "I hope I see you again."

Rhydin smiled warmly. "I have a feeling that I will, but even if I don't," he paused momentarily as he realized what he was unintentionally implying, "er…regardless of what happens, thank you for being my friend."

I gulped. "Don't mention it."

"Rayna, I…I did not mean it that way, I swear-…" He clutched my hands tighter.

"I know," I whispered past the frog in my throat, desperate to play it cool. I gently pulled my fingers out from his grip as Mathiian reappeared. "I'm glad to have met you."

Rhydin Caldwell had a forlorn expression on his pale face as Mathiian gallantly scooped me up, and we disappeared in a flash. The white void in between destinations seemed extra fast with me lost in my thoughts, wondering whether I really *would* see the real Rhydin again, and we reappeared in mid-air.

We were high above the slow-marching column of rebels inching their way through the Lunakan countryside to the southwest. The rebellion had just passed the western turnoff toward the city of Lun, and our numbers were still growing as more and more pockets joined up along the way. Hundreds of Ranguvariians now flanked each side of the main line of rebels with dozens more in the air lower than us; their existence was certainly never going to be a secret ever again. I didn't see many Aatarilecs yet, but I'd overheard someone saying that most of them would transport to the source of the river that fed Spenser's Lake which then turned into the two main rivers that serviced eastern Lunaka.

Mathiian was scanning the ground, searching for a good spot to land. I was still gazing at my parents' kingdom, never having been this high up in the air before, when I noticed something dark so far away over the mountains that it looked like an ant. I squinted, trying to see better but to no avail. The spot was in the very same direction we were heading.

Just as Mathiian tried to make his descent, I pointed and said, "What is that? Over there?"

The teenage Ranguvariian boy shrugged awkwardly with me still in his arms. "Good question. I could ask my mother to check it out?"

I rolled my eyes. "Oh, come on, we're already up here. Just transport over there real quick to get a good look at it."

Mathiian groaned. "Fine! But you're explaining this to my mother if we get into trouble!"

Instantly, we transported as close to the magic-less boundary of the mountains as Mathiian could manage. The gargantuan rocky faces were now blocking the view of whatever dark thing I had seen, so Mathiian flew upward, straining to get up high enough to see over Caden's Peak. He gasped with the effort, and I found myself breathing a little harder too as the air thinned and chilled.

At long last, Mathiian was able to shift enough to the side that we could see beyond Nerahdis's tallest mountain, and my heart plumb left my body and plunged to the grassy foothills far below.

"I think Aunt Rachel is going to be the least of your problems," I panted as Mathiian's eyes seeped through every color before landing on a dark, golden color like the shade of an ancient gold coin.

It was no longer one dark spot on the horizon. While it was still dozens of miles away, it was still clearly crossing the boundary where the mighty trees of Mineraltir abutted the southern edge of the grassy heart of Nerahdis.

Emperor Rhydin's armies were going to beat the rebellion to the northeastern high ground of Caden's Plain.

Chapter Twenty

Lina

"You're telling me that *all this time*, the greatest man in Nerahdian history is actually *not*, and his mysterious murder was actually due to a quarrel between lovers and not some big conspiracy against him?" Frederick levelled his gaze at me as he spoke for the first time in several minutes after listening to my story with his mouth agape. He was astride a large, white stallion while I walked the road to Caden's Plain alongside him, having only just arrived moments earlier.

"I know," I chuckled as I answered the one part he hadn't said out loud. It did sound crazy.

Frederick's icy eyes narrowed from atop his horse. "And we're *sure* we can trust this…this ghost? *Rhydin's* ghost?"

"I know it sounds completely insane," I admitted, my eyes trained on the dirt of the road ahead before I began to ramble, "but yes. Every detail of his story makes sense and links with what we already know. And he's not a *ghost*. I mean, he is Rhydin, but a different, younger-looking Rhydin, and I think he is *technically* alive but-…"

"Wait, you saw him?" Frederick was so surprised he nearly caused his horse to come to a halt. "I thought only Rayna could see him?"

I shrugged. "I guess he's gained enough power back as the Rhydin we know degenerates that all the Allyens can see him now. We all have created magic. Rayna is just more so since she wasn't born an Allyen."

"I see," Frederick mused. "My ancestors have always been born with magic since the very beginning of time. Or at least, so I'm told. With how much the Gornish land-hopped over so many generations, first to Rounia and then to Nerahdis, their history of Gornan's beginnings is completely forgotten."

"Hmm," I uttered absent-mindedly as I stared at the mountains ahead of us. They were growing closer, but it would still be two days before we reached them and managed to reach the far side at the rate we were marching.

I became so lost in thought that I almost forgot Frederick was there until he suddenly chided himself. "Ack! I apologize, I do not mean to make you walk! Would you like to ride with me?"

He extended a hand, and his stallion slowed. I glanced at his hand briefly; I was more than capable of mounting that horse all by myself regardless of how tall it was. Frederick knew that. The thought of him wanting to hold my hand even just for a moment felt warm in my mind, even as guilt arose in my chest. The shame only concentrated more as I realized I wanted to hold his hand, too.

Without a word, I accepted his hand, placed one foot in the stirrup recently abandoned by Frederick's boot, and swung my leg over to sit behind him in the saddle. As he squeezed his horse back into its leisurely walk, I contemplated what to do with my hands before settling them innocently on either side of his hips rather than wrapping my arms around his waist. Surely, this was harmless, right? Practically all human beings who rode behind another on a horse had to hold on somehow.

I'd pretty much mentally talked myself into that theory aside from the fact that I felt like my palms were burning with shame where the leather of Frederick's belt rubbed. My face flushed, and I was instantly thankful that Frederick was in front of me and not behind me where he could see. Although, I desperately wanted to know what his expression looked like.

I'd come to accept that Sam would want me to be happy. Even the people of the rebellion were in favor of this new marriage so quick after Sam's death. I used to be afraid of whether I could grow to love Frederick the way he seemed to already love me. My care for him was indeed growing…but would it ever be love?

It was a moment before I realized there was shouting, my line of sight blocked by Frederick's tall frame directly in front of me. The long, lumbering line of rebels, horses, and wagons came to a halt. Frederick's horse turned to the left a bit, which allowed me more of a view.

We were near the front of the now stilled mass of people, and to my surprise, I saw Rayna and Mathiian. They were standing just a few feet away with Rachel and Xavier, who had been in the lead, and the two redheaded adults rapidly shared the teens' wide-eyed fear. Rachel and Xavier immediately sprang into action as those around them suddenly began to panic. Rachel's *matrii* glowed as she rattled off directions to Jaspen, and Xavier rushed to calm those around them.

One by one, the rebels began to abandon their traveling cloaks, unbuckling them right where they stood in the road. Some began to rummage through their bags for any last-minute supplies while others checked whatever armor they happened to wear or put on more. My heart hammered faster and faster until the message finally reached us as it traveled through our caravan.

Emperor Rhydin's forces were already enroute to meet us, and as of now, they would beat us to the high ground we so desperately needed on the northeastern edge of Caden's Plain.

My breath left me as if I'd been punched in the gut. I gasped as Frederick rotated around in his seat to face me, "What are we going to do?"

"If I know Rachel," Frederick answered as he slipped off the horse and shrugged off his own cloak, "I am sure she has a plan. We better follow everyone else's suit."

I nodded numbly as I swung my leg back over the horse, and Frederick gripped my waist to steady me on my descent. His eyes latched to mine for only second, like he was testing the waters between us to see if that touch was okay, before he turned his attention to making sure he had everything he needed for battle. I busied myself with shedding my cloak, triple-checking the buckles of my armor, and ascertaining that my sword and all my throwing knives were accounted for. Then, I chugged a few mouthfuls from my water pouch before doing as the rest of the rebels were doing and setting it and whatever else we didn't need for battle on the ground at my feet.

The rebels around us had erupted into chaos and panic as Frederick and I readied ourselves, but they came to a stop in an instant as dozens of shadows suddenly started racing across the ground unlike anything I'd ever seen. My gaze shot to the sky, and my jaw dropped to the earth.

Hundreds of Ranguvariians were darting back and forth overhead, even more than had originally been accompanying us on this march. The bulk of the Ranguvariian population was to meet us at Caden's Plain in two days, but now they all zigged and zagged over our heads, transporting in with their bright tunics like bursts of color. They began to land all around us, choosing spots at random to touch down, grab the nearest readied rebel, and vanish in a blink of light. Then, minutes later, the same Ranguvariian would reappear in the midst of the crowd and transport another rebel, all happening so fast I could barely register it.

"Where are they going?" I yelled above the ruckus of people murmuring, great Ranguvariian wings beating, and the *poofs* of transportation.

My question hadn't been aimed toward anyone in particular, but a nearby Ranguvariian happened to hear as she threw her long, lanky arm around a middle-aged man and prepared to transport. "Are shorten the journey to Caden's Plain, we. Shall lose the high ground, otherwise," the fierce warrior rattled off in a thick accent before disappearing with her passenger.

The wind left Frederick's sails. "If we don't have the high ground on the other side of the mountains, we will never stand a chance. The battle will be over before it even begins."

My stomach flip-flopped. I glanced left and right as rebels were plucked and transported instantly without another step, any belongings not needed for warfare left behind where they once stood. Any wagons we didn't need were abandoned while the ones containing weapons were hefted into the sky by five or six Ranguvariians pumping their powerful wings before speeding them up and over the mountains.

I wondered what they could see now at our final destination.

We were supposed to have two more days just to get to Caden's Plain. It could have been as much as a week before Rhydin's forces came to meet us from their base in the Great Desert. We were supposed to have time to get there at our own pace, establish our position, and rest.

It wasn't supposed to happen like this!

The Ranguvariians only reappeared long enough to touch their next rebel – after all, there were thousands of us and only hundreds of them – and they soon began to show the strain of their efforts. Their eyes were golden with fear, brown with nerves, red with anger, and gray with exhaustion. Once or twice, I saw a Ranguvariian I knew; Jaspen, James, Bartholomiiu, Rachel. I never saw Arii, but perhaps he was already at Caden's Plain.

As the number of humans began to dwindle, the older, more experienced Ranguvariians began taking the horses. They'd fling themselves into saddles far too small for them or hug the horse's neck before they vanished into the white void of transportation. I couldn't imagine how adept at transportation a Ranguvariian would have to be in order to transport something as huge and heavy as a horse.

The rest of the Royals were already gone, along with all our teenage children. I never even saw Rosetta and Erikin, despite my plans to find my sister and finally talk to her about everyone during the journey. Frederick and I scanned the road and the horizon, making sure nobody was being left behind even as we deserted enough possessions and other gear to keep traveling bandits busy for weeks. The elderly and the youngest of children were huddled under one of the larger trees with one of the covered wagons nearby. In a way, I was thankful they would be left here and not present if we lost.

As the last dozen or so stragglers – all of fighting age – waited for their turn, I noticed that Frederick had turned to face me. His voice was almost unreadable as he said, "It looks like our battle is about to begin."

"I think you're right," I murmured as I turned toward him, my voice betraying the emotions I was feeling. "What if we aren't ready?"

Frederick took both of my hands in his. I barely felt it. "I am proud to fight beside you. I know the circumstances of our marriage were not ideal…but if I fall today, I want you to know that I have never regretted any part of it. In fact, I wish I could have been your husband for much longer than I had the privilege to be."

I couldn't look at him. Seconds turned into hours. What magic allowed him to be so eloquent and kind all the time? Pressure was mounting in my chest as I pondered my response. Part of me wanted to lean forward and kiss him for the first time. For real. The other part of me panicked at the thought, so instead I met his gaze and said firmly, "When will you get it through your thick head that I'll never let you fall?"

The king paused as he absorbed the hidden meaning to my words, and a flicker of hope danced in his sky-blue eyes as his mouth crept upward into a small smile. Before he could reply, two Ranguvariian warriors popped up nearby and barreled toward us. I couldn't help but grin in return just as I flung my arm out in the direction of the Ranguvariians. The male latched on the moment he could reach, and the world immediately became white.

When we landed, the rebellion was in chaos. The ground was now a rocky slope beneath our feet as we scanned the southern foothills of Lunaka's mountains. Frederick had already put on his king voice and was barking orders at anybody within earshot, and the rebels, who were scrambling like ants desperate to find their hill in a rainstorm, suddenly slowed before setting off determinedly.

As Frederick headed off to help them find the wagons to make sure all our weapons were passed out fairly, I noticed another large group of rebels staring at me expectantly with wide eyes. My heart shuddered, and my breaths became shaky. I'd never been in *charge* before. As a young Allyen, I'd frequently fought on my own with maybe one or two others, or I made decisions in conjunction with Rachel. I was Kidek in Sam's place *very* briefly during the war, and that was a disaster. As a rebel fighter, I'd led a very small team, of which June was one, and now served as Kidek in Kylar's place, but none of the decisions thus far had remotely been on this scale. Not life and death. Not for the *entire* rebellion.

Now, I wasn't just Lina, Allyen Linaria, or even the Kidek's wife or mother.

I was Queen of Lunaka. The crown on my head said so.

Instinct kicked in. I knew the battle plan. The entire rebellion had been present for that Council meeting a while back. I bellowed, "If you still need your weapons, go after King Frederick! Archers, set up your lines here. Everybody else, move toward the plain!"

I spent the next several minutes repeating the same instructions until there were no longer any rebels near me appearing lost and confused. The air was becoming eerily silent as people found their positions and their peace before the storm. Soon, only the archers were around, and once I entrusted them to Mira's command, I began to skid down the silty hill toward the rest of the action. As I did, I noticed the end of an abandoned bow poking out of a cropping of rocks, so I snagged it on my way down. Just as I looped it over my head after testing its strength, I caught a glimpse of a darkness growing upon the opposite end of the grassy expanse of Caden's Plain.

They were visible now, and they were approaching at an unhuman speed. The sun was almost directly overhead.

I rushed down toward the main body of the rebellion even faster, giving directions to anyone I happened to pass. All the horses the Ranguvariians had brought were now wearing their protective gear, and the foothills were teeming with nervous energy. The grass was brown and crisp, but new growth was peeping out from underneath with the coming of spring. The four wagons that had been flown over were spaced evenly among the troops, and people were lining up on either side. When I spotted Evan at the center left one, I made my way toward him.

"Lina!" my brother called when he noticed my approach. He was already done up in his armor, his sword sheathed at his side, and he eyed the bow over my shoulder. "Want some arrows to go with that? I hear you're quite the shot."

I chuckled darkly as I accepted the full quiver handed to me. "If only it was just one Einanhi dragon, eh?"

He shrugged. "At least there's no Darkness to worry about."

"Where's Rayna?" I asked as I caught a glimpse of Evan's part of the Allyen locket around his neck.

"She's over there at that wagon with Taisyn and the other kids." Evan nodded at the next wagon over. "Don't worry. She'll find us when it's time. We need to get her part of the locket first anyway. I sent her over there to tell Aron and the heirs to head up the mountain."

"Good idea," I whispered. Then, I meaningfully met his eyes and put my hand upon his shoulder. "I didn't know you existed for the first twenty years of my life. I'm glad to have you as my brother."

Evan balked. "Don't get sappy on me. You're a halfway decent sister," he said sarcastically, and then asked, "Do you think our father would be proud?"

Robert's face flashed in my mind from the last time I saw him before Kino killed him. Gaunt, his formerly empty Allyen eyes with a spark in them once again. He may have been disillusioned by Rhydin's false promises of power and protection for him and his children, but at the very end, he finally saw through the fog and tried to make it right. I answered thoughtfully, "Yeah, I think he would. All he ever wanted was for us to be safe, and all of Nerahdis will be safe once Rhydin is destroyed."

My brother nodded bashfully, his eyes a million miles away. I squeezed his shoulder wordlessly and set out for the front of our mass. I waded through a sea of soldiers, no longer just regular men and women. They stood in clumps, either muttering to each other or standing in silence. Some were making their peace while others chewed grass. Weapons were sharp, armor was tight. There was nothing more to do except wait for the war horns.

Some people reached out to touch me as I passed, patting my shoulders or the hilt of my sword. The Rounans pounded their chests in salute, and the Gornish gave the custom half-bow. They knew the role I must play in this battle, the Allyen key to our victory. It was like each one them passed a bit of their strength to me as I went, and I bottled it all up against the butterflies I was beginning to feel in my stomach.

Frederick was reunited with his horse now, and he stood in charge of this section. Down the line, I could see Xavier on one end and Sabine on the other, each of them flanked by rebels and Ranguvariians. As the wind picked up, the clouds high above our heads began to grow thicker and grayer. I was just noticing that the Aatarilecs were beginning to trickle over the hill from their watery grotto when someone tapped me on my shoulder yet again.

Clariion Arii stood tall and magnificent in his warrior's regalia; decorative beads and threads were too numerous to count all across his robe. My brow furrowed. "What are you doing down here? Most of the Ranguvariians are up the hill to be air support as long as they can until more Aatarilecs are here to cancel out the effect of Rhydin's magic."

"I have placed Rachel in charge," Arii answered in his mellow voice as he touched one of his large, pointed ears. "I am here to help you get Rayna's locket piece back."

A wave of emotion threatened to overtake me. "Thank you," I responded breathlessly, suddenly feeling like the invisible burden I bore was just a few ounces lighter.

Arii nodded and flew away to give Rachel one last set of directions. I turned to find where I wanted to stand when it began when I suddenly recognized the head of dark blonde and gray hair tied in a low bun in front of me. I touched her shoulder, and Rosetta rotated to meet my eyes, dressed in armor just like everyone else. I asked in confusion, "What are you doing down here? I thought you were going to be up with the archers."

My little sister shook her head and smiled sadly. "Mikael taught me to fight, and I want to be down here with you. I made Erikin go up the hill though."

Her words touched my heart, but I wouldn't let myself cry now. I needed to get my truth out in the open before it was too late. Time to rip off the bandage. "Rosetta, I've been meaning to tell you...*I'm* the one who killed Mikael. It was an accident, I swear. He was trying to kill Frederick, I was only trying to disarm him...but I'm so very sorry. I never wanted to hurt you, or Mikael."

Rosetta's hazel eyes widened. A flurry of emotions crossed her face, ending with grief. She took a minute to breathe, her eyes fluttering closed, and I felt like I was holding my breath the entire time. She measured my terrified expression and replied quietly, "I know you would never hurt me. I've had a lot of time to think about this.... Even if things had played out differently, he would have still died…whether it was a different rebel who killed him or Rhydin for losing Lunaka Castle. I…could never get him away from Rhydin like I wanted. I forgive you. My son and I are free thanks to you."

My heart swelled with relief, and I flung my arms around her, holding her tight. "Thank you," I choked as I tried to keep from crying, months' worth of stress vanishing from my shoulders.

The air was split by the blare of a war horn, and Rosetta and I jumped apart. Others replied to the signal, adding their long blasts to make the sound carry even farther on the cool wind. Everyone around me stilled, and in unison we all faced our approaching enemy.

Rhydin's army numbered in the thousands, and it had paused in its marching perhaps half a mile away, stationed in the heart of the flattest portion of the plain where a cluster of stones stood. The same rugged rocks where Bartholomiiu saved my life from Rhydin during the War of the Three Kingdoms and sustained his mental injury. Judging by the soldiers' bland, look-alike faces, ninety percent of the army was made up of Einanhis dressed in matching black uniforms. Rhydin himself was at the front of the line wearing a sleek, black and purple trimmed with gold that looked ideal for dueling. He was too far away to read his expression.

At least he planned on joining the fight then, for once.

Our people turned to each other. Fear trickled through the rows of rebels like a slow-moving creek, all the way from the lead horn-blowers to the archers in the rear, and my gut told me we had to do something to stop it before it was too late.

I had to do something.

I yanked my sword from its sheath and threw the latter on the ground, not needing it anymore. Hefting the shining blade into the air, I yelled, "*This* is the moment for which we've waited for so long! Remember whom we fight for!"

The people around me suddenly quieted as my words reached them one by one, but the seconds crept by as no one uttered a syllable. Then, a roar behind me from Frederick coincided with the *shiiiiing* of another sword drawn, "For Cornflower!!"

The rebels began to shift. Xavier lifted his Mineraltin battle-ax and cried, "For Taisyn!"

"For Dathian!" Sabine bellowed as she spun her twin blades once, and the people began to shout their approval.

An Auklian man stepped forward and raised his sleek club over his head. "For King Daniel!"

"For Suze!" someone I couldn't see yelled.

Soon, the air was choked with names. Most of them were likely dead, but I heard a few names I knew had sustained permanent injuries due to Rhydin and his Followers, like Taisyn's blindness. I didn't recognize the overwhelming majority of the names I could hear, but every so often I heard one or two that I did.

Rosetta added the names of our parents, Liam and Elaine, as she clutched my hand.

Frederick added Cassandra and Gloria.

The Rounans began a chorus of Sam's name, which brought tears to my eyes.

Evan added Robert, Uncle Jed, and Aunt Marie.

Rachel added her father Viincen, her brother Luke, and a stream of other Ranguvariian names I didn't know.

I called out my own names. Sam, Grandma Saarah, cousin Keera, Bartholomiiu, and Kelsi, Sam's sister.

Arii remained silent through it all, although his eyes glimmered with approval, and my heart tremored at the fact that he likely could have stood here for a week yelling every name he knew.

The change in our people was palpable. Terror transformed into determination, helplessness into strength, and despondency into ferocity. Their eyes contained the fire of one thousand stars. We were ready.

And not a second too soon because at that moment, a flare of shadow magic streaked into the sky above our enemy, and they began to charge.

Chapter Twenty-One

Rayna

The other Royal children and I were halfway up the main foothill, wading through the rebels as they sang their chorus of loved ones, when our war horns blew a much longer blast. All around us, rows suddenly snapped back into formation, and shields lifted and locked into place. I whirled around just in time to see all those on horseback in the very front rear up and take off. They raced across the field, led by the Three Kings and Queen, as the flow of those on foot slowly swept forth like a dam broken. Time stood still for me as our force made first contact with Emperor Rhydin's: a spear piercing an Einanhi's sand-filled chest.

The sound level on the plain quadrupled as weapons clanged and horses bawled on top of the previous noises of jingling armor, battle cries, and the thunder of thousands of boots and hooves.

"Rayna, come on!" I heard Kylar wheedle over my shoulder. Aron's voice added, "We were told to stay up by the archers!"

I could feel the weight of multiple sets of eyes on me, so I turned. Chretien was ushering young Lyla up the hill toward her mother, but Kylar, Aron, Erikin, Dominick, Willian, Nathia, and Taisyn remained where they stood even as the rest of the rebels flowed around us until they were gone to the plain below. I set my jaw as I decided. "I'm going down there to help. I'm not just going to wait up here until I'm needed for the spell. It's not like I'm an heir or anything."

Kylar opened his mouth to object, but Taisyn was faster. "I'm going with you."

"No, you're not," I answered stubbornly, grasping for a reason other than my own secret desire that he stay safe. "You're too important to Mineraltir-…"

"I told you, I don't want to be king," Taisyn insisted, his hands beginning to glow as he faced me and repeated, "I'm going with you."

"I'm going too," Nathia suddenly announced, which caused Dominick's blue eyes to practically pop out of his head. She turned to him and said, "Don't even think about it, blondie. Frederick would murder me if I let something happen to you. And Willian, we all know you're too much of a fraidy-cat to come even with your big crush on Rayna, so why don't you escort my 'brother' on up the hill?"

Willian turned beet red, and I stifled a laugh. *That* explained a lot. Apparently, I owed Mathiian an apology.

"Rayna," Kylar groaned as worry pinched his brow into the usual shape of our father's. Aron and Erikin, behind him, had eyes like windows.

They really were my family.

"I have to do this, and you know it," I insisted. I stilled my anxious fingers as on the hilt of my trusty dagger and took one step toward the battle. "Stay safe, Kylar. The Rounans need you."

With that, I hurried down the hill as fast as I could manage without rolling down it with Taisyn and Nathia by my side. All the rebels in their neat, orderly rows were now gone, subsumed into the fray that lay ahead aside from the archers stationed above our heads. At each of Queen Mira's commands, the archers fired a volley of iron rain ahead of our people to thin their oncoming opponents or to redirect any flank that split off from Rhydin's main force.

I paused for a moment on the last small knoll as arrows whistled above our heads and *booms* reverberated off the mountains at our backs. I scanned the battlefield, which was rapidly becoming consumed by dust kicked up from the dry ground by all the activity.

"I see the emperor," Nathia snarled, her green eyes pinned to the cluster of tall stones in the direct center of Caden's Plain as her upper lip curled upward. "His forces are sweeping around him, but he's staying put in the rocks. I don't see your mother or uncle, it's too chaotic in there. What are you thinking, Rayna?"

"He must be making the Allyens come to him." Taisyn frowned.

I stroked my chin and nodded. "We catch up with my mother and Uncle Evan, and we help them get my part of the locket back. Otherwise, all of this is for nothing."

Nathia and Taisyn both hesitantly bobbed their heads. Then, we raided one of the wagons for a few shields – all the weapons were already gone – and hurried to join the dusty cloud of battle.

We quickly lost visibility. For the first ten minutes or so, we were just mindlessly scuffling around smaller fights within the fracas, trying to make our way with as few obstacles as possible. When I tried to look up for any sort of direction, the wood of Nathia's circular, Mineraltin-style shield was nearly cleaved in two by the thin, midnight-blade of an Einanhi. Taisyn immediately charged a ball of flame in his fist and flung it overhead at the enemy still enshrouded in dust. He added another round seconds later before becoming satisfied, and from there on out, Nathia and I easily agreed that Taisyn would lead the way.

At that point, time ceased to contain any sort of meeting for us. Had it been six minutes, six hours, or six days? Taisyn led us through the battle as best he could as I honed in on my mother's presence in my head. For the most part, we were able to avoid any other unpleasant encounters, as small as we were in such a gigantic, dust-filled space. The sounds of warfare were deafening all around us, and the new grass of spring was littered with the sand of innumerable Einanhis. I cast my eyes to the side whenever a dark lump of a body appeared just ahead of us, too afraid to check whether it was one of ours or one of the slim human minority in Rhydin's forces.

After what felt like miles of inching this way and that, my senses felt like we were practically on top of my mother and Uncle Evan. I motioned for Taisyn and Nathia to wait for a moment – after all, there was no way they'd ever hear me over the chaos around us. The sun had begun its descent now judging by what I could gather from its filtered light shining above. Nathia and I scanned all around us, and while there was no one to be seen, I did notice that in one direction, the ever-hovering dust seemed to be thinner. In unspoken agreement, Nathia nodded at me, I took Taisyn's hand, and we began to creep toward where the powder of the earth kicked up by so many thousands of soldiers had started to settle in the absence of fighting.

We saw the flashes of light first. Golden orbs of Allyen magic and long snakes of crackling amethyst power. After a few more steps, I could make out the forms of my family members flying in and out between the dark, towering stones as they flung spells at Rhydin and narrowly hid from his replies. The emperor wasn't wearing any traditional armor, which was like spit in the face of the rebellion. Instead, he wore a slim, black tunic decorated with his imperial crest in golden thread, which left his pale, sinewy arms bare. His black-trousered legs poked out of slits on either side of the tunic, which nearly reached the ground, and his boots were the only lick of leather on him. My third of the locket hung around his neck plain as day.

He obviously didn't expect his life to be threatened today.

I didn't realize I was still walking forward until there was a tug on my sleeve of chainmail. Nathia's eyes were fierce as she hissed, "Do you *want* them to see you? If you want to get your piece of the locket back, we need to come up with a plan and take Rhydin by surprise!"

"Point taken," I huffed, trying not to feel like she just wanted to make me look stupid.

So, we began to wait. It was like agony watching my mother and uncle fight with every inch of their life while I only stood on the sidelines, especially with Rhydin's magic obviously benefitting from the amplification of my locket. I tapped my fingers impatiently against my elbow as I studied every one of their moves for any sort of opening to allow me to steal it back. Taisyn's hands continued to glow, magically watching the situation around us as we stood in silence. As the minutes ticked by, the Mineraltin prince became more and more antsy, his anxious tics increasing in number until I couldn't take it anymore.

"Taisyn," I yelled as loud as I dared simply so he could hear me over the metallic clashes and magical booms all around us, "what is it?"

"I can sense every being on this field," Taisyn answered, his copper brow furrowed. "It's not looking good for the rebellion right now."

Nathia's mouth fell open. My heart dropped to my toes and then perhaps a mile more into the earth. "What?"

"We're going to lose this battle if the death spell isn't done soon," Taisyn said, a hint of a quiver in his voice. "Rhydin's soldiers are drawing the rest of our forces toward this spot. We don't have much time before this area is thick with fighting again."

Resolve suddenly settled like a blanket over my shoulders.

We couldn't wait any longer. Yet, no opportune moment was revealing itself. The emperor and the two Allyens were just as entangled in their fight as they had been the entire time, chasing and dodging each other in circles around the stones. I bit my lip as turmoil threatened to swallow me whole. The sounds of war were beginning to get louder again.

My foot moved on its own accord to step out of the residual dust cloud and into the clear air where the stones stood. But just before I could shift my weight to it, a small shadow made the earth flash black around us. My leg froze, but my eyes shot to the sky.

Circling high above our heads was Clariion Arii, his large wings beating resplendently. In fact, he was so high up that none of the three mages in front of us had noticed his presence, busy as they were in their fight and not paying attention to their senses. It was then that I realized that Arii was here to do the exact same thing we were. He, too, was waiting for the perfect moment to swoop down and snatch the locket from Rhydin's neck.

Then why alert us to his presence? I wondered. Arii was intently gazing down at us as he flew like he was sending some sort of message that I couldn't understand.

Nathia, who was also staring straight up into the sky at Arii, suddenly gasped. "He's trying to do what we're doing. Rayna, we need to become a distraction!"

"A distraction?" I scoffed. "Isn't his fight distraction enough?"

"It wasn't for us, nitwit!" Nathia growled. "The only chance Arii has is if he can sneak up on Rhydin, and that means we need to make him hold still long enough to give the Clariion a chance!"

"But what about his senses? Wouldn't Rhydin still sense Arii coming up behind him?" Taisyn asked anxiously as the dust began to encroach upon us again with the coming armies.

Nathia groaned and smacked her forehead. "I think we're just going to have to trust that the three-hundred-some-odd-year-old mythical creature has *thought of that!* Now, *move* Rayna!"

With a nod from Arii that one usually used in conjunction with the words "go on," the three of us rushed forward several steps together. For a second or two, the warring adults didn't notice us, but that didn't last long. After ducking under a huge violet blast, my mother whirled to face us first, her Allyen eyes wide and her earth-colored hair poking out of her braids like newborn tree branches. Uncle Evan had to jump in and knock her to the side to keep Rhydin from taking advantage of her distraction, but soon the emperor caught wind of us too.

"What are you three doing here?" Mama shrieked, her gaze darting back and forth between us and Rhydin, just as Uncle Evan shouted, "Go, now!"

The edges of Rhydin's lips twitched upward as he laughed in an unhinged manner, "Excellent! Now all the Allyens may die together."

Rhydin stepped forward to move or turn again, and I cried out to keep him in place. "Wait! I have a message for you!"

All three mages in front of us looked at me like I was crazy, but none of them moved. I could see Nathia out of the corner of my eye glancing upward as discreetly as possible to check Arii's progress, and I had to consciously fight to keep my eyes down. If I so much as looked up, it would all be over. Nathia whispered through open, barely moving lips, "Almost."

"From Rhydin Caldwell!" I yelled again as the evil clone's attention threatened to turn back to my family. "He wants you to know something really important!"

Something seemed to snap in Rhydin the Einanhi upon hearing that name. He roared chaotically, "Caldwell is no more! I shall end him myself once I have the rest of the locket. There is *nothing* he can possibly have to say!"

Then, it was me who smiled, as Arii dropped down low enough in his approach for me to be able to see him directly behind Rhydin. For a moment or two, it looked like it was Rhydin with the glowing, crystalline wings growing ever larger behind him. I couldn't help the smugness in my voice as I said, "He says goodbye."

Several things happened in the course of the next two or three seconds.

One, Clariion Arii overcame Rhydin with his hand outstretched, narrowly grasping the chain at the back of Rhydin's neck from which hung my piece of the locket.

Two, Chelsea, fierce in her lavender-skinned, fanged Aatarilec form, appeared from between Arii's beating wings. A thick leather belt around her waist linked her to a harness Arii wore over his arms like a rucksack, her presence masking his from Rhydin's senses. She plunged a barbed, seashell-looking spear downward at the same moment Arii snatched the locket.

Three, Rhydin howled with rage as he felt the locket leave him and Chelsea's spear enter his shoulder. The entire area from his collarbone down to his armpit caved in like crumbling rock, but not before his other arm swung his blade around and shoved it deep into Arii's gut.

I felt sick as Arii listed to the side off his perfect flight pattern, blood dripping from his wound. Panic overcame Chelsea's impish face, and she snatched my piece of the locket out of Arii's weakening hand with her long claws and threw it in my direction as they glided uncontrollably over our heads. I jumped to action and lunged forward, narrowly catching the gleaming silver necklace as a huge *thud* resounded behind me.

"*No!*" Rhydin bellowed as Arii and Chelsea skidded to a halt on the hard, dry ground. Arii's wings didn't disappear like Ranguvariian wings normally did; they broke apart, the crystal feathers falling away from their invisible form one by one until there was nothing left by a pile of dull, diamond-shaped shards on the ground.

I tried to run to Arii, but my uncle was shouting my name. I could barely hear him over the abrupt sounding of dozens of war horns at once over the strengthening thunder of the approaching armies. A gigantic wind then came out of nowhere and whipped all the floating dust out of the air and far, far away. Suddenly, Caden's Plain had clarity again.

King Frederick was several yards away from us, his hands still held upward from his wind spell. Behind him were several small groups of rebels with hundreds of Einanhis in between them, the fighting still going strong. However, with the new visibility, everyone seemed to pause a beat, and the source of the horns became apparent.

Half a mile away where the grasses of the plain sloped downward toward the Kingdom of Auklia was a huge battalion of Ranguvariians and Aatarilecs with Aunt Rachel and Chieftess Doona at the helm. Then the horns sounded again, the two rival, mythical races raised their weapons with a booming war cry and charged.

"*Rayna!*" my mother cried in a voice I'd never heard before. "*NOW!*"

I scrambled to get my footing and sprinted toward where she, my uncle, and Emperor Rhydin all still stood among the stones of Caden's Plain, looping my locket around my neck with shaking fingers. Rhydin started screaming unintelligible words, his ruined shoulder unable to move. As I approached, Uncle Evan rushed him with another barrage of magical attacks to keep his one good hand too busy to cast a transportation spell, kicking up more dust.

Taisyn and Nathia rushed up behind me as I got into position, and the two of them unleashed every ounce of power they had. Taisyn flung fireballs at Rhydin to take over for my uncle as he rushed to get into position as well and keep him from moving anywhere, and Nathia used her invisible Rounan powers to immobilize Rhydin's good arm. Behind us, King Frederick stood at attention between us and the rest of the soldiers on the field while Chelsea hovered over the wounded Arii.

Rhydin growled in frustration, unable to move either of his arms due to Nathia and Chelsea to cast any magic. He couldn't even run, lest he suffer a hit by Taisyn's fire, so the three of us Allyens began our magical dance of *Alytniinaeran*. Stepping out with our right feet and raising our right arms as the first formation, we circled each other right in front of Rhydin, arcing our arms and sweeping our feet slowly in broad, unified motions. The three stars of light appeared on cue as we returned our hands to center, and Rhydin's violet eyes doubled in size as he furiously wriggled back and forth against Nathia's magic. Our little orbs of light grew and grew as our hand movements became more complicated, and I found myself minutely engrossed in every twitch of my fingers, which were beginning to feel numb despite my best efforts. Then, the three of us began the march to the center of our circle, cradling our orbs the size of large fruit.

Rhydin began to scream, "*Stop!* You do not know that which you are doing! R-Robert…he tricked you! This spell will not destroy me; only preserve me! *Stop at once!*"

I found myself involuntarily hesitating as I listened to his words. I had to shake my head to regain my focus. *He* was the trickster, and one grasping at straws now. Wind picked up as the three of us came together, pushing against us with such force that I could barely see with all the dust coming into the air again.

I felt the moment our three magics combined. The release of tension rippled throughout my body to the point where I weakly fell backward. The colossal globe of light magic shot a beacon of light into the sky before the glow seeped into a brilliant green color. The beacon ceased, and from within the globe grew vines. Dozens of healthy green vines riddled with leaves unfurled from the globe, growing in size until it was like a human-sized cocoon. As the vines reached toward Rhydin and he grunted with the effort of trying to get away, beads of sweat racing down his pale face, the cocoon parted to reveal a young woman clad in a beautiful white dress that flowed about her form in an ethereal fashion. The ocean-blue hair was unmistakable on top of her head.

"Amelia," I breathed. My mother and uncle gasped while Rhydin seemed to shut down altogether.

Vines, glowing with our Allyen magic, began to coil around Rhydin's body, and both Taisyn and Nathia stopped their magics. Amelia's arms made intricate motions as she worked a powerful magic that had been dead to Nerahdis for hundreds of years. Her angel-like face was fixed in determination as she commanded her magical vines to crush the Einanhi that had murdered both her and her lover long ago.

Rhydin could no longer speak. Cracks erupted all over his body as if the veins were constricting around a marble statue. The dust was rising rapidly, and we were quickly losing our visual of Caden's daughter and his sons' usurper. I heard the *twang* of a bowstring behind me, but the arrow moved so fast I barely saw it. In a panic, I groped for Rhydin Caldwell's vial in my pocket and rushed toward where I could barely see their silhouettes. Surely, I wasn't too late to reclaim the stolen magic!

Another great gust of wind came up from King Frederick. I glanced back at him and saw that the rest of the plain had fallen still and silent; everyone on both sides waited for what the settling of the dust would show us.

When the air was clear again, all eyes went to Rhydin. An arrow protruded from his heart, and the vines gripping him, holding him up, were slowly grinding him into nothing more than the sand of a destroyed Einanhi. The amethyst fires of Emperor Rhydin's eyes were snuffed out.

Vial in hand, I scrambled up toward the stones as the rest of the Einanhi that had plagued Nerahdis for centuries dissolved into sand. I yanked the jeweled stopper out and thrust the gaping, slender tube toward the pile, muttering the words "no" and "please" over and over again as nothing seemed to happen.

That was when I felt the hand on my shoulder.

The sea stared back at me in Amelia's eyes. The young woman in her white dress still glowed with the golden light of our Allyen magic. When she smiled, she looked her age – only twenty-one when she died. She beckoned with her other hand to the short, brand-new grass where all that was left of Rhydin lay. To my surprise, strong green blades poked up from underneath the sand, and upon them were tiny, glittering bits of purple. I gasped and desperately pushed my vial toward them as I exhaustedly drew upon whatever stores of magic I had left after the death spell, but they were already flying in with flashes like lightning.

Relief soared through me. When I turned to thank Amelia, she finally spoke in the clear, light voice I'd already heard so many times before through Nora's ears.

"Thank you," she said, before she suddenly burst into millions of leaves floating away on the breeze.

Chapter Twenty-Two

Lina

I could hardly believe it when Rhydin dissolved into sand like every other Einanhi I'd ever fought and destroyed. When he did, I heard cheers of victory rippling through the plain behind me, and I turned just in time to witness a good three-quarters of Rhydin's imperial army turn to sand as well.

Could it really be true? The enemy who'd been after me my whole life was truly gone?

Evan looked downright joyous when I looked at him. Frederick, utterly relieved. We all watched with rapt attention as Rayna began to collect the remaining crystallized magic in Rhydin Caldwell's vial with Amelia's help. It was uncanny to watch the two young women together; Amelia seemed to be far more than just the "image" the real Rhydin had believed would appear, but I didn't know exactly what she was.

Caden's daughter had just transformed into a multitude of crisp green leaves when there was a loud scuffle behind me. I tore my eyes away from the disappearing Amelia to see one of Rhydin's few human Followers sprinting toward Evan and I, his blade aimed for the kill. We scrambled around, searching for the swords we'd dropped at the beginning of the death spell.

My chest heaved as the Follower grew close enough that I could see the whites of his eyes and his dust-encrusted sweat, but try as I might, I could conjure no magic into my palms. Helpless, I involuntarily squeezed my eyes shut.

There was a *clang*, and then a *thunk*.

The Follower lay dead on the ground only feet from my brother and I, Frederick standing just behind him with a bloodied sword. He stared at me and then nodded as he relaxed from his stance, as if that were all. I couldn't help but leap up from the grass and into him, knocking his sword to the ground as I wrapped my arms around his neck. Frederick clutched me tightly as we stood there a moment in silence, my feet dangling due to his height, letting the fear of what nearly just happened wash over us.

When I could feel him beginning to extricate himself from my embrace, my hands moved to his chest, and I found myself whispering, "I love you."

"What?" Frederick asked, his blue eyes framed by dusty cheeks and forehead.

I flushed with embarrassment that I had been too quiet to hear. "I lo-…"

"No no, I heard you," he replied, "I just…. Are you sure? You don't have to love me just because I saved your life."

"No, I-…" I shook my head as my words tripped over each other, my hands tremoring. "I really do…love you, Frederick. You have always been there for me as my friend and now, and I…I swear I have come to love you."

Frederick's golden brow tipped upward in the center and gave the briefest of glances at my lips, but a shriek split the air. I jolted, afraid to look over my shoulder and see another Follower with a death wish, but instead, I saw Rachel hurrying to Arii's side where he still lay a small distance away. A crimson stain was blossoming ever larger upon the belly of his orange robe despite Chelsea's best efforts.

"Oh no," I breathed before scrambling over to them.

Rachel's short red hair was slick with the sweat of battle as she collapsed to her knees at her grandfather's side. She whipped out at least three Ranguvariian feathers from within her armored vest and began to sing the healing incantation with a shaking, breathless voice. My eyes wandered to the ruined front of Arii's robe, wondering how extensive the injury was, and Chelsea suddenly caught my gaze. She shook her head.

As if in agreement, Arii reached out with a long, weathered hand. Just as James scurried into the huddle, Arii curled Rachel's fingers back around the feathers and pushed them down and away from him. "No, Rachel," he rasped, his Ranguvariian eyes beginning to turn gray, "I have thwarted death long enough."

"No!" Rachel gasped, "No, please, just be with me a little while longer…I'm not ready."

James's eyes fluttered closed. He knew it was no use.

Arii smiled even as his eyes waded in and out of sleep. "You shall be a magnificent Clariion, Rahchii-thii. Create the best world you can."

I opened my mouth to say some sort of thank you – even though words could never suffice after everything Arii had ever done for me and all the Allyens – but he was already gone. A lump rose in my throat as both Rachel and James wept, one a little more audibly than the other, and my hands balled into fists. Surely, he knew how grateful we all were…but it killed me that I couldn't have said it before he left the world. Frederick's hand alighted on my shoulder, and I fought to keep it together.

As the surviving rebels around us rounded up the few remaining Followers and put them in shackles, the air around us abruptly filled with humming. Several hundred Ranguvariians trickled in from all directions, their blades and other weapons sparkling clean as if we hadn't all just fought the largest battle in Nerahdian history. They created a large circle around us complete with multiple rows as the humming became deafening.

"No," Rachel wept and shook her head, "he deserves better than this."

I walked forward and put my arms around my longest friend. I whispered in her ear, "This is exactly what he would want."

Hundreds of Ranguvariian wings appeared and spread wide. As the sun dipped toward the western sea, its light caught their shards and cast a beautiful pattern of colors on the grass beneath their feet, transforming the simple plain into a tapestry of stained glass. Several younger Ranguvariians bearing wide, war drums began a rhythmic heartbeat, and my memory of Luke's funeral came roaring back. I scanned the crowd, remembering all too clearly what happened next.

No one had bothered to bring an actual torch to a battle of course, so James stood and walked the field a moment, all while the humming and drumming filled our heads. Finally, he stooped when he found what he was looking for: a human-sized spear. Then, he tore a swatch of fabric from his own red tunic and wrapped it around the head of the sphere before returning to the center of the circle.

"He died for all of us," I said to him as I continued to crouch next to his sister, "so who lights it?"

James was monotone as he responded, "When the Clariion dies, it is customary for his or her heir to light the torch and the pyre."

"Pyre," I repeated absent-mindedly, suddenly wondering how we were going to build a pyre in the middle of a field. However, it seemed the Ranguvariians had already thought of this dilemma, for a half dozen of them led by Jaspen flew away from the circle and returned with one of the wagons we'd brought with us from Lunaka Castle, its cover removed. They set the wagon down in the center of the circle, and James and Rachel watched as Jaspen and the others carefully hefted their fallen leader into the bed of the wagon. Jaspen then took his place next to Rachel while the other Ranguvariians rejoined the circle.

By now, the rebels had finished shackling the last Followers and had come to add even more rows to the circles, even though probably only half of them had been present at Luke's funeral back when the Dome was first established. Rachel took the torch from James wordlessly, and I watched intently, wondering how her musical Ranguvariian magic would create fire. Using my light magic to create fire had been difficult enough when I did it at Luke's funeral. Rachel sang a low song full of staccato notes that seemed like a mix between a dirge and a fight song, and after a few moments, to my immense surprise, fire popped into existence upon the makeshift torch.

The moment the flame flickered to life on the head of the spear, the humming and drumming halted. Silence ensued for only a beat before the Ranguvariians began a chorus of long, low words I didn't understand. Rachel approached the pyre hesitantly, her blue eyes shining, as James said the traditional words along with their translation. "*Uny calou, etne Clarii, uny calou*. Well done, my soldier, well done."

By now Rayna was next to me too, Rhydin Caldwell's vial corked tight and shining bright between her fingers. She gazed at Arii's sleeping face forlornly, and I squeezed her to me. Frederick, too, touched her shoulder and spoke in her ear that he was relieved she was alright. Rayna nodded and smiled at him in response.

"*Anoet'v vas naeran dii ntae nten, etne Clarii.* You vowed you would die for us," James went on. "*Aiin'v ran, nten. Ba, eht raniin ii shae iiba Shaelen, iiba Alyen. Iiba C'calou chaldnii*. You gave your life song. So that the Allyen may live and destroy the evil one. The greatest sacrifice."

I noticed the addition of the words concerning Rhydin, and I found myself nodding in hearty approval.

Rachel threw the entire spear with its now large, healthy fire into the wagon bed with the body of her grandfather, and the dry wood of the wagon caught better than I would have expected. Rachel said the next words in unison with her youngest brother. "*Eht anet iivan dii jaenou, eten shnetran.* May your blade remain sharp for eternity."

With that, the Ranguvariians' song ended with a high note as the drum beat softer and softer into silence. All of Caden's Plain remained still and watched the fire for several moments as it consumed the entirety of the wagon and Arii's body, the smoke billowing high up into the sky as a signal to all of Nerahdis.

I looked around, thinking it was over, but I was wrong. There was a flash of silver in Jaspen's hands, and I realized he carried the band of silver Arii had worn around his head as the Ranguvariian version of a crown. He positioned himself squarely in front of Rachel, holding the band with only his fingertips and declared in the loudest voice I'd ever heard him utter, "*Ja aiin eten shnetran jorentiim iiba Ranguvariians, nten Rahchii Owiins Coralii da?* Do you devote your blade to guide the Ranguvariians, Rachel Owens Coralii?"

Rachel, still on her knees, adjusted herself into more of the kneel of a soldier rather than a distraught granddaughter. Her voice was strong once more as she replied, "*Prii anet iiba Ranguvariians jaenou ii bru, eten shnetran.* My blade shall remain the Ranguvariians' forever and to the finish."

Jaspen placed the crown on her brow and beckoned for her to rise, a proud smile on his long face. He shouted at the top of his lungs, "*Iivanchal, ntii Clariion!* A new Clariion has ascended!"

The Ranguvariians erupted into shouts of victory as they cast off their somber expressions. I knew in all reality they would be mourning Arii for years, but I could physically see their joy giving Rachel strength again. Her color returned, and her fear melted away even if her sadness did not. I gripped her hand tightly, unable to tell her how proud I was with the sheer volume of those around us. Then, Rachel gave me a quick hug, took one last look at the burning wagon still fully engulfed, and then wandered off toward her people with James and Jaspen in tow.

I was about to strike up a conversation with Chelsea when I felt Rayna tapping my arm repeatedly. She seemed about ready to explode with impatience when I faced her and asked what she wanted.

"We need to take this vial to Rhydin Caldwell *right now!*" she whined, the glowing vial and its jeweled stopper barely visible between her tight fingers.

I scoffed, "Rayna, we *just* came out of a major battle. Can't we have a minute to take a breather and get ourselves organized?"

My daughter shook her head rapidly. "He said I needed to bring it to him *directly!* I don't want to mess this up, Mama, please?"

Sighing, I weighed the desperation in her eyes. I supposed I really didn't know how long the vial would keep his magic contained, even as I looked around at all the battle-weary rebels – many exuberant with victory but many grieving those who fell too – who were obviously looking for some sort of direction.

"You should go," Frederick said to me softly, "but you should give everyone the option to go. To hear his story for themselves."

"Yeah!" Rayna was suddenly excited. "That way they'll all *know* that he really is good! And his existence can never be hidden again!"

I couldn't help but smile. "That sounds like a great plan. Hopefully, Mr. Caldwell is ready for some company."

People were uncertain when we announced the open invitation to come along to the Archimage Palace and witness the restoration of Rhydin Caldwell. I couldn't say I really blamed them; they were the products of generations of teaching that magic was to be shunned and feared. The Archimage Palace had been kept a secret from all aside from the Three Kings for centuries. Slowly, the façade around Nerahdian history was beginning to fall, but really, we needed as many witnesses as possible. Caden was not the gold standard. The

Archimage sort of supervised the Three Kings, but he or she was never in charge. Rounans were not evil, and neither were Ranguvariians or Aatarilecs. Royals could be good people and create governments allowing for input from the people.

Ultimately, about half of the rebels agreed to go along while the other half opted to remain at the battlefield to begin the burial of those we had lost, reclaim lost weapons, and sort out what to do with the few dozen human Followers left. Chelsea and her mother, Chieftess Doona, agreed to come on the Aatarilecs' behalf while the rest of the watery creatures made their way home, the uneasy alliance with the Ranguvariians having fulfilled its final need. Rachel, on the other hand, was not ready to leave the plain, but she gave free leave to any of the Ranguvariians who wished to go. Those who did wearily helped transport each and every human who desired to go as well until we had all arrived at the camouflaged front gates of the Archimage Palace.

Everyone except the Royals who had been here before gaped. I cringed as they approached the disguised palace, and I hoped this obvious deception didn't sharpen their fear of Royals. Rayna was bouncing on her heels, barely able to wait as the slow-moving mass of people entered the gigantic throne room, still in a state of destruction from that battle long ago lost.

Sabine seemed to hesitate and soak in the sight more than anyone else; she had not been back to the Archimage Palace since she left as a girl. I touched her shoulder cautiously, and she tucked her short, green hair behind her ear. "I'm fine," she huffed, trying to put up her usual steely exterior, "it's just been a while."

It was then that I looked up and saw him. Rhydin Caldwell was standing timidly at the other end of the throne room, one hand clutching his other wrist, as he gazed at so many hundreds of people in both disbelief and terror. When Rayna saw him, she excitedly sprinted the length of the entire hall, but Rhydin held up a hand to stop her a short distance away from him.

Meanwhile, the people continued their approach deeper into the throne room, having absolutely no clue that an invisible man was yet present. The Ranguvariians crowded the very back of the room, likely fearing the unknown effects the true Rhydin's power could have on them.

As Rayna and Rhydin exchanged a few words up ahead, I whispered to Frederick next to me, who was confused by the sight of Rayna talking to no one, "He's up there with her. They seem to have become friends through all this."

"It still just all seems so hard to believe," Frederick replied quietly before trailing off.

"I know," I said as I gently took his battle-stained hand into mine. "That's why you all need to see him. I know I didn't truly get it until I saw him." In response, it looked like his heart jumped into his throat, but he kept his hand firm on mine.

As the only other person in the room who could currently see Rhydin, I decided to take the lead and stop the rebels once they were most of the way through the throne room. I didn't want them to get too close to the dais and become terrified when someone who very much looked like our long-time nemesis materialized from nothing.

Rhydin straightened his ancient tunic and nodded at Rayna. She held the vial out at arm's length, uncorking it with her thumb, and the gleaming stopper rolled away on the floor. Instantly, a myriad of glowing, purple globules flew up and out of the vial, and they collided with Rhydin's chest. He grunted from the impact, and his translucency began to disappear for me as full color first returned to his head and core before spreading outward to his arms and legs.

For everyone else, he came into full visibility, as evidenced by a chorus of gasps and a few screams. Frederick stiffened next to me, and I squeezed his hand once to remind him that everything was okay. Then, there was a crash of what almost sounded like thunder above our heads, and everyone looked up to see the faint, lavender mist had transformed in a far larger, brighter, and more purple version. It churned above our heads at the same strength as Dathian's blue version once had.

The First Archimage was fully returned.

Next, something happened that I was not prepared for in any shape or form. It took my mind a second to recognize that I was feeling a weight disappear from my body. More specifically, from around my neck.

I looked down just in time to see the last of my locket dissipating into dry soil, which rained down onto the ruined marble floor of the Archimage Palace, leaving only the thick, old chain Sam had once given me so long ago.

Chapter Twenty-Three

Rayna

"I cannot believe you did it," Rhydin murmured, his eyes glued to the glowing vial in my hands with a strange mixture of awe and fear. "After all this time…but why have you brought so many here? Are they here to stone me?"

I laughed and shook my head. "No, of course not! They're here so you can tell your story, Rhydin. Clear your name! No one will ever forget any of this happened ever again."

The specter cleared his throat as he attempted to straighten and smooth the poor, white tunic he'd worn for centuries. "I do not think my name capable of being cleared, but I appreciate the opportunity. Needless to say, I am forever in your debt."

"Learning the truth of history is payment enough." I waved my hand back and forth. "Now, are you ready?"

Rhydin Caldwell took a deep breath before nodding. I held the vial out away from my body, slightly fearing what was inside, before uncorking it. The crystals of magic instantly returned to their true owner after being separated for so long, and seconds later, the entire room behind us was gasping and shouting. The Archimage mist returned full force up in the rafters with a boom. Then, the room stilled into such an eerie silence, it was almost like all life left the place. Rhydin's hands fidgeted in front of him like an actor struck with stage fright, but as I moved to help him, I felt a weight disappear from my neck and dirt sprayed my feet.

I numbly touched the leather cord that now bound nothing around my neck, not understanding. My piece of the locket that Arii had sacrificed himself for had dissolved into dirt!

As Rhydin stepped further forward onto the dais, unaware that anything was amiss, I scanned the crowd for my mother and uncle. Both of them stared back at me with frightened eyes, and I noticed Uncle Evan attempt to summon a charge of light magic in his palm to no avail. I, too, put my hands together like a bowl and tried with all my might to create any sort of light whatsoever, but the flesh basin remained dark.

What happened to our magic? Why can't I use it?

I slipped off the dais as unnoticeably as possible while Rhydin began his story, retelling how he'd grown up in Diagalo and been chosen as the First Archimage when his father signed him up even though it meant leaving behind his one true love. My uncle now stood raptly listening to the story, so I made my way toward Mama, who had heard it before. As people gawked at the idea of Emperor Caden not having one illegitimate daughter but *two*, I met her against the far wall of the throne room. I failed to keep the panic out of my not-so-hushed tone. "What happened? My locket turned to earth! I can't use my magic-…!"

"I know, neither can I," my mother hissed in an attempt to get me to lower my voice. "Evan and I's locket pieces are gone too."

"Does…does that mean our magic is gone forever? That we aren't Allyens anymore?" I asked, fighting to stop the tremor in my voice. I could no longer feel any presences around me either.

"I don't know, but we'll figure it out, I promise," my mother answered as soothingly as possible. "Let Rhydin tell his story for now."

I nodded, even though I didn't really want to. Mama returned to where she'd been standing with King Frederick in the crowd, and he eyed me for a moment to make sure I was alright before returning his attention to Rhydin's story. Now, Rhydin was telling how Caden gave him more magic than he could control and how being so torn about whether to go after Amelia or remain in his position to protect Nerahdis was his downfall. His narrative was riddled with apologies and embarrassed explanations. It wasn't easy to tell a few hundred people that the reason their lives had been so ruined by a dictator was because one young man was star-crossed in love.

Every once in a while, someone would interrupt with a question, but those were few and far between. It seemed that Rhydin had been practicing this speech for a number of years, if not decades. Before long, his story came to an end, and after a few more questions, silence filled the throne room. After a few minutes of nothing, Rhydin straightened a mite, probably assuming that his part was done until one last question echoed around the room from an unknown origin.

"So, what happens to you now? We killed the other Rhydin."

The temperature in the room suddenly shifted. The tone of patience and willingness to listen had transformed into one of anger and bloodlust.

"You have every right to be furious with me. You have every right to have the desire to hurt me," Rhydin said softly, clutching his elbow. "I have been furious with myself and desired to punish myself for over three hundred years as I watched the world deal with the problem I created. I know I have no right to request anything, but my life is rapidly expiring. I have lived beyond my bounds, my heart has beat for far too long, and now that my flesh has returned to me, my time approaches. All I ask is for the ability to leave this place. I have not stepped foot off its stone since the day I was sentenced here so long ago. I wish to feel the sun on my head and the wind in my face. Then, I shall disappear from your world forever."

The room was quiet, and I couldn't help but walk back closer to the dais as if to protect him.

"Please," Rhydin added, his voice becoming a little breathy as his pale hands folded in front of him in the manner of a small child apologizing for knocking something over.

After a few more beats of silence, the rebels and Ranguvariians in the room sort of just began to turn around and leave. It sent the message of "we don't care what you do," likely due to the fact he was dying anyway. The thought of him disappearing for good was a pang in my heart, but deep down I knew that I'd never known how long my friendship with him would last. I took another step in the direction of the dais to speak with him once more when a battle-worn person stepped into my path.

Nathia had re-braided her long chocolate hair upon the blonde top of her head, but her face was still smeared with dirt and sweat. She touched the back of her neck awkwardly as she said, "You did good today, Rayna. I'm sorry I've given you so much trouble since you came."

"Uh…thanks," I replied in shock. "I, uh, couldn't have done it without you, really…but why did you decide to help me? What changed?"

Nathia sort of shrugged. "I guess I just knew that the Allyens were the only ones who could defeat him. We may butt heads, but we've always been on the same side, Rayna."

I let that thought wash over me, let the gratitude sink in, and then chuckled, "So, are you going to be nice to me from now on?"

The young woman cracked a sly grin. "Oh…I won't hate you at least."

"Eh, works for me. Same to you," I said nonchalantly, and then Nathia joined the last vestiges of humans awaiting Ranguvariian transportation to wherever they so desired.

Their destinations varied widely. Solăna, Coliare, Tredeno, Canis, Rondeau, Tranini. Caark. Some of them nervously mentioned that they were headed home for the first time since

Rhydin became emperor or since they joined the Dome years prior. As I continued on my way toward Rhydin Caldwell, I realized with a jolt that I didn't really know where home was. Caark was the only home that Kylar and I remembered, but that wasn't my mother's home. She was Lunakan and was now married to the King of Lunaka. Did that make Lunaka Castle my home?

My mother and Uncle Evan were furiously whispering to each other as I climbed the stairs of the dais once again. Rhydin had his arms crossed over his chest as he stared out over the now empty, still trashed throne room and the swirling mist above it. His breathing was becoming labored as he whispered to me without turning, "This place should be burned to the ground."

"I don't blame you for thinking that, but I think Arii would be disappointed in me if I didn't ask to remove the books first." I cracked a grin, trying to cheer him up.

Rhydin replied quietly, "I doubt I shall still be here that long."

My brow furrowed. "How long do you think you have?"

"Perhaps an hour or two? I cannot be sure," he said as if it was the simplest thing in the world.

I fought to maintain my composure through the shock. I had expected longer than that although the sound of his breathing definitely made it believable. "I'll set light to it myself after all the books are saved," I promised.

Rhydin finally faced me, his violet eyes sad. "Thank you, Rayna. I am afraid I must trouble you for one more favor before I go."

"What is it?" I asked, before glancing over my shoulder at my mother and uncle who ironically were now headed to the vast Archimage library themselves.

"Will you accompany me to Diagalo?" Rhydin queried like a gentleman. "Through the Archimage's mist, I have seen the entire world evolve over the centuries. The entire world save one place, for there was never any point in any of the

Archimages checking in on a place erased from existence. My home. I would like to be there when I go, even if the buildings are gone. I have wanted to go home for so long."

I stuttered, "Y-Yes, of course, but…how will we find it? Diagalo isn't on any map."

"I would know my home anywhere." Rhydin finally smiled, but I felt my own heart sink a little at the thought.

The two of us approached three or four Ranguvariians before finding a couple who were willing to take us to the southeastern bank of Spenser's Lake, and Rhydin never looked back. They didn't stay hardly more than a second, just long enough for me to ask one to tell my mother where I'd gone really, and Rhydin and I were soon all alone.

I instantly began looking for any sort of remains of this town, so it took me a moment to realize that Rhydin seemed to be frozen in place. Lunaka's wind pushed and pulled at his clothes and his midnight hair, and he continued to stand there with his eyes closed. I took a second and closed my eyes too, and I appreciated the feeling of the wind caressing my arms, the sound of the prairie grasses rubbing together and the nearby lake lapping its shores, and the smell of the newly arrived spring.

What must it have been like to be trapped in a secret palace for so long? The stillness, the quietness, the constant musty odor. It must have been like suffocating.

Rhydin was taking rapid deep breaths when I opened my eyes again, which semi-confirmed my suspicions. He stared at the sky now as the sun sunk toward the horizon, the entire expanse opened to him. Then, he collected himself, and without a sound aside from his heavy breathing, we began to walk the shoreline.

Only minutes passed before Rhydin suddenly stopped. "We have arrived."

Surprised, I looked around for any sort of hint that a town was once here. "How do you know?"

"I would know this stretch of the lake anywhere. My mother would bring me here every day as a small child, before I could even walk," he replied before moving away from the lake's edge and studying the few trees and the ground. "These trees were not here then, but…" – he abruptly fell to his knees and started digging through the soft soil – "Ah…here it is, then…."

I cautiously crept up behind him to see what he had unearthed. A large, perfectly square stone sat just beneath the soil level, and when I looked up, I could see other block-like shapes or piles lurking beneath the dirt and grass, covered up by centuries of wind and growth.

"Our manor was the only stone building in all Diagalo," Rhydin explained quietly as he stared at the stone. "The rest of the town was still made of wood. That's why there was nothing left when he burned it. Judging by this broken edge and those piles, he must have toppled the house."

"I remember you said he was trying to erase every reminder of you," I replied softly, my heart beginning to truly understand what that meant.

Tears streaked down Rhydin's pale face. "The people of Diagalo were kind people. They did not deserve such retribution."

I crouched down next to him and took his hand for the first time, still amazed to feel the weight of it within my own. "You didn't mean for this to happen." Rhydin didn't respond, and I could tell the guilt was eating him alive. I pulled him to his feet by his thin arm and guided him back to the serenity of the lake as his footsteps started becoming uncoordinated.

It was truly a beautiful evening. The sun was touching the horizon now as the wind died out for the night, and I knew it wouldn't be long before it was dark but didn't know how much longer I had with this man who had become a friend. I decided to distract him as I forced him to sit next to me on the damp, gritty shore. "Tell me how you met Amelia."

"My father was a lord, the main patron of Diagalo. He insisted that I go with him one day when he traveled to Soläna to get supplies for the town, to my great disdain I might add, and…well, Amelia was difficult to miss," Rhydin chuckled through his tears.

"Her hair?" I asked, smiling.

Rhydin could only nod through a sob. "She was delightful to talk to. I went with my father on every single one of his next trips, even though I despised spending time with him. It was not long before I was sneaking to Soläna on my own, or she came to Diagalo after she forced Nora to meet me." He was quiet for a second, and then he finally pulled his eyes away from the rippling water. "What was she like?"

Amelia and all her beauty and prowess flashed in my mind. "You were right when you said she was rather adept with vines."

He couldn't help but laugh.

"She was amazing, she really was," I continued on. "I don't think she was just an image though. She actually helped me gather up your magic. I couldn't have done it without her."

Rhydin's eyes tripled in size. He breathed heavily. "Perhaps, this means she has forgiven me? Oh, how I wish I could have seen her."

Trying to make him feel better, I replied, "I think she has-…" I cut off as I transitioned my gaze from Rhydin to the lake.

Far out on the water, two figures had appeared. I blinked a couple times and rubbed my eyes, certain the sun's reflection on the water was playing tricks on me. When they grew closer, slowly walking across the water's surface, my eyes about popped out of their sockets.

Amelia in her white dress just as she had appeared on the battlefield only hours ago walked toward us arm and arm with none other than Nora, who wore a flowy gray tunic over trousers and bare feet. I'd seen so many of her memories that I'd know that tall, muscular frame and mud-brown ponytail anywhere. Her face reminded me of my mother's a little bit, but her golden Allyen eyes were the dead giveaway.

I delivered a swift elbow into Rhydin's ribs next to me, and he jolted from his thoughts to see the two women out on the lake. He paused for a moment, obviously not believing his eyes, before leaping to his feet so fast that he stumbled forward onto his knees. He staggered to the water's edge before a shudder went through his body, and he groaned between gasps for air, "The time has come…after so long." Then, he seemed to suddenly remember me and turned around to face me one last time. "Rayna, I can never repay you or your family for freeing me-…"

"I know." I interrupted him as I stood with a grin on my face, even as my eyes filled with water. "What are you waiting for? Go!"

The edges of his mouth twitched into a relieved smile. He said "thank you" firmly before another shudder racked his body. Then, he waded out into the water as fast as he could, but it was slow-going. The darkening lake was up to his chin by the time Amelia and Nora reached him. The blue-haired young woman extended her hand down to Rhydin, and as he grasped it, I thought I saw a shadow slip beneath the gentle waves. Afterward, Rhydin stepped up onto the golden surface of the water, his white tunic crisp and fresh again while his black trousers had become tan, and his boots were nowhere to be seen. Then, he flung his arms around Amelia, and she wrapped her arms around his neck. Judging by Nora's averted gaze, I felt it safe to assume that the two lovebirds were finally getting that long-awaited kiss of reunion.

When they separated, they turned back around and walked out of my sight, but Nora still remained. She watched as the couple faded away before turning to look at me with that ferocity of hers, and it was then that I realized something rather important.

She wasn't here for Rhydin. She was here for me.

My heart quivered with fear as Nora walked toward me with the grace of a hunter, and the sun finally disappeared. The air turned cool around me, winter's last grip on the world, and I fought to tell myself that I had nothing to fear. In the light of the rising twin moons, Nora was aging as she approached me. With every step she took, her skin became more weathered and more gray hairs overtook her head. She was maybe six feet away from the shore when she stopped, now looking about the age she would have been when she died, perhaps mid-fifties. I'd never seen her this old before, but her hands were free of the scars the evil Rhydin gave her.

Abruptly, she gave me a cocky grin, and she bowed at the waist. "Well done, young Allyen. My magic's purpose is now complete," she said in that deep, feminine voice I knew all too well.

Understanding struck me like a slap in the face. I asked anxiously, "Is that why our power is gone? And the locket turned to earth?"

Nora, the First Allyen, nodded. "I created my magic to avenge Amelia. Yet, that required not just destroying whom I thought to be the real Rhydin Caldwell, but undoing what he had done to his creator as well. Now that that has been rectified, the Allyen magic is no longer needed. I hope the memories I sent you aided this mission. You were the only one I could reach."

I nodded awkwardly, unable to really feel my neck, trying to absorb everything she was saying.

"Good. All is finished then," Nora declared, and she gave me a wink before turning around and walking the same way Amelia and Rhydin had gone. Then, before I knew it, I was left alone under the black, starry sky.

Once I was on my own, surrounded by nothing but the sound of the lake lapping its shores now that the wind had died, something came unraveled within me. I sat back down on the damp, gritty ground and clutched my knees to my chest, weeping quietly. Not just because I'd never see my friend again, but because now I had no idea what to do.

As I thought to myself, I remembered that I still had Taisyn's metal bird in my pocket. I pulled it out, cradling it in my hands as I studied the fine details he'd painstakingly put into it. For my entire life, I'd known I was the next Allyen. I'd painstakingly awaited the awakening of my power so that I could help my parents rather than remain sequestered away in Caark. Now that magic was gone after not even having it half a year. Forever. It wasn't coming back. I'd only ever dreamt of being the best Allyen I could be, and now I was washed up at only fourteen. I'd never imagined myself as anything else.

"Rayna?"

I dove forward, terrified out of my skin, and drew my dagger. Then, I saw Taisyn cleaned up from battle and dressed in a traveling cloak, aglow with a small ball of flame held in one hand. Inwardly, I sorely missed the ability to sense people coming as I sheathed my weapon and plopped back down on the rocky shore, clutching my bird. "What are you doing here?" I asked, my voice betraying my tears.

Using his magic to see, Taisyn wordlessly came to my side and sat next to me, still holding his little fire. I realized abruptly that the light wasn't for him; he didn't need it. It was for me, so that I could see him. He whispered softly, "Are you okay?"

"Yes, of course I'm okay!" I half-shouted, half-blubbered. "We've accomplished what Allyens have fought to do for centuries, and Rhydin Caldwell is free and happy!"

Taisyn pressed his thin lips into a line, his flame making the freckles on his face look like they were dancing. "I know you better than that, and you know it. Please tell me."

I groaned and flung myself backward to lie on the ground, not caring if I got wet pebbles in my short hair. For a few beats, it was silent, before I finally murmured, "What am I supposed to do now, Taisyn? I have no future."

The Mineraltin prince's copper brow knitted together even as he stared unseeingly off into the distance. "That's preposterous. Of course, you have a future!"

"No, I don't!" I rebuked loudly as I stared at the stars above. "I was supposed to be an Allyen, and I got to be one for like two seasons, tops. I spent every waking moment for the past fourteen years either wishing my magic would awaken or practicing it like crazy for the death spell. Now, that's all over. So, what do I do from here?"

To his credit, Taisyn stayed quiet for a few moments, although that just made the fact that I started crying again worse. He sighed, and to my surprise, he gently took my hand, which happened to have the bird in it, and just held it, the warm metal encased between our hands.

"I suppose you can do anything you want now," he replied softly, shrugging a little. "The world doesn't have expectations of you anymore. Your role is fulfilled, so you can pick something to do that you love. And thanks to you and the other Allyens, Nerahdis is now the best world to ever do anything in."

I jutted out my chin as I considered that a moment. While I still had no idea what that would even be, the thought was still comforting. "I guess I'll just have to figure out what that is," I mused. Then, I rolled my head against the damp ground to look at him, my fingers tightening on his and our bird. "Will you help me?"

"I'll always help you." Taisyn smiled.

"I know," I whispered. "Thank you for coming with me during the battle. Nathia and I would have definitely died without your superpower senses."

The teenage boy chuckled as he let himself fall backward flat on the sand beside me. "Yeah. You definitely would have."

We laughed together. Then, I took a few minutes to tell Taisyn all about what I'd just witnessed with Rhydin, Amelia, and Nora. Aside from my mother, he was probably the only one I could tell who wouldn't think I was insane afterward. He was astounded and asked a couple questions, but then we settled into silence once again.

"Taisyn," I asked hesitantly after a few minutes, "do you think this means I won't suffer the same fate as Nora and the real Rhydin?"

"What do you mean?" he asked confusedly as he lay next to me.

I sighed. "The evil Rhydin told me that no forger has ever had a happy ending. That they're to be pitied. Rhydin Caldwell spent centuries imprisoned in the Archimage Palace, and Nora was hanged."

"Sounds to me like he was just trying to scare you," Taisyn replied softly. "Sure, they both had hard lives, but they both also experienced happiness too. Amelia had a short life, but she wasn't a forger, just like plenty of other people. I wouldn't put any stock into anything Emperor Rhydin said."

A weight lifted off my chest that'd been there ever since the evil Rhydin uttered that curse. "I think you're right. Thanks."

After a couple seconds of silence, Taisyn whispered, "I'm glad you like the bird."

I blushed, the item in question still cocooned within our hands and hot with their warmth. "Yes, I do," I answered anxiously before sighing and choosing my next words carefully. "I suppose we should probably go home. I don't really want to sleep here. Um…did your Ranguvariian wait for you, or are we walking?"

Taisyn snorted at the thought of walking that far. It was probably a three or four days' walk to Soläna. "I asked Mathiian to bring me, and he claimed he'd wait for me anyway. He's just beyond that tree."

"Good ole Mathiian," I chuckled. "Can he uh, see us right now? I don't see him, but uh…it's too dark."

"Er…Probably not. I don't know, why?" the prince asked as he leaned forward on his elbows.

In response, I squashed my nerves, rolled myself toward him as small, wet rocks stuck to me and fell, placed one hand on the back of his neck, and pressed my lips to his. The flame in his other hand grew larger and spit sparks. Taisyn froze, and when I finished, I jumped to my feet, tucked my bird back into my pocket, and said, "C'mon, fire boy. Let's get out of here and let the dead sleep."

Taisyn, a little breathless and his cheeks the color of his hair, responded as he stood, "Yeah, I think you have a pretty great future ahead of you."

I cackled and gave him a friendly shove before we raced to where Mathiian awaited.

Chapter Twenty-Four

Lina

I'd never seen so many people in my entire life. All of Nerahdis was here dressed in their best clothes with either a full meal in tow, or whatever they had to spare to share with everyone. Thousands filled Caden's Plain, the central location we had chosen rather than having three separate coronations in the stuffy castles. They stood and talked, ate, drank, and danced to the music the Ranguvariian musicians played on a scale I'd never before seen.

Several weeks had passed since the battle that decided Nerahdis's future, and spring was in full force, its heat sometimes hinting at the coming summer. A small section of the plain around the center stones had been swathed to help with the ceremony, so the air was ripe with the smell of freshly cut grass. Three small pavilions in each kingdom's colors had been erected like points of a large triangle, each nearest its respective kingdom, and I peered out from the Lunakan one at all the people, butterflies wreaking havoc in my stomach. Finally, I had to close the flap and clutch the front of the embroidered bodice of my dress.

Frederick was watching me carefully as he helped Dominick finish donning his ceremonial attire behind a screen. They both wore a suit of white and gold velvet with Lunaka's twin moons perched on a wheat stalk emblazoned on the front surrounded by delicate scrollwork. The only difference was the silver crown of wheat heads that still sat on Frederick's brow, the twin of my own which had been left at the castle. Frederick appeared healthier than I could remember him looking for a long time; the color had returned to his skin, his gauntness had vanished, and the sparkle had returned to his blue eyes. "Are you alright?" he asked.

"So many people," I replied like there wasn't enough air in the tent.

"Last time, you were the one who crowned me, and you didn't seem that nervous," Frederick laughed as Dominick finally emerged from beyond the screen.

"For starters, I was *extremely* nervous! But it's still different," I groaned as I began anxiously smoothing my dress, "I wasn't wearing one of *these*, and I *certainly* wasn't one of the people *being* crowned with an official crown!"

To be fair, the dress I wore was *not* the one originally presented to me, the one that Queen Gloria once wore when she was made Adam's queen. That one would have made me look like a cream puff. The dress I'd chosen was Lunakan white and flowed over my skin like water. The skirt had many layers, but the other dress had been so full, it would have never fit through a doorway. Mine had long, slender sleeves of delicate lace that were nice and cool in the sun, and the bodice had been embroidered with the same Lunakan crest as a compromise with the castle staff who had overseen the last three Lunakan coronations. Sam's Kidek bandana was tied around my shoulders today; Kylar had his own now.

"Stop fretting," Frederick said with a smile on his face as he came to my side, and then he dropped his voice so that Dominick wouldn't hear. "You look beautiful."

I cringed and snuck a peek outside again. It was almost time to begin. "That's not what I'm worried about. But thanks."

"I swear I won't let you trip." Frederick grinned, holding up his hand in promise. "Besides, remember this is different. This isn't absolute monarchy anymore. It's a new era."

"I'm not sure whether that makes me more or less nervous," I muttered pessimistically.

The horn sounded sooner than I anticipated, and the Ranguvariian musicians suddenly changed over into a different song. The roar of small talk grew quiet in response. That was our cue, and suddenly my lungs felt restricted.

"Just look at your family up there and no one else. You'll do great." Frederick said encouragingly, still seeming happier than he'd been in decades. Then, he gently took my hand in the fashion of an escort, the one wearing the pearl ring he'd given me, and the three of us exited the pavilion together.

Across the large, mown area, I could barely see the Mineraltin and Auklian pavilions – the first forest green and the other ocean blue, both with gold accents. Somewhere in between them and the tall, standing stones in the middle of it all were their respective Royals. Aisles from each tent extended toward the stones, and as the music played, each family made their way to the stage and the stones in the center. I clung to Frederick's hand so tightly I was probably cutting off the blood flow while my other hand, which still wore Sam's silver ring, remained firmly glued to my side in an effort to stop myself from hiking up the skirts to where I could see my feet and *know* I wouldn't trip over them.

Thousands upon thousands of faces ogled on either side of me, and their weight threatened to crush me. I couldn't decide whether it was better or worse that I could no longer sense anyone around me. I tried staring at the ground, but that caused me to take clumsy steps, even in my trusty boots hidden under my skirts. When I felt Frederick squeeze my hand, I remembered what he said and fought to look up.

At the very end of our aisles, among the stones where Nerahdis won her freedom, were several people. The other Nerahdian leaders were present – Clariion Rachel of the Ranguvariians, Chieftess Doona of the Aatarilecs, and Chancellor Aver of Caark, who was recently voted into power after Rhydin killed the last chancellor at the start of his reign.

Alongside them were a handful of nobles and commoners, Gornish and Rounan alike, who would serve as Nerahdis's first senators. A few weeks ago, the rebellion and its Council, which would continue to exist, had *finally* come to a united decision concerning how Nerahdis's politics would transition from an absolute monarchy, while still maintaining the stability and familiarity of the Royal families. These senators would have two-year terms to allow the people to replace them if needed, and governance of the kingdoms would be split equally between them and the Royals in a system of checks and balances.

Lastly, among all those people awaiting us at the stones were my family. Cayce had been nominated as one of the new Rounan senators, so she stood proudly next to Evan in a new dress that befitted her new Lunakan citizenship. Evan wore a dignified suit of silver and red, probably the last time he'd ever wear the Allyen colors. The last time we spoke, he had expressed the desire to go back to playing his violin.

Rayna stood next to him in a matching dress, a silver bodice with a floral design that stretched down in a few vines along her scarlet skirt. I'd braided her auburn hair just a few hours ago, and how beautiful she looked put my heart at ease after such a rough time with her appearance since Sam's death. Last but certainly not least was Kylar, who stood with the other world leaders, and my heart swelled even further with pride at the sight of him in Sam's ceremonial Kidek outfit. He wore a navy satin tunic with a purple, golden-starred sash, and Sam's Kidek bandana was tied around his head.

I kept my children and my brother in my sights, and before I knew it, we'd managed to make it to the stones, Dominick trailing behind us. A circular platform had been erected around them, all the important people already standing upon it, and we walked up the stairs to join them. Sabine and Chretien mounted the stairs on the Auklian side, and I did a double take when I saw that it was Lyla who accompanied Xavier and Mira to the Mineraltin side instead of Taisyn. I scanned the crowd and saw him standing on the ground near where his family stood on the platform with the other Royal children who weren't being named heirs today, Nathia and Willian.

What did that mean?

Once we were all in place, Evan cleared his throat and announced in his loudest voice, a decibel unheard of from him, "Thank you, Nerahdis, for making the journey to be here today. Your presence is more important than ever as we make the biggest transition in rulership since Emperor Caden's time."

The entirety of Caden's Plain erupted in cheering.

"Today, we return the Three Kingdoms to their rightful rulers, but we also give them to you, the people, in the form of your chosen senators before you," Evan continued, sneaking a proud glance at Cayce before gesturing back to the Royals. "These people have taken vows for Nerahdis before, underground in the Dome, but now we make them official under the Nerahdian sun with the true crowns of the Three Kingdoms."

Evan and Rayna circled the platform until they reached the Mineraltin side, and there was suddenly a small wooden chest in my daughter's hands. Evan declared, "Xavier and Mira Rollins, do you both so swear to not only lead, serve, and protect the people of the Kingdom of Mineraltir as their king and queen, but also to partner with their chosen senators to uphold their freedom until your final breaths?"

The vows are different, I thought to myself as Xavier and Mira both wholeheartedly answered, "We so swear." *But they reflect the new world perfectly.*

Xavier bowed his copper head, and Evan removed the small silver crown designed like a tree branch. Evan placed it in

Rayna's box for a moment before withdrawing the heirloom emerald-studded, Mineraltin crowns and bestowing them on Xavier and Mira's brows. Xavier's eyes were a million miles away before he closed them briefly, and I couldn't imagine what it must have felt like for him. Xavier's mother died bearing him, and when his father remarried Queen Jasmine and had Princess Ren, who both made his life utterly miserable and even tortured him, he likely wondered for years whether he'd sit on his rightful throne. Mira gazed at him lovingly and took his good hand. For once, the other arm, badly mauled in the avalanche during the war, wasn't tucked away in a cloak.

Evan continued, taking the silver crown back out of the box, "And now, to ensure stability for the line of Mineraltir and as a reminder that your rulership is not permanent, whom shall you name as your heir?"

Adam was probably the reason for that, I mused inwardly. The whole reason he joined Rhydin was because he wanted more power and never wanted to pass his crown to his son. He even tried to kill Frederick shortly before Duunzer struck.

Xavier took his old silver crown of branches and set it on his daughter's copper head that matched his own. "My daughter, Princess Lyla."

Whispers popped up in the crowd, and more than one person shot glances at Taisyn among them. Mineraltir had always been a more old-fashioned kingdom and had never passed the crown to a girl before, much less to one over her firstborn brother.

To dispel the rumors, Evan said, "If an heir does not wish to be ruler, then they should not be made to. Even Royals deserve new freedoms in our new system."

Rayna was beaming, and Taisyn looked more relieved than I'd ever seen him before. Their happiness was contagious.

Evan and Rayna continued on around the circle to the Auklian side and repeated the same vows to Sabine and Chretien. Evan settled the beautiful sapphire- and aquamarine-encrusted crown on Sabine's short green hair, and she in turn placed her former silver, wave-shaped crown on Chretien's rose-red head. He was the elder twin of her wards by only a few minutes, but what little experience I'd had with Chretien and Willian told me that she had made that choice on purpose and not just because he was technically older.

Sabine reached up and touched her new crown absent-mindedly. Unlike Xavier and Frederick, she had never remotely dreamed of wearing it. It would have been Daniel's birthright, if we had not lost him in the battle of the Archimage Palace – the same event that took Archimage Dathian's life, who was Sabine's father and Daniel's uncle. I nodded at her when she happened to glance at me; she was steady, wise, and was already one of the best rulers Auklia had ever had.

As Evan and Rayna made their way around to us, the last to be crowned, my heart seemed to hammer faster and faster out of control. But then, Frederick was abruptly murmuring in my ear to distract me. "Remember when you crowned me in the Dome?"

"Yeah, the world went crazy and let a farm girl like me put a crown on a king's head," I hissed back, "yet now it's gone even more nuts and is about to put the *real* one on my own head!"

Frederick couldn't help but smile. "I will never let you forget that you were the one who first made me want to be king as a boy when I was in the middle of running away. And now, you will officially be my queen."

For a moment, time seemed to freeze. My eyes seemed to move on their own accord away from Frederick and down to where Kylar stood, wearing Sam's clothes. In another life, that was where I would have been standing on this day. If Sam wasn't dead, I'd be standing with him. If he wasn't cut with that poisoned blade, becoming Frederick's wife and Lunaka's queen would have never happened.

But he was.

It was Kylar's strange look in response that woke me up. His eyes darted from side to side as he tried to figure out why I was staring at him so intensely. I turned back to Frederick, and he too seemed to be trying to understand where my mind was. I took a deep breath and soaked in how healthy Frederick looked. How happy he looked. How relieved he seemed to be that he was not taking on this mantle alone like he'd done for years after Cassandra's death.

Even though Sam was dead, good had still been born of that. Out of the darkest hour of my life had come something special in its own way, and Sam would want me to live it to the fullest. I gave Frederick a small smile and replied, just as I did back in the Dome, "It is my honor."

Evan and Rayna finally made it to our corner, and Evan repeated the vows as he took the silver crown of wheat heads from Frederick's brow. "Frederick Tané and Linaria Greene, do you both so swear to not only lead, serve, and protect the people of the Kingdom of Lunaka as their king and queen, but also to partner with their chosen senators to uphold their freedom until your final breaths?"

I met Frederick's eyes, and we said in unison, "We so swear."

My brother withdrew the traditional Lunakan crowns, which I'd never seen so close up in my life. The king's crown was a thick band of gold etched with a swirling design like the wind magic of the Lunakan Royals and sprinkled with diamonds and pearls. The last time I'd seen this crown, it was on Adam's head, and I couldn't imagine how heavy it must have felt. Frederick was solemn as he accepted it, but there was no denying the relief I saw in his eyes to finally have a chance to put his father's wrongs to right for all of Lunaka.

When I turned back to Evan, he stood there waiting with the queen's crown cradled in his fingertips. It was gold as well, but far more delicate in design. Great loops and swirls dusted in diamonds created the body of the tiara, and large pearls dangled from the empty spaces and danced whenever the crown moved. My brother's eyes met mine as my breath left me, and while all of the other Royals had needed to bow for

Evan to crown them, I shared his short stature. I dipped my head the tiniest of bits as an invitation, and he gracefully settled the crown on my head, tucking its wings into my braids. When I faced him again, his Allyen eyes seemed a little misty, and Rayna gazed at me with a smile on her face. Frederick looked like he'd never been happier.

"And now, to ensure stability for the line of Lunaka and as a reminder that your rulership is not permanent, whom shall you name as your heir?" Evan asked as he reclaimed the silver wheat crown from Rayna's box.

Frederick released my hand and put his arm around his son's shoulders to bring him forward. Dominick was his father's spitting image, but he had his mother's eyes. I placed one hand on my step-son's shoulder as well, and Dominick gave me a sheepish grin. He'd always taken this new marriage extremely well, likely because he couldn't remember Cassandra. Once I'd shared all my stories of her with him, he'd accepted me even more so. Frederick beamed with pride as he took his old silver crown from Evan and placed it on his son's head. "My son, Prince Dominick."

With that, Evan and Rayna returned to their starting point on the circular platform, but they remained facing the Royals rather than turning toward the audience. My brother declared loudly, "Until your dying breaths, you all are the sovereigns of your respective kingdoms! May you serve Nerahdis well, or not at all."

The Mineraltins in the crowd erupted, "Long live King Xavier and Queen Mira!"

The Auklians boomed, "Long live Queen Sabine!"

And the Lunakans roared, "Long live King Frederick and Queen Lina!"

My ears rang from the cheering for several hours afterward. Caden's Plain became the site of a festival celebrating the defeat of Rhydin and the creation of our new world late into the night; people could stay as long or short as they wished. I found Rosetta in the crowd, and we found ourselves reminiscing about the festivals in Soläna we used to go to as girls. Soon, however, she was ready to go try her hand at finding a dance partner, and I wasn't interested. Frederick was off giving pointers in the Lunakan corn-bobbing game to Dominick, so I found a quiet place to sit on the edge of all the activity to soak it all up in my own time as the sun crept toward evening. I was watching two men who'd imbibed a bit too much attempt to play a Mineraltin game I wasn't familiar with but consisted of some throwing knives and a tree stump when someone suddenly sat down next to me and scared me out of my wits.

"Oh, sorry," Rachel said with a smile on her freckled face, still decked out in her new Clariion regalia. "I forgot you can't sense me coming anymore."

"Heh, yeah…it's going to be a while before I get used to not knowing who's around me again," I replied quietly, trying not to let her remark feel like salt in a wound.

But Rachel, having been my friend for decades now, knew exactly what was going through my head. "I know it's hard. I never dreamed the Allyen magic would ever come to an end after how hard we've fought to preserve it. At least it ended for the best possible reason. It accomplished its job."

I nodded slowly. After all, I'd had weeks to come to terms with Rayna's message from Nora. "There's a lot of things that have turned out far differently than I ever remotely dreamed they would. I mean, you're Clariion, and Arii is gone. Sam is gone, and now I'm a magic-less Royal married to a friend I'm coming to love."

"It's a relief to hear you say that," my red-haired friend responded as she smoothed her orange robe. "Nothing in life ever goes the way anyone thinks it will."

"I know, and I was reminded today that I can't live in the past and keep asking 'what if?' For either my magic or Sam," I said as I looked down and studied the traditional Lunakan embroidery on the bodice of my gown. "I spent the first nineteen years of my life without magic. I can learn how to do it again. It'll be okay in the long run."

"Good." Rachel grinned facetiously. "And Frederick?"

As if on cue, I looked up to notice that Frederick had left Dominick to his own devices and seemed to be slowly combing the crowd, not spending much time with anyone he happened to stop and talk to. He seemed to be discreetly searching for someone, and I wondered if it was me. After all, I didn't put off a strong magical presence anymore, just one the faint strength of a non-magical person, only perceptible when facing them.

I replied softly as I spun my rings around my fingers, "This story will be good too, I think. A different kind of love story than Sam's…but still good."

As Frederick finally caught sight of me off away from all the activity and began to walk towards us, Rachel stood and said, "I'll leave you to it, then!"

"Hey, Rachel," I called after her before she could transport away. "Thank you. For everything. I think you're going to be a great Clariion."

Rachel ducked into a gallant bow. "Thank you, Your Majesty."

I rolled my eyes and laughed, "Okay, you can fly away now."

Frederick strolled up just as Rachel was cackling and disappearing simultaneously. He eyed where she'd just been confusedly before offering me his hand. "I was just coming to see if you were ready to eat. What was that about?"

"Nothing important," I chuckled and shook my head before taking his hand. "Yes, let's go."

All of the Royals stayed for the dinner, which we funded and provided for everyone there after the potluck lunch that had been before the coronation. It lasted several hours as people ate their fill and left to find their way home. Thankfully, there were no more speeches or great displays; just community and breaking down the barriers between the Royals and the commoners, of which I still considered myself to be both. Afterward, Frederick and I corralled our four teenagers along with my sister and Erikin, and we imposed upon the Ranguvariians' kindness to transport us home to Lunaka Castle.

After the last several weeks since our victory at Caden's Plain, Frederick and I had worked to clean up Lunaka Castle the best we could in between all our other commitments to our people and our children. Slowly, some things were beginning to return to normal. The people of the Dome left in their own time to go find their homes again. Some left immediately, and others continued to stay on and help out, like Rosetta and Erikin. Around the time we finally got all the chicken droppings washed off the main staircase a week or so in to the process, a good number of the former castle workers started to come back, re-hired at a fair pay of course. Thankfully, the mines were kicking back into full production while the planting of crops was underway, which meant both the Lunakan economy and the Royal stores were beginning to recover after years of neglect. Emperor Rhydin had tried to just send resources wherever they were needed without the exchange of money rather than let the Three Kingdoms haggle and potentially fight for them, but all the senators ensured that the old trade systems were resurrected at reasonable rates.

As we arrived late at night, the castle seemed empty without people loitering along every hallway and random crates of supplies everywhere. Rayna was glum after bidding good night to Taisyn, who went home to Mineraltir with his family, but Kylar, Dominick, and Erikin were still boisterously laughing about some joke I'd evidently missed. Nathia simply rolled her eyes at the boys as she kicked off her sparkly shoes and scooped them off the floor to continue on to her room barefoot. It only reminded me of how badly my own feet ached even in my old faithful boots hidden under my gown after being on them for so long.

The boys and Rayna disappeared to their respective rooms, all having their own since the majority of the former rebels had gone home, but Frederick waited at the next landing of the stairway as I bid goodnight to Rosetta. She wore a pale blue gown that complemented her fair complexion well, and she too had her shoes slung over her shoulder as she giggled groggily, "Oh, Lina, I *still* cannot believe you're the queen. It's just too weird."

I touched the crown still on my head absent-mindedly. "I know. I'm still not used to it, even weeks later."

Rosetta reclaimed some focus and clasped my hands in hers between us. "I think you will be a splendid queen. I just wish Mama and Papa could see this because they would agree with me."

"You think so?" I asked anxiously. "They…they've been gone so long, it's hard to imagine what they'd think about all this."

"Definitely," Rosetta replied softly, her hazel eyes fluttering closed in remembrance. "No doubt about it. They'd be so proud."

I smiled. "They'd be proud of you too, Rosetta. You're the most loyal person I've ever met."

My little sister – who was taller than me – threw her arms around my neck and rested there for a moment. Then, she whispered "thank you," detached herself, and promptly left me to go find her bed. I watched her go briefly, thankful that we were under the same roof and I could know she was safe after so long of having no idea.

I climbed the last rotation of stairs slowly and carefully up to the landing where Frederick still waited. I had no qualms about hiking up my skirts now in order to see as each foot throbbed numbly on each stair. The new king was rubbing his eyes when I reached him, and while he simply turned to walk down the hallway next to me, I slung my arm around his waist as we walked, too tired to even attempt to reach his tall shoulders or even his back. He responded almost immediately by putting his arm around me, and we walked wordlessly down the hall like two battle-weary soldiers leaning on each other to stay upright.

My eyes were barely open when we reached the end of the hall and pushed open the big double doors that led to our separate quarters. Frederick left me to light an oil lamp on his desk, which was no longer hidden under a mountain of papers as usual. Instead, a manageable stack sat neatly in the corner, the rest delegated out to the six new Lunakan senators – one from each Lunakan city as well as two Rounans.

Frederick's room as a whole was tidier than it'd ever been before, but then again, I couldn't remember the last time I'd bothered to look at it on my way through to my inner chamber. We'd been so ridiculously busy the last several weeks that I didn't even remember the last time we had headed to our respective beds at the same time. I found myself hoping that the absence of the mess was just more proof that Frederick was doing better mentally.

When my hand touched the handle of the inner door leading to the queen's room, I found myself stuck in place. My mind raced, but my thoughts were jumbled and unclear. After a moment, I pushed the door in and wandered into the dark room, my mind still lost in a haze, leaving the door cracked behind me. I studied the purple florals on the walls, the empty bookcase in the corner – after all, I certainly hadn't had time to read during my time here even if the castle tomes had been remotely within my reading level – and the bare writing desk. Nothing in this room was mine, save for Rhydin Caldwell's history book hidden under the mattress now and the Lunakan moon plant in the window.

Mindlessly, I extricated myself from the coronation gown and tossed it on the bed I'd made just that morning. I gently took the crown from my head and set it on the desk before donning the long, plain tunic that reached to my knees that I'd taken to wearing at night. The plant Sam saved for me caught my eye as I picked out all the little pins keeping my hair in its updo. It looked much stronger now in the real sun after our experiment of growing it under the Dome's Ranguvariian-made crystal light.

Out the window, I could see the rolling Canyonlands around Soläna, and I imagined I could see my old farmstead. The barn where I'd cared for my goats when they came in from pasture. The field where I'd sown my wheat. The little shack where I'd grown up with Rosetta and our parents – Liam would always be my father too. Sam's farmstead right next door.

What if Rhydin had never split in two? What would our lives have been like if I'd never left the farm? My parents would have never died in the Epidemic. Robert would have never left; my mother never remarried Liam and had Rosetta. I would have grown up with Evan instead. No Allyen magic, no Duunzer, no war, no leaving our children in Caark for a decade, no rebellion, and no becoming a widow so young.

No marrying Frederick. No becoming a leader, a fighter, or one of the most powerful mages in Nerahdian history. No new world where people no longer had to live in fear and had representation in their government. My son would *never* have had to fear being discovered as a Rounan and being hanged for it like every Rounan before him. My daughter could choose any path for her future.

Perhaps, everything did happen for a reason.

Feeling suddenly emboldened, I inched back toward the barely ajar door. I'd been putting this off for weeks, if not months. Originally, it was because the thought sickened me. Then, it was because I wasn't ready. After that, it was my embarrassment that I still sometimes woke up screaming, thinking that Duunzer was coming for the castle. The night terrors had become less frequent since Frederick and I's little talk late that one night, but they hadn't ceased plaguing me either.

Still. I was ready to no longer be alone. Even at night.

When I re-emerged into Frederick's quarters, he was still dressed in his white and gold coronation attire, although his crown now sat on a shelf. He sat at his desk with one long piece of parchment in his hand, angling it awkwardly at the oil lamp so he could see it well enough to read it.

Frederick didn't notice my entrance at first, but when he seemed to see me out of the corner of his eye, he pulled at his tight, tall collar and said, "Oh, Lina. Could I perhaps bother you to unhook this for me? I can't see it and can't seem to…" – he finally tore his eyes away from his parchment and quieted when he saw me standing there in my nightgown with a nervous expression on my face – "…are you alright? Missing something?" He set down the parchment almost immediately.

"I'm fine." I shook my head slowly. "I…uh. I don't want to be like your parents, Frederick. I don't want to live separate lives."

Frederick was quiet for a moment, trying to understand what exactly I was saying. "Neither do I. They had an awful relationship."

"Good," I said a little too quickly, clutching my hands tightly in front of me, "then I-…."

The blond-haired king stood abruptly and came to stand in front of me. He met my eyes and took my hand before saying calmly, "Several months ago, I told you that I had decided to love you. That was true at the time…but as time has gone by, I can honestly say now that I love you fully. You…you mean so much to me. You're not just the little girl who made me want to be king. You've helped make me a better person. To see when I'm unintentionally acting like my father. How to be partners with a woman in a way he never was…."

Frederick paused, looking away. He remained quiet even as I stared up at him, like he was trying not to expect any sort of response from me. As I mulled over the words I'd thought about ever since the battle one final time, I reached up and grasped his stiff collar that was so tight against his neck it was no wonder he'd been unable to undo it himself. I undid the little hook within that kept the two halves closed neatly, and

Frederick automatically rubbed his neck where it had chafed all day long.

"I meant what I said on the battlefield," I said softly as one of my hands dawdled on the scrollwork on his chest, "and I wasn't just saying it in the heat of the moment or because you saved my life or any of the other dozens of things you've done for me over the years. I really do love you, for who you are. I don't want to be alone anymore. I don't want a marriage like Adam and Gloria's-…."

I had started to ramble awkwardly, but Frederick stopped me with a radiant smile. He touched my cheek lightly and whispered, "As long as I'm here, you'll never be alone."

My face suddenly felt hot with embarrassment. "Well…before you agree to this, you should really know that I still have nightmares sometimes. I-I've been seeing Duunzer a lot…being here in the castle. Other times I see your father or our friends who died because of me…. I've been afraid you'd be sleep-deprived if I joined you in here."

Frederick's face went slack. I'd never had a chance to tell him of what exactly my nightmares consisted before. We'd been so busy for so long. His hand on my cheek readjusted to the back of my head as he pulled me against him and kissed my hair. "I'm sorry you see those things. But I'd rather have you in here with me more than anything else. I have my own memories that keep me awake anyway, you know that-…."

I tugged his chin down and silenced him with a kiss. Frederick seemed to melt with relief when I pulled away, and I grinned tiredly. "Can we go to sleep now?"

He nodded quietly before stealing another kiss like he just couldn't help it. Then he disappeared behind his screen to change out of his fancy clothes as I went back to the queen's room just long enough to grab what little clothing I owned, the book, my crown, and my plant. After throwing my clothes into the drawer of an empty armoire in the corner, setting the book and crown on a shelf within, and finding a new home for my plant on the sill of the one vast window, I closed the doors to that room for good.

The king's four-poster bed had to be the largest bed I'd ever seen in my life, but as I pulled the covers up around me and Frederick blew out the lamp across the room, a rather uncomfortable thought occurred to me. "Frederick…this isn't *Adam's* bed…is it?"

"Definitely not," Frederick's voice responded from the dark, my eyes not adjusted to the moonlight yet. "I threw that one in a room downstairs for others in the rebellion to use. This is mine from my old room."

"Oh, good." I breathed a sigh of relief as I finally allowed myself to sink into the soft pillows.

When the bed jostled from Frederick's weight, I rolled over in search of him. He was waiting, and we fell asleep instantly, wrapped in each other's arms.

That night was the deepest I'd slept since we'd left the Dome. Every part of me was finally able to rest, even my mind. While Frederick and I never did vanquish the terrors that came for us especially at night over the rest of our years, their powers over us were halved by the fact that we never woke up alone again.

Epilogue

Rachel

After the Battle of Caden's Plain, Nerahdis entered an era of unprecedented peace. There was never such a time before that not only all the rulers strove toward agreement but also that the commonfolk had so much say in how their kingdoms operated.

While the heroes of that time are all gone now, I – Clariion Rachel Coralii of the Ranguvariians – have been given permission to record the rest of their lives here in the Allyen journal, entrusted to me by Allyen Rayna before her death, in order that Nerahdis may never forget the Story of the First Archimage. It is my solemn duty to keep this journal safe as the original iteration of the story, so that historians may document their own histories accurately. Herein lies the stories of my friends, our heroes, after the Battle of Caden's Plain.

Allyen Linaria and King Frederick remained married for the rest of their years. They learned to love each other powerfully, despite their opposite upbringings. Lina adjusted to the loss of her magic slowly but surely, and she threw herself into being the best queen she could be. She told me that Frederick continued her reading lessons until she could read every book in the castle library on her own. While queen, she worked very closely with her son, Kidek Kylar, to ensure that Rounans received equal rights and representation within Lunaka in honor of her first husband, Kidek Samton Greene. Lina never returned to her old farmstead again, but she maintained a small field just outside the walls of Lunaka Castle. She tilled, planted, watered, and harvested it until the very end, sharing its produce with the people of Soläna.

A few years after the Battle of Caden's Plain, Lina and Frederick welcomed a daughter into the world, whom they named Allana. As she grew, her talent as an aeromage like her father before her was obvious, and Allana spent her adult life as a bodyguard for her elder brother, King Dominick, and a magic tutor for his children. Lina died at the age of seventy-six in her sleep, and Frederick followed her before the sun had set at the same age. It is my belief as their close friend that after having found peace in one another after so much trauma and spending over four decades at each other's side, one could not live without the other.

King Dominick assumed the throne perhaps ten years before his father passed to allow him to retire. He was a level-headed and kind king like his father before him, and he married a common woman called Katherine, who worked as a seamstress in Stellan. They were very popular rulers and had several children, Todderick, Cornflower, Andromeda, and Gilbert. Dominick's adopted sister, Nathia, ended up marrying Chretien, the heir to Auklia's throne, which made the Rounan community very excited. When Queen Sabine perished following a riding accident, Chretien and Nathia were as strong and fierce of leaders as she was before them. They had one son together, who later became King Dathian.

Meanwhile, in Mineraltir, King Xavier and Queen Mira were able to put the kingdom back on the right track after so many years of poor leadership by Jasmine and Ren even before Emperor Rhydin. They updated more infrastructure than any past king or queen and helped people displaced by Rhydin get back on their feet. Their daughter, Lyla, continued this work after her mother died and her father retired soon after. Prince Willian of Auklia became one of her suitors, but it was obvious he was only searching for a throne. Lyla ultimately married the son of a nobleman named Declan. He was a quiet prince consort, but he served Lyla well as an advisor and a father to their two children, Gloria and Samuel.

Because Lyla stepped forward to become the heir to Mineraltir, Prince Taisyn was free to move to Lunaka where he and Allyen Rayna married in their early twenties. As newlyweds, they settled in Soläna where Taisyn opened a specialty blacksmith shop, using his fire magic to power the forge. While most of his business consisted of the usual blacksmith wares such as fixing horseshoes and selling wagon parts, he became renowned for his metal sculptures that he created with his magic. Erikin, Rayna's cousin, acted as his eyes and maintained the storefront of Taisyn's shop from the beginning.

Rayna told me once that she struggled to decide what she would do with her life after the disappearance of her Allyen magic. During the time she and Taisyn lived in Soläna, she worked a variety of short-term jobs before becoming a schoolteacher with her aunt, Rosetta. Rosetta and Erikin created a new life in Soläna, and Rosetta remarried after a few years. Rayna was well adept at being a teacher after so many years of honing her skills of description in aiding her blind husband, and she naturally gravitated toward history in order to ensure that the events concerning Rhydin's dark reign were recorded accurately. Rayna and Taisyn had three children over the years, whom they named Nora Linaria, Christopher Samton, and Andrew Rhydin. The youngest's middle name is only known to a small handful of people.

Later, Taisyn and Rayna fixed up the old Allyen farmstead to live there when one of their sons became interested in farming; however, they were only there a few years before Taisyn was taken from us due to a forge explosion in his mid-fifties. After Taisyn's death, their daughter took on the blacksmith forge, having inherited the same fire magic and artistic skills. Rayna remained at the farm with her adult sons, but she quit her job as a teacher and became Lunaka's official historian for her step-brother, King Dominick. Allyen Rayna lived to be a ripe ninety years old, seeing her great-grandchildren come into the world before she passed.

Her brother, Kylar, was Kidek for many decades. He was the first Kidek to ever be on the same political level as the Three Kings and Queen, and he was at every Council meeting. He married a local girl with whom he had two daughters, and he was proud that his heir was middle-aged by the time she took over as Kidek. Sam had always wished to keep the burden of being Kidek from Kylar as long as possible, and Kylar was able to honor that desire with his own child. Nowadays, a few generations later, there is still a Kidek, but they serve as more of a cultural leader rather than a political leader. Rounans have become so interspersed in the Royal families that they are no longer differentiated from Gornish; everyone is simply Nerahdian.

Allyen Evanarion spent the rest of his days as a musician, frequently playing his violin at Lunaka Castle for various events. Cayce spent several terms as a Lunakan senator before the family returned to her home in Auklia, where she became a representative for the Aatarilecs in the Auklian government, ensuring their promised fishing rights. Their son, Aron, upon adulthood, also served as a senator during the reign of King Chretien. Evan died of a coughing sickness before the age of sixty while Cayce and Aron lived long, healthy lives.

No descendant of either Evan or Lina was ever born an Allyen again. Rayna was the last Allyen. The magic was dead and buried, its purpose of avenging Amelia by defeating the Rhydin clone and restoring the true Rhydin Caldwell complete.

Neither was there ever an Archimage again after the tragic death of Princess Cornflower. Every so often, the people of Nerahdis would suggest the idea, usually during a disagreement between the kingdoms or the threat of war. However, those who knew the Story of the First Archimage vehemently opposed such an idea. Rayna kept her promise to Rhydin Caldwell, and the Archimage Palace was burned to the ground after its library and other treasures were removed. Rayna also saved his copious charts of the stars and constellations, which she copied and dispersed to all the kingdom libraries. She felt proud that Rhydin's work could be useful to anyone who depended upon the stars.

These are the final stories of our heroes. Thus, their story is at an end. May Nerahdis never forget.

"There you have it," Rachel announced as she laid the book down in her lap, "we have finished the Story of the First Archimage for this year."

This night was much cooler than the nights before it; a sign that the world was slowly spinning toward autumn once again. The twin Lunakan moons hung low in the sky, their light illuminating all of the Ranguvariian village in the northeastern corner of the kingdom. The night air was filled with shining stars, the smoke of the torches encircling the fire in the middle of the group, and the salty smell of the ocean just over the mountains. Rachel gently closed the delicate pages of the Allyen journal. The hard leather tome was many centuries old now, containing every Allyen's story from Nora to Rayna. It was all that was left of Rachel's friends, who were all long gone, so it was never far from her side.

"Wow," Reviin, a teenage Ranguvariian boy exuded. "That's really the end?"

Sunlii, Bartholomiiu's some-odd-great-granddaughter, cried in Ranguvariian, "I'm sad it's over!"

"Were all your questions answered, dear ones?" Rachel asked kindly, and after a few moments of silence, she went on, "Today is the one hundredth anniversary of the Battle of Caden's Plain, and Nerahdis has continued to be at peace for every one of those years. We must continue to tell this story so it is never forgotten, by us or the humans."

"But…Clariion Rachel," another child of the dozen piped up, "the journal never said your story at the end."

Rachel was in the middle of standing and straightening her elaborate Clariion's attire when she suddenly froze. Sadness overcame her faster than she could process. Of all the hundreds of times she had read through the journal with the children of the Ranguvariian camp, this question had never been asked before. "Well…my story isn't in the journal because it hasn't ended yet. I chose to stop my aging when I turned fifty just like my grandfather to make sure history wasn't forgotten after Allyen Rayna passed away. My mate, my brothers, my son, even my grandchildren are all gone."

"Oh," the child replied disappointedly, but that only lasted a few beats. "What about our people?"

"Ever since the Battle of Caden's Plain, Ranguvariians have been welcomed in all spheres of human society," Rachel responded proudly. "However, we are still a warrior people who prefer to stick to our territory, although a few Ranguvariians have moved to human towns."

"Can you read the story to us again? Starting with Allyen Linaria again?" Sunlii gushed again.

"No, child." Rachel shook her head, her long red hair threaded with gray. "We'll read it again next year like we always do. It is time for you all to go home to your families."

The Ranguvariian children all groaned as they stood from their places around the fire before they scampered off in a dozen different directions. Once alone, Rachel doused their fire and quietly set off toward her own home, lost in thought. She felt like stopping her aging had been what Grandfather Arii would have wanted her to do, but it was definitely the hardest thing she'd ever done. To watch every one of her friends meet their ends, natural or otherwise, as well as a large part of her family. Jaspen was long gone, and so was Mathiian, her son. On the flipside of the coin though, Rachel wouldn't have otherwise gotten to meet her currently nine-year-old four-times-great-granddaughter.

Rachel reached the gigantic tree in the center of the Ranguvariian camp and rounded it until she stood beneath the front entrance of the Clariion's Lodge. She whistled her musical magic to summon her bright Ranguvariian wings just long enough to fly up to the landing and then immediately on up to the next floor through the large hole in the ceiling. Rachel had largely made the Lodge her own over the decades, redecorating many things from Grandfather Arii's time there aside from the traditional first level and its Ranguvariian historical items.

The second floor was Rachel's pride and joy. It was a very tall room with a ceiling of glass panels to let in natural lighting and a view of the millions of leaves above. Various drapes of colored fabric hung every which way across the ceiling, dangling in haphazard ways from one wall to another. Every wall was lined with shelves, and Rachel had filled one entire wall with books in honor of her grandfather's fascination with them. Another wall was dedicated to the very first volumes of Ranguvariian work, which Rachel was most proud of. Before now, Ranguvariians hadn't possessed a written language and only passed things down orally or by song, but Rachel had made it her mission during her frozen old age to put down their stories and songs using the Gornish alphabet she was taught as a child by her human grandmother, Princess Emily of Mineraltir.

Rachel wandered around a corner to her bedroom where she sat thoughtfully by a window of tree branches, staring at the village down below that pulsed with activity like a beating heart.

One hundred years. Almost sixty years since Lina passed; a whole lifetime. Every single one of those years, Rachel had drawn the Allyen journal out of its protective case and shared the Story of the First Archimage with the Ranguvariian people over the course of several weeks. Now, every Ranguvariian in the camp knew the story, and most humans were taught the story in school. Rachel had vowed to stop her aging until she could be sure that the story would never be forgotten.

Had that time come? Was the threat of history repeating itself completely over? Was the story really complete until Rachel closed her eyes for eternity like everyone else who had lived it? Just like the Ranguvariian child suggested?

Memories of light and darkness overtook her. Faces flashed in her mind's eye. The Ranguvariian faces of her family: Jaspen, Mathiian, Luke, James, Grandfather Arii, her father Viincen who died protecting Lina and Evan as children, and her mother Laveniia. Her human friends: Lina as both a young woman with Sam and the old woman she became with Frederick, Xavier, Mira, Cornflower, Evan, Sabine, and Daniel. Rachel remembered all the happy times with these people, but there was no shutting out the faces of the people who had caused her inconceivable pain. Rhydin, Kino, Adam, Robert, and the Aatarilec who murdered her mother.

In some ways, Rachel remembered all these people and the events of the story like they were yesterday. Her heart lifted with the happy memories, but her hands often tremored with the trauma.

Nobody else remembered them that way anymore. They were only characters in a story. Heroes and villains. Not real people in real life.

Rachel took a deep breath as she turned back toward the dimness of her bedroom. Perhaps, it truly was time. Grandfather Arii had led the Ranguvariians through their darkest era. Rachel had restored them to their former greatness. Before Arii, the Clariion had never magically ceased their aging. The only other person in Nerahdian history who was frozen in time had not been a good experience for the world.

Yes, Rachel thought. *It is time to join my friends. No one should live forever, so no one should meet me and try to pursue it.*

Drawing upon her magic, Rachel reached deep within herself and removed the dampener that kept her blood frozen in time. Now, this wouldn't end her life immediately; it would simply begin her aging again. Rachel sat upon her fur-lined bed and jotted a list to herself of the things she needed to accomplish before she drew her last breath, most notably to give a little more instruction to her great-granddaughter who stood as her current heir.

Feeling at ease for the first time in weeks and more tired than usual, Rachel kicked off her boots and settled into her bed. When she slumbered, she was transported back to Caden's Plain, which looked more resplendent than it ever had before. The tall grasses shimmered like they were spun of gold while the cerulean sky was clear, but the sun wasn't too harsh. The wind blew sweet smells of wildflowers and the sap of the distant trees of Mineraltir onto the plain, and the tall stones in the center looked less rugged than usual.

Normally when Rachel dreamt of Caden's Plain, it was a nightmare of her grandfather's death and all the different ways she tried to prevent it. Regardless of how she tried to play things differently, his demise never changed. Whether it was Rhydin's blade as it happened in real life or the weapon of a random Einanhi or crash-landing to the earth or a heart attack, he always died. However, the Caden's Plain of Rachel's nightmares was always dark and gloomy. Nothing like this.

Rachel approached the stones cautiously, and as she did, she happened to pass a small pool perhaps from a recent rainstorm. A young Rachel stared back at her, her hair as red as ever and her freckled face devoid of any wrinkles. She touched her face in surprise, and then she heard laughter. The stones were still several yards away from her, but the forms of people now loitered among them. The tall silhouettes of Ranguvariians and the average-sized ones of humans. From afar, she couldn't make out many faces, but there were some faces that she would recognize anywhere.

Jaspen and Mathiian stood the closest to her, both looking young and healthy, with her brothers, Luke and James, standing with them. Lina's familiar face was just beyond them. She looked nineteen again, the age she had been when she first became an Allyen, and she smiled and laughed between two tall men, one wearing a bandana and one with a head full of blond hair.

They've been waiting for me. All this time. The words came unbidden into Rachel's mind as she happily rushed down the hill the rest of the way to the stones and her loved ones. She didn't know whether this was a dream, a vision, or something else entirely – she could feel herself smiling even in her sleep back in the Clariion's Lodge –

but she welcomed the peace that she finally felt after more than one hundred years.

Now, truly, the journey on which they had all been thrown in together – the Story of the First Archimage – had found its end at last.

THE END

Acknowledgments

Michaela

Wow. There it is. "The End." The series I first developed when I was only thirteen is now fully finished and published. This story and these characters have occupied my mind for fourteen years, and they have grown with me during some of the greatest and darkest times of my life. I am so incredibly grateful to everyone who has supported me during this amazing journey, especially my readers! Without you all, none of this would have ever been possible.

To my husband, Olin, thank you for always supporting my writing and encouraging me. You've always gone above and beyond to help me at author events, and this dream wouldn't be possible with you.

To my babies, Cassidy and Wyatt. Thanks for napping at the same time, so I could stick to my publishing goal for this book. I'm excited to show you two someday that childhood dreams *can* be accomplished!

To Rachel Evans Clark, your help in this story was invaluable. You are the Rachel to my Lina. You designed the Ranguvariian language all on your own and created their entire culture. You should be proud, my friend!

To Hannah Robinson, thank you for always being there to crush my writer's block and be my soundboard. Without you, this book probably still wouldn't have a title. Thanks for being my writing bud!

To Daphne Olson, my faithful editor. You keep me in check when my mom-brain skips words, forgets a character, or creates a brand-new grammar rule. Thanks for saving me every time!

To Magpie Designs, Ltd., thank you for creating the most beautiful of covers for this series. Each one surpasses the last, and I appreciate you dealing with my nit-picking and going above and beyond on the stuff I never think about!

To L.N. Weldon, thank you for creating my map, even though it's not in your normal skill-set. It takes a special person to take a sketch of mine and spend hours digitizing it. Plus, adjusting its locations for every book. My books wouldn't have a map without you!

Above all, thank you to my Heavenly Father for everything He has given me. I give You all the glory.

I feel so very sad to say goodbye to these characters – to let go of Lina, Rayna, and their adventures – but I know they'll always be with me in some form. I am *beyond* excited to get to move on to new projects in a couple years – to allow myself a break after steadily publishing six books in five years as well as let my young children grow a little – some nearly as old as this one. Thank you all so much! If you want to keep up with me and new projects when they come, definitely check out my author page on Facebook or visit my website!

Visit my website to learn more!
www.michaelarileykarr.wordpress.com

www.ingramcontent.com/pod-product-compliance
Lightning Source LLC
Chambersburg PA
CBHW030537310726
48979CB00010B/1942/J
* 9 7 8 1 7 3 5 5 0 7 1 0 1 *